PADDLE.

LIVE.

LOVE.

KAAREN SUTCLIFFE

Author: Kaaren Sutcliffe

Title: Paddle. Live. Love.

Genre: Fiction, Sports Romance

ISBNs:

978-1-7636624-1-4 (hardback)

978-1-7636624-0-7 (paperback)

978-1-7636624-2-1 (ebook)

Published by Just So Fiction

Dedication

This book is dedicated to Andrew Sutcliffe, my very own Justin.

He didn't run away from my initial diagnosis of breast cancer in 2005, providing unlimited support and TLC.

Andrew stepped up even more in 2021 with the diagnosis of a recurrence in my spine, becoming my special 'baby driver' (watch the movie) by taking me to countless appointments and supplying even more love, support and care. In particular, with excellent humour, he chauffeured me to a number of survivor regattas, allowing me to enjoy the inspiration and camaraderie of Dragons Abreast Australia events.

Unbelievably, in 2022 he gave me the money to participate in the International Breast Cancer Paddlers' Commission regatta in New Zealand. Talk about a bucket-list experience, and I am eternally grateful.

On top of all this, he put up with me being constantly late for dinner once I'd got it into my head I needed to set myself a target of writing a fantasy with romance trilogy to keep myself focused. Yes, it might contain dragon boats. With bonhomie, Andrew assisted with the organisation and running of several book launches, while restraining himself from commenting on the costs.

Together, we produced two beautiful daughters, Elena and Mara, and we are proud of both of them.

Andrew, love you heaps, and could not have made it through any of this without you. Thank you for the fabulous life together.

Kaaren Sutcliffe AE

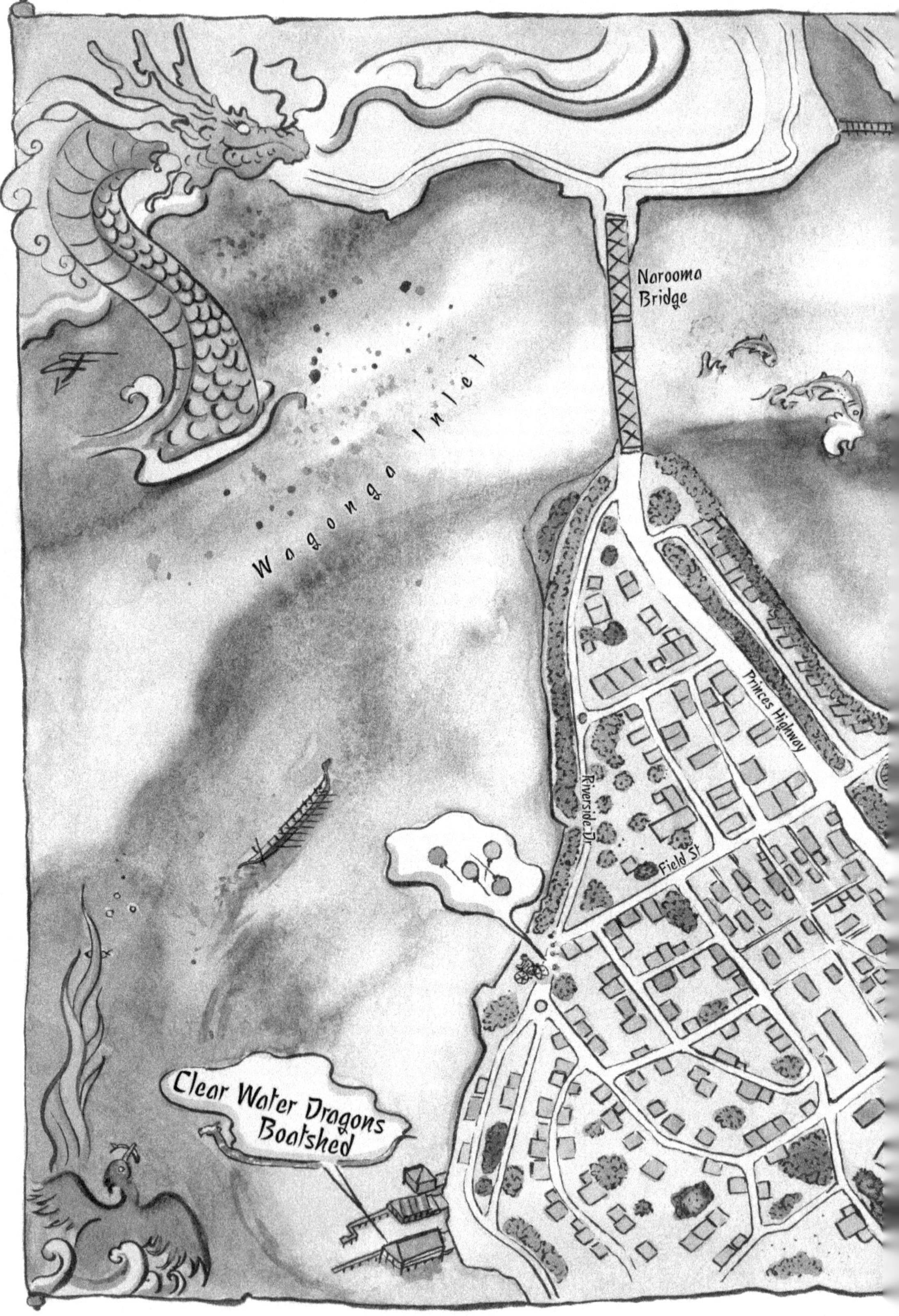

Narooma Bridge
Wagonga Inlet
Princes Highway
Riverside D
Field St
Clear Water Dragons Boatshed

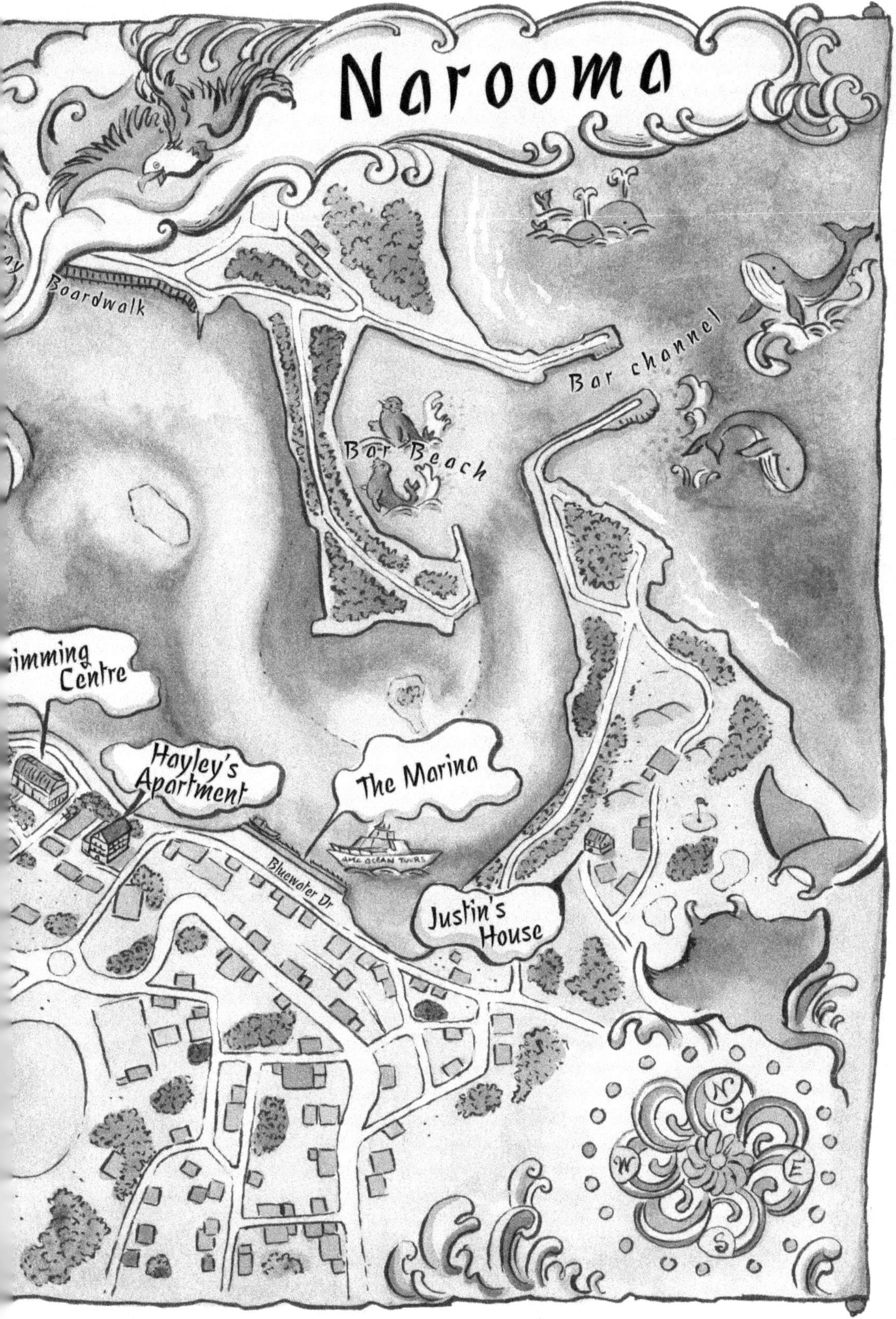
Narooma
Boardwalk
Bar channel
Bar Beach
Swimming Centre
Hayley's Apartment
The Marina
HMS OCEAN TOURS
Bluewater Dr
Justin's House
N
W
E
S

CHAPTER ONE
Hayley

The numbers in the table rows all blur together. Rubbing my eyes, I sigh and look out the office window. The view from my desk on the fifth floor overlooks the lake. A wave of fatigue washes down from my head, making my limbs feel awkward and heavy. I blink a few times and focus on the blue-grey water of Lake Ginninderra and the trees huddled along the shore, branches waving in a blustery spring breeze that's shaking off the newly budded blossoms.

A few runners jog up to a chap standing at one end of the wooden bridge, huddled into his jacket and holding a clipboard and watch. My legs feel even heavier. Of course, first Tuesday of the month and it's the Lake G. Handicap, a monthly seven-kilometre timed run of one lap of the lake with a trophy for most improved each month.

"Not running today, Hayley?" asks Rob from the next desk over, having followed my gaze out the window.

I shake my head, not trusting my voice to speak without wavering.

"You'll get back to it," he says sympathetically and tactfully refocuses on his computer screen.

Everyone has been so kind, giving me space, trying to resume the work banter and camaraderie as if I hadn't been away for nine months. Hadn't come back altered, inside and out. Four months back at my job and I'm still struggling. My brain is sluggish; slow to grasp the program evaluation data and narratives. No longer snapping out insights about meaning and significance, nor teasing out just the right words to succinctly convey the important facts.

Eat, prompts my stomach. So, I open my desk drawer and take out my lunch box, eyeing the rice crackers, small tub of hummus, apple and cheese wedge.

"You need to eat more," suggests Rob, his face creased in a fatherly smile. "You're even thinner than when you were in marathon training."

I nod. He means well, but it's hard. How do you explain you've lost your appetite … not just for food but for life?

Rob gives me a pointed look, rummages in his drawer and reaches over to hand me a Kit Kat bar. "A bit of sugar won't hurt. Go on." He thrusts the bar at me.

I take it and summon a smile. *But cancer likes sugar*, my mind rushes to remind me. *You can't eat that.*

"I'll need to see the empty wrapper," says Rob around a grin. "We evaluation types like evidence and concrete data, remember."

"Very funny." My smile turns genuine. "Speaking of which, I'd better get back to grappling with this executive summary."

"Yeah, rather you than me. The new Minister is so picky. Good luck." Rob swivels his chair and gets back to work.

Putting the Kit Kat in my lunch box, I peek out the window again. More runners are gathering by the bridge, the arrivals becoming progressively leaner and faster-looking as the back markers appear. I glance at my watch: twelve-thirty. Only four minutes until

I'd be heading off, with a best run time of twenty-six minutes for the seven kilometres. The handicap works so everyone comes in close together at one o'clock. *You could run, you know. It just won't be fast.* My pulse lifts. Am I being too cautious? Maybe it is time to resume training.

Jonathan cruises across the bridge to the start line, the wan sunshine reflecting off his tousled golden hair, his feet flowing effortlessly over the ground, not an ounce of fat on him. *Nope, correction. No running events. No going anywhere he goes.* Anger burns in the pit of my stomach and bitterness crawls into my mouth. After four years together, he ditched me with no warning. Then, he didn't even come to the hospital or contact me when I was busy fighting for my life. Sure, we weren't together then, but who does that? The self-absorbed, ego-centric coward... Fine. No running. No men either; way too unreliable. Tossing my hair back over my shoulder, I glare at my computer screen. And reach for the Kit Kat, rustling the wrapper loudly as I peel it off.

Rob laughs. "That's the spirit! Go Hayles. Nail that brief."

An hour later, I'm staring at the same table. There has to be a pattern here, some trend worth highlighting. Come on, come on brain, get with it. I know the data, know how important the Adult Migrant English Program is to the Department and Minister. It's always a good news story, something positive the Australian Government does for new arrivals, especially refugees, the proud story to counter the flack the Department routinely cops. Are there more Croatian participants than last year? Less Sudanese? The past trends hover listlessly in a fog at the edges of my brain, refusing to reveal themselves.

I lean back in my chair. Maybe I need ten Kit Kats to reconnect the synapses. What am I doing here at this desk? The work is hard, no longer interesting. Somehow less important than before. Closing my eyes, I see the oncologist's face at my last appointment. She's kind, an expert, saying gently, *'You're in the higher risk group for a recurrence so we'll need to keep monitoring you. Yearly scans for a couple of years at least.'*

I swallow a surge of dizziness. How far I've fallen from the immortality of running a sub-three-hour marathon, making the ACT team for the nationals and a state team silver medal to … this. From having a handsome, talented partner who I thought loved me to … alone. *Just think how much faster you might've run if you hadn't had a tumour growing in your breast sapping oxygen and energy,* suggests my mind, trying to be optimistic.

'Be kind to yourself. Don't underestimate how long it will take your body, mind and soul to recover.' Now I see the kind McGrath Foundation breast care nurse in her pink uniform giving us survivors the farewell briefing at the end of almost a year of treatment. *'Some people use the experience as an opportunity to make changes to their lives. Review their priorities.'*

My eyes snap open and I stare at the lake, watching the wind ruffle up the surface. Maybe that's what I need, a sea change … literally. Summer's coming, so why not? Think of running barefoot along a beach, letting salty water heal me. Practising my Tai Chi on a balcony facing the rising sun over a vast glittering ocean. My pulse races. *That* would be healing. Can I afford it, though? Would be tight, but what's the point of having money if I'm not here to spend it? I can barely afford my current townhouse solo anyway. *Do it, Hayles.*

"Earth to Hayley!" calls Rob. "Earth to Hayley!"

"What?" I swivel my chair to face him, my cheeks warming.

"Boss wants you in his office. Now. He's called for you twice."

Shit! I grab a scrunchie and pull my hair back into a neat ponytail. No doubt the boss wants a draft of my executive summary. Which is going nowhere. I grab a notepad and pen and hurry across the open plan space to Noel's office. Through the glass front wall, I see he's on the phone. I hover at the door, nerves rising. Ask him for more leave. Before I chicken out. Tell him I'm not coping. I gulp. Do I want to admit that? *Who cares? Get your priorities straight, like the nurse said. Value yourself. Your life. You only get one.*

Noel hangs up and waves me in. I scurry in and perch on the chair in front of his desk. The bland white walls and faded grey carpet look even more sterile than usual as I tense, preparing for a tonne of stress to land. My fingers clench like they're trying to snap the pen in half.

"The Minister needs our briefing urgently," Noel says. "Apparently there's a press conference tomorrow. Where are you up to—" Noel stops speaking, tilts his silver-mop-topped head, assesses me with his steel-blue eyes. "Are you alright? You've gone white as the proverbial sheet."

Tears prickle the back of my eyes. Am I that obvious? Gripping the pen tight, I say, "I'm sorry, the brief's not going well." I blink rapidly to block my tears. "I can't seem to focus as quickly as before." I pause to take a breath.

Noel pushes a box of tissues across the desk. "Hayley, that's understandable. You went through a lot, especially for someone as young as you are. Is breast cancer at thirty-two some kind of record?" He steeples his fingers together and peers at me over the tips. "I need you to finish that brief because you're still the most talented writer I have despite your setback. How about you finish it and then we can talk about anything else the team can do to help you?"

I rub my nose with my knuckles to stop a sniff. Noel is a good manager and I'm lucky to work for him, but I can't possibly ask the team to take on more of my tasks, they're already being as supportive as they can. They'd be better off replacing me … until I'm ready. How long will that take? *Forever,* nudges my subconscious. *Not affordable,* I push back. I clear my throat and surprise myself.

"Yes, I can finish the brief. After that, I think more time off would be good. I need … about three months. Is that long enough for you to backfill my job?"

Noel's bushy silver eyebrows lift and he taps his fingertips together. "You want more time off?" He stops steepling his fingers and adjusts his pen into a neat line beside his blotter pad, a legacy of ancient public service times that suits him because he's ancient too. "Not ideal, Hayley, but I'd rather not lose you from the team." He looks sad, the corners of his mouth turned down. "If we make your leave to mid-January I can advertise for a fill-in."

Breathless, I nod. Holy wow. A massive weight levitates off my shoulders and I sit straighter.

"Put your leave application in," Noel says, "*after* you send me the brief. *Before* you go home today. Deal?"

"Deal!" I leap to my feet, a strange tremor rippling through me. "I'm onto it."

I almost run back to my desk and open the report again. It's two o'clock. If I stay until six, can I do it? I scroll back to the troublesome table. Whoa! Now the numbers are clear, the trends virtually shouting at me. I open up a brief template, title it and start typing. Three pages churn out and I pause typing to scroll back over them, checking my arguments and data are cogent, crisp and lucid.

"Seems this worked. Our Wonder-Writer is back," quips Rob. A Kit Kat bar plonks onto my desk beside my right hand resting on the mouse. "Go Hayles, finish it off."

I flash Rob a grin, letting him think my frenetic productivity is due to the chocolate and not impending freedom, and he lumbers back to his desk and slumps into his chair. I focus again, typing fast and furious, already tasting salty sea air on my lips.

At five forty-five, I'm crafting the cover email and sending the brief to Noel, who is still in his office, waiting. He sends me back a thumbs-up emoji. Right. I glance around. Rob has left, and so have the other two in our team. Pushing aside a surge of guilt, I open

Google on my phone and type in 'apartments available by the sea, South Coast, New South Wales.'

The screen fills with a number of options. Okay, these are way too expensive, I should have specified one-bedroom. I refine the search parameters. The options dwindle to a few in Batemans Bay, doable and I think there's a Parkrun there so I could meet new runners … one in Moruya Heads, no view of the sea though …

I open up the details for the next one and my heart gives a jolt. Narooma. I scan the description: 'This modern, third-floor apartment faces east and looks out over Wagonga Inlet and the sea, all the way to Montague Island.' The turquoise water in the photos is simply stunning. My chest heaves in a sigh, my body wanting to sink into the water and float staring at the sky, doing nothing but watch teeny clouds scud by. No pressure to do anything, no deadlines, no-one feeling sorry for me, no bumping into Jonathan — just me and time to heal, get fit again, redefine, find the 'after BC' me.

I read more details: 'Close to shops, charter tours, restaurants, parks … and only a three-hour drive south of Canberra. Five hours from Melbourne.' So, close enough to drive to Canberra Hospital for my monitoring tests and also closer to Dad in Melbourne. Maybe he'd visit me while I'm there. It would be good to see Dad, especially with so much free time. My lips twitch. I could even let him take me fishing or hiking. He'd like that.

There's a discount for a monthly rate, less again if I take it for three whole months. And it's available from Thursday next week. I feel an invisible nudge to my shoulder, like serendipity or karma is calling. I wish Mum were here, what would she say? I see her sparkling green eyes and hear her voice, 'Oh Hayley, such an adventure. You should go.' My finger hovers over the rental booking form. *Do it. Book it now. New priorities, Hayles. Second chance and all that.*

I press the box to check the three-month option and enter my details and credit card number. I can almost hear my bank account wailing as the hefty deposit goes out. My heart is hammering. Okay, I'm committed.

Next step is to call up a personal leave form. Before common-sense returns and I change my mind.

CHAPTER TWO
Justin

The alarm jolts me out of a delicious dream. I'm at the Dragon Boat Championships and there's a drop-dead gorgeous paddler in our mixed team. She's smiling at me seductively. Rolling over, I turn off the alarm, sit up and scrub at my face. Get a grip. What are the chances? Besides, never date in the boat. Way too many possible complications.

Five-thirty and it's still dark. I groan. A month of hard work to make sure I pass all the test elements for the regional team tryouts. Dragon boat racing is a whole-of-body sport and the tryouts are cunningly designed to detect any weakness. Do I really need to make the team for the fifteenth time? Yep, or I'll never hear the end of it from my father and brother about how living in Narooma, such a small backwater town, has made me soft, how the competition in Sydney is so much stronger.

Right. Get up, Justin. Keep proving them wrong. I do not need them, nor their lifestyle. I am fine here, managing my own life, thank you. Rising, I put swimmers on beneath shorts and a simple tank top. Gotta get to the beach before the retirees arrive for their early morning swim. Too many are my physio clients and love to chat. I swig down an acai berry energy shot, followed by a plain croissant. Okay, good to go. Slipping on my sandals, I yank the small towel from its hook and set off down the porch steps.

Walking briskly, I'm at the entry to the Bar beaches just as the sun's rays lighten the tops of the rock walls. I pause at the top of the steps to the beach and look left then right. Yep, mainly surfers at the longer, open Bar Beach North at this hour. The shorter, sheltered Bar Beach South is deserted, apart from a handful of seagulls and a seal cruising the shoreline looking for fish in the shallow water. The tide is out, leaving an inviting stretch of firm sand. Perfect. I skip down the steps and park my towel and sandals by the rock wall. The water looks good, a light swell and no jellyfish visible.

Easing into a jog, I plan out the session. Two laps at an easy pace to loosen up, then two laps with sprint intervals before a triple set of twenty push-ups and thirty sit-ups. Followed by a brief swim. Should be doable in forty-five minutes. Then bolt before the retirees arrive. My first physio client is at eight-thirty. Note to self: Schedule a day a week when you start at nine so you don't have to rush. Tell your boss. I grin. Okay, the boss says yes. Make it Wednesdays. Note to boss: tell Simone to adjust your calendar.

The sand scrunches under my toes and there's a crisp tang in the air. The Bar channel to the sea is almost flat between the two rock walls embracing it like cuddling arms. Several seals are hunting breakfast in the middle of the channel, the occasional bark echoing across the water as they squabble. I breathe in deeply, filling my entire chest: why would I live anywhere else? I turn at the end of the horseshoe-shaped beach and pick up the pace for the return lap.

The water surface is glinting with silver-gold lights now and my heart pangs. It would be nice to have someone to share this with. To get close to, instead of being the local physio and club coach, always keeping a professional distance. Father would find me a Chinese bride with a snap of his fingers. An *appropriate* bride, to go with running his *appropriate* multi-million-dollar business. Being the oldest son is a curse I can't seem to outrun. I swallow, and run faster.

Lap three and I start my sprints, pushing up onto my toes, stretching my legs out, driving for speed. Again and again, until my legs, arms and lungs are burning and my frustration slips away with my drops of sweat.

I jog a lap to cool down, find a dip in the sand dunes and start my strength work, tucked away from any prying eyes that might arrive. Some of the paddlers like to swim early too. Sit-up ninety … sweat trickles down my torso and my stomach is groaning. Okay, that's it, session complete and it's already six-thirty. Stripping off my shorts and top, I run into the water and dive under. Clear, refreshing water closes over my head and I surface, easing into a relaxed freestyle. A seal glides past on my right and lifts his nose to bristle his whiskers at me. "Hey, bud." The seal flips his tail and effortlessly passes me. "Show off." Once my arms and legs feel lighter, the lactates shaken out, I head to shore.

"Hey, Justin." Sandi, the other sweep in our dragon boat club, is standing at the water's edge, tugging her swimming cap on and pushing her grey hair in at the edges. "Training for regionals again?"

I nod.

Shaking her head, Sandi says, "I don't know how you do it, year after year." She grins. "You need a good woman to distract you, divert some of that nervous energy."

I summon a laugh, knowing she's not really joking.

"Seriously," she says, wagging a finger at me. "Life's short and you're not getting any younger Justin, no matter how hard you train." She pokes me in the chest. "All these muscles … too good to waste." She brushes past me and wades into the water.

Speechless, I watch her dive under. Does the whole club think this? Mortified, I sling the damp towel over my shoulder and walk home.

At my front gate, I pause, regarding my modest cottage-style weatherboard home, unease swirling through me. Am I 'too good to waste' as Sandi says? She's sixty-eight and can afford to tease me. The women in the boat seem to like me, well, okay, I know they respect me as a paddler and coach. Do they actually *like* me as a person, a *man*? Hard to tell. Been a while since I've tried to date. Maybe I don't give off the right vibes. A knot forms in my stomach. Maybe they think there's something wrong with me — thirty-four with no partner, not even a girlfriend.

Opening the gate, I move down the path. Between the dragon boat paddlers and my clients, I'm surrounded by women. Just not inspired to ask any of them out. Am I too fussy? My chest grows heavy. No, let's be brutally honest here, it's more about how any partner I choose will be judged — and rejected — by my family. Wait. Why the hell am I so busy justifying myself this morning? Must be the impending competition against Father's team at the regionals.

As I make my lunch, a glance out the kitchen window shows the first golfers arriving at the golf course on the other side of the road and teeing off. I slap cheese and lettuce on the bottom slice of bread for my sandwich. My phone buzzes on the benchtop. *Father.* My nape prickles. I must have sensed he was going to call. Answer or not answer? Sighing, I pick up the phone.

"Jun Jie," Father's voice says firmly, insisting on using my Chinese name. "How are you? How is your training?"

"Good, and good," I reply. "How are you, Father? How's Mother?"

"We are wondering when you will next visit us. My cousins are coming from Beijing."

He's straight to the point, as usual. "When?" I croak.

"They arrive in three weeks, staying for two. You will come?"

"Of course," I say, ever the dutiful son. "Straight after the regional tryout."

"Text me the exact date. They are looking forward to seeing you. As are we." Father's tone is dry.

"Yes, Father. I will see you soon."

"Train hard." The call ends.

I slump over the benchtop. His cousins. The ones from Beijing who have several daughters. No doubt they will bring at least one eligible daughter with them. Maybe my brother will choose one. Hope rises in my chest and just as quickly vanishes. He can't. As the oldest son, I should marry first. All enthusiasm for the day dissipates, and I feel gloom descending like a grey sea fret.

Straightening, I slap down the top slice of bread and wrap my sandwich. Resist the urge to throw it across the kitchen. Now I have to excel at the regionals *and* dodge all attempts to impose a Chinese bride on me. Which will be relentless.

I seriously need to find the courage to choose someone, to risk losing my heart, and at least *try* to establish some boundaries around my life.

Man up, Justin.

CHAPTER THREE
Lollipops?

I'm quivering with nerves as I wait outside the front of the apartment block. I can't believe I'm doing this! The building is attractive even from the outside, off-white with slate-blue roofing and an oversupply of pristine windows, and the surroundings — the place lives up to the tourism photos. As advertised, the apartments look out over a stretch of inlet and the two curved rock walls forming something called the Bar, which is described as 'infamous', not sure why, and beyond that stretches the alluring sea.

I hear running footsteps and a blonde heavy-set woman rushes around the corner.

"Hayley?" she puffs. "Sorry I'm late."

"No problem," I reply, my nerves jingling in time with the set of keys she produces.

"Let's go up," she says. "I'm Jane, by the way." She charges through the double glass doors and presses the lift button.

We get out at level three and the ache in my chest alerts me I'm holding my breath as Jane fits the key into the door to number

311 and pushes it open. I so need this to be the sanctuary I crave. Taking a deep breath, I march into the space and stop dead, blinking rapidly. Oh. My. God. I love it. Mist-green walls stretch up from pale-grey timber floorboards to a crisp white ceiling. The space is filled with light and sunshine and the view is absolutely to die for. I swallow hard.

"The bedroom is this way," says Jane, heading towards a side door.

Tearing my gaze from the glittering ocean, I follow her into a spacious room, the décor the same, with a shaggy white rug by the king-sized bed, which looks Japanese in design with its slanted beige wood headboard.

"I hope you like a firm mattress," she says, pushing her fist into the doona cover.

Speechless, I follow her to the ensuite. Oh. My. God, again. There's a Japanese bathtub-spa against one wall, and a large, modern shower backed by mist-green tiles with a seashell pattern on the other side of the vanity.

"You fill the spa bath when you want to use it," explains Jane, showing me a hose attachment that can be attached to the sink taps. "It's o-furo-style, meaning you sit in it, on the bench there, with your legs down."

I nod. "I'm familiar, I've been to Japan."

"Oh, right," she says. "I'm told the spa jets are powerful."

"The place is perfect, thank you." I smile at her.

"So glad you like it." Jane hands me the keys and a business card. "Call if you need anything. Enjoy your stay." She pumps my hand briskly and charges out.

I wander back to the lounge area and plonk down on the moss-green leather sofa, staring out at the turquoise water of the inlet. Three whole months … I may never want to leave. But I don't know anyone, don't have a job here. Can't afford to stay longer.

Shut up, practical side. Do you have to remind me of reality all the time? Relax, Hayles. You're here to recuperate, recover, find yourself again. Everything else can wait. *Not your luggage, which is still in the car. And don't you need food?* Okay, good points. Grumbling, I push to my feet.

By the time the setting sun is casting golden glints across the ocean, I've lugged my cases and boxes up to the apartment and packed everything away. Thank God the lift goes down to the underground carpark, and the unit comes with a designated space. As I stand with my hands on my hips, mesmerised by the view, my stomach rumbles. According to the information folder the owners left on the glass coffee table, there are a number of hotels, pubs and restaurants nearby, within a five to ten-minute walk.

My energy drains away: I don't fancy walking into somewhere by myself. It's been a long day. I see the breast care nurse's face in my mind: *'Be kind to yourself. Don't force anything, not for a while.'* Okay, instant noodles and salad it is. With a glass of alcohol-free Pinot Gris to celebrate. Ten minutes later I'm seated on the sofa, slurping up the noodles. Lifting the glass of fake wine, I salute my reflection in the dark window — I made it, I'm here, ready to open a new chapter.

~

I open my eyes, my whole body heavy, anchoring me to the sheets, and see primrose light rippling on the ceiling. My pulse rises; my bedroom is usually shadowy in the morning due to the trees outside. *Where am I?* Sitting up, I spy the azure ocean stretching away to meet bluebell sky. Narooma! New chapter, second chance. Get up, Hayles, Carpe Diem, seize the day! *And do what?* prompts my subcon. *Something, anything,* I hurl back.

My phone screen reveals it is six-fifteen. I squint at it. Can that be right? It means I slept for … nine hours! That's a first since my diagnosis. Most nights I wake several times, brain and stomach churning with what-ifs. This place is good for me already.

Energised, I leap up and prepare my breakfast of neatly chopped fresh fruit, topped with organic almonds and dollops of natural yoghurt. A daily habit since the cook at the health retreat told me the importance of starting the day with fresh, raw fruit due to the enzymes and that dark red berries contain some kind of anti-cancer agent. I eye my mug of coffee; not recommended, but some things are harder to let go of.

Breakfast concluded, it is … seven-thirty, Saturday morning, day one. Hmm. Some exercise and exploration? I pad to the bedroom and don knee-length shorts and a simple T-shirt, then stand with my gaze flicking between my running shoes and my sandals. My heart pangs painfully. No point running with such limited strength. Don't want to shuffle along looking pathetic. Walk, then. Better than nothing. I grab my comfy Keen sandals and slip them on.

Once outside, I open up Google maps and select the satellite imagery. Which way is more attractive? So, right leads to where the fishing and charter boats are moored and then the golf course. Left follows a bike path along the foreshore, crosses a road and goes deeper into the inlet, past a park with picnic tables and further along leads to some waterfront cafes. Worth checking them out.

As I pass the indoor fifty-metre pool, I peer in the full-length glass windows at the lap swimmers powering up and down. Maybe I should treat myself to a new swimsuit and do a few laps too. That might stretch my chest open again, help dislodge this horrible, scrunched feeling.

Striding faster, I follow the path along the foreshore, cleverly designed to look like a natural wetland, complete with short boardwalks heading over the water so you can stop to watch the marine and birdlife. Crossing the road, I take the path heading along

Riverside Drive. Pausing, I check the Google map. Yes, the green park with picnic tables should be eight hundred metres ahead, and then, past several whacky-looking boatsheds, there are the cafes hugging the waterline.

I stride out again, and out of nowhere my mind shows me sitting at a café table by myself, looking all forlorn and playing with the froth on top of a coffee. The backs of my eyes prickle. *Not now. No random tears on day one.* Holding my chin higher, I gaze around at the scenery. *Focus. Enjoy the walk.*

Allowing the path to roll by beneath my feet, I lap up the sprinkle of warmth from the sun on my face and arms. Definitely warmer here than in Canberra. *Be in the present, breathe in the here and now. In for four, out for four. Again.*

A cyclist whizzes past on my right and my heartrate gallops. *Idiot.* Doesn't he have a bell? The bicycle clunks over a bump and several brightly-coloured objects tumble out of the rider's pocket. Not noticing, the cyclist keeps going. I glare at his back until he pulls up with a screech of brakes at the first boatshed, dismounts and props his bike against a tree.

On reaching the trail of scattered colourful objects, my lips twitch. Lollipops? Why would a man need so many? Retrieving them one by one, I form a vibrant bouquet in my hand. Taking a deep breath, I approach the blue-and-white striped boatshed, which is a hive of bustling activity with people going in and out and carrying paddles of some sort. The man has removed his helmet and is changing his shoes. I hover, twisting the lollipops in my hand. What should I say?

The man glances up, and I find myself staring into almond-shaped dark brown, almost-black eyes in an alert and fit-looking face topped by wiry black hair in a sporty bob.

"Er, you dropped these." I thrust the bouquet of sweets at him.

"What?" He pats his pocket. "Oh. My lollipops."

I thrust my hand at him again, insisting he take the lollipops and he gives me a sheepish grin. Should I ask why he needs so many? Tempting, but I don't know him. He cups his hands and I drop the lollipops into them.

"Thanks." He pushes the sweets back into his pocket, then his gaze sweeps down to my feet before travelling back up to my face. "You look dressed for paddling. Have you come to join us?"

My eyebrows pucker into a frown. Join them? Oh, they're all dressed for paddling, in royal-blue matching tops with a pattern on. A uniform? "Are you going kayaking?"

"No, no." He flaps a hand at the sign above the open shed doors. "We're the Clear Water Dragons."

I stare at the sign, with its image of what looks like a turquoise seahorse and, none the wiser, blow a wisp of stray hair away from my mouth.

"We're a dragon boat club," he says with a welcoming smile that reveals neat white teeth. "We're about to take the boat out."

A dragon boat club! The breast care nurses said in our final debrief session that dragon boat paddling was really good for recovery and regaining strength. Should I go? I flex my fingers, considering.

A tall woman with strawberry-blonde hair brushes past the man, heading towards the shed. "Are we giving lollipops to random pretty girls now, Justin, or do we still have to earn them?"

Heat flames up his neck and he coughs. So, his name is Justin. His offer seems sincere, and I don't have anything else to do. I chew my lower lip. *Go on. It's a sport. But I'm a runner, no upper body strength. What if it's too much for my arm?*

"We have space in the boat today if you'd like to give it a try." Justin smiles encouragingly. "What you're wearing will be fine. Let's find you a paddle."

My courage arrives. "Alright. Why not?"

He looks delighted I'd agreed. My heart skips a few beats.

Dragon boating! Alexa and the other breast care nurses will be proud of me. Justin races into the shed and I stand outside watching the super strong and fit crew, mainly women, pushing a massive boat out the back of the shed. Seriously? After major surgery, chemo and radiation? This looks like hard work. Am I about to make a fool of myself?

"Here." Justin emerges from the shed and hands me a wooden paddle. "Put the blade on the ground, yes, like that, and slip the handle under your armpit. Yep, perfect. That's the right length." His eyes bore into me. "Can you swim or do you need a lifejacket?"

"Swim? Will the boat tip over?" Maybe I shouldn't have been so hasty, I don't know anything about water sports.

Justin shakes his head and a lock of hair slips into his eye. "No, no. Never so far. Just in case."

"I can swim."

"Good." He slaps his forehead. "Ah. As a guest paddler you need to complete a waiver form, for the club's insurance."

"Are we going today, Justin?" The tall woman with strawberry-blonde hair approaches. "The boat's ready."

"Funny. I'm briefing our new paddler. Can you get her a waiver form?"

The woman rolls her eyes, then turns to me. "I'm Natalie. I assume you have a name?"

"Hayley." I suppress a smile at the discomfort crossing Justin's face when he realises he'd neglected to ask.

"I'll seat you in row ten, at the back of the boat where I can see you," says Justin, quickly adding, "I mean so I can see your style and give you tips."

Natalie arches an eyebrow at him and then gives me a measured look. "I'll be your bench buddy. Follow me."

First, she takes me into the tiny shed. Amazed, I stare around at the volume of equipment all impeccably stowed along hooks and shelves. The narrow shed's a bit like the Tardis, seems much bigger on the inside. I balance the clipboard on my knee and complete the waiver form, momentarily panicking when I can't recall the name of the apartments. The View? No, that's not it. The Wharf? Sounds right. I scrawl that and add number 311.

"Thanks." Natalie takes the form and slides it into a clear sheet inside a ring-folder. Then with a tilt of her head, she sets off down the side of the narrow shed, steps down a small sandy ledge and wades into the water.

I follow, wincing at the cold water rising over my ankles, and round the back of the shed. *Wow!* A lifelike dragon head beams at me, stretching into a long boat with multiple wooden benches. The sides of the boat are painted with blue dragon-like scales. Now the image in the sign makes sense, it's not a seahorse, but a river dragon — they don't have wings like the ones in many fantasy novels do. It's meant to look like a Chinese dragon. Tentatively, I pat the dragon's head. *Wish me luck.*

Justin splashes past, now clad in a royal-blue singlet with a swirling turquoise dragon pattern on the front and back, and climbs into the boat. The muscles in his legs ripple as he takes confident strides over the benches until he reaches the back, where he picks up a long oar. Then the muscles in his shoulders and arms bulge and ripple sinuously. *Er, wow.* He looks like an Oriental warrior from ages past.

"The back of the boat boards first," says Natalie. "Let's go."

Gulping in some air and courage, I climb into the boat, which feels narrow and tippy, and carefully step over the benches until I can thump down on the last one beside Natalie. It's snug, with our hips brushing each other. While the others board, Natalie shows me how to hold the paddle with my outside hand down low, just above the broad part which she tells me is called the blade, and my inside hand curled over the handle at the top, ready to plunge the paddle down.

Warm, chai-scented breath flows over my cheek and shoulder and Justin's words are right near my ear. "We swap sides regularly. Are you okay to start on the left side?"

My throat tightening, I nod. Has he noticed something? Are my uneven boobs and wasted left arm that obvious? Shit. I want to get off the boat, but the benches are now filled with paddlers, chatting to each other and adjusting their position.

"If you feel tired or get sore, pull your paddle out of the water, okay?" The chai scent wafts around me again.

Natalie nods. "The most important thing is to be in time. Watch and mimic the arms of the two at the front."

"They're called the strokes," advises Justin, his face still close behind my shoulder.

When Natalie's lips quirk up like she's itching to make a smart remark, Justin retreats and stands up tall.

"Paddles back!" he calls.

Observing the others, I put my paddle blade back behind me and hold it just above the water. When Justin calls "Go!" I copy everyone and pull it through the water, lift it high and swing it back for the next stroke. Energy seeps into my arms and body.

The boat slips backwards past the wooden pier, gliding over golden sand and waving jade seagrass below crystal clear water. The sound of the paddles and water swishing is rhythmic and soothing. Calm steals over me. I can do this!

~

Keeping the boat straight as we reverse, I run my eyes over Hayley. Slim, tall, looks fit but somehow fragile … Why does she appear fragile? Got it. It's the way she's kind of curling her left side in, protecting it. Some strength work would do her good. Should I recommend my physio practice? *Bit soon for that, Justin.*

At the edge of the pier, I swing the boat around to head towards real estate bay, with its verdant sloping lawns and elegant waterfront houses. Although there's only a light wind, I want Hayley to have a good experience first time out. She mightn't come back if we aim for choppy water and a hard paddle.

"Paddles up! Go!" The crew fluidly change direction and paddle forwards, with Hayley gamely copying them, her shoulders tight with tension. She's trying too hard, but that's usual for newbies. Natalie's a good buddy, providing lots of encouragement and technique tips.

"Stop the boat!" After ten minutes, I call for the paddlers to change sides. While the front of the boat is swapping seats in pairs, I lean forward. "Are you okay?" I ask Hayley.

She half-twists to look up at me, her hazel eyes wide with exhilaration. "Yup. Good, thanks."

My heart races for several beats. Just like that, she's taken to paddling! "Great." I smile and her cheeks turn a delightful shade of rose.

Natalie diverts Hayley's attention by telling her how to swap sides and I breathe out. *Focus, man. She's just a new paddler.*

"Paddles up. Go!" This time, I steer the boat around several sheltered bays in the inlet, changing up the drills for longer, stronger strokes, then shorter powerful ones, then a pyramid of getting faster and faster. Hayley only clunks her paddle against the paddle in front of her twice, keeping excellent timing. Her shoulders still look tense, though.

"Sea eagle at eleven o'clock!" yells Amelia from the front.

With a sigh I call, "Stop the boat." Got to keep the ornithologists on board happy. A young white sea eagle with grey wingtips soars above us on the left, waiting for a fish to jump. Hayley is craning her head around at one o'clock. Tipping forward and holding the oar with one hand, I tap her shoulder with my other hand. She jumps.

"Your other eleven o'clock," I murmur. "To your left."

"Oh." She quickly glances the other way. "I see it!" She flashes me a broad grin.

I give her shoulder an encouraging pat. "You're doing well, just try to relax."

Natalie lasers an astonished look at me and I give her a level look back. What? I'm the coach, encouraging a newbie. Working the oar, I turn the boat's nose for home. What was Nat's look about? She knows I don't date in the boat. Complicates the team dynamics.

While the crew paddle back across the inlet, I hold my chin high, telling myself I do not need to keep watching Hayley, she's doing just fine. Two-thirds of the way across, I drop my gaze to check her form. My eyebrow lifts. Hayley's still paddling in good time, actually pulling a fair amount of water with each stroke, and her shoulders have relaxed. Okay, so she's not as fragile as she looks. Maybe we do want her to come back.

I turn the boat in a wide curve so we can glide in straight alongside the pier and stop just out the back of the boatshed. A perfect run in and the boat's nose slides smoothly onto the sand in the shallow water just behind the shed.

Natalie turns to Hayley. "Well done. Not bad for a first outing. Now we clean the boat and do warm-down stretches." Nat flicks her head back at me and adds, "The coach is a stickler for stretching."

Hayley peers over her shoulder at me, her mouth curving up at the ends. "Stretching is good."

The look in her eyes suggests she has experience from another sport. Well, that could explain how she managed to breeze through an hour's paddle. Interesting. I travel my eyes over her physique. She's not too muscled, so maybe an endurance sport. Running or cycling? We could use another fit paddler for regattas.

The crew efficiently hose and wipe down the boat, with Hayley pitching in and chatting happily. Not that I'm looking. When two paddlers hold up the sleeping bag that houses the boat's dragon head, Hayley steps forward and gently pats the forehead, an admiring look on her face. My breath catches: she acknowledged the dragon! A shiver runs down my spine. Does she know the significance of the dragon in Chinese mythology or is she intuitively responding to the ornate and boldly carved head?

Hayley looks up and catches me watching her. Better go and speak to her.

"Are the boats expensive?" she asks before I can say anything.

I nod. "The boat we went out in is a twenties boat — twenty paddlers plus a sweep to steer it, that's me, and in races we have a drummer to help us keep in time and egg us on. This boat cost us 14,000 dollars new. It was shipped from China."

"China? Wow." She gives me an intent look, like she wants to ask something else.

When she doesn't say anything, I beckon to the crew and head for the patch of grass near the front of the shed. "Gather round, and I'll take us through some cool-down stretches. Then it's lollipop time."

The crew form a ragged circle and I begin with holding my arms above my head and circling my wrists. Hayley winces when she lifts her arms. Hmm. Hope she won't pay for this too much tomorrow. She gamely tries all the stretches, and I observe her tiny winces of discomfort. No upper body strength, but some underlying toughness there. When I get the lollipops out and bunch them in my fist Hayley gives me such a spontaneous Cheshire cat grin that my fingers fumble and I drop the lot. Cheeks hot, I bend over to retrieve them, pretending I can't hear the crew's laughter.

"Alright, that's enough," I croak, standing tall and avoiding looking at Hayley. "The yellow lollipop for good timing goes to Sonja. Nice work," I say when Sonja collects her lollipop.

"The green lollipop for best bird spotting goes to eagle-eyes Amelia. Again."

I award a purple lollipop for the best long and strong strokes, an orange one for most power shown, a white one for smoothest changing sides, and a blue lollipop for excellent buddying to Natalie. "Great job, Natalie. Hopefully she'll come back."

"And finally," I fix my eyes on Hayley, "the red lollipop goes to our new paddler, Hayley, who did really well today."

As Hayley crosses the circle, with everyone clapping, the sunshine casts warm glints in her wavy brown hair. She stops in front of me, a little breathless, and I notice the lines of freckles sweeping up over her nose in elegant curves. *Focus, man!*

"Good job, Hayley." I hold out a bright red lollipop in a courtly manner.

She prises the lollipop from my grasp, her fingers brushing mine, and my hand tingles.

"Will you come back?" God, that sounds too hopeful. "We can always use a new paddler."

"Can I? I think I'd like that." A somehow lost look flits across her face.

"Well, if you're not too sore …" I hesitate. Too much too soon? Maybe, but let her decide. "Tomorrow we're going for a social picnic paddle … from nine to about eleven. Bring snacks and a water bottle."

"From here?" Hayley waves a hand at the shed, flinging her red lollipop with the motion. "Oops. Sorry, I do want that."

Laughing, I dive to retrieve it. "The lollipops sure are lively today. Here." I give it back to her with another courtly flourish. "Tomorrow?"

Hayley swallows. "Sure. Couldn't pass up the opportunity to earn another lollipop!"

Laughter surrounds us. The crew! Better be more professional tomorrow or I'll never hear the end of it. I push down a groan.

"Thanks for making me go in the boat," Hayley murmurs with a shy smile. "See you tomorrow."

"Good. You're a natural." I watch her walk away, a lightness in her steps, wavy brown hair bouncing between her shoulders, looking happier and stronger. A lump clogs in my throat. Can paddling make that much difference to someone? If so, I'll have to coach her through carefully, make sure she builds gradually and doesn't get injured.

Do I need to know whether she has a physical issue? Maybe, but let's see how she goes.

CHAPTER FOUR
Picnic Paddle

I flutter my eyelids open and lay on my back for a moment waiting for the square, strong jaw with blond stubble and planed cheekbones below searing blue eyes to fade and be replaced by pale gold light playing on the ceiling. A tear trickles from my left eye and I brush it away. I haven't dreamed of Jonathan for a while. An ache builds in my chest. *He left me. Right when I needed him most.* I brush another tear away, my throat tightening painfully. *Come on, Hayley, move along.*

Why am I thinking of Jonathan? An image of Justin standing at the back of the dragon boat, the breeze ruffling his dark hair and his arm muscles rippling drops into my mind. Huh? Is this my mind trying to distract me with an alternative man? Talk about chalk and cheese, one blond and pale and the other dark and mysterious. Does Justin have hidden depths? *Nope, don't go there, Hayles. Find yourself first before you even think about it.*

Beep! Beep! Beep! I bolt upright and switch off my phone alarm. The picnic paddle! I swing out of bed and stride to the shower. The warm water sluicing down my neck and back eases the dull ache in my shoulders and arms. Bit of an ask, expecting my body to paddle again today. Cautiously, I rotate my left shoulder. Good, no sign of swelling or anything more sinister than my triceps grumbling they've been worked hard. My pressure stocking … I should wear it for the longer paddle, but then everyone will know there's something wrong with me. Sighing, I dip my face into the running water. Does it matter? *Yes. It does. You want people to accept you as you are, not feel sorry for you.* I flex my fingers. Fine. No pressure stocking. Brave face; bold front.

At 7:40 I lock the apartment door and skip down the stairwell, mentally running over what's in my lightweight backpack. Spare hat, sandals for paddling, water bottle, fruit and nut mix, protein bar, an apple, sunscreen. Long-sleeve running top in case it gets too sunny or breezy. Too much to take in the boat? I guess Natalie or Justin will say.

Walking briskly, I try to recall the paddlers' faces and names. Natalie my bench buddy, Justin with the almond-shaped eyes, Amanda the strong one, Justin with the shiny black hair, Amelia who likes birds, Justin the Oriental warrior … *cut it out, Justin,* I shake my head. Focus on the other paddlers — who are potential friends — get to know the crew.

As I approach the blue-and-white-striped shed my footsteps slow. The doors are shut; no sign of any activity. Did I get the day wrong? Wait. Justin said from 9 am. and it's only eight-fifteen. I guess a warm-up jog won't hurt. I tuck my backpack under the table to the left of the boatshed doors and set my Garmin watch to 'run' mode. Back along the path to the pool and return should take me about twenty minutes. I touch my toes a few times then set off.

For the first few minutes my legs and chest feel heavy. My Garmin shows six-minute kilometre pace and my eyebrows tug into a frown. *Not awesome.* I cross the road and pump my arms, feeling my stride lengthen. On reaching the pool car park I turn around. Five-thirty kilometre pace now. *Better.* Halfway back along the stretch of foreshore, a surge of energy fills me and my legs lighten. A salty sea breeze blows into my face, lifting my hair. I stretch my chest taller and my feet lighten further. *Now* I'm running. I revel in the familiar and much-missed movement, the sun bouncing off the water and the seagulls flying above. *I am alive.*

"Extra warm-up?" A voice on my right brings me back to earth. Justin. On his bike. Of course. He's cycling by my side, matching my pace, his dark eyes peering at me from under his helmet rim.

I nod. Speechless, not breathless.

"Impressive," he says, continuing to ride beside me.

Heat crawls across my cheeks as he glances over, watching my feet, my legs and then my arms. Is he assessing my running form? Does he have to be so obvious about it? I relax my shoulders and lengthen stride so he has to pedal faster. He grins.

"I'd race you to the boat shed, but you'd better save some energy." He waggles his fingers at me and forges ahead.

As soon as he's out of sight I drop back to a walk. Good grief. Please tell me he's not a running coach too. Curiosity rises. What does he do when he's not in the boat? He seems very focused on fitness. *Well, you have two hours in the boat to find out.* Speaking of which, I'd better jog again and make sure I don't miss the boat.

I walk the last bit to cool down. The boat shed is bustling with paddlers, many I recognise from yesterday and a few faces I don't recall.

"Hi Hayley!" Natalie waves at me. "You came back, good job."

I smile at her and retrieve my backpack from under the table, dodging all the paddles propped up against the side of the table.

"Oh good," says Natalie. "I was worried you hadn't brought a drink."

I take out my sandals and hat and show her my water bottle. "Do I sit next to you again?"

"Depends." Natalie glances at the open shed door. "We have

two sweeps here today, Justin and Sandi. Follow me and let's see where they've put you."

On reaching the shed door I see there's a whiteboard pinned up with a list of the paddlers present. A woman I don't recognise looks up at the mingling paddlers and adds Amanda's name as number nineteen. On the right-hand side, there is another list forming, marked left and right, bench one to bench ten. I watch as she writes Sandi in the sweep position and then puts Justin as the front right-hand paddler.

"Oh oh," murmurs Natalie. "The first half is going to be brisk. Sooner we put him at the back the better." She pats my shoulder as if in sympathy. "Remember, pull your paddle in if you get tired."

I swallow, but my mind's eye is already showing me Justin's sculpted body paddling powerfully at the head of the boat. I'd better be put at the back again so I can't be too mesmerised.

Natalie clears her throat. "Morning, Sandi." She tugs me forward. "This is Hayley, a new paddler who started yesterday. I'm happy to sit at the back with her again, if you like."

Sandi turns assessing grey eyes on me, then her weathered face crinkles into a smile. "Welcome. Good plan," she says to Natalie, turning back to write our names down at bench ten.

"Thanks, buddy," I whisper. The scent of chai teases my nostrils and sensing Justin behind me, I turn around.

He solemnly hands me a wooden paddle. "This is the paddle you used yesterday. Did it feel alright?"

I take it, making sure my fingers don't brush his. "I think so." I mean, how would I know? He tilts his head and hands me a clip-board and a pen. "You need another waiver form for today, so we're covered under DBF rules."

"Dragon Boat Federation," supplies Natalie.

"You're allowed five free paddles," continues Justin. "Then," he scrunches his fingers and cracks his knuckles, "if you're enjoying paddling, we need you to join up." His eyes focus on mine, like he's waiting for me to yell: Where do I sign?

Trying to balance the paddle with the clipboard, I'm all fingers and thumbs. "Thanks," I murmur.

Justin nods and backs away and a ball of disappointment rises in my throat. He seems more serious, more formal today. I prop the paddle against the shed wall and hurriedly complete the waiver form.

"I can take that," says Sandi kindly and I hand her the board and pen.

Nat taps my elbow. "Grab your paddle, we'll be boarding first again."

I follow her around the side of the shed, my heart warming at the sight of the ornate boat sitting in shallow water waiting for us, the dragon's lower jaw dropped open in what looks like a grin. Placing my hand on the smooth wooden forehead, I silently murmur, *Wish me luck again, river dragon.*

"I like that you greet the dragon." Justin materialises beside me, the skin around his eyes crinkling in a warm smile but there's an unfathomable depth in his dark eyes, like he's peering into my soul. "In Chinese mythology the river dragons are protectors of the people and bring rain to makes the crops grow."

My eyebrows quirk upwards. "They control the weather?"

"Uh huh. And in exchange, the people race their boats fast and furious and beat their drums loud and long and ply the dragons with offerings, especially before harvest time." Leaning in so close his breath washes over my cheek, he whispers, "The young dragons love to hear the drums."

I stare at him, tasting the salty air washing into my open mouth. Is he trying to wind me up? I love reading fantasy, adore dragonlore, but even so … His eyes turn even darker, shielding mysterious secrets. "Are you from China?" my lips blurt before I can think it through.

"My family is, yes." He waves a hand at the boat. "You'd better get in."

The thousand questions forming dissipate on seeing Sandi at the rear holding the oar with a what-the-hell expression and Natalie perched on the back bench beckoning impatiently. The rest of the paddlers are queued behind me. Mortified, I scramble into the boat, high-step over the benches and sink down beside Natalie, ignoring her look of curiosity. The other paddlers pile in, and I recognise Amelia's red ponytail in front of me. Justin looks a long way away right at the front.

"Paddles back!" calls Sandi. "Go!"

Like yesterday, calm steals over me as I copy the others, enjoying the energy seeping into my arms and shoulders, feeling my chest open and fresh, tangy air filling my lungs. The water is a more vivid turquoise than yesterday, if that's even possible, and a shoal of narrow silver fish darts under the boat, their fan tails wiggling frantically as they pull away on the far side.

"Focus on the strokes," mutters Natalie. "Watch Justin. See how high his inside arm rises? Match his movement as he drives his paddle down. Mimic his arms, not his paddle."

I gulp. *Watch Justin's technique, not ogle his muscles, Hayles.* Even as a newbie, from the back of the boat I can tell Justin's technique is neater, stronger, somehow more perfect than everyone else's. His shoulders ripple fluidly with each stroke he takes. He is, I imagine, a model of the Chinese paddlers of old. "Is Justin a good paddler?" I ask Natalie.

She flicks me a dry glance as she lifts her paddle for the next stroke. "Way too good for our club. He's going to try out for the southern team for the regional champs."

A regional team? No wonder he comes across as so intense. Cold shivers across my nape. Competitive … like Jonathan. Like me. Or how I was. Before. My heart gives a strangled throb. I miss the competition, the adrenaline of the races. How soon is Justin's tryout? Before I can ask Natalie, Sandi yells, "Give me a lift! Three, two, one … lift!"

After several rounds of drills, which Justin effortlessly leads the crew in, my arms are burning, particularly the left one, but I grit my teeth and keep paddling.

"See the island ahead?" says Natalie. "We're stopping there for the picnic. You've done well, buddy."

I give her a thankful grin, relieved when Sandi directs the boat to a grassy bank and with some tricky paddling forwards and back-wards, we align the boat so we can get out.

~

I splash a handful of water over my face. It's hot for September; the place will be flooded with tourists over the school holidays. Jumping out first, I take the rope and tug the boat's prow snug to the bank, then loop the rope around the closest tree trunk and tie a sailor's knot. Can't have *Ming II* heading home across the inlet without us. The others are plonking themselves down on the tufty grass in a large circle. Skimming the group, I see Hayley is between Nat and Simone. Nat catches my eye and gives a brisk nod, letting me know our newbie is doing well. Okay then.

Pulling my bag of snacks from my waist pouch, I join Greg and Andrew. This is a good time to talk to them about the imminent spring regattas.

"Hey, Justin," says Greg. "How's your training going? You look strong."

"When's the tryout?" asks Andrew, his words muffled around his muesli bar.

"Second weekend in October," I reply, my stomach rumbling as I eye the almonds and dried apricots in my palm. "The week after the first regatta in Canberra. Speaking of which, will you two come? We need at least six men so we can go in the open races."

Andrew hurriedly pushes the rest of his muesli bar into his mouth and grimaces.

Greg tilts his head. "I guess I could. You think I'm strong enough?"

I nod, crunching on almonds then washing them down with water. "We'll practise. Most of the girls have said they'll go and it would be good to have a Clear Water team without having to combine with another club."

"Well," says Andrew slowly, "if you're one short I suppose you can twist my arm."

Greg laughs. "You sure you want Justin twisting your arm? Look at his muscles!"

Flexing my biceps, I grin at them. Then, out of the corner of my eye, notice Natalie and Hayley staring at me from across the circle. Nat looks at Hayley and they both giggle. *Crap.* My cheeks flaming, I lower my arms. "Thanks guys, I'll add your names."

"Who's the new girl?" asks Andrew, his eyes sliding across the grassy expanse to rest on Hayley. "She's pretty."

"Not sure," I say a tad too brightly. "Turned up out of the blue yesterday."

Greg elbows Andrew in the ribs. "Mate, maybe she'll go to the regatta. Extra incentive for you."

I lift my water bottle and take a long drink. *Don't say anything.* My chest feels cramped and I swallow hard, the water searing the back of my throat. Andrew's always chatting up the girls. Suddenly, I don't want him anywhere near Hayley. Whoa! Where's that coming from? *You're the coach*, nudges my mind. *Keep her near you.*

"Justin?" says Greg.

I blink my mind back into focus. "What?"

"Andrew asked what the distances are at the regatta." Greg

gives me an odd look. "You alright? You've gone a bit pale. For you."

"Fine." I paste on a grin. "Water went down the wrong way." I look at Andrew, trying not to acknowledge his bushman, rugged square jaw and bright blue eyes. "There'll be a two-kilometre turn race followed by two-hundred metre heats."

Andrew grimaces. "Urgh. A long race and then lots of fast ones. I suppose we have to train for both?"

"Yep." I nod, the sly idea occurring that I could try to deter him in the training. No, wait, that's not fair on the team. Besides, that could deter Hayley too. Should I mention the regatta to her? Bit soon, she hasn't even joined yet! I glance over and she and Nat are looking at me again. What's going on? "Excuse me," I say to the boys. "I think Natalie wants to ask me something."

I push up to my feet, relieved to see Nat is actually now beckoning to me. I cross the grass casually, munching on more nuts. They instantly lodge in my throat. I gulp twice, forcing them down and try not to cough as I stop in front of Nat.

"Sit." Nat points at the grass before her, gesturing as if she's commanding one of the dogs she trains. "Can you tell Hayley how much it costs to join up and so on?"

I sink down cross-legged, glancing around to see where Sandi is. Nat could have asked her to explain. Okay, Sandi is busy showing Simone and Amelia something. A flower? I turn to Hayley, whose hazel eyes are latched on my face. "You think you might join up? Already?"

"Maybe." She gives me a nervous smile. "It would be good for me."

My eyebrow arching, I nod again. "Paddling is excellent for overall strength and fitness." Okay, wise guy, enough of the advertisements already. What next? Does she live here?

Natalie jumps in as if she's read my mind. "Hayley will be living here for three months, maybe longer. If she goes back to Canberra, can she transfer to a club there?"

Three months. My heart misses a beat. Long enough to get to know her, but then she might leave. *Never date in the boat, Justin. Just give her the facts.* I look into Hayley's eyes. "Well, it's not a neat transfer because we're different states, but they allow dual memberships now so it is doable. There are several clubs in Canberra."

"You could do dual membership and then paddle with us whenever you visit," Natalie adds.

My heart pounds as Hayley glances from me to Nat and back to me, her eyebrows pinched in a frown. *Come on. You want her to join, right?* I touch her knee lightly. "The team would love to have you, even if it's not long-term."

Her eyes fill with light and she runs the tip of her tongue over her rosebud lips before giving me a smile. "Okay. I'd like to. Thanks."

Astonished, I watch Natalie give Hayley a brief hug. Since when was she so friendly? She's usually all business. I arch an eyebrow at Natalie and she gives me an amused, knowing look. What the hell? Never mind. I shake myself and turn to Hayley. "I'll explain how to sign up when we get back. It's all online these days."

"Thanks, coach!" Hayley snaps me a salute. Is that a hint of mischief glinting in her hazel eyes above her pert, freckled nose?

My heartbeat skitters. Is she making fun of me? Natalie is positively *smirking.* Unease slides through me, I'm out of my depth here. "Anything else you need to know?" They both shake their heads. "Okay then. We'll get ready to paddle back." I stand and head towards Sandi, trying hard not to listen to hear if Hayley and Natalie are giggling behind me.

Soon, we're all back on board. Manoeuvring the oar, I steer the boat away from the bank. "Listen up," I call above the chatter. "Sandi and I reckon we'll do some endurance work on the way back, so we're going to move into a pyramid." I glance down, noting the worried look Hayley gives Natalie. "This is meant to be a fun day, so we'll keep the power and rate down a notch but practise continuous paddling. Keep going at a gentle rate while I explain to Hayley."

Leaning forward, I wait until Hayley tilts her head, indicating she's listening to me. Gods, her ear is a perfect shape, nudging out from her wavy hair. *Focus.* "A pyramid is as it sounds. We do ten strokes at a set rate, then twenty at a higher rate, building up to fifty strokes at the highest rate, then working back down." I wait for Hayley to nod.

"Remember, any time you feel tired or sore, pull your paddle in, rest a bit and join back in when you're ready." Hayley nods, but I'd wager she won't be pulling her paddle in any time soon. I'm reaching the conclusion that the fragile look is a mere shell. Or temporary. I stand tall. "Alright, start with ten strokes at fifty per cent, twenty at sixty per cent and up from there. I'll count it in. Starting in three … two … one … fifty per cent now."

The boat swishes forward at an easy rate. "Sixty per cent for twenty." The boat lifts, not a bad transition with everyone in good time. Even Andrew. "Seventy per cent for thirty." The boat lifts again. Tapping my right foot to keep count, I glance down at Hayley. Her form is still good, she's reaching forward and sitting up. Bubbles flow from her paddle, so she's pulling some water.

We reach fifty strokes at ninety per cent. Okay, I'm officially impressed. Hayley is reaching and pulling along with the crew as if she's always been in the boat. My pulse races. Maybe she *would* like to go to the regatta. She seems determined, and in another month she'd be ready.

"Fifty!" calls Natalie.

Oops. Lost count. "Forty strokes at eighty per cent," I call. I count the pyramid back down. "Great job, everyone! Let it run, have a drink and swap sides."

While the others are swapping, Hayley stretches out her left arm and then holds it above her head, opening and closing her fingers. A circulation issue? Pushing down the urge to ask if she's okay, I take a swig from my water bottle. Did she tell Natalie why she's moved here for three months? Should I ask? No, not appropriate. Give her space, let her paddle. Just be a good coach and bring her through.

Soon, we're back at the boat shed hosing *Ming II* and putting her away. I look away when Hayley strokes the dragon's head again and murmurs thanks to it. How does she know to do this? *Ask.* I grab a copy of the page with instructions on how to join the club and make my way towards Hayley. "How was that?" I ask neutrally.

"Great!" says Hayley, beaming at me. "Thanks so much for inviting me."

"You seem to be getting the hang of paddling really well," I say genuinely. "Glad you enjoyed it." I turn the piece of paper over in my hands. "Can I ask … why do you greet the dragon?"

A rosy flush stains Hayley's cheeks. "I read a lot of fantasy … and I love dragons. I also used to ride horses, and I always patted my mount before and after." She shrugs. "Habit, I guess."

"I see," I say, although I'm not sure I do. I hand her the sheet of paper. "Here are the instructions on how to join, and the club's bank account details. I'll add you to TeamApp." Her eyebrows lift quizzically and I add, "It's a special sports app. It lets you register for training sessions and any events. I'll talk you through it."

"Thanks." She bestows a coy smile on me. "I appreciate your help. Coach." She snaps me another salute, then backs away.

I watch her thank Sandi and Natalie then stride away along the bike path. The way my mind is churning, it's going to be a long three months.

Or a short three months — then she'll be gone.

CHAPTER FIVE
Morning Interlude

Even before I open my eyes, I groan. My arms are throbbing. As are my shoulders, lower back and hamstrings. What was I thinking? Over three hours doing a totally unfamiliar sport in two days. Was it worth it, though? Gently, I roll my head from side to side on my pillow to stretch my neck, considering. I think so. I've met way more people than I expected to already, Natalie seems really nice, I like her, and Justin is … intriguing. And the strength work will be really good for me, once my body adjusts. *Stick with it, Hayles.*

Sitting up, I glance out the window. The sun is only just clearing the horizon, casting glints across the surface of the sea as if someone has sprinkled jewels over it. Perfect for Tai Chi on the balcony. Wincing, I get up, pad to the fridge for a glass of cherry juice, down that, then open the sliding glass door and step out onto the balcony. The tiles are cool, refreshing beneath my feet and the air has a tangy, crisp edge to it.

Facing the rising sun, I put my right foot forward, angle my body and begin the first movement 'playing with water'. Lifting both arms, I bring them down, shifting my weight to the back foot and waggling my fingers as if I'm playing with a waterfall. Five times. Pivot and put the left foot forward, repeat. Hmm. The back of my left arm and under the armpit is tight. Hope it eases. Breathing in, I move into the second movement, legs apart, swinging both arms in a wide circle and then pushing out first to the right, then a big circle back the other way and pushing to the left, 'pushing away troubles'. I love the names the health retreat gave the movements. It makes the sequence easier to remember, and helps to visualise healing thoughts, like literally pushing away negativity and bad luck.

I complete the set of seventeen movements and stand for a moment assessing my body. Better, looser, but my right hand goes to my left armpit and prods it. Still tight. Is that a bit of swelling? A bud of anxiety forms. No, no, no, this can't stop me from paddling. It'll adjust. It has to. My gaze rests on the tranquil inlet water. The breast care nurses encouraged swimming as a way to offset lymphoedema, something about the weightless movement and the pressure from the surrounding water. A swim it is, then.

After changing into my worn swimsuit, slipping shorts and a tank top over it and strapping on my sandals, I check the information folder. I'm sure I saw a reference to a nearby safe beach … page two, here it is — Bar Beach South, a small beach sheltered by the rock walls and with a netted area for swimming. It's about a fifteen-minute walk. Grabbing my phone and a beach towel, I set off.

The bike path is fairly deserted, just a few early dog-walkers and ad hoc seagulls resting on the grass verge. On reaching the road crossing, instead of going left to the boatsheds I keep going, taking the slim footpath beside the narrow two-lane bridge across the inlet, then swinging right towards the sea, following yet another bike path. Over a crest, then downhill to a really cool boardwalk. I amble along the wooden slats, peering into the clear water searching for fish. The soldier crabs are so cute with their bright blue bodies, there's a few different types of fish, and then my heart thumps. Oh wow, that is the biggest manta ray I've ever seen! A good metre across, it glides effortlessly past.

The boardwalk ends at a car park. There's a boat ramp on the right, with a few signs about various diving, snorkelling and nature tours. That could be fun, wonder how much they cost? Next, there's a grass and tanbark children's playground, and then I reach some steps looking out over a long, open surf beach to the left, a handful of wet-suited surfers bobbing in the swell, and to my right is the promised sheltered swimming beach. I can see someone running at the far end, and one — no, maybe two — swimmers in the netted area.

I head down the steps and walk a little way along the firm sand, until I spy a natural dip in the sand dunes at the back of the beach. I trudge through the softer sand to get there and put my towel down on the slope, between a clump of wiry bushes. Sitting down, I unstrap my sandals. A flash of movement makes my breath catch. Oh. It's the runner, now sprinting. That is fast! Shading my eyes with my hand, I watch the runner ease back, touch the rock wall and turn around for another lap. The sun shines into his face, screwed up in concentration, and my heart jolts. Justin.

I shrink into my towel as Justin sprints back past me, his arms pumping and up on his toes, driving for speed. He's shirtless, and I can see every muscle and sinew in his shoulders and back working. Oh. My. God. With difficulty, I swallow. *Get a grip, Hayles. Okay, fine, he is magnificent — and he's the coach. Keep it simple. Just paddle. Recuperate. Get stronger.*

My stomach has barely stopped squirming when Justin sprints back past. I close my eyes. Hopefully he'll finish soon. If I sit quietly, he mightn't notice me. A brief peek shows Justin touching the rock wall and turning around, this time coming back at a steady lope. Sweat glistens on his shoulders and down his arms. I huddle into myself as he draws closer. A seagull glides down to land near my feet and screeches at me with bright eyes, hoping for scraps.

Justin glances across and his stride falters. *Oh oh.* He runs a few more steps then stops, turns and walks towards me. Scrambling to my feet, I fix my eyes on his face, resisting the desire to watch his well-defined chest muscles rising and falling with his breaths.

"Hayley?" he says. "Good morning." He looks down at my towel. "Going for a swim?"

"That's the plan," I reply brightly. Okay, he knows I saw him training so don't dodge it. "You're training pretty hard."

Justin runs a hand across the back of his neck and slicks sweat off. "Yep." He pauses and I can see him deciding how much to say, then his dark eyes meet mine. "I'm going to try out for a regional team, the trials are in four weeks."

"You have to run?" I ask, my curiosity piqued.

"It's part of the test, along with doing weights, pull-ups, sit-ups and, of course, paddling. Lots of paddling." He brushes sweat from his forehead and a lock of dark hair falls forward. A shiver ripples down his arms. "Do you want to walk a lap, by any chance? I shouldn't just stop."

Walk a lap? My heartbeat hitches. But he's right, he shouldn't just stop after strenuous exercise and I am interested to know more. "Yes, okay. Sorry to interrupt your session." I bend over to grab my sandals and jump when he taps my shoulder.

"Barefoot is better. Works all the foot and ankle muscles. Besides," he grins, "it feels good."

Feeling chastised, I drop my sandals and fall into step beside him as he heads back to the firmer sand along the water's edge. Assuming he wants to cool down briskly, I stride out.

"Whoa!" he says, lengthening his stride. "Do you always walk this fast?"

"Apparently," I reply, not slowing. "My friends are always complaining." I bite down the words, *I'd rather be running.*

"Okay, then." Justin grins and walks even faster, forcing me to lift my stride rate.

I snort, amused, and subtly drive with my arms. He has no idea how much practice I've had at this. I even considered becoming a race walker once. He matches me, his lips curved in a goofy grin, and I take it up another notch. He matches me again. My lips twitching, I start to wiggle my hips like a pro race walker and truly stretch out, chin high.

Justin tries to imitate me, fails, and breaks into a jog, laughing. "Okay, I surrender. I'll jog and you do whatever you call that weird thing you're doing!"

His laugh is infectious and I giggle, dropping into an easy jog beside him. We jog in silence to the end of the beach, where he slows and touches the rock wall. I stop and turn around.

"Hey," he says, mock-serious. "No shortcuts. Touch the wall."

I hasten to brush the grey boulders with my fingertips. "Agreed. Distance runners *never* take shortcuts."

Justin starts to walk back along the beach, but his expression sharpens. "You're a distance runner? How far?"

I shrug. "Did a few marathons, quite a bit of cross-country but I'm better on the road."

He looks astonished. "As in an Olympic-length marathon?"

"Yep, the full forty-two kilometres." I glance at him sideways, tempted to show off by revealing my times. No, no, my pulse skitters. If I do that he'll ask when my next race is. Better deflect him, fast. "So, back to the regional tryouts," I aim for a casual tone, "tell me more about these? How do dragon boat competitions work?"

Gee, that was easy. Justin is successfully deflected for another full lap of the beach while he explains the usual distances raced, how clubs compete at local, regional, state and national level, and tells me the Australian team that competes overseas is called the Auroras. Such a cool team name. Intrigued by this very different form of sport, I brush my fingers over the rocks at the end near the steps while he's still explaining.

When he starts another lap, my eyebrows rise. He sure is passionate about his sport. My mind drifts, unable to absorb any more dragon boat information, and I can't help but eye his sculpted shoulders as he walks, or the way the sunshine puts rainbow hints in his raven-black hair, just like a real raven's feathers. A large boat comes into view from behind the inner rock wall, bouncing over the small waves in the channel. It's packed with people decked-out in life jackets, and my feet falter as I twist to watch it line up preparing to make a run out through the Bar channel.

Justin pauses beside me, but I'm absorbed by the boat, which idles for about a minute, then revs its engine and races out between the rock walls. By the lift-up at the front I realise it's a hovercraft. The boat races up an incoming swell, dips down the other side then powers up the next wave. Four or five bounces, then it's speeding out to sea.

"Wow," I murmur. "That looks like fun." I turn and find Justin studying my face. A rosy heat spreads up my neck.

He clears his throat. "That's one of the more popular charter tour boats. They go out to Montague Island." He hesitates, and I notice he's scrunching his fingers by his side. "Have you ever seen a whale? Up close?"

"A whale?" I gasp. "Here?" I wave my hand at the sea.

Justin nods. "The whales swim south after they have their calves. It's the start of whale-watching season."

"Calves, as in baby whales? Wow, I'd love to see one." My mind starts trying to picture a baby whale. "How big would it be? Do they have only one?"

A troubled frown pinches Justin's eyebrows, then his facial muscles relax and smooth it away. "Okay, then," he murmurs so softly I barely hear him. He looks me in the eye. "I'll take you on a tour. In another week or so, when there are more whales."

My mouth falls open and I feel my heart thudding against my breastbone. Did he just say he would take me? To see the whales? Words of delight are forming, curling around my tongue, but none of them seem able to pass my lips. I try to smile. "Awesome," comes out as a croak.

Justin smiles, fine creases forming around his eyes. "I'll book it. Let you know. Probably a Friday morning."

I nod, still speechless.

Justin looks at his watch. "Crap!" Panic crosses his face. "I'm late, gotta go." He backs away, walking backwards. "See you at paddling. Thursday afternoon, 4 o'clock, at the shed." He spins around and runs, almost as fast as when he was sprinting.

Dazed, I watch him grab up shoes and clothes from the base of the wall, then bound up the steps and out of sight. What just happened? My mind whirring, I walk back to my towel. Did Justin just ask me out? Or is he merely being kind? My heart swells with a sigh. Guess I'll have to wait to find out. *Keep cool, Hayles. Seeing the whales will be reward enough if he's only being nice.*

I'm still trying to convince myself of this as I swim.

CHAPTER SIX
Justin

"You can sit up now." I sneak a glance at my watch while the client is manoeuvring himself to sitting up on the physio bed. Nearly three-fifteen, time to wrap up the appointment. Will Hayley remember I said four o'clock for training? And if she does, will she come? She seems keen enough. I can't believe I blabbed at her for so long about the regional training! She must think I'm boring as batshit.

"That does feel a bit better," murmurs Gerald, one of the active octogenarians in the area.

"Just rotate the left shoulder for me … good … now the right one."

"Much better," says Gerald with a thin grimace. "Can I resume swimming?"

"Yes," I advise, "but maybe skip it on days when the water's too choppy or the pull is strong. Give it another week before you fully load it."

"Sounds fair," grumbles Gerald. "Should I book in again?"

I look at him, assessing the slight rotation visible in his left shoulder. "You decide, but a follow-up in a fortnight might be good." I don't like to encourage dependency, but these older clients need a fair bit of maintenance to help their bodies keep pace with their enthusiasm. They're so full of life it's impressive.

After Gerald has left, I clean the table with disinfectant wipes, check my calendar to see how full tomorrow is and am about to log off when I remember to check the tour availability for Friday next week. I go to the 'Ama Ocean Tours' website, run by Kraig and his Japanese wife Akiko. I like their options best and they're fun, lovely people. I scroll through their schedule. Gosh, there are only four places left on the 8am tour Friday 29th September already. Must still be school holidays. Reserving two slots, I print out the tickets and tuck them into my desk drawer. Then I block out the morning in my physio calendar, scrawling a post-it note to remind me to tell Simone, my receptionist, that I won't be in.

I log off and stand blinking at the blank screen. What if Hayley doesn't really want to go? My mind replays the astonished and de-lighted look on her face when I said I'd take her. I swallow. What am I doing? My heart gives this kind of strangled throb. I hardly know anything about her other than she's randomly here for three months and runs marathons … wait. Does she still run marathons? How fast is she? She didn't elaborate … oh, hang on, I see what she did, asking me about dragon boat races so I couldn't ask her anything more! Subtle. Clever. Well, I won't fall for that trick again, and she'll be trapped on a tour boat with me for two hours. Plenty of time to come up with a few questions. My watch beeps. It's time to leave for training.

Pulling up outside the boat shed, I park my bike against the tree, take my helmet off and survey who's here. Amelia, Sandi, Nat, Greg, Andrew … and Hayley emerges from the shed clutching a wooden paddle. She remembered. My heart gives another of those strangled throbs. I clip my helmet to the bike handlebars and tug off my shoes so I can put on my paddling ones.

"You want to sweep or paddle?" Sandi approaches me with the whiteboard pen in her hand.

I tilt my head to ease the kink in my neck and consider. Probably better if I'm not watching Hayley, and I could use the training. "Paddle, if that's okay with you. Do you want to coach or shall I coach from the middle?"

"You can coach. I assume we need some race starts." Sandi walks off and continues assigning paddlers to seats on the board.

In almost record time we're all boarded. Sandi has put Greg with me in row five and cunningly seated Andrew in front of me so I can give him extra tips. His tense shoulders tell me he's not thrilled. Rose and Pippa are the strokes. Good call, they're both strong and can be relied upon to listen up rather than chatter and will smoothly change the rate or power when asked. Sandi has put Hayley next to Nat again, but moved them forward to row eight so Hayley can develop a feel for different seats in the boat.

Sandi takes us for a long warm-up, then calls for us to stop the boat in a sheltered, secluded bay with almost emerald water and houses I wish I could afford perched on sloping verdant lawns.

"Justin, do you want to take us through the race start?" she calls from the back of the boat.

I put my paddle across the gunnel and slowly stand up and turn inwards so I can see both the front and the back of the boat. The front rows half-swivel so they can hear me. "Okay, we have a month until the first regatta in Canberra. We've got twelve names down so far and it'd be great if another eight or ten can join us. Spread the word to those not here."

I run my eyes over the crew. "The regatta will be a two-kilometre turn race, followed by two-hundred metre heats. I'd like us to practise some fast starts, then do a steady paddle and practise some turns. Take note of which side you're more comfortable on and tell me after." I turn to Sandi. "We doing drinks and nibbles after training as usual?" She confirms with a nod.

"Okay, then," I glance to bench eight and rest my eyes on Hayley, who is sitting tall, listening eagerly. *Once a racer, always a racer.* "The start we've been using is five, short, deep powerful strokes to get us moving …" I pause when Natalie puts her paddle blade in the power zone to show Hayley, "yes, like that, then ten brisk strokes in the same zone, about level with the seat in front of you, then over the next ten strokes lengthen it out and settle into a sustainable rhythm."

Everyone nods when I sweep my eyes over them. "Let's do just the start twice, then try a two-hundred metre stretch at pace. We'll take a breather, swap sides and repeat." I sit back down and everyone shuffles their hips snug against the boat sides and digs their paddles in deep.

"Paddlers, sit ready, attention … go!" yells Sandi.

One, two, three, four, five, I bury my blade deep, challenging myself to pull ever bigger bubbles of water past the boat with each stroke. Ten brisk strokes and the boat is powering along, the nose lifted. I lean forward to lengthen my reach and bump my nose on Andrew's back. "Hinge and lean," I grunt and he takes the hint, leaning and reaching forward.

"Let it run!" calls Sandi, and we all sit up. "Justin?"

I half stand. "Not bad, the timing was good. Felt like we could do better in the lengthen phase. Remember to hinge it forward from your hips, use your whole upper body to bury your blades and pull that water. Let's try again."

The second effort is better, smoother, and the whole race practice goes well. It would be good if all these paddlers came to the regatta. We swap sides, and in the race start I detect a slight wobble in the boat, so someone is definitely better on the other side.

The sun is sinking lower and the faint breeze drops altogether as Sandi heads the boat back towards the shed. I relax into the rhythm of the boat, considering where to put people to optimise our performance. Depends on who else commits to the regatta. Did Sandi put her name down? Must check because then I could be a stroke rather than the sweep. Or we can alternate for the two distances. That would be good.

Once the boat's been cleaned and stored away, the paddlers mingle around the table in front of the shed. I change my shoes, slip on a fresh T-shirt and retrieve the rice crackers and hummus I brought from my bike pannier. Others are putting out cheese, salami, biscuits and other dips. Rose and Nick have both brought a bottle of wine to share and are pouring measures into plastic cups. Opening the crackers and hummus, I put them on the table and catch the tail end of Natalie explaining to Hayley that this is usual for Thursday evening training and not to worry that she didn't bring anything. Hayley puts her backpack down and moves closer to the table.

Before I can say anything to Hayley, Amelia sidles up to her and starts showing her photos of birds on her phone, explaining which ones are more common around the inlet.

"Coach," says Nat, bumping my elbow with hers, a cup of Rosé in her other hand. "Hayley has paid up and joined. That brings us to forty-two members."

"Great." I grin at Nat. "Good work, bench buddy. Maybe we should hold a Come and Try day to get you some more people to persuade."

"Good plan." Natalie takes a few sips of wine and doesn't move away. "After the regional tryouts is better for you, right?"

I nod and grab a few crackers, debating whether to ask Nat to persuade Hayley to come to the regatta. A sigh builds. No, let her volunteer if she's interested. Don't push her.

"Listen up, folks," calls Sandi. "I'd like to welcome Hayley to

Clear Water Dragons." She lifts her glass in a toast and everyone follows suit, beaming at Hayley with a chorus of 'welcome'.

Hayley blushes and fiddles her fingers together. She slides a subtle glance at me and I smile. How am I going to tell her about the tour next week without the others hearing? Maybe wait until everyone is leaving and grab a quick word.

I chat to the others, talk Rose and Jeannie into coming to the regatta, reassure Andrew he'll be fine if he remembers to hinge forward more, then glance at my watch. Almost seven! Everyone is enjoying the unusually balmy evening. Dusk is falling. I should go or it'll be hard to get up early for training. I sketch a wave at everyone and go to my bike.

I've just clipped my helmet on when Hayley approaches with a shy smile. "I didn't want to ask in front of everyone, but ..."

My pulse races while she twists her fingers together. What is she going to ask?

"... do you think I'd be ready to go to this regatta you're training for? I mean, I wouldn't want to slow the team down or anything. Natalie said I should ask you." She presses her lips closed.

"Er..." *C'mon Justin, words, man, words!* I clear my throat. "Judging by how quickly you're picking things up, I'd say you'd be fine." I find a smile. "Plus, from what you've said, you're already fit."

Her eyebrows retain their worried tilt.

"There's no medals at these season regattas, no sheep stations at stake, so they're a good place to start."

"Okay." She relaxes her eyebrows. "I'll put my name down." She goes to take a step back.

"Wait." I swallow. "The whale-watching tour ... does Friday next week suit you? It'll be early, before the wind picks up."

Her hazel eyes fill with light and her whole face radiates happiness. "That would be wonderful!" She takes a breath. "I can't wait."

Hard to speak with my heart doing this strangled throb thing again. "Send me a text, my number's on the club Facebook page as head coach, and I'll text back when and where to meet."

"Thanks, Justin." She looks like she wants to say more, but Natalie arrives by her side.

"Did he say yes?" Natalie asks, giving me an undecipherable look.

Hayley grins at her. "You might regret this if you have to sit next to me in a race."

Nat laughs. "I can bribe Justin to put you elsewhere, he's a real softie underneath this stern coach façade."

What the? My turn to laser Natalie with a fathomless look, which will have to do as no smart reply comes to mind.

Hayley shrugs on her backpack, the curve of her mouth betraying that she's trying not to laugh. "Thanks so much for making me welcome. See you on Saturday." She waves and sets off along the path with brisk steps.

I look away from her receding back and find Nat still standing there, her lips twitching with a barely suppressed smile.

"This is going to get interesting," she says vaguely, waggles her fingers at me and heads to her car.

Closing my eyes, I lean on my bike handlebars and ease in a slow breath. This is exactly why I never date in the boat. *Too late,* quips my heart. *You're in deep water now.*

I open my eyes. Maybe not. Hayley will be gone in three months — I can maintain control until then.

Yeah, good luck with that, my heart whispers.

CHAPTER SEVEN
Whale Watching

Pre-dawn gloom coats my bedroom walls and the shadowy curtains flutter in a gust of breeze. *Finally*, it is whale-watching day. But it's barely light and my forehead is throbbing. Sleep eluded me for most of the night, my brain intent on agonising over whether the tour with Justin is a date or a simple act of kindness. Two hours on a boat with him … my heart skips with excitement, rapidly chased out by anxiety. He's bound to ask questions. Lots. How much do I tell him? I flex my feet, stretching my calves. Is honesty the best policy? My chest muscles snap taut.

Stop stewing and get up. I throw off the covers and head straight to the balcony. Tai Chi literally watching the sun peek over the horizon, it is. The health retreat would be proud of me, given that they made us get up in the dark five mornings in a row, insisting we repeat all the moves facing the rising sun until we'd memorised all the poses. Unlocking the glass doors, I step out onto the balcony. Blinking, I encourage my eyes to adjust to the gloom. The green and red lights marking the edges of the rock walls and the width of the Bar channel wink reassuringly into the hazy sky. A handful of lights are moving along the channel towards the Bar and the distant chugging of motors reaches me. Fishing boats, heading out to sea. The magic of this place has wrapped itself around me already.

Standing with my legs apart, a breeze caressing my face, I move into the first pose. I manage not to think about Justin until pose four, 'peeping at the moon and sweeping earth'. As I swing my arms back up to my right, peering at the hazy sky from under my right armpit, Justin's face looms, his dark eyes assessing me. I swing my arms down, brushing my fingers across the floor to 'sweep earth' and swing up to my left. *Focus on the now. Breathe in wellness.*

The horizon shimmers with silvers and greys as I move through the poses until the tip of the sun rises, casting a rosy puddle on the distant waterline. Thin clouds scud above, reflecting a reddish tinge. Not a sailor's warning, I hope.

By seven, I'm striding along the bike path, my backpack bouncing on my back, lumpy with all the items Justin suggested I bring. Even through my lightweight spray jacket, the air brushing my arms is cool and more clouds are scudding in. As the boardwalk slats speed by under my feet, a ball of tension tangles itself in my stomach. I force myself to think about whales. And baby whales. That's what I'm here for.

I approach the end of the boat ramp and my heart thuds at the silhouette leaning against the post of the tour-guide sign. Justin. Here early. He sees me, pushes away from the post and cracks his knuckles. He's nervous too. My ball of tension yanks tighter.

"Hi Hayley. You all set?" Justin greets me with his professional coach smile. He's wearing a black bomber jacket, which accentuates his dark hair and eyes.

"Yes, coach," I say brightly.

"It's breezy so Kraig wants to set out as early as possible. But," he hurries to add, "the whales like it windy. They're more likely to breach, so the choppy water will be worth it."

"Okay." Excitement ripples through me; this will be a brand-new life experience. Lap it up. Enjoy. Be in the now. Stop stressing about the future. And how short it might be.

Justin turns around and walks down the boat ramp. Distracted by the *amazingly* intricate Chinese dragon embroidered right across the back of his jacket in silver and red thread I catch my toe on a ledge and stumble. Oh. My. God. I want a jacket like that. Luckily Justin doesn't notice, busy heading towards a tall man wearing navy trousers and a light-blue shirt with 'Ama Ocean Tours' embroidered across his left chest.

The silvery-cream boat behind the man has *The Ama Diver* in flowing navy script on the prow, and below the words is a painted image of a slim woman swimming downwards with dark hair fanning behind her, like she's free diving. Ama diver … I know this term from my Japanese studies. Got it, these are the women who free-dive for pearls and abalone. Why is—

"This is Kraig, the boat captain." Justin flaps a hand at me. "This is Hayley, one of our new paddlers."

Kraig shakes my hand, his grip strong and confident, matching his square jaw and steel-blue eyes. He looks vaguely familiar. When he gives me a crooked smile and tilts his head, an image of Matt Damon in the same pose flits into my mind. I blink. So, I'm surrounded by a Chinese warrior and a Matt Damon look-alike. The tour is shaping up well already.

A slim woman, who looks Japanese, with waist-length, straight, black hair pushes past Kraig and hands Justin a red lifejacket. "Hey Justin. You are training hard as usual?" Without waiting for his reply, she hands me a lifejacket. "I'm Akiko. Welcome aboard." She glances from me to Justin and back and lifts an eyebrow.

My cheeks warming, I smile at her. She is so very pretty, and buzzing with contained energy. Is she the woman in the image on the boat prow? "Hayley," I say. "One of Justin's paddlers."

Akiko gives me a sceptical look, lightly punches Justin's shoulder and heads back to the pile of life jackets near the boarding ramp. I find Justin watching me.

"Put it on over your spray jacket. It'll be colder when we head out to sea," he says, although I see his lifejacket is under his jacket. Didn't want to squish his dragon? Waving a hand at the narrow boarding ramp, which is rising and falling with the slight swell in the inlet, he adds, "There's no assigned seating so we can board first and choose."

Picking up my backpack, I follow Justin across the short ramp, carefully not admiring the intricate dragon to focus on my footing, and gratefully take his hand to step into the bobbing boat. A breeze hustles through the open sides. There are several rows of seats, five across, in the centre of the boat, all facing forwards. Justin heads to the front row. Trailing him, I realise this row will be more sheltered because the seats are right behind the captain's cabin. How many times has he been on this tour? How many women has he brought? My stomach knots. Was that why Akiko punched his arm? Is a tour his go-to move? A taste like unripe limes seeps into my mouth.

"You can take the outside seat," says Justin, "so you can see better." He taps my upper arm. "Are you alright?"

Damn, he is perceptive. I swallow the urge to shriek, *No, I am not alright. A long way from. I like you but what if my cancer comes back?* His expression turns serious and his eyes brim with concern. With effort, I flatten the overwhelming desire to throw myself into his arms and instead sit on the seat he suggested. That was rude of me, but I can't dredge up a single thing to say. Behind us, more people are boarding and choosing seats, chattering excitedly. A couple of young boys run a loop around the boat. Justin perches on the seat beside me, his shoulders tense. I need to rally and not ruin the tour for him, especially given he wouldn't even let me pay for my ticket.

Lifting my head, I raise a smile. "Sorry. Too much breakfast. The swell kind of got to me. I'll be fine. Honestly." His dark eyes assess me, as if the image I saw while doing my Tai Chi was a premonition. "I'll be right as soon as we see a whale."

After a dubious look, he says, "Kraig is very skilled at finding whales, he's lived here most of his life."

I shiver as cool air brushes across my cheeks. "Is Akiko his wife? She's Japanese?"

Tilting his head, Justin gives me a smile that looks kind of wistful. "They got married last year. Akiko's Japanese husband was killed in a car accident nearly three years ago and she came here to recuperate, with her daughter Miki." Humour lights his eyes. "I'll let Akiko tell you how they met, it's hilarious and she tells the story so well."

"Tell me Kraig didn't drop lollipops at her feet?" I say, laughing at the instant blush that stains Justin's cheeks.

"Very funny. No, Akiko's story is way more embarrassing." He glances at Akiko, who is moving smoothly among the passengers, greeting them and checking their life jackets are snug. "After the tour I'll introduce you properly. She runs too, you'll like her."

"Good morning, folks," Kraig's voice booms through a microphone. "Welcome aboard *The Ama Diver* for today's tour. It's breezy and choppy, so we're likely to see a few whales. If it gets too rough, I'll bring us back earlier. I'll hand you over to Akiko, who is brimming with fun and useful facts, including where your sick bags can be found."

A nervous tittering fills the boat while Kraig hands the microphone to Akiko and retreats to his captain's cabin. The boat engine stutters to life and the smell of diesel wafts around us. I grip the rim of my seat while the front of the boat swings away from the mooring pontoon and then chugs towards the entry to the channel.

"Good morning, everyone," says Akiko. "There is a toilet at the rear of the boat if you simply can't hold on, and the all-important sick bags are tucked in a pouch beneath your seats, although I hope you won't need them." She waves a hand at the inlet. "Please enjoy our close-up journey through this land and water, and we pay our respects to the people of the Yuin Nation, the traditional custodians of this beautiful area. Did you know Eurobodalla, the name of this shire, means 'land of many waters'?"

There are several murmurs and shaking of heads among the passengers.

"This area is blessed with many beaches, rivers and big lakes teeming with wildlife."

"Excellent for water sports, and the water is warm," murmurs Justin leaning towards me. "Unlike the water of Lake Burley Griffin. If you capsize there you'll have to be thawed out." He gives me a sly look. "And disinfected due to the algae."

A thrill chases through me as his arm brushes mine. Is he trying to persuade me it's better down here and I should stay? "Sooo encouraging to hear for my first regatta, coach." I quip back, arching an eyebrow. "Do we need wetsuits or Hazmat gear, then?"

Creases form around his almond-shaped eyes with the breadth of his grin. "We Clear Water Dragons are tougher than that. Sandals and shorts all year round." The corners of his mouth curve up. "But I hear some of the Canberra paddlers have special heated booties in winter."

Now I know he's trying to wind me up. I stare at him. Such an enigma; so intense but so much fun. Much more fun than Jonathan ever was … *no, don't go there. Keep it light.*

An 'oooh' sounds from the passengers on the left side of the boat and some of them stand and rush to the side railing.

"On our left we now have a pod of dolphins," informs Akiko. "They are likely to race the boat for a while, so please enjoy."

Justin grabs my hand and tugs me to my feet. Every nerve in

my fingers afire, I'm pulled to the side of the boat and lean on the railing beside him. He releases my hand, but before I can feel disappointed, I spy the sleek dolphins leaping alongside the boat. Their happy chatter fills the air as they bound effortlessly over the swell.

"Oh wow." I lean further out, peering at the closest one, admiring its grace and power.

"These are Common Dolphins," says Akiko, "often found in the waters around here. We used to see them regularly from the shore, but unfortunately as the supply of fish diminishes, we must go further out to see them."

I realise we're already out at sea and the rock walls are a blur behind us. I didn't even notice when we went out through the Bar! The boat is travelling fast now, rising and dipping as it crests each swell. The breeze is stronger, and becoming colder.

"Okay?" murmurs Justin. Suddenly swinging his gaze away, he points way ahead and to the left of the boat. "There. Whale spume."

Following the line of his finger, at first, I see nothing but choppy grey water, then there's a sense of a shadow and a spurt of white water. "I see it!" I yell and he gives me a pleased look. Beneath me, I feel the engine tone alter and the boat changes direction. I'm going to see a whale! Excitement flooding me, I grab Justin's hand. He jumps, then his fingers squeeze mine.

My heart hammers my breastbone as the boat draws nearer the whale, then Kraig cuts the engines and the boat bobs silently. I realise I'm holding my breath and let it out with such a whoosh that Justin laughs.

Akiko's calm voice surrounds us. "This is most likely a Humpback Whale. They are between 14 and 16 metres long and are the most frequently found around here. They are playful, and because it is windy, we should see it leap and roll and thump the water with its tail. Sometimes, the male whales range ahead, so we'll wait to see if this is a male or a mother with a calf. We are not allowed to go closer than this, but if we are lucky the whale might come to see us."

It feels as if the whole boat is holding its breath as we wait, scanning the water. Justin flexes his fingers and I realise I'm digging my fingernails into him. "Sorry," I mumble, and he squeezes my hand.

For a while we bob and sway in silence, with the whale spurting jets of water as if it is teasing us: 'I'm here but you can't see me'. Then it surfaces and leaps half out of the water, waves a massive fin at the sky in a half-roll and drops back down with an enormous splash. I want to take a photo with my phone, but then I'd have to let go of Justin's hand … which I grip hard to stop myself from squealing when I spy the smaller shadow right behind the enormous whale, its back just breaking the surface. "Is that … is that a calf?" I gasp.

Justin gives me a delighted smile, proud that he has delivered on his promise. I feel like kissing his cheek and hurriedly look back to the whale before I do despite telling myself not to. The boat drifts sideways with the current, and a cold wind gusts into our faces, moist with spray from the waves. Other passengers mutter and shrug on extra layers. Damn. I should have brought a thicker jacket. Determined not to waste a second of this magical experience, I clench my teeth and fix my eyes on the whale. Wait. Is that burst of spume closer?

"It's coming," says Justin. "Don't be afraid if it goes under the boat."

Under the boat? One look at his face tells me he's not joking. I imagine the massive creature surfacing under the boat and tossing us all into the sea. My teeth start to chatter and I feel as cold as if I've already been dunked.

"Hey," Justin says, starting to shrug out of his jacket. "You're going blue. Doesn't suit you."

I grab his arm. "My fault I didn't bring another jacket. You need yours as you have regional team tryouts. I'll be okay." My teeth chatter annoyingly.

His eyes grow immeasurably deep and a flash of something, could be resignation, crosses his face. Shrugging his shoulders back into his jacket, he says, "Okay, then. Go back to holding the railing. I'll keep you warm."

Unsure what he means, I face the sea and grip the railing so tight my knuckles are tinged white-blue. The boat is rolling rather than bobbing, and spray showers the railing as each swell slaps the boat's sides. None of this matters as I gaze at the massive, majestic whale sluicing towards us — and Justin leans his chest snugly against my back and envelops me in his arms. Hot elation washes through me, and I lap up the strength in his arms and his easy balance as he flexes with the pitching of the boat. I feel safe. Secure. Wanted. Overwhelmed. Burning tears slide from my eyes to mingle with the spray coating my cheeks.

The whale surfaces about a hundred metres away, revealing its throat and barnacles and white-ridged chest, then curves down, glides slowly towards us and dives under the boat, the baby whale shadowing her side. Tears are rolling down my cheeks but I can't wipe them, my arms are pinned by Justin's. I feel his cheek rest against the top of my head and a strange tremble runs down his arms. Stupid life jackets, I wish he could get closer. Did his lips just brush my hair? Another tremor runs down his arms. I'd swear Justin is having a major moment. He's smart, strong, magnificent, intense, funny … and seemingly romantic too. How can he not have a wife or girlfriend?

My heart is breaking as the tail of the baby whale and then the rest of the mother whale and her tail disappear under the boat. Talk about a bucket-list moment. Silent, cold tears are dripping off my chin. Disentangling one arm, I brush them away. I'm a mess of roiling emotions. I can't face Justin. *Get a grip, Hayles. Fast.* This is a moment, that's all. It has to be. He's far too good to get tangled with me, with my uncertain future and high risk of recurrence. But it feels so good in his arms, which are hugging me closer, if anything. His chest presses against my back with the depth of his sigh. I drag my hand across my nose and sniff. Is he being a gentleman and giving me space to get it together? Or maybe he doesn't want this moment to end either. I close my eyes, despair lurking. I can't let him fall for me. Not fair. How can I deflect him gently?

"Today we are very lucky to see a mother and calf so close," Akiko's voice breaks the moment. "I hope you got good photos. Kraig apologises, but the wind is rising too fast at Barunguba Montague Island and he is going to head the boat back now. We must get back through the Bar before it gets too rough. To compensate, we'll give you a discount for a seal tour on a better day."

The engines splutter back to life. The delicious presence of Justin edges away from my back and his arms unwrap from around me. My heart wails. He gently squeezes the tops of my shoulders — difficult through the lifejacket — and steps back. I still can't look at him. I don't know what he's feeling. Did he go and sit down or is he waiting behind me? I can't bear to check.

The boat has turned right around and is picking up speed. I glance towards the cabin and find Akiko frowning at me. When she sees my messed-up face, her frown lifts and she nods. What does that mean? I look away and rummage for a tissue to blow my nose. Take three deep breaths. *You can do this. Go back to paddler and coach mode. Just be nice to him.*

I lurch my way back to my seat and thump down beside Justin. Give him a bright smile. "That was incredible. I can't thank you enough."

He reaches into the pocket of his jacket and hands me a red lollipop. I can't read his expression at all, but my heart is breaking all over again — a red lollipop, like how we first met. Overriding my despair, I summon an imperious look. "You're not going to throw it at my feet first?"

He looks startled, then gives me a crooked grin. "That only works once." He pushes the lollipop at me. "This is to celebrate seeing a whale."

"But we saw *two* whales …" I say cheekily. Phew, we're back on safer ground.

Justin slaps his forehead. Then draws out more lollipops, gives me the yellow one and keeps the green one. "Technically, one point five whales, but you can have two anyway."

"So generous," I quip. Quick, get him talking about dragon boating. "What do we get if we win a race at this Canberra regatta?"

"How about the glory of winning, Miss Sweet-tooth?" After a beat, while I'm still composing a smart reply, he gives me a measured look. "Are you used to winning? How fast can you run?"

I squirm on my seat. Part of me wants to dodge, the other part yearns to impress him. He waits, his eyes glued on my face, genuinely wanting to know. I swallow, but he doesn't give in. I swallow again. "My best times are thirty-seven minutes for ten kilometres and two-hours-fifty for a marathon."

"Okay, then." Justin's expression softens. "That's impressive. When?"

"When what?" I stammer.

"When did you do these times?"

"Year before last," I murmur. My breathing and pulse grow thready with anxiety: please don't ask why I didn't run last year. Justin scans my face, frowns slightly, and I can see the words forming in his mind: What happened last year? He flexes his fingers, cracks his knuckles, then gives me such a tender smile that I can't breathe at all.

"Okay, then. How do you feel about being trained to be nearer the front of the boat for the two-kilometre race? Your endurance is just what we need."

Air rushes into my chest as the bands of tension snap loose. He's let me off the hook. Deliberately. "Seriously?" I imagine what it would be like near the front, seeing the back of the dragon's head, feeling the boat prow skimming the water. "I'd like that."

Justin smiles, but somehow looks sad at the same time. I've let him down by not revealing more about myself. I glance out the side of the boat and see the rock walls looming ahead. We're almost back. Anxiety swamping me, I twist the lollipops around and around in my fingers. This is so unexpected, so unlooked-for, and I've only just got here. But I *need* the paddling, Justin's coaching, his friendship — just being with and around him. He makes me forget my possible death sentence. My pulse skitters. *Be brave, Hayles. Salvage this. But how?*

I square up my slumped shoulders and twist to face him. He's waiting, eyes on my face, no surprise there. He's being brave; so must I. "Coach … Justin … I appreciate everything you're doing for me. I do, honest." *Come on, spit it out.* "I've had a few setbacks, but I'm working on it." *Okay, shut up now.*

Justin rests a hand on my knee. "You're incredibly brave, Hayley, I can tell. You'll get there."

The concern on his face conveys his unspoken offer to help. He goes to remove his hand and I clutch at it, loving the way his strong fingers curl warmly around mine, and I know I don't need to say anything more.

For now.

CHAPTER EIGHT
Coach Mode

The half-eaten fish and chips are congealing on the plate. My stomach hasn't stopped churning since the tour. It was a miracle that none of my afternoon physio clients fell off the treatment table I was so barely present — Gerald almost did, but I managed to grab his arm in time. Gave me a fright and didn't help my nerves at all. I couldn't face cooking dinner and now it seems I can't eat it, either. Pushing the plate aside, I gaze at the sheet of paper with the benches numbered, ready for me to assign paddlers for tomorrow morning's training and our two-kilometre race practice. I need to tell Sandi I'd like to move Hayley forward in the boat, and why.

Hayley. My stomach does a spectacular triple backflip. What have I done? She obviously has a lot going on, and I'm probably only making it worse. Why, why, why did I have to hold her like that? I lean against the hard chair back. Man, the magic of the moment, the whales, the wild wind and sea, the searing chemistry between us. My stomach double backflips back the other way. I'm sure she was crying but hid it from me. I wanted to hold her forever, kiss away her troubles. Except I don't know what they are. I scrub at my face. It's something big, that much I can tell, and I should paddle as fast as I can in the other direction. But I don't want to.

Buzz. Buzz. My phone jangles on the table. *Father*. Talk about timing … I ignore it. Last thing I need right now. Come on, Justin, decide. What to do? Let it happen or back off to coach mode? That would be simpler, safer … *don't want to*, says my heart sulkily. Closing my eyes, I relive how Hayley lifted her chin and pert freckled nose when Akiko announced their range of tours, including Ama diving. As soon as we'd disembarked, Hayley marched over to Akiko to book in for Ama diving! Akiko did pause and glance at me in query, but I shrugged; not unless Hayley asks me and maybe it's better to let them form their own connection. How does she go from being devastated one minute to bouncing back like that? *She's different, could be special.*

Buzz. Buzz. Buzz. Father again. Damn it. I snatch up the phone.

"Jun Jie. You didn't get back to us. What days are you coming?"

Hello to you too, Father. I shove down the urge to actually snap this out. "I'll come straight from the tryouts in Nowra, so Saturday 15th October."

"Be in time for dinner. You stay a week?"

A week? On what planet does he think I can take a week off from my physio practice? "I have to leave Tuesday afternoon. Too many clients booked in." I bite back the automatic apology forming on my lips.

A grunt comes my way. "You need to make family your priority, Jun Jie. We have much to speak about and your cousins want to spend time with you."

"Understood, Father. Anything else?"

"Bring smart clothes. Xin Li, Meng Yao and Li Na are also coming." He hangs up.

I put the phone back on the table, eyeing it like it's a venomous snake. Oh man, I'm in deep, deep trouble. Father wants to talk about my involvement, or lack thereof, in the family business and his cousin is bringing *all three* of his eligible daughters. Maybe I could crash my car so I can't go. No, he'd send me a plane ticket. It's only an hour's flight from Moruya to Sydney. Why don't I stand up for myself? Why can't I just walk away, forever? Change my address and phone number? Ethan is welcome to have the empire. And his pick of the girls. I don't care that he's four years younger than me, why should Father?

Shame flooding me, I bow my head. What am I thinking? This is my family, my ancestry, my honour. *Their* honour. Mother must be sorrowful, and my actions are holding Ethan back, and that's not fair. I have to resolve this. Somehow. Soon. My hands shaking, I stand up and tip the slimy fish and chips into the bin, for once wishing I had a bottle of wine stashed in my fridge.

Maybe my troubles are as bad as Hayley's. Wait. What? Where did that come from? My heart pounding, I stand gripping the rim of the dirty plate. Talk about doomed if we *both* have such massive hurdles to overcome. But at least she's trying to overcome hers, whereas what am I doing? Being compliant, as usual. I slide the plate into the dishwasher.

Okay, then. How about I help Hayley overcome her troubles and learn from her? Observe her impressive courage and try to absorb some. Sitting down, I pull the sheet of paper to me, pick up the pen and tap it on the kitchen table. Hayley ran, no, *raced* marathons. That took dedication, courage, strength, the will to succeed, the desire to win. Something happened last year, and she seems to have lost herself. Yet she's brave enough to relocate and try to start again.

What if … what if paddling could refocus her? New sport, new goals. What if I could coach her all the way to regional level paddling? Despite whatever her 'setback' is. Excitement jolts into me. I'd have to spend loads of time with her … in coach mode … and I'm positive gaining strength and fitness would help her. It has already.

The more I think about it, the more I like the idea. A new challenge for me too, given most of the Clear Water Dragons are not that competitive. I'd love to have someone with real potential to coach. I chew on the end of the pen. Maybe I could even, after a bit, talk to her about my situation; I could sure use someone to brainstorm with. She comes across as sensible and smart. A different perspective would be helpful.

Wait, hang on. I almost forgot: she might not be in Narooma for long. My chest feeling hollow, I put the pen down. *Just try. It doesn't hurt to try, and maybe she'll stay. See where it goes.* And if she doesn't stay, she might prove to be the best person to confide in, given how private I've kept myself so far.

I pick up the pen.

~

"Okay, gather around for a chat before we board." I wait until the eighteen paddlers have clustered in a small circle and Sandi moves to stand beside me. "Right, we only have two weeks before the first regatta of the season but Sandi and I think it would be great if we can aim to attend most of them this season."

Sandi nods. "For once, we nearly have the numbers to register a club boat. I agree with Justin, let's give it a go. Doesn't matter if we don't win any races, in fact it's unlikely, it's about the training and aiming to improve our times and form over the season."

I skim my gaze around the circle and see most of the paddlers nodding, some more keenly than others. Andrew looks dismayed. "We still need two more paddlers for the regatta so if you can think of any other members who might join us, please encourage them."

"What about Gianni and Giulio?" asks Rose. I've seen them working in the family restaurant so I know they're still around."

"That would be great," I reply. The Italian brothers are strong but they play multiple sports so it might be hard to get them to commit. "Can you ask?" Rose gives me a thumbs-up.

"So today, we're going to start moving you around in the boat to find out who's best sat where for the long race. It's too late to achieve more fitness, but we can analyse our efficiency. Sandi will stroke and I'll sweep so I can watch you all." Out of the corner of my eye I notice Hayley stand taller. So, she hasn't forgotten my comment about moving her forward, but I'm not going to start her there. She's going to have to earn it so I can't be accused of favouritism.

We set off for a relaxed warm-up and I put the crew through a few technique drills, chipping people for not having their inside hands high enough or for not hinging at the hips and reaching forward when I ask for longer. Andrew will no doubt hate me before long, but a few of the others smarten up. Hayley and Nat are paddling well in bench eight. They're a good match height-wise, although Hayley is slimmer.

"Stop the boat." Here goes, and most of them are not going to like it. "A 2K race is about endurance." A few shoulders tense. Hayley slips me a small smile over her shoulder. Nat raises an eyebrow.

"We're going to do five and ten — five powerful, deep strokes then ten long and strong — repeat until I say stop." That earns me astonished looks over shoulders.

"Until you say stop?" asks Amelia. "Seriously?"

"Yep. I'm mean coach today." I try to snarl but end up grinning. "When you get tired, rest for two sets, then come back in. Extra lollipop to whoever doesn't pull their paddle in."

"Gonna need a gin and tonic with that lollipop," mutters Andrew sourly and everyone laughs.

"Remember your timing, I'll be watching closely. Paddles up. Go!"

Sandi and Rose dig in, the crew following suit, and the boat moves forward. I work the oar to keep us in a straight line running with the current, making sure we have a clear run for about a kilometre.

"Five power!" I remind them during the fourth set. "In a longer race we must keep momentum. I should feel the change. That's it. Good."

The crew does better than I expected. After ten sets no-one has pulled their paddle yet, although Amelia and Andrew's inside hands are starting to droop. I watch Hayley and Nat. Hayley is trying hard, and when her inside arm comes up, she glances inward, subtly goading Nat, who is paddling more strongly than usual. Unexpected. My pulse skips. Maybe I'll move them forward as a pair.

"Set twelve, keep it up. Doing well," I call, feeling the boat lift as they refocus.

"Are we winning yet?" gasps Greg.

"Sure are," I reply. "Power, power, power."

Okay, then. It took twenty sets before Amelia, Andrew and Ellie all suddenly pulled their paddles in. Nat is scowling at Hayley and paddling with gritted teeth. I watch Hayley for a while, crimping back my grin. As a marathoner she sure knows how to pace herself. In bench three Chloe yanks her paddle in. Perfect. Just the slot I need.

"Let it run!" I call. "Slow the boat and have a drink." Above the groans and grunts, I add, "Well done, everyone." I reach down for my water bottle and take a swig. The sun's already warm, and the whole crew is glistening with sweat.

Sandi half-turns to speak to me. "Good coach speaking, are we moving anybody, *mean* coach?"

A giggle ripples down the boat. Fair enough, I deserve that. "A few. I'd like Natalie and Hayley to move forward to bench three, please."

Natalie chokes on her mouthful of water and sits spluttering until Hayley thumps her on the back. I barely catch her muttered, "You'll keep," to Hayley.

I move another six paddlers and firm up my balance as the boat wobbles while they change benches.

"If you haven't swapped sides, do that now, starting from the front."

"We're not going to do that all over again, are we?" moans Andrew.

"Nope. I'm mean coach not terrible coach. We'll just do three sets so you can tell me whether you feel better on the right or the left. Paddles up, go!"

The boat feels smoother and a tiny bit faster. Hayley is now on the right and still paddling well, although her left arm doesn't punch her paddle down as strongly as her right one did. I realise that she's still paddling with an old, wooden paddle, which is heavier. Should have thought of that, she'll need to borrow a newer, lighter one. We practise a few turns and sudden stops, then I head the boat in.

After the cool-down stretches, I give everyone two lollipops for great work, which goes over well and everyone thanks me as the 'not-so-mean coach'. Although Andrew still wants to know where the gin and tonics are.

As the crew begin to disperse, I mime a phone call to Sandi, who nods, and beckon to Nat and Hayley. "Are you two good with being in row three?"

Hayley beams at me. "Love it, coach. I can really feel the water."

Natalie groans. "Can I dunk her after the regatta? Please say yes."

I laugh. "This is the reward for all your excellent buddying."

"Fine. You owe me at least two drinks after the regatta then."

"Deal." I shake Nat's hand, then turn to Hayley, whose gorgeous hazel eyes are fixed on my face. "Two things. First, did you feel better on the left or the right?"

Hayley tilts her head. "My left arm is not as strong, so I might be better sat on the left with my right arm driving."

"Good call, and we can put you on the other side for the two-hundreds. Second thing, we need to lend you a lighter paddle."

Hayley arches an eyebrow. "My paddle's heavy? Oh wow, *mean* coach!"

I grimace. "Not intentional. My second paddle is adjustable, so I'll bring it on Thursday for you to try."

Natalie's mouth drops open. "You're going to lend her *your* paddle?"

Hayley looks between us, a question mark on her face. "Is this a problem?"

"No," I say quickly, giving Natalie a shut-up glare. "The length is adjustable, hence my offer. You might be able to buy your own paddle at the regatta, if you want to, that is. Sometimes there are gear stalls."

"That sounds good." Hayley smiles, oblivious to the WTF look Nat is lasering at me.

Beginning to wish I'd never sat them together, I say, "Okay, I have to go. All good?"

"*Fascinatingly* good," says Natalie primly.

Haunted by the confusion on Hayley's face, I bolt to my bike. I sure hope Nat doesn't tell her that I ordered my second paddle especially from China.

And I've never lent it to anyone.

CHAPTER NINE
Ama Diving

Akiko and Kraig are waiting as I hurry down the boat ramp to *The Ama Diver*. There are three other people there, adjusting their life jackets.

"Sorry, I overslept," I gasp out when I reach them.

Akiko smiles. "You're right on time, and it's a beautiful Monday morning with calm sea, so don't stress." She passes me a red lifejacket.

I hastily strap this on and follow aboard the other three, who look like university students. My feet take me straight to the front row, where Justin sat us only three days ago. His absence surrounds me like a dull ache. *Be strong. Own two feet.* The students file into the row behind me. "Will we see a whale again?" I ask Akiko as she passes me to stand at the front of the seats.

"Maybe." She tilts her head prettily before leaning over to open the lid to a wooden box and pulling out two laminated A3 sheets, handing one to me and one to the student seated behind me. "This is a list of the species of fish we find around here. When we reach our dive spot, we'll do some snorkelling first so you can get the feel of the water. Count how many species you see."

The engine thrums to life and the boat slips away from the pontoon and chugs along the channel leading to the Bar. Through the window at the rear of the captain's cabin, I can see Kraig's back and his easy movements as he steers the ship.

Akiko slips into the seat beside me. "How long have you been here?"

"Three weeks now. I came from Canberra."

"Ah soo. I lived in Canberra for ten years before I came down here." Her gaze flicks to Kraig's back. "And never left."

Justin said I should ask how Akiko and Kraig met, but it feels a bit soon for that. "You're from Japan? Which part?"

"Ise, in the south of Honshu." Akiko's face lights up. "It is famous for the Ise Shinto Shrine, which has the purest water in Japan running through it. Ise is also famous for the Mikimoto pearl factory and the Ama divers. My grandmother was one, and she taught me how to dive as a child." She twists her fingers together. "Sadly, the tradition is dying out as the Ama divers grow old and die and the younger women are not so interested."

Sadness resonates off her and a chill runs up my arms. "That's a shame," I murmur, wondering if her grandmother is still alive. A chill crawls across my nape; I'd prefer not to think about death. "I studied some Japanese at University," I offer, "as part of my degree in Asian Civilizations."

Akiko claps her hands like an enthusiastic child and flashes me a delighted smile. "Tsugoi! We must practise. I am trying to teach Kraig, but he struggles." Dimples form in her cheeks. "Miki makes much fun of him, poor Kraig."

"Your daughter?" I guess.

"Yes, she is eight now."

Kraig turns around and taps on the window and Akiko promptly leaps up. "I have to prepare the group. We must talk more."

Absorbed, I listen while Akiko explains that Kraig will moor the boat in a sheltered bay on the side of Barunguba Montague Island more protected from the wind. She tells us the island is nine kilometres from Narooma's shore, covers some eighty-one hectares, and that the lighthouse was built in 1881 and remains pretty much intact as the original. Barunguba is the Yuin Nation name for the island and it has significant traditional meaning for them.

"We expect to see many, many seals, some little penguins and hundreds of fish." Akiko hands around sets of snorkelling masks and flippers for us to try for fit. "Don't worry if the seals decide to play with you." She grins. "Just don't chase them as they can bite."

"Are there sharks?" asks the tallest student with shaggy ginger hair. He sounds nervous.

"Unlikely in the bay we will dive in, but of course they do live in these waters."

The dark-haired student claps ginger-hair on the shoulder and laughs. "Good one, mate."

I choose a pale blue snorkel set. My pulse races with anticipation. Another brand-new experience. I'm sure packing life in — this sea change has been such a good idea. So far. I feel a twinge of guilt, I should ring Dad tonight and reassure him I'm okay. Better than okay, for the moment. Justin's intense, handsome face flashes into my mind and I swallow. Should I have asked if he wanted to Ama dive too? Maybe, but I don't want him to feel he has to escort me everywhere. And if things become awkward … I need to be able to manage on my own.

To divert my thoughts, I look out the side of the boat and focus on the large island looming closer. It looks rugged with craggy bays, a white lighthouse and sparse vegetation. Birds are wheeling with raucous cries and I hear seals barking. Was that a dolphin? I move to the railing, delighted to see a pod of dolphins has arrived, as if they are here to guide the boat in. A shiver ripples down my back, thinking of how good it felt with Justin's powerful arms wrapped around me, his strong presence behind me. A warm awareness blossoms in my groin, something I haven't felt for two years. *Oh God, do I want this?* Want it or not, can I deflect it? I shake my head.

Kraig steers the boat into a stunning, secluded bay with white crags rising steeply out of aquamarine water. I blink at movement on the shore, then realise it is seals flopping along the rocks right by the water. Above the central ridge of the island, seagulls and other birds teem in crowds. Even higher, a bird of prey circles against the pale blue sky. I draw in air, stretching my lungs and ribcage to capacity. *This* is living. How can I ever go back to my desk? Whoa, Hayles. One day at a time. For however many I have.

Kraig feeds the anchor off the stern, then straightens up and says, "Gather round."

The three students and I huddle closer.

"The rules are pretty simple." Kraig eyeballs each of us. "This is a protected Marine Park so enjoy the wildlife but do not touch, chase or harass it in any way. There are hefty fines if you do." He gives his lop-sided smile. "Or I might just leave you here and it gets pretty cold overnight."

The students mutter nervously and Akiko smiles at me.

"Akiko and I are both qualified divers, we must have at least one on board. For snorkelling and a brief taste of Ama diving, you don't need a qualification as we won't be going too deep. Unless any of you can hold your breath for ten minutes?"

I tilt my head. My lung capacity should be way above average, even after all my treatment. I eye Akiko, wondering if I could keep up with her.

"Right, strip off," says Kraig with a twinkle in his eyes. "Put your masks on and let's sample the water." He tugs his shirt over his head and I look away from his rippling six-pack and well-defined shoulders and arms. No wonder Akiko fell for him. Matt Damon face aside.

My pulse racing again, I climb backwards down the ladder and step off into the water. My breath catches at the brisk temperature. Akiko treads water by my side, seemingly having assigned herself to me and leaving Kraig to manage the boys. We practise blowing water through the snorkel and then Akiko points towards the shore. I nod. She swims away and I follow her gently kicking legs, reminding myself to breathe evenly and calmly.

The water is amazingly clear and I startle as a shoal of silver fish flashes so close beneath me I could grab one. I slow my kicking, entranced by the undersea landscape of craggy rocks laced with seaweed and prettily coloured anemone. A black-and-white angel fish flits past. Hovering above a clump of weed, I spy several greeny-blue fish with stripes. Tiny, narrow golden fish zip around them. It's like swimming in an aquarium.

Swirls of water attract my attention, and I find Akiko beckoning. She leads me up close to a rocky spur and points. I blink for a while, then spot the pair of seahorses curled around a strand of seaweed. Oh wow. A flat silver-yellow fish drifts towards me, with a snub above its nose that reminds me of a unicorn. This is better than a fantasy realm. I drift behind Akiko's flippers in a daze, absorbing every sight.

In what feels like nanoseconds, Akiko makes a 'turn-around' swirl with a hand and swims back towards the boat. We've finished snorkelling already? My legs wobble as I climb back up the ladder. This is good exercise.

We sit in the sun, towels draped over our shoulders, while Akiko explains how we will Ama dive. I can't help but notice the adoring look Kraig gives her as she stands before us with erect posture, clad only in a white linen loin cloth and wrap around her breasts, her black hair cascading over her shoulder. She is gorgeous.

"First, we must try the *isobue*." Akiko points to her mouth. "Stretch your top lip over your bottom one and breathe out with a whistling noise."

Intrigued, I try it. I get it! A clever way to release air slowly and evenly. Akiko gives me a pleased nod. The three boys clown around with wolf whistles and Akiko rolls her eyes.

"This is important! When you surface you must release the pressure evenly. We do this between dives and, if your chest is pressured, you can start to do this whistle as you surface." She waits patiently while the students try again. "Before you dive, you will be tempted to take a massive breath in," she pauses as ginger-hair puffs his chest full and thumps it, reminding me of an orangutan, "but this will slow your descent. Better to take two-thirds of a breath and sink faster."

Kraig stands and we all scramble to our feet. "We're going to start down in the water, and if you master that successfully, you can try a dive in off the boat."

Akiko doesn't have swimming goggles, but I decide to use mine. I want to see everything. When Akiko beckons, I hasten to follow her down the ladder.

At the bottom she leans in and murmurs, "Kraig will keep the boys closer to the boat. Just in case. We'll swim a little away then dive."

Thrilled by her confidence in me, I follow her back to near where we saw the seahorses. I tread water while she mimes breathing in deeply, putting her hands above her head in a dive position, and flipping her bottom up to swim straight down. I give her a thumbs-up. She grins and flips her hand up and down in a go signal.

Inhaling through my nose, I fill my chest, but not too tight, point my arms up and somehow flip my butt up and dive downwards. Using breaststroke, I swim almost straight down, counting my strokes. The water feels heavier when I reach thirty strokes, but I keep pushing. Akiko reaches my shoulder, matching my swim rate. I manage to get to forty strokes, deep enough to see there are actually six seahorses wrapped around the strand of seaweed, then my lungs begin to ache. Carefully turning to face the surface, I release a few bubbles and kick upwards. I can see the boat bobbing in the sunshine above the rippling surface. My chest grumbles and I start the *isobue* whistle, releasing air as evenly as I can.

My head breaches the surface and I gasp in some air. Akiko bobs up beside me, not at all out of breath.

"Not bad." She smiles and peers at her dive watch then adds, "Almost five metres for a first go."

The next hour passes quickly and I'm sad after we're rounded up and passed towels to shiver into, as Kraig heads the boat back to Narooma. That was so much fun, and I reached six metres on my last dive. Another bucket-list achievement. A massive yawn catches me by surprise, and I realise how tired I am. My upper left arm is throbbing. I'd better rest it for a day or so and stop pushing my luck with it.

While Kraig is lining the boat up with the pontoon back in the inlet, Akiko slides onto the seat beside me. "Would you like to go have lunch? I have a while before I collect Miki."

I sit up straighter, energy zinging into me. "I'd love to."

～

Thirty minutes later, I'm cold-showered, changed, and sitting opposite Akiko at a small table by the window at the ice-creamery, my stomach rumbling in anticipation of my tempura prawns, chips and salad. I'm starving. The place is busy, and Akiko explains the food is always good, the service fast and friendly. My cappuccino is good too. I'm impressed. Akiko twirls her teaspoon through the froth on her coffee and I can sense her questions forming.

I get in first. "What made you move down here from Canberra?"

Her lips curve upwards and cute dimples form. "This is a bittersweet story." She sips froth off her spoon. "I came from Ise to Canberra with my husband, nearly eleven years ago. Satoru was a research scientist at the university, and I was a librarian. We had Miki, and I worked part-time." She starts to run her spoon in circles around the mug. "Satoru loved fishing, and we came down here many times. Miki and I enjoy the beach, so it was happy times."

The serving lady places my food in front of me and I absently thank her, absorbed by Akiko's wistful face and tone.

"Then Satoru was killed in a late-night car accident. Suddenly," she makes a puff motion with her hands, "it was Miki and me."

"I'm so sorry," I mutter, a hollowness consuming my chest.

Akiko dips her head. "I was sabishii … you know this word?"

I nod. "Melancholy."

"So, I brought Miki down here on the anniversary of Satoru's death, to remember him. Do you know Dalmeny Beach?"

I shake my head.

"It's close by. There's a wooden footbridge and a large sandy oval running along the narrow channel before it reaches the open beach."

"Okay." I try to visualise it, wondering why this detail is important.

Her face neutral, Akiko says, "So, I'm sitting on the sandy beach feeling incredibly sabishii, and Miki is running free." Her lips twitch. "Miki spies a flock of seagulls lying on the sand and runs at them, her long hair flying behind her."

I pause with a chip halfway to my mouth. This must be it. How she met Kraig!

"The birds scatter and fly up screeching, Miki is running and flapping her arms, and a man comes striding around the corner, the sun and sea behind making him a shadow-man. I'm holding my breath, willing the birds to wheel the other way … but the flock flies straight at the man. He ducks and flings his arms up and drops something."

Mesmerised, I watch as she weaves her hands expressively.

"I run over to apologise to the man. And to make Miki apologise." Stars of delight twinkle in her eyes. "Oh my. I see he has dropped his ice-cream … all down the front of his shorts." She claps a hand over her mouth. "I can hardly help him with that."

I burst out laughing and nearly choke on my chip. Justin was right, she is hilarious.

"The poor man, he's dabbing at his crotch and I'm bowing and apologising. We are both red with shame. Miki," she says dryly, "is skipping around us, oblivious."

I dab at my eyes with my serviette, vowing to find this Dalmeny Beach so I can visualise the scene properly.

"I'm lucky, Kraig is nice and says not to worry. So, I offer to buy him a replacement ice-cream." She pauses theatrically. "He agrees, but only if Miki and I will join him."

"Nice one," I say. "Clever Kraig."

"He orders banana, Miki insists on strawberry." She pulls a deadpan face and I hold my breath. "Then I remember I left my purse at home. I am bowing even lower and apologising again."

"Oh my God," I gasp. "Way to make an impression!"

"Yes, right." She shrugs. "Kraig says he will buy the ice-creams, but only if I buy them the next day."

"Such a smooth operator," I say, grinning.

Akiko takes a sip of her coffee. "It turns out his wife had left him after their unborn baby died and he was also melancholy. Many ice-creams later, we are married."

"That is an awesome story," I say, recalling the wistful look on Justin's face when he said I should ask how they met. Is he hoping such an epic event will occur for him?

"Your turn," says Akiko. "How did you meet Justin?"

Encouraged by her humour and openness, I spin the incident out into a story like she did, explaining how I was at a loss on my very first day here and was walking along the path when a cyclist barged past me then dropped all these lollipops over the path at my feet, and when I handed them back to him, he made me get in the dragon boat.

Akiko claps her hands in delight. "That is so Justin. He's such a sweetie." She peers at me intently. "You like Justin?"

My cheeks flaming, I dip my head ever so slightly and shrug. "But I don't really know him, I've just got here."

There's a silence while Akiko takes a few mouthfuls of her chilli chicken wrap, then she says slowly, "Everyone here adores Justin, the always kind, happy, professional physio and coach … but now you speak the words, I'm not sure any of us really know him." She puts her half-eaten wrap down. "He never says much about himself."

Unease prickles across my nape. Does Justin have dark secrets too? "He isn't married, or anything?"

Akiko shakes her head. Then she gives me a kind smile. "You are melancholy too? This's why you are here?"

I fight my instant surge of discomfort. I would very much like to be friends with Akiko. But I don't like talking about it. Her eyes are widening as she waits; she realises she's asked a bigger question than she thought. *Come on, spill it out. Once. Briefly.* Clearing my throat, I murmur, "I was sick last year. Very sick, breast cancer, the whole treatment." I shrug. "I'm recovering, but it's hard. I'm … changed. I don't like to tell people."

Akiko pats the back of my hand. "So young, but you are strong, Hayley. I can see this." She lifts her hand away and waves it around. "The sea is healing and the light here is special. You have done a good thing, coming here. Your body is speaking and you are listening." She gives me a reassuring smile.

I chew my lower lip. Many people have told me I am strong, that I'll be fine, but how can they possibly know? Is this just what they want to believe because the alternative is unthinkable, uncomfortable? And if I'm 'strong' they can leave me alone to 'get on with it'. Blinking back to the present, I realise by her worried face that Akiko had said something. "Sorry, what?"

"Does Justin know?"

I shake my head rigorously. "I … I want people to just treat me as they meet me and not feel sorry for me." *But he suspects something, he's too perceptive.*

"I see," says Akiko slowly. "I'm good at secrets." She mimes zipping her lips, but her forehead is furrowed. She drums her fingers on the table. "When it is right, tell him. Hayley, I *saw* the expression on Justin's face when he was holding you on the whale-watching tour …" She swallows. "He will not run away."

"No," I whisper. "But my last boyfriend did … and Justin is so nice, how could I …" My throat closes up.

Reaching across the table, Akiko grabs both of my hands, her dark eyes intense. "You are so brave, such a good person to think of his needs." Her grip tightens. "I nearly let Kraig go because who would want to be saddled with a widow and somebody else's child?" Her dimpled smile returns. "But he and Miki adore each other, she has the father she needs, and both Kraig and I have a new start, a new chance at love. Maybe let the universe decide."

Hollowness swirls inside my chest and I feel like crying. Not here. Not in public. I get what she means, but … it's too soon. I'm too raw. And anyway, why isn't Justin already taken? That is so odd. Impossibly odd.

"I think we need ice-cream," says Akiko brightly. With a final squeeze of my hands, she pushes her chair back. "Come, they make it here, and …" She gives me a triumphant grin. "… they even have green tea flavour ice-cream, just for me."

Rallying, I summon a weak smile and follow her.

CHAPTER TEN
Regatta

I take a breath, buzzing with optimism. Twenty-one paddlers are gathered before me outside the shed for the final training session before the regatta. The Italian brothers have managed to dig out their Clear Water Dragons uniforms and paddles. Mara has taken the weekend off from her horse training job and, even better, has talked her sister Elena, who fell off her horse a while back and hasn't paddled since, into being our drummer. We've filled the boat! Unbelievable. Hayley is subtly hefting my second paddle, feeling its weight and balance, oblivious to Natalie and Sandi glancing at her with their lips compressed. I sigh. Hopefully she buys her own paddle at the regatta or I'm likely to have a lot of explaining dragged out of me.

"Right, let's board," I say. "We'll warm up then paddle two kilometres at a steady rate as a confidence booster and to practise maintaining rhythm. Sandi will sweep this part, then I'll take over for a few two-hundred metre race starts. Just a couple," I add, seeing alarm forming on a few faces.

The session goes smoothly; we're as ready as we can be for this regatta. Hayley is more comfortable with the lighter paddle, lifting her left arm a smidge higher. My smile fades when I think of the awe on her face as she ran her fingers over the intricate pattern on the blade of a blue-and-gold dragon cresting a Hokusai-style wave. My special good luck paddle. How am I going to take it back from her?

In what feels like no time at all, we're putting *Ming II* away and collecting around the table for drinks and nibbles. Sandi bangs a teaspoon on her plastic cup until everyone shushes and looks at her.

"Has everyone got transport sorted? Remember, we need to be on site by 6.30 am to set up our marquee, thank you Giulio and Gianni for lending one, even if it does advertise your family restaurant." Sandi pauses while the boys bow and everyone giggles. "The first race is at 8 am sharp so we'll be doing a crew warm-up on land at 7.30." Sandi looks at me.

"Okay, then." I clear my throat. "I'll print the race schedule and peg this to the edge of the marquee. Pay attention to which heats we're in and where you are in the boat — both the bench number and which side — as this will vary from the 2K to the two-hundreds." Feeling the pre-regatta buzz, I grin broadly. "I am *so* proud we're fielding a Clear Water Dragons boat! Be focused but enjoy the day. I haven't entered us in everything, just the open 20s races."

"Don't forget to bring chairs, blankets, lots of layers, snacks, water and sunscreen," chips in Sandi. "Canberra weather can be variable in spring."

That earns her a few rolling of eyes and 'yes, Mum'.

I mingle among the paddlers for a while, checking everyone is feeling good about this, then grab the protective case for my second paddle and drift towards Hayley. My heart skips several beats when she turns to face me before I've even said anything. Her hazel eyes are shining and the soft dusk light is accentuating the rows of freckles that march up and over her cute nose. My tongue all tangled, I pass her the paddle case and the soft rubber strip to protect the edge of the blade.

"Oh, to keep it safe?" She arches an elegant eyebrow. "Thanks Justin, I mean coach." She fingers the blade protector, her eyebrows drawing together.

"Here." I take it back and slip it over the edge of the paddle blade. Then I slide the paddle into the case and Velcro it closed. "Keep this with you. You have a lift?"

Hayley nods. "I'm going to drive up tomorrow afternoon and stay with a friend, reserve my energy for the races."

"Good plan," I force out, immediately wondering whether this friend is a male. *None of my business. Coach mode, remember?* "Drive safe, see you Saturday."

"Justin." Hayley's voice wavers. "Thank you for this … the paddle … everything." Her chest heaves in a breath. "I'm looking forward to the regatta. To racing."

My heart melting, I squeeze her slim shoulder. "I know you'll do well." I hesitate a beat. "After, let's talk about a strategy for your training. You have real potential."

Her hazel eyes flicker with more than glints of the setting sun while her brows furrow but then relax, as if she's reached a decision. Lifting her chin, she meets my eyes. "I'd so like that."

Oh man. Are we now positioned to cross some invisible line? I smile briefly then head straight to my bike before the emotions tumbling through me render me legless.

~

Right on 6 am, I pull up in the car park at Grevillea Park. A light mist is hovering above the surface of Lake Burley Griffin, and the first rays of sunlight are hitting the side of Kings Avenue Bridge. The boats are all parked on the grassy expanse between the sheds, their covers still on, although almost immediately a couple of volunteers for Dragon Boat ACT emerge from the shed and approach a boat to take the cover off. I eye the trees along the shore, sprouting their spring leaves. Nothing is moving, a rare calm morning. I hope it stays this way. My team — whoa, not really *my* team, although it feels like it — need a good experience today if I'm going to convince them to keep racing. We do not need a typical Canberra spring gale and cold, choppy water.

Getting out of the car, I walk to the boats. "Want some help? Until my team arrives?"

A woman with a clipboard looks around and I recognise the Chief Official, Gillian. "Hello. Justin, isn't it? That'd be great. We need twelve boats today."

I help one of the volunteers fold the cover down from the tail end of a boat. After uncovering five boats, I turn around and see Delizioso's large, royal-blue marquee, with its white motif of a crossed pair of wine glasses, being erected near some trees. It's double the size of the usual team marquee and I swallow. Our presence will be hard to miss. Better not embarrass ourselves. Sandi is scurrying around, no doubt barking instructions, so I head over.

"Morning, team," I call. "Er … nice tent," I say to Gianni.

Gianni flashes me a smile. "Papa said we could take it but only if we have flyers for the restaurant too. I hope that's okay."

"Sure," I say, trying not to wince, but then an idea occurs. "Maybe he'd like to sponsor the team?"

The brothers crack up. "For when we go international?" gasps Giulio.

"Who's going international?" demands Sandi, materialising beside me. The brothers laugh even harder.

"Never mind," I murmur. "I'll grab my gear and the race schedule."

Jogging to my car, I go to grab my sports bag and paddle from the boot but pause to double-check I have water bottles and my snacks in a handy place.

"Morning, coach!" says Hayley brightly from right behind me.

I stand up too quickly and bang my head on the open boot door. Ouch. Such an idiot. I grit my teeth against the stinging.

"Are you okay?" asks Hayley. "Is this part of the tradition?"

"Very funny," I grunt, my eyes watering. Part of me is pleased everyone is in such good humour, another part of me is thinking this could be a very long day. Shutting the boot carefully, making sure I don't catch my fingers, I look Hayley over. Man, she looks great in the team uniform. The turquoise, jade and white offset her wavy brown hair, fair complexion and hazel eyes perfectly. "Uniform looks fabulous on you." Shit, did I say that out loud? By the rosy blush staining Hayley's cheeks, I guess I did. I rub at my stinging head.

"Just hope I can do it justice, coach," she says softly. Frowning, she adds, "Do you want me to check your head? Make sure you haven't cut it?" She gives me an impish smile. "Check you don't need a Hazmat helmet, given the algae and all that?"

"No … yes … no …" Can I cope with Hayley touching me? She has a point about the algae and an open wound, though. "Okay. Yes, thanks." Putting my bag down, I bend over towards her. She moves closer and next thing her warm fingers are delicately feeling the top of my head, gently parting my hair. A shiver tingles down my spine. That feels good. I close my eyes. Hayley moves even closer and a hint of cherry blossom shampoo teases my nostrils and, beneath that, a scent that is uniquely her: fresh, alert and somehow zesty.

"Your hair is so soft," she murmurs, "and so very black. Like a raven's feathers." Her fingers creep towards the crest of my skull.

She traces a finger right over where I hit my head and I wince. Then hold my breath as she stands on tiptoes while carefully parting my hair this way, then that. Goosebumps race down my back and my mind unhelpfully presents me with an image of Hayley washing my hair, her lithe body in the shower with me …

"Hmm. You'll have a fair lump but there's no blood, and I can't feel any broken skin."

When she removes her fingers and takes a step back, a sense of loss washes through me. Maybe I should ask her to check it again later?

"Good. Thanks," I croak and flap a hand, indicating we should go to the team tent.

Hayley gives me a nervous smile and picks up her gear.

I round the corner of the tent and find the whole crew massed out the front, looking formal. What now? Hayley snags my elbow and drags me back a few paces, still facing the front of the tent. Alarm flutters in my chest as Sandi and Natalie move to stand in the centre at the front carrying a bunch of rolled up cloth. The Italian boys, both about six feet three, are hovering.

Sandi looks me in the eye. "Justin, super coach as well as mean coach, depending on the day of the week, the team wanted to acknowledge your persistence and training in getting us here. This is for you."

My pulse is hammering in my throat. Most of them are wearing goofy smiles, but Natalie looks all emotional, gripping the cloth tightly. What have they done? I feel like my eyes are bulging out of my face as Sandi and Natalie slowly unfurl a long banner with Clear Water Dragons emblazoned across it in elegant, bold turquoise letters, and our sea-dragon logo at each end. Speechless, I watch the tall brothers pin it to the front of our marquee.

"For when we go international," quips Gianni, and the crew laugh.

Adrift, I stand blinking at the banner. No-one has ever acknowledged me like this before. No-one. Never. Who the hell's idea was this? From the strangled look on her face, I suspect Natalie. In collusion with Sandi. And who else? Say something! But what?

"I think he likes it," says Hayley, casting me a concerned glance.

"Well," says Sandi briskly, putting her hands on her hips, "good job I'm sweeping the first race as Justin seems to have lost his voice."

I press my hands together in the universal sign of thank you and bow low to the team, twice. "It's fantastic," I rasp out.

"Must've hit your head harder than I thought," murmurs Hayley, her hazel eyes still brimming with concern. "You sure you're alright?"

I weakly flap a hand at the banner. "So unexpected."

Hayley gives me an assessing look, opens her mouth and closes it, instead giving me a push towards the tent.

The shore is teeming with paddlers clad in a vibrant array of uniforms and the boats are now neatly lined up in the water, gilded dragon heads facing the shore. The mist has spiralled away, and pale blue sky stretches above. My knees tremble as I pass under the banner, park my gear and get my paddle and gloves ready. The day feels special, magical even, as if anything could happen. *Get a grip, Justin. This is a normal first-season regatta.* Just try not to capsize or come last.

Within moments, Sandi is gathering us for the warm-up routine. Standing in a circle out the front of our marquee, we start by running on the spot. The restaurant logo and our banner are attracting many looks, nudges and grins from passing paddlers. I glance around the circle. "Where's Hayley?"

"Loo. Again," replies Natalie, rolling her eyes. "Nervous."

On cue, Hayley comes jogging back and joins the circle. I arch an eyebrow at her and she nods back. All okay. As we conclude our warm-up, I hear a number of other teams screaming a team war cry. Perhaps we need one of those too for next time. My heart thuds. Next time. Let's get through today first.

"We're marshalling," calls Sandi. "Grab your gear and line up in lane six, alphabetically by surname. Chop, chop!" She claps her hands.

Once we're lined up, I run my eye over the other five teams in our heat. No quarter will be given here; they are all strong and well trained.

"Abandoning us, hey Justin?" says the stroke for the composite South Coast team in the lane beside us, one of their Aurora-level paddlers.

I shrug at her. "We managed to fill a boat. See you for the regionals, though."

"Sure thing." The stroke smiles. "Nice uniform."

The team in lane six files out of the marshalling tent and heads to their assigned boat. I wait until lanes two to five have followed and it's only us left in lane one. "Team, listen up. Some final reminders. It's 2000 metres, with three tight turns around the 500-metre course. It's a staggered start. We're going to be setting off first and the other teams will be chasing us. Do *not* stress when a boat passes us. Eyes and ears in *our* boat, listen to Sandi, and do not get sucked into racing faster. We have a plan and we need to stick to it." I almost add, 'we're not international yet', but think better of it.

"Keep focused on Justin and Rose," adds Sandi. "Watch their inside arms and whatever you do, keep in time. Listen to Elena's drum, no-one else's."

"Let's go, lane one!" calls the marshal.

In no time, we've boarded and have paddled almost to the start buoy, and Sandi is positioning us. A light breeze has risen, but conditions are good. Elena wedges herself firmly in the drummer's seat then checks her blonde hair is securely tied back. She gives me a thumbs-up.

"Remember, not too fast," I mutter to Rose. "We want to come home strongly." Nothing worse than having the team collapse in the home straight with nothing left.

"Paddlers, sit ready."

I dig my blade in deep, ready to pull water, feeling tension ripple down the boat behind me.

"Boat one move up. Ready … attention … go!" The hooter blasts and Rose and I plunge our blades deep for five powerful strokes, quicken for ten, then settle into a long and strong stoke. Elena is drumming loudly and grinning. We're away, and the start felt good and smooth. No wobbles, no hitches. Too soon, I hear the horn blast again and the boat behind us is in pursuit.

"Reach for twenty!" yells Sandi. "Keep the power."

I feel the boat slide forward faster. Good. Sandi and I want to try to keep ahead to have clear priority through the first tight turn at 500 metres. Plus, we don't want the team demoralised too early.

"Bring it back for twenty, keep the power," calls Sandi. Soon, she calls, "Give me a lift for ten!"

Damn, the next boat is gaining. I dig in hard, Rose copying, and we drive hard for ten. The boat surges forward, so far so good. Sandi calls for three more lifts and I flick my glance up to see the priority buoy is only fifty metres away. Hope rises. One more lift and … yep, the Water Marshall, Deb, calls to Sandi, confirming we have priority, then we're nudging our nose ready for the tight turn.

Elena tilts forward, still drumming. "Boat coming up just outside our tail."

I nod my thanks.

"Back left dig in! Front left paddle short, outside long!" screeches Sandi. "My buoy," she yells to the other sweep.

I reach forward to pull water longer past the outside of the boat. The nose is turning beautifully tight. We're around!

"Normal paddling! Give me a lift for twenty!" yells Sandi.

The boat drives forward, but relentlessly, the South Coast team goes wide and draws alongside, paddling deeper and faster than us. I feel a hitch behind me.

"Timing!" admonishes Sandi. "Watch Justin."

The wobble settles and we flow forward. "Stay relaxed," I mutter to Rose. "We can't match them."

"Reach for twenty," calls Sandi, and I feel the boat strengthen. We're heading for halfway. Can we maintain priority at the 1000-metre turn buoy before the next boat catches us too? If we could, we'd be on for a decent time.

Sandi manoeuvres us out of the wake of the South Coast team and continues to call for reaches or lifts. Sweat is trickling down my face and back, but the boat feels okay. We're still working together. Amazing. In an almost repeat sequence, we get the call we have priority, with another boat's dragon head almost on our tail. Elation surges through me. We are definitely not disgraced. Only two boats have caught us so far. With proper training …

We dig in for the third leg and I wonder how Hayley is doing. It doesn't feel as if anyone has pulled their paddle at all, so we've got our pacing right.

Elena tips forward. "Another boat coming."

"Give me a lift for twenty!" calls Sandi.

Time passes in a blur of lift, reach, plunge, pull water and repeat. Massive balls of white bubbles are surging away from my blade. Blinking sweat from my eyes, I glance ahead and see we're closing on the third turn priority buoy. Sandi's trying to hold onto the inside turn again. Extraordinary. "Drive," I say to Rose. "Until the buoy."

She nods and matches my extra oomph. After a breath, Elena beats the drum harder. "Go! Go!" she exhorts the front pod.

"Your buoy, boat one!" calls another Water Marshall.

Sandi nudges our nose in. "Draw water inside left front! Dig in at the back. Go!"

We're turning early so this must be really tight.

"Oh my God!" squeaks Elena. "They nearly clipped our tail."

I grunt and drive harder. We've barely completed our third turn when a team clad in black vests with silver dragons on the back surges alongside, the sweep yelling. They power past us imperiously and our boat's nose rises and dips as we ride in their wake.

"The home leg," calls Sandi. "Five and twenty. Five and twenty. Go, go, go."

Five power, twenty strong, we settle in, with Elena calling, "Power!" each time we start the five. My chest is heaving and I can hear grunts and groans behind me. The team is giving their all.

"We got this!" calls Sandi, breaking my focus. "A boat coming at us but I can see the finish."

I hear the fast tempo of the other boat's drummer. A bit too early to bring it home but I flex my fingers, getting ready. A shiver travels across my neck; I can sense the boat looming by our tail. I dig in, thrilled to see Rose copy me, then sense the whole team trying harder. The other boat's nose draws into my peripheral vision.

"Bring it home now!" screeches Sandi.

Elena drums faster and harder. "Go! Go! Drive! Drive!"

I give it everything I've got, but it feels as if the back of our boat is tiring. The other boat noses past the finish buoy, with us one mere breath, a dragon head, behind.

"Let it run!" calls Sandi. "Great work, everyone." She sounds so pleased. Then she shrieks, "Paddles up, twenty strokes forward."

I realise we're getting out of the way of the other two boats. Once we've actually stopped, I look around and see one boat just finishing, the other one a few seconds behind. Okay, then. We might not be the slowest.

We climb out of the boat and hover on the beachy shore. Natalie grabs Hayley's sleeve and drags her towards me. Oh oh. What now?

"Coach," says Natalie firmly. "That was *not* fun. Can I dunk her now? Say yes."

Too late, I remember Natalies's threat to dunk Hayley because

I'd put them together in row three. Hayley throws me a pleading look. Then I catch Natalie's wink. Holding out my hand, I say levelly to Hayley, "You'd better give me the paddle. I don't want it getting wet."

Hayley's expression turns to panic and she tries to pull away.

I can't do it to her. Laughing, I say, "She's joking. You two did really well." I wag my finger at Natalie. "Good job. You're both glued to bench three."

"Coooaaach," groans Natalie, before she grabs Hayley in a hug. "Great work, bench buddy!"

Hayley is so shocked she drops my paddle. Retrieving it, I brush the grit off and hand it back to her. "More races to go, remember."

Blushing furiously, Hayley grabs the paddle, her fingers brushing mine. She looks at me with wide, dark eyes and I so want to pull her into my arms and hug her like Natalie did. For a heartbeat, we stand with our hands locked around the paddle and I see my longing mirrored in her eyes. Swallowing, I release the paddle. I'm saved by Natalie linking her elbow through Hayley's and tugging her away.

Back at the tent, I wait until everyone has had a drink and a quick stretch, then gather them around. "Team. The Clear Water Dragons have made their mark. Give yourselves a round of applause. We finished fifth in a time of thirteen minutes thirty. Most respectable for a first ever 2K." I pause while everyone claps and nudges each other.

Gianni and Giulio high-five each other. "We're going international!"

The whole team laughs and a warm feeling spreads through my chest. I shake my head. Must be getting soft. "Grab some early lunch. There's the open 2K final to go, then a short break before the two-hundreds."

I grab a water bottle and head down to stand on the beach level with the finish line to watch the final of the open 2K. The first two boats have started when I hear soft footfalls and Hayley comes to stand beside me.

"What are we looking at, coach?" she asks.

"The final." I smile at her. "Canberra's best plus the South Coast team. They're strong and a few of them are likely to be in the southern region team, the one I'm trying out for."

Hayley arches an eyebrow at me. "Okay. So can you tell me which boats look good and why, so I can learn?"

"Sure." A thrill runs through me at her level of interest. We stand companionably while I point out various aspects of technique, such as how burying the blade deep gives more strength and is often better than paddling faster, especially over distance."

"Pacing is everything in distance running." She squints at the distant boats. "I see it now. They're all strong, but that boat gaining on the others is digging deep and reaching way forward. Wow."

"Hayley?" says a female voice.

Hayley spins around. "Alexa! Glad you could come." She turns to me. "Justin, this is my friend Alexa; Alexa this is our coach and sweep, Justin."

Alexa gives me a kind of knowing look and Hayley's cheekbones turn pink. Have they been talking about me? Is this the friend she stayed with? She looks a fair bit older than Hayley. "Hi Alexa, nice to meet you," I say politely, wishing she hadn't interrupted us.

"How did you go?" Alexa asks Hayley.

"I made it!" Hayley beams at her. "It was great."

"Lovely," says Alexa. "Your arm's okay?" She frowns. "No pressure stocking? Or did you take it off after?"

Hayley shakes her head and gives Alexa what can only be interpreted as a warning glance. I feel my eyebrow lift and look away, uncomfortable. Pressure stocking … that's ringing bells. When do people need a pressure stocking? Got it. For lymphoedema. But

Hayley doesn't seem to have lymphoedema. Blinking, I try to refocus on the race.

"Well, enjoy," says Alexa, patting Hayley's elbow. "See you back at my place about three? Good. I'm going to say hello to my ladies." Peering past Hayley, she says to me, "Bye Justin. Good luck for the other races."

I nod and smile, hearing the horn blare in the background. The first boat has finished.

"Is that the coast team coming second?" asks Hayley, shading her eyes with her hand.

Squinting against the light bouncing off the water, I see she's right. "Uh huh." Subtly glancing over my shoulder, I watch Alexa striding towards a turquoise, cream and pink team tent. She enters and I catch the numerous cries of welcome. Lifting my gaze, I read the team's name: Dragons Abreast Canberra. Known as the 'pink ladies', they're all breast cancer survivors or supporters. Prone to lymphoedema.

My throat closing tight, I stare back at the boats. My legs feel far away, my heart heavy in my chest. How can Hayley possibly have breast cancer? Isn't she far too young? Where does Alexa fit in? If she knows them all, is she a nurse or doctor? For the second time this day I am adrift.

"They look strong even just paddling back to shore," says Hayley, apparently still watching the South Coast crew. She looks at me and does a double-take. "Does your head hurt? You look a bit pale. Can I get you a coffee? Chai?"

The concern in her eyes makes me want to cry. Beautiful, brave, amazing Hayley, so focused on going forward. *Go forward with her. You know you want to. Let it happen.* Go on. Ask her out and find out more, find out if you're right. The bands of tension around my chest snap and I breathe again. "A Chai to pep me up before the two-hundreds would be great. Thanks."

Hayley goes to walk away, and I feel a rush of panic. *Do it now, before the moment, and my courage, evaporate.* I clear my throat and she pauses, eyeing me expectantly. "We should celebrate your race. How about dinner … on Wednesday?"

Her eyes startle wide, but the smile that slowly spreads across her face is stunning. "You should hit your head more often! It's shaken some great ideas loose. Dinner would be nice. Thanks, coach." She gives me a cheeky salute and walks away, a bounce in her stride.

Okay, then. We're crossing the invisible line.

CHAPTER ELEVEN
Dinner

Wednesday takes forever to roll around, then the day is suddenly here. Waiting out the front of my apartment block, I twist my fingers nervously. Am I looking for Justin in his car or on foot? He didn't say. I tug at the edge of my jade top. Will the crumpled material and pinch pleat in the centre hide my uneven breasts? I tug at the edge of my bra too. Damn thing is perpetually uncomfortable. Maybe I should have got one of those bra inserts, after all. Wait, what am I thinking? This could be a coach and paddler casual dinner. Don't be stupid. The look on his face when I said yes! This is a date, so find some courage.

Panic shivers through me. He's going to ask about my arm. Curse Alexa for mentioning my pressure stocking. I know he heard, saw his shoulders go rigid. Was that why he went pale? He's a physio, of course he knows what a pressure stocking means. *Wait.* Hope flutters in my chest. Justin asked me to dinner *after* that. Akiko said he wouldn't run away … I cross my fingers and close my eyes, so hoping she's right.

Something brushes my elbow and I leap back with a yelp. Justin retracts his hand and gapes at me, looking amazing in a navy shirt, rolled up to mid-forearm, smart black pants and the awesome dragon bomber jacket draped over his arm.

"Sorry, I was miles away." My smile feels weak, my pulse erratic.

"Dreaming of your next race?" Justin's smile creates fine wrinkles at the edges of his almond-shaped eyes.

"Something like that," I mumble before summoning a brighter smile. "So, where are we going, sometimes-super and sometimes-mean coach?"

"The mean coach will keep you in suspense until we get there. This way." He grins and extends a hand, pointing towards the main road that leads up the hill.

"We're walking?" I ask, falling in beside him and thinking we're lucky it's such a balmy evening. "Good idea, in case you hit your head on the boot again."

Laughing, Justin shakes his head. "As a bonus, it saves petrol." He hesitates a beat. "Maybe you could check my head again after dinner? It kind of hurts still."

I gasp. Is he flirting now? "Good idea, we can't have our coach keeling over," I tease back. He falls quiet, and I concentrate on keeping up. Just as well I opted for my casual, billowy grey pants and flat shoes.

Five minutes later, he's taking my elbow, his hand warm and strong, and guiding me into a Chinese restaurant perched on the top of the hill. "Chinese food okay?"

"Yum," I reply. "Love Asian food."

The waiter hurries over. "Justin, good to see you. Your favourite table?" Without waiting for an answer, the man leads us to a table by the window tucked into the far corner, with a clear view of the inlet, the Bar channel and rock walls. The hanging Chinese paper lanterns reflect in the glass. The walls are laden with inked landscapes on silk hanging scrolls. The ambience is delightful, and I relax a notch.

I slide onto the chair the waiter, who actually looks Chinese, is holding out and admire the view of the red-gold sunset and hazy dusk descending to meet the darkening water. Similar to the view from my apartment, but the restaurant is higher up so more of the vast ocean is visible.

"What do you like?" Justin asks, settling into his chair.

I glance at the menu, but the dish names are all blurring into each other and my stomach gives a nervous roll. Didn't he say his family was from China? Looking up, I say, "Why don't you order? You must know what's good here."

"You sure?" At my nod, he waves for the waiter and without looking at the menu rattles off several sentences in Chinese.

Fascinated, I watch his face and listen to the way he intones the words. The waiter responds a few times and I become certain they're chatting beyond the ordering of a few dishes. Intrigued, I watch the way Justin's lips and the planes of his face move with the words. He looks and sounds like an Oriental warrior. An extremely handsome one. The soft light from the lanterns plays rainbow hints across his glossy black hair. My fingers tingle, remembering the feel of his sleek hair, and burning to play with it again. I put my hands in my lap.

The waiter suddenly looks at me. As does Justin.

"What would you like to drink?" asks Justin.

My mouth runs dry. God, I've been avoiding alcohol since my diagnosis, but Justin said we were celebrating. What to do? He's so sport-focused, maybe he doesn't drink? I wish I knew more about him. Now he's arching an eyebrow at me, confused by my failure to respond to what is a simple question. I can't say 'whatever you want' because that will look insipid. I used to like cider … actually, a glass of that would be good right about now. "Do you have pear cider?"

Justin beams at me. "Excellent choice. For me too." After the waiter has left, he adds, "I like cider. It's good for muscle and joint recovery." Tilting his head, he says softly, "You look nice. Jade suits you. It is a good luck colour in China."

Feeling warmth along my cheekbones, I smile at him. "I liked hearing you speak in Chinese. Are you fully bilingual? When did you come to Australia?"

Justin fiddles with a sleeve for a moment, then answers. "Yes, I'm fully bilingual. My family came from Beijing to Australia nearly twenty years ago, when I was fifteen. My father decided to relocate his business, and us, to Sydney." Before I can ask a follow-up question, he adds, "I studied physiotherapy in Sydney, worked at a practice there for two years to raise some money, then moved to Narooma. There was no physio here, so it was a good place to open my own practice." Now he fiddles with his napkin. "And there was a dragon boat club here."

My mind buzzes with questions. Why Australia? Why Narooma? He already paddled? Something niggles below these concepts. *My father decided …* something about the way Justin said that feels significant. At that moment the waiter arrives with two tall glasses of cider and puts them in front of us with a flourish.

Immediately, Justin lifts his glass and says, "Cheers. Here's to your, and the Clear Water Dragons', first regatta!"

I clink my glass against his. "And to Justin, super coach, for making it happen." He looks pleased, his dark eyes gleaming in the mood lighting. The cold cider slips down my throat, the taste fruity and refreshing. Maybe I should relax more, allow myself some of the things I used to enjoy. *Don't do it*, prods an inner voice. *Big stakes here. Protect your body.* I put my glass down and blow at a stray wisp of hair in frustration. I need to switch this inner voice off. Live properly.

Putting his glass down too, Justin gives me a smile, but above it his eyes are serious. "What do you do in Canberra? Your work, I mean."

So, the questions begin. Come on, Hayles, this is a fair one. "I'm a public servant, I work for the Immigration area of Human Services. Have done more or less since I graduated from university there."

"Okay," says Justin, his expression alert. "What does that mean you actually do?"

"I progressively evolved into an evaluation expert. I like writing, and my boss says I'm a good, clear writer. So, I look at data from survey results or other research and try to pull out the key trends, the main story, and write it into a report and briefing for the senior executive, and sometimes the Minister."

"Wow." Justin looks impressed. "So, you're an analyst, kind of."

"So are you." I tilt my head. "As a physio, you analyse what's wrong with people and the best way to fix them." I grin. "I bet you analyse all your paddlers too. You know everyone's strengths and weaknesses."

"Sprung!" He lifts his glass at me. "There's no escape from the super coach."

I laugh. He's really taken this super coach and mean coach teasing on board. An image of him blinking at the team banner, shock all over his face, flits into my mind. So not the reaction we were expecting. "Justin," I finger the base of my glass. "The team banner ... that meant a lot to you, didn't it?"

His eyes become fathomlessly dark. "Sprung again," he murmurs so low I have to tip forward to hear him. His fingers tap on the table. "No-one has ever done anything like that for me before. I was humbled and moved." A shine grows in his eyes. "I've never felt so optimistic about our small team here."

The waiter arrives with a woven bamboo bowl and lifts the lid to reveal a neat ring of steaming shumai. I inhale the wonderful aroma, my mouth watering while the waiter puts down small bowls of various sauces. I copy Justin as he expertly picks up a shumai between his chopsticks, dips it into a sauce then pops it into his mouth. Fragrant flavours burst over my tongue, a mix of herbs and vegetables. "Divine," I mutter, and Justin nods.

While I'm still trying to decide which one to eat next, Justin waves a chopstick at me. "Okay, Miss Analyst. My turn. What brought you to Narooma?"

I pause with the shumai perched between my chopsticks. "Complex question," I say, dipping the shumai into a sauce but then putting it on my plate and trying to coax air into my chest, my heart rate rising. Be fair; he deserves to know. And he's probably guessed anyway. My left shoulder is curling in, trying to hide that part of me. Justin's forehead furrows, but he waits me out.

"I … I was sick in 2022. Breast cancer." My hands flap about on the table. "With all the treatment works, surgery, chemotherapy, radiation." I can see Justin is holding his breath, his eyes fixed on my face, calm, non-judgemental. "I went back to work, but even after nine months I couldn't really focus." I shrug. "It didn't seem fair on my boss or team, so I decided to take a break and focus on healing." Air whooshes into my chest. *There. Done it. Told him.* My shoulders felt lighter and I tip my chin up, observing his face.

Justin's forehead relaxes and he gives me his wise coach smile. "That's a lot to go through. Very brave, Hayley, to focus on you. And a good idea." His smile becomes tender. "I'm glad you chose Narooma."

My heart thuds against my breastbone. So, he's not going to make a big deal of it? My legs feel like they are floating away under the table. "Does this …" My voice is all squeaky. I start again. "Does this make any difference to my paddling, your coaching strategy?" I desperately want to add 'to you and me' but the words clog in my throat.

Reaching across the table, Justin pats my hand, his expression intent, eyes in shadow. "We'll work on balancing your strength and posture. Otherwise …" His eyes glint and his lips curve in a wistful, uneven smile. "… this doesn't make a difference … to anything."

My ribs are trying to strangle my heart. Oh my God, how did I manage to stumble across a man like Justin? This is *way* too good to be real. Panic bubbles. There has to be a catch. *Crap. The side-effects of all that treatment!* The tablets I have to take for another four years that make certain parts as dry as a desert. What if my body *can't* respond, no matter how much I want it to? How could I do that to him?

"Hayley," Justin squeezes my hand. "Breathe. It will be alright." When I blink back my focus, he releases my hand and sits back. "Okay, your turn for a question."

My thoughts tumbling every which way, I absently reach for the shumai and put it in my mouth, chewing carefully. How can he possibly be so calm when I feel like screaming? Questions. What else do I want, need to know? His family … "Is your family still in Sydney?" Before he can answer, a second question blurts out. "You said your father is a businessman. Was he a business migrant?" Wait. Why did I ask that?

One eyebrow arched, Justin nods. "You know about business migrants? Yes, he was. Father makes and exports medical equipment."

I remember analysing some of the business visa class mandatory survey data for a major report to parliament. Anyone who migrated with that visa back then had to be successful, and very rich. Like multi-millionaire rich. But Justin is a physio in Narooma … I look at him and find him studying my expression.

A shadow races across his face and his expression becomes guarded. "And no, I don't want to live in Sydney. I like it here."

This feels like a massive understatement. Maybe of the century, but he didn't push me, so I won't push him. "Just as well," I say lightly. "Where would the Clear Water Dragons be without you!

Wait …" I lift a finger. "One more question. Did you paddle before you came here?"

I have to wait for his answer while the waiter swoops on our table with a dish of fried rice, a whole fish covered in spices, and a sizzling beef dish. Justin banters with the waiter in Chinese then looks at me.

"He says you will paddle much faster after eating the ginger barramundi."

I grin at the waiter, who bows and retreats. Justin expertly jiggles pieces of fish off the bone and I hold my plate up to receive them.

Mid-transfer of fish, he says, "I paddled in China as a child. My father and brother are both strong paddlers, and the regional team I'll be in will take their team on in the regional championships."

I catch the underlying tension in his voice and abruptly remember his regional tryout is this weekend. A sudden desire burgeons to go and watch the championships, to see his battle against his family. Too soon to ask, surely. "No wonder you're so strong." My words feel inadequate.

The food is delicious and the dishes complement each other; Justin has chosen well. As if we'd both uncovered what we most needed to know, the rest of the meal passes in chatter about whether I enjoyed the Ama diving and how much fun Kraig and Akiko are. And Justin makes me laugh with his descriptions of some of his clients, unnamed of course, but beneath his humour I can tell how fond he is of them. He must be an excellent physio.

Entranced, I watch the array of emotions that pass across his face, the way his eyes can go from dark, bottomless wells to gleaming with light and life. The way his full lips move and fleet from a smile to serious to a mock pout. The hanging lanterns highlight the planes of his cheekbones, the bold, chiselled jaw, the glossy black hair. The muscles in his forearms ripple with his hand movements.

I'm transported back to how good it felt on the tour boat with his arms around me, his chest pressing against my back and the majestic whales gliding beneath the boat. A warm pulse passes between my legs. If only he'd hold me like that again … forever.

"Er … Hayley?" Justin waves at me. "Where did you go?"

Swallowing hard, I meet his eyes. "I was thinking of the boat … the whales …" I don't need to say 'you' because his eyes widen, grow dark and he swallows too.

Putting his chopsticks down, he folds his serviette. "Maybe a walk, to help dinner go down?"

A shiver running down my spine, I nod. "I'll just go to the ladies." I head in the direction he indicates and find the toilets. I go, then stare in the mirror while I wash my hands, which are shaking. *It will be alright.* I rinse my mouth and apply a trace of lipstick. *Will it? Am I ready?* Once we cross that line from coach and paddler to dating … what if it all goes wrong? Am I sure I want to do this? I so need Justin as a friend. Can't lose that. I lean my forehead on the mirror and breathe in slowly. A girl has to live, otherwise what's the point? If it goes wrong, I can scarper back to Canberra. I straighten up. Okay. Let him lead. See where he goes. And hope he goes slowly.

I emerge and find Justin waiting by the reception desk. Oh crap. He's paid! I didn't mean to dodge that part. As I approach, he moves to the door and holds it open. Hesitating, I say, "Justin, I meant to pay my half."

"Next time." He shakes his head and gives me a nudge through the door. "You can surprise me where we go."

He's already thinking of next time? A warm glow fills me. "Thanks," I murmur. "Dinner was delicious."

Slinging his bomber jacket over one shoulder, he takes my hand with his free one. "This way, there are two things I'd like to show you."

"Okay." Instead of walking back down the hill towards my

apartment, he takes a side road that heads towards the inlet and ocean. Intrigued, I look at the houses lining the street. After a few minutes, we pass a school on the corner and I see a road running downhill, parallel with the main road, and on the far side of that is a massive expanse of verdant lawn and beyond that, moonlight glimmering on the sea. "Lucky kids," I say. "Talk about classes with fresh air and a view!"

Justin laughs. "This clifftop golf course has featured in many lifestyle ads. It's pretty special." He turns left, leading me down the hill for a few hundred metres, then stops and turns me to face a cottage. "This is my house. Number twenty-two." He peers into my face, his shadowy in the gloom. "If you need anything, you know where I am."

Before I can react, other than to register how quaint his place looks, he spins me around and takes me across the road. The grass is dewy and slippery, so I walk carefully, glad Justin still has a grip on my hand. As we approach the cliff edge and the sea, the house lights fade behind us and the sky above seems to expand, stretching to infinity. I become acutely aware of the thousand pinpoint stars twinkling down upon us and the moon casting silver beams across the rippling water. A shiver ripples down my spine. This is magic.

"You're not going to throw me over, are you?" I ask when Justin appears intent on going right to the edge of the land. I hear the hiss and swoosh of waves breaking on the rocks below.

"Funny," says Justin. "Although Natalie might. I don't know how you do it, but I like how you push her to paddle harder."

I don't know what to say to that. A tremor of relief fills me when Justin stops about two paces from the edge. I can see white water swishing and swirling over jagged rocks. A light sea breeze caresses my face and lifts stray strands of my hair to tickle my cheeks and neck.

"Not cold?" asks Justin.

"No," I say, then eye his dragon bomber jacket. "Or maybe yes if I get to try your jacket."

A gleam in his eyes, Justin steps behind me and drapes his jacket over my shoulders. The material is soft, cosy. I hold my breath, willing him to wrap his arms around me. For a few heartbeats neither of us move. I lean back, feeling for him, and his arms fold around me, pulling me to his chest, and he rests his chin on my shoulder. Bliss. I sigh and press into him.

His words are almost in my ear. "Look ahead. The moon is sending a path for you to walk on."

Glancing up, my heart gives a jolt. Oh my God! The moon is throwing a swathe of silver light straight at us and I feel as if I could step off the edge and walk on water to touch it. How does he know this?

"Sometimes, I sit out here to think." His words are deep, measured. "And one night, I found this."

"It's magic," I say. Could this moment possibly be any more romantic? How can he not have a partner? What am I missing? Is it something to do with his family? I push the unwelcome thoughts aside. *Be in the here and now. This is another bucket-list moment.* Justin chooses this moment to gently kiss my hair and my legs float away again. *Turn and kiss him. Do it now.* I'm frozen; my muscles are simply not present. Warm, soft lips brush my ear and heat rushes through me. My neck unlocks enough for me to twist my face towards him.

Small moons are reflected in his dark eyes, moonbeams play along his cheekbones and put a silver sheen on his lips. My knees feel weak and an ache builds in my heart. My kind, mysterious, gorgeous Oriental warrior. I tilt my chin up, can't quite reach his mouth, and he slides around me to press his mouth on mine. I am lost, gliding on moonbeams, revelling in the taste and touch of him.

Vaguely, I feel him clasp me to him, his powerful arms

tightening across my lower back. His tongue gently probes my lower lip, bringing with it an aftertaste of ginger. I part my lips and gasp when his tongue slides into my mouth, exploring. Waves of heat scorch down my torso and pool in my groin. I caress his tongue with mine, and feel his body heating too. We are so not coach and paddler anymore.

Time stands still. Until I can't take the heat building and pull back a little. "Need air." I bury my face in his shoulder, breathing him in. After a while, my heart rate slows and I can feel my legs again, my feet on the dewy grass. I don't want to speak, break the magic, can't find the words, and neither can he. More time passes, and I shiver as a breeze wafts in from the sea.

"Hayley." My name rumbles from deep in Justin's chest. "I should get you home."

Disappointment and relief tumble through me. I don't want this magic to end, but am glad he's content to take things slowly. One step at a time. I peer at him from beneath my eyelashes. "Thanks, coach."

His face unreadable, Justin tugs his jacket snug around my shoulders, takes my hand, walks me back to the road and heads us down the hill. Ten minutes later, we're stopping outside the front of my apartment block.

I shrug his jacket off my shoulders and pass it to him, my fingers giving the intricate dragon one last caress. He puts it on, oblivious to how it accentuates his essence and how unbelievably desirable it makes him. "Thank you," I mumble, more words failing to arrive. I try to say the rest with my smile and eyes.

Justin smiles tenderly, leans in to kiss my forehead. "See you at training tomorrow."

Then he's gone, striding away back up the hill.

CHAPTER TWELVE
Family

It's amazing I make it to Nowra in one piece. Lucky my car knows the way because I sure as hell am not steering it — how can Hayley have been so sick? How does she go forward? Should knowing about this change anything? What should I do? My heart throbs. She remembered to bring my special paddle to training yesterday and handed it to me after, wishing me a cheerful good luck and adding, "Go get 'em, Tiger!" Not sure that was the right thing to say for a dragon boat event, but the others overheard, and in a heartbeat, they were all chanting: "Go get 'em, Tiger!" Gripping the steering wheel tighter, I grin. How can one new paddler lift the dynamics of the whole team?

I shake my head. Hayley is special, but she doesn't seem at all aware of her effect on others. Is it her positivity? Her determination? Or that gorgeous hint of mischief? Despite everything. My heart sinking, I indicate and pull into the motel driveway. Breast cancer is serious. Potentially terminal. I sit for a moment, drumming my fingertips on the steering wheel. What does it mean when the survivor is so young? Do some research, physio-man, you got all evening. Okay, then.

I check in and organise my paddling gear on the table in the room, ready for the early start. Staring at it, I feel flat, all enthusiasm dissipated. Has making the regional team become too routine? Am I tired of the competition? The struggle to keep up with Father and Ethan? Or … are my heart and mind diverted? To matters of more significance. My legs bend and plonk me onto the edge of the bed. Big decisions here. Closing my eyes, I replay Hayley's delicious mouth pressed against mine, the ends of her hair tickling my neck, the way she leaned into me. She needs me. I just didn't think I'd need her so much. Every fibre of my being yearns to be with her.

Flopping backwards onto the bed I stare at the ceiling. No way will Father sanction me being with Hayley. Ever. This is going to be a long three days. What will Mother think? Hope blossoms briefly. Mother *might* warm to Hayley's resilience … and my wishes, anything to get me married off … but enough to influence Father? I scrub both hands over my face. Pointless agonising over this now. I should eat.

Sitting up, I order a take-in lasagne and salad, something simple and full of carbs. After demolishing the food and a hot shower, I crash.

~

My dream of walking hand-in-hand along the beach with Hayley under mystical, silvery moonlight is shattered by my phone alarm. Dawn already. Dressing, I start on my toast, trying to muster some enthusiasm. My phone pings. Hayley. She's sent an image of a tiger pouncing. Cheeky. Two bites of toast then my phone pings again. Natalie has sent a tiger. Rapidly followed by one from Sandi, Rose, Chloe, Gianni with the speech bubble 'international tiger', then even Andrew and Greg send one. Energy buzzes through my veins. *My team.* Ping. Hayley again. This time it's a GIF of a cute kitten meowing and waving its tail. Laughing, I choke on my toast. When

I've recovered, I text back: *OK already! Ggrraow!*

Buoyed, I gather my gear and drive to the Nowra club's boat shed, right on the river. I will do this. For my team and their belief in me. I check my name off, then look around for the other South Coast paddlers trying out. Wow. There are so many paddlers here this year. A couple of hundred; many familiar faces and many new ones, all looking fit and fierce. I'd better value my spot — if I get one.

Time passes quickly as I do the sprint, the sit-ups, the push-ups, the jump-squats, the rowing machine and the erg machine tests. So far, feels good. Most of the test officials greet me by name and give a pleased nod when I complete the test. Encouraging. I grab my paddle and gloves and head to the pontoon. This is the critical test — paddling a 20s boat solo for 100 metres. A measure of power, strength, reach and technique, with a top-level coach observing. Grant, a paddler from Moruya, joins me as the pair to balance the boat. "Good luck," I murmur. He's been on the regional team a few times.

"You too," Grant says quietly.

I imagine Hayley giving me a push and saying, 'Go get 'em Tiger!' and suppress a smile. *Focus.*

The boat comes in and the previous pair step out, then hold the front of the boat steady while we step in. I take the right side of bench two — my name was first in the pair — this is my marginally stronger side. Grant and I paddle together to take the boat up to the start buoy, where I breathe in deeply, stretching my ribs and lungs, while the sweep moves the boat into position. The coach sitting up front in the drummer seat gets her stopwatch ready. A shiver ripples down my spine.

"Paddler on the right, sit ready," calls the sweep and I bury my blade and take a firm grip with both hands.

"Go!" calls the sweep and I plunge my paddle down and back. The boat nose moves. Six deep, strong strokes later we're moving smoothly. I focus on lifting my inside hand high, twisting and reaching, plunging deep and pulling water. Silver bubbles flow from my blade but there should be more. *Do better.* As my inside arm comes up, I think of a tiger coiling, waiting to spring, then lift my torso higher and pounce forward to grab the water. An extra pull runs up my arms and shoulders and I drive hard with my legs, repeating the pouncing tiger image over and over until the sweep calls, "Let it run!"

Grant gives me a respectful nod. We paddle back to the buoy, then it's his turn. Grant is strong too, and I find myself hoping we both make the team. "Nice work," I murmur when he's done. We reach the pontoon, jump out and hold the boat for the next pair.

"Want to join us for coffee?" asks Grant. "There's ten of us from Moruya trying out."

I shake my head. "I would, but I have to go to Sydney now. Thanks for asking. Next time?"

He wanders away and disappears into a throng of paddlers. Ten here from one small club. That's impressive. I wish I had club buddies here. An upturned nose with lines of freckles in a heart-shaped face framed by wavy brown hair hovers before my eyes. I sigh. Can Hayley train hard enough for a regional team with her issues? I mentally slap myself on the wrist: *Don't judge. Don't assume. Help her try.* My feet reluctantly move me to the large shed so I can rinse off in the club showers and get changed.

A three-hour drive — then I face Father.

~

The Sydney traffic is a nightmare, as usual. The stop-start with red lights every four hundred metres drives me nuts. A far cry from Narooma and its two traffic lights! It's nearly five o'clock when I pull into the curved driveway of my family's three-storey house in McMahons Point. I'm in time for dinner. Phew. Ethan's Lexus is already here, parked behind a shiny black sedan that looks like a hire car. The cousins. Easing past the vehicles, I slip my Subaru into the short kink that edges down the far side of the house, out of the way. I carry my bag to the front door.

The gardens are immaculate, with glossy camellia trees adorning the white-washed house walls, neat beds of lilies and azaleas running along the base of the wall. To the right of the elaborate red front door, a fountain tinkles into a small goldfish pond, a couple of white water lilies floating on the surface, against a backdrop of rising layers of rocks and Bonsai shrubs, a small jade temple perched at the summit. An elegant miniature landscape in itself. Mother has an excellent eye for form and colour. The tiny temple is special, I remember Mother packing it very carefully when we migrated. Was it a wedding gift from her mother?

Stepping onto the front step I'm surrounded by the melodious tinkling of the wind chimes and hanging bells. I lift my hand to knock when the door flings open and Ethan steps out.

"Brother, good to see you." Ethan bows then punches me on the shoulder. "How did the tryout go?"

I arch an eyebrow at him and shrug. He is remarkably ebullient, for him. What's going on? "Okay, I think. Have you done yours?"

"Last week." Ethan grabs my bag. "A formality."

Slipping my shoes off and sliding my feet into the pair of slippers lined up ready, I follow Ethan down the hall. The aroma of orange blossom floor wax teases my nostrils, and beyond that the distinctive smell of duck roasting. My mouth waters.

"You go greet everyone and I'll put your bag in your room." Ethan disappears up the flight of stairs, taking two at a time.

Nerves rippling through my stomach, I hesitate outside the lattice doors to the lounge room. *Don't be stupid. Family. And you have met Father's cousin before.* Taking a breath, I enter. My eyes are immediately drawn to Father, seated stiffly upright in his customary armchair of white leather with dark mahogany arms and legs. Bowing respectfully, I clasp my hands in front of me. "Ba."

"Jun Jie, come in." Father stands and nods to me, then sweeps an arm to the grey-haired, wiry man seated to his left. "You remember my distant cousin from Beijing?"

I bow again. "Of course. Nice to see you again."

The cousin stands and bows. "You look fit and well, Jun Jie."

I bow several times more as Father introduces me to the cousin's wife, and to their three daughters in order of age. Xin Yi is stocky with a round face, not helped by her hair being wound on top of her head, held in place by ornate jade pins. When she smiles coyly at me and flutters her eyelashes, I wonder how much pressure she is under to woo me. My stomach recoils and it's an effort to keep my face neutral.

Meng Yao is a few years younger, slimmer and more relaxed in appearance. She gives me an assessing look and a confident smile. I nod politely.

Li Na, the youngest, is really pretty. Her glossy hair frames her oval face attractively, and her eyes are large and brown. She exudes a happy demeanour. After giving me a brief smile, her eyes flick away to watch Ethan as he enters. Ah. Does she explain Ethan's buoyancy? My heart weighs heavy; if he likes her too this will double the pressure on me.

Mother pats the space beside her on the lounge and I approach, bow before sitting, and accept the cup of steaming Jasmine tea she immediately pours. She runs her eyes over my attire of a crisp white shirt, open at the neck, above my best charcoal suit pants, and gives a subtle dip of her head. *Passed test one.*

The conversation is light, discussing what the cousins have done in the week they have been here and what they enjoyed most. I sip my tea, conscious of the two older girls giving me subtle glances. Li Na is captivated by something Ethan is saying. My brother is animated, his eyes alight. I feel a groan building. *Don't be mean. They look good together.* After a while, Mother stands, saying she must check on the meal. I half stand to ask if she needs help and she puts a hand on my arm, the dangerous glitter in her dark eyes daring me to move. I sit. Okay, then. Understood. I am expected to seriously consider these girls.

Soon, we are seated at the formal dining table. Father is at the head, Mother on his left, with the cousin and his wife next to her. I am at Father's right, the oldest son, and, no surprise, Xin Yi is beside me, then Meng Yao, then Li Na, which places her next to Ethan at the far end of the table. The table is adorned with a banquet of seafood soup, Peking Duck, scallops in the shell on a bed of glass noodles, fried rice and a sizzling, spicy fish dish. I smile at Mother; my favourites. Ethan's favourites – crispy pork and mushrooms with greens – are included. And steamed rice, making it eight dishes in total. I know an ornate fruit platter will follow.

Dishes are passed from right to left, and I try not to become irritated at the way Xin Yi coyly flutters her eyelashes each time I hold a dish for her. I can feel Father's eyes on me. Once our bowls are full, I ask Xin Yi, "What do you do in Beijing?"

"I am a dressmaker," she says proudly. "For one of the large boutique shops." She eyes my shirt. "Nice silk. Good quality."

I worry that she will run her fingers up my arm and look past her to Meng Yao, not wanting her to be left out as Ethan is busy flirting with Li Na. "How about you?"

She smiles prettily. "I work in a florist. We specialise in high-end floral arrangements and cultivate a Bonsai collection." After a pause, she says, "What role do you play?"

"I'm a physio, I manage my own practice."

Both girls look at me, confused.

"What about in the business?" asks Xin Yi.

The business? I swallow my mouthful of duck pancake while

they both regard me expectantly. Oh. They mean Father's business. Zhao Medical Enterprises Pty Ltd. Unease rises. What has he told them? Crap.

Just then, the cousin raises his glass to Father. "We must congratulate Chiaoxiang on his imminent expansion into the Hong Kong horse racing market. This is a major achievement." He nods respectfully. "Wishing the venture every blessing."

I lift my glass to toast too, then take a sip of the rice wine, the taste searing up my nose. Father regards me intently over the rim of his glass and guilt slides through me. I am such a bad son that I do not know about this. I tilt my head respectfully. The horse racing market … equipment for jockeys. No, more than that. Wait. Is he expanding into medical and recovery equipment for horses? Whoa. His empire will increase ten-fold. I turn to Ethan and find him giving me a sour look. I lift an eyebrow. What? He looks down, but I sense his anger.

Meng Yao leans forward. "Will you go to Hong Kong? How exciting!"

"I appreciate the blessing," says Father. "Tomorrow, I have a special outing for us. We will go to the Top Star racing stables to demonstrate the new line on their champion racehorses." His eyes glint with steel. "Jun Jie, with his physiotherapy and scientific background, will explain to the trainer and head groom exactly how the products stimulate the muscle enzymes and the positive effect on training."

My throat constricts. The noose is drawing tight. Father is too clever. Has he named me as the potential Hong Kong manager? Is that what's annoyed Ethan? Blinking back panic, I look down. Filial piety. There is no graceful refusal.

How can he do this to me?

Woodenly, I manage to get through the rest of dinner. Both Xin Yi and Meng Yao are keen to prove their prowess and by the time we're finished eating, I know far more about types of cloth, fashion and flower arranging and Bonsai trimming than I will ever need.

Using the excuse of the long day and drive, I head to my bedroom on the third floor while the others are enjoying post dinner tea and sweets. Once comfortable in my boxer shorts and T-shirt, I sit cross-legged on my double bed and stare at the ornate wall panel behind the bedhead. The two river dragons fighting in the image look as fierce as ever, their golden horns gleaming, whiskers bristling and eyes pure slits of rage. Is this me and Father? Are we destined to lock horns forever? Can there be no compromise? I scrub at my face.

Ethan is a good brother, a good friend. But if he wants to marry Li Na and I'm in his way will that change? Does Ethan want to be the Hong Kong manager? Am I in his way there too? I will become the sole dragon fighting two irate ones working together. Man, this is a mess. Then there's Hayley … How could I go to Hong Kong and leave her before we even get started? With whatever we have. What do we have? Too soon to tell, and I don't have much experience to go on, but Hayley feels different. I won't tire of her after a handful of dates. My heart and soul know this; they are shouting it.

Sighing, I glance around my room, my eyes coming to rest on my old laptop, sitting on the study desk built into the bay window alcove. Retrieving it, I sit back on the bed and fire up Google search, keying in 'anatomy of a racehorse'. No matter what, I will not disgrace Father tomorrow. Not in front of these horse people and not in front of his cousins. Are they potential investors in this new enterprise? Ah. That would explain the timing of their visit. Bringing the daughters is a bonus — invest in *and* marry into Zhao Enterprises. What a coup that would be.

The computer screen shows me the outline of a horse with all the different muscle groups colour-coded. The picture even shows where the rider would be positioned. Focusing, I begin to memorise all the major muscle groups and to understand how the whole musculoskeletal structure works in this four-legged creature as opposed to a human.

At midnight, voices and car doors disrupt my research into the other equine training products available. The cousins, going back to their hotel. I rub my eyes. Okay, then. Horses are quite interesting — on paper, anyway. I know enough to be credible. Before I climb under the sheets, I bow to the river dragons on the wall.

"No fighting tomorrow, Father. Jun Jie will be your dutiful son."

CHAPTER THIRTEEN
The Noose

Rosy light shining through the window wakes me. Seems I forgot to pull the curtains. Rising, I stand looking out the window. Pale sunlight ripples across the grey-blue harbour water, the Sydney Harbour Bridge standing out in contrast. The ferries are already active, carrying people to their workplaces. Around the shoreline, imposing buildings stretch for the sky, vying to outdo each other: look at me. My eyes are drawn to the greenery and trees, the glimpses of lawns and parks. I miss Narooma already, the turquoise water, the balance between nature and people. Swallowing hard, I long to be with Hayley, to speak with her, watch her face and the emotions that fly across it. Can I confide in her?

"Justin!" Ethan bangs on my door then bounces into the room. "Good, you're awake." He eyes my boxer shorts and shakes his head. "Hurry up. We leave in twenty minutes."

"Good morning, brother," I say with a respectful bow and a less respectful grin.

Ethan laughs. "Funny man. Get dressed." He throws a dark red polo shirt at me. "Wear this."

Catching it, I spy the gold embroidered logo on the left breast: *Zhao Enterprises, Equine Performance Division*, and a stitched running horse below it. Of course, Ethan is wearing one too.

"And boots." Ethan plonks a pair on the end of my bed. "Borrow my old ones. These creatures weigh more than a dragon boat, so you don't want to be in runners if they step on your foot." He bestows a lop-sided grin. "Then there's the piles of dung … you can wash my boots if you find one of those." Bounding out of my room, he leaves a trail of aftershave in his wake. I take it the girls are coming on this venture too.

Minutes later, I walk into the kitchen. Mother puts a plate of toast and mug of chai tea on the benchtop. Seeing the question in her eyes, I say, "I was up late researching horses. I'm ready."

A trace of relief crosses her face and she nods approval. Her expression hints she wants to say more, but she doesn't.

"I know this is important," I reassure her and reach for the plate.

Father strides into the kitchen and ignores my hasty bow. "We will go in Yichen's car. You can read the product documentation on the way. Ready?"

I swig down the tea, scalding my throat, and bolt down the toast. Passing the cousin's wife on her way in, I race outside to see Father's cousin and the daughters in the sedan, ready to follow Ethan's car. Sliding into the back seat of the Lexus, I pick up the folder full of leaflets with glossy images and photos. Throughout the drive, Father does business on his phone and I catch Ethan intermittently watching me in the rear vision mirror, his forehead pinched in a frown. I so need to talk to him. Properly.

By the time Ethan turns the car off the main road and passes between two ornate stone walls with bronze statues of galloping horses on each post, I am impressed. According to the leaflets, Father has subtly improved the design compared to the existing equine products. His are lighter and more malleable, making it easier to move the saddle-blanket arrangement all along a horse's spine, including near the hindquarters. Twisting in his seat, Father explains this trainer is interested in the products and was happy for the cousin to attend. Father doesn't explain, but I well understand: this is a test of my capability. And loyalty.

The Lexus glides past white post-and-rail fences containing glossy horses of various shades of brown grazing in verdant paddocks with water troughs and clumps of trees for shade. The gravel driveway finishes in a large courtyard, surrounded by a multi-barn wood-and-brick stable complex. A man, dressed in blue jeans and a cream polo shirt, points to a designated visitor space and Ethan parks there. Glancing at the main product leaflet one last time, I breathe in. *Coach and physio mode. You can do this.*

The man shakes Father's hands. "Mr. Zhao, welcome. We are looking forward to seeing the products. Thanks for coming over on a Sunday, our quiet day."

"This is Dominic, the trainer," says Father. To Dominic, he says, "This is Jun Jie, my oldest son. He is a physiotherapist and highly trained in science and physiology. He will explain the products."

I bow respectfully.

"And this is Yichen, younger son, my assistant sales manager. If you are interested, please speak with him after."

Ethan bows while Father rapidly introduces his cousin and skims over the presence of the three girls.

There's a clatter of hooves and a tall, bearded man emerges from the nearest barn leading a large, skittish horse. Dominic says, "This is our head groom, Nigel, and Windsong, one of our rising three-year-old colts. He raced a two-mile handicap yesterday and is probably sore today."

I regard the prancing horse, my pulse rising with each thud of its hooves on the gravel. Magnificent as the horse is, will it stand still long enough for me to fit the saddle-blanket product to its back? I don't fancy being bowled over while trying to clip the chest buckles shut.

Turning to Ethan, I say, "Can you bring the *Elevator* back product please?" Ignoring his arched eyebrow, I then approach the horse, keeping back far enough not to be knocked over, and say to Dominic and Nigel, "Let me explain how the science works. Are you familiar with any of our human medical class II products?"

They both shake their heads and I smile. "Your jockeys might like to know about those." They laugh and Father almost smiles. I continue. "Anyway, the equine *Elevator* back pad and the smaller *LightTouch* device for specific trouble spots are both based on the same cycloid vibration therapy, known as CVT. This unique circular vibration action provides deep tissue stimulation, essential for improving circulation, lymphatic drainage, removing lactic acid and muscle tissue repair."

Ethan comes to a stop beside me with the pale gold saddle-blanket device *Elevator* hanging over an arm. I can see the wireless control poking out of his jeans pocket.

To my relief, the horse has calmed somewhat and is chewing on the groom's shirt sleeve. "Can you hold him still so I can feel his back?"

Nigel takes a firm hold on the cheek strap of the head collar and strokes the horse's shiny mahogany neck, murmuring soothing words.

I crack my knuckles then rub my palms together to warm them, and approach cautiously. The colt is no doubt a magnificent creature — lithe and superbly muscled, not an ounce of fat on him. Gently, I place my hands on either side of the little ridge called a wither and pause, gauging the level of muscle tension where the front of the saddle would sit. The horse's head lowers a fraction.

Nigel grins. "He thinks you're an equine bodyworker about to give him a massage."

Okay, then. I lower my eyes and focus on the feel of the horse, the way the long muscle equivalent to our trapezius muscle feeds down the neck, over the wither and along the spine. Standing balanced, I absorb the warmth of the horse and allow my fingers to somehow extend into the horse, probing for trouble areas. When I touch where the back of the saddle would sit, I sense a small knot. When I knead it Windsong shivers and gives a grunt. "He is sore here. Ethan, bring the *Elevator* please and we'll start here."

Ethan sidles next to me and we gently lower the arch of thick blanket over Windsong's back. Dominic steps in to do up the chest buckles. I ask him to do up the belly strap too, so I can focus on making sure the pad is in the best spot. *So far, so good.* I step back and press the power button on the remote, starting at the lowest intensity. The colt jumps and snorts when the pad vibrates, but then realises the sensation is pleasant.

While we are treating the horse, I show Dominic how the controls work and detail more of the science behind it. I point out how the *Elevator* can be held in place over a horse's hindquarters to give relief to the massive muscle groups there, needed for galloping. By the time I have turned the intensity to level four, Windsong's head is lowered level to his chest and the horse's bottom lip is hanging loose.

"By God, he's falling asleep!" Nigel exclaims. "This is magic."

"It is good for relaxation too," I say seriously. "You can use the products for injury prevention as well as to just relax the horse ready to race."

"This is marvellous, Jun – Jun…" says Dominic, his face alive with interest.

"Call me Justin, and my brother Ethan. Easier to remember."

Next, we demonstrate the *LightTouch* machine, which can be used either hand-held or strapped to a horse's leg in a tendon boot. By this time, I am certain Father has a sale. Dominic and Nigel ask several questions, which I field easily. Windsong remains calm while we treat all along his back and all four lower legs.

Finally unstrapping the tendon boot, I stand up. Ethan is looking at me like I'm a stranger. Father dips his head imperceptibly, and the three daughters are staring with wide eyes. What? Why? Ah. Father and Ethan have never seen me doing physio work before. Do the strange looks mean they're impressed? Or have I done something stupid?

Nigel leads the sleepy colt away and even my inexperienced eye can see how relaxed the colt is, the long loping reach in his stride, the back muscles rippling smoothly.

Dominic grabs my hand and pumps it vigorously. "Thanks, Justin. Such a comprehensive explanation. You've convinced me."

Ethan steps forward, bows and hands Dominic a business card and a folder of leaflets. "Would you like me to call you later this afternoon?"

Dominic shakes Ethan's hand, all smiles. "Say around five o'clock, after evening feeds. Let me look at the prices and do some sums."

We say polite farewells and climb back into the car. My stomach rumbles loudly and I realise it's past lunchtime. A wave of fatigue tumbling over me, I lean my head against the window and close my eyes. Thoughts flit in and out of my mind against the backdrop of Father and Ethan's low voices. Did I do well? Could be a mistake: Father will be more determined to appoint me. Does Hayley like horses? The way she gently pats or strokes the dragon's head before she gets into the boat reminds me of how someone would pat a horse before mounting. Actually, didn't she tell me that's why she does it?

The car jolts to a stop and I blink at the surroundings. Looks like Darling Harbour.

"Are you with us, brother?" says Ethan. "Lunch at the Chinese Gardens."

Soon we are seated at a table overlooking the large pond at the café in the gardens. I somehow become wedged between Xin Yi and Meng Yao while Father rattles off an order to the waiter. Ethan and Li Na are sitting close together, heads almost touching as they confer. I feel pressure along my right forearm.

"That was *so* interesting," says Meng Yao. "How did you calm the horse like that? Do you ride?"

I am pinned by her hand on my arm. Trying to relax, I answer truthfully. "No, but I work with injured or elderly people every day and the principles are the same. Just a different anatomy."

"You must have a gift," Meng Yao murmurs, gently squeezing my arm then running her forefinger down to the back of my hand, tracing my knuckles. "Such strong hands." She smiles coyly and lowers her long, dark eyelashes seductively.

My mouth runs dry and I feel a powerful urge to snatch my hand away and crack my knuckles. Several times. Maybe I should as this habit seems to annoy people. There's a tug on my left sleeve.

"Jun Jie," says Xin Yi in a husky voice, "have you ever been to Hong Kong?" She tugs my sleeve again so I have to look at her. "We went last year. Such a magnificent city ..." She regales me with a long story, while Meng Yao is still tracing my knuckles.

I look across the table, directly into Ethan's amused look. I glare at him and he shakes his head. No help there. The lunch is interminable with the two girls pulling me between them and talking incessantly. I can feel my pulse beating in my throat. When the waiter brings tea, I stand abruptly and mutter about watching the koi in the pond.

Escaping, I lean on the red wooden railing and stare into the water, willing my heartrate to calm. Numerous massive, colourful fish glide between the lily pads. A few pause in front of me, silently gulping with their mouths, but I have no food for them. A giggle floats across the water and I look to my right, glimpsing Ethan and

Li Na, hand-in-hand, disappearing behind some rocks and maple trees. Will he kiss her? My brother is not one to waste time. Never has been. A bubble of envy rises in my chest and I quickly squash it.

A presence looms behind me and I hurriedly stand straight.

"Jun Jie." Father's hand lands — fleetingly — on my shoulder. "You made me proud this day."

"Thank you, Father," I respond. He watches me, waiting for more. "Your products speak for themselves. I am sure they will be most popular."

A glint lights his serious eyes. "With the right team managing them, this is my wish." His gaze lingers on my face, endeavouring to scrutinise my inner thoughts. "Tonight, we celebrate, and tomorrow morning we talk business. Zhao business." He pats my shoulder and turns away, calling to his cousin that it is time to go.

A chill runs from my head to my toes.

~

Sleep eludes me for most of the night. My stomach roils from the rich food of the banquet Mother prepared, my mouth tastes sour from too many toasts of Chinese wine, and, above all, I'm unable to shake the sensation of a large hand trying to squeeze all life from my heart. Light is eking over the windowsill. Maybe a run would help.

I slink downstairs carrying my running shoes and slip out through the front door. The morning is bright with the promise of a sunny spring day. I jog down the street and take the laneway heading to the edge of the water. My chest is tight and my legs heavy. On reaching a narrow strip of park, I drop back to a walk. How can I escape this? What can I do or say to persuade Father to let me live my own life?

Spying a bench overlooking the water, I sit and put my head between my hands. I am such a bad son. Ethan enjoys working in the business, so why can't I? It's not the objective or the products themselves, those I believe in, so what is it? The office? The data and sales? *Uggh.* I enjoy working with people, helping them, improving their lives. *Hayley.* I want to help Hayley. Be with her. I promised to coach her. My lips tingle, remembering our kiss. No, I promised her way more than coaching. A groan thrums in my chest. I haven't even texted her since the tryout! What am I doing? Letting *everyone* down. Filial piety trumps everything. But we're not in China now.

An hour later, with nothing resolved, I head home. There is no way out of this meeting. I creep back inside and am tiptoeing past the kitchen when Ethan strides out of it.

"Where have you been? Running?" Ethan's look is incredulous. "Father will skin you alive. He's meeting with his cousin now, wants us in there at 11 am."

"Got it." I flee upstairs and spend an eon in the shower. I pack my bag ready, and feel a bit better. I should leave by 3 o'clock. It's at least a six-hour drive and I have clients booked in all day tomorrow. Just another four hours …

"Justin!" bellows Ethan from downstairs.

My phone buzzes in my pocket. I pull it out. *Two* missed calls from Natalie? What? She never rings me. Are they that keen to know if I made the team? They'll have to wait. I start down the stairs, drawing in deep breaths. Halfway down the bottom flight, my phone buzzes again. I let it ring out. Then check. Natalie again. Unease stirring, I send a quick text: *What's up? I'm in Sydney.*

From the bottom step, Ethan hisses, "Put that away. Father's waiting."

He pushes open the lattice door to reveal Father poised at the head of the coffee table. As well as a coffee pot and biscuits, there are three piles of papers, neatly arrayed. One before him and two where I presume Ethan and I will sit. My breath catches in my throat. Despair floods my veins.

My phone buzzes. In a trance, I reach for it and skim the

message from Natalie: *Sorry. Urgent. Bumped into Hayley at shops. Looks tense. Pried out of her she's going to Canberra for health checks. Tomorrow. Do you know what for?*

My vision blurs and I blink hard. Read the message again. And again. She didn't tell me. Must be serious. How serious?

"You going in or what?" Ethan nudges me.

I take a step backwards, letting the doorframe obscure Father. If I leave now, I can be in Narooma by dinner time. Hayley shouldn't be alone, not with this looming. Pain stabs into my heart. How bad is this? I have to go to her. Turning around, I run back upstairs and grab my bag from the end of the bed. Charge out the door and sprint back downstairs, car keys in my hand. Stick my head in the study door.

"Father. Sorry. Crisis in Narooma." I bow low and retreat before he can register what I've said. Dodging Ethan's hands, I run to the front door, yank on my shoes and literally sprint to my car.

Ethan pursues, in his socks, and grabs the door handle. "You can't do this!"

I throw my bag on the back seat, then grab him in a fierce hug. "Commit to Li Na. You look good together. Go for it." I hold him at arm's length. "Take the Hong Kong initiative. You'll be great at it."

Ethan's mouth is working, no sounds issuing.

I nudge him away from my car. "Tell Mother I am deeply sorry. I must go."

I jump in my car and reverse. Ethan has the good sense to stand out of the way.

Before I reach the end of the street, my phone is buzzing on the passenger seat. I clench the wheel. Terror mingles with exhilaration. I stood up to Father!

But will I survive the fallout?

CHAPTER FOURTEEN
Revelations

My small suitcase is packed for three days in Canberra. I tuck it near the wardrobe door and wander back to the kitchen. I should prepare dinner, but my stomach is robustly telling me it isn't interested. My phone buzzes — Dad, confirming he's booked us adjacent rooms at The Hyatt. Nice. He knows I'll use the indoor pool to help me unwind. The next buzz confirms his flight details, arriving in Canberra 5.45 tomorrow afternoon.

My phone clock informs me it's only 5:30 now. I sigh, anxiety budding. It's going to be a long, slow evening. The downside to not knowing anyone down here well enough to ask them around or to go visit someone to take my mind off the two days of scans — let alone the results.

Leaning on the benchtop, I turn the phone over in my hands. *Should have told Justin.* A tremble quivers through my fingers. *No, it was right not to, not fair to distract him.* I haven't heard from him since his tryout. Should I text him? Doesn't feel right. Is he regretting the dinner? Our kiss? What would I say, anyway? I put the phone down. I'll be alright once Dad arrives in twenty-four hours.

I just need to keep occupied until then.

Grabbing one of my favourite books, I slump on the lounge. I'm still staring at page one when my phone buzzes again. Has Dad forgotten something? I glance at the caller ID and my heart skips a beat. Or three.

Justin: *Are you at home? Can I drop by?*

Yes and yes. Should I be more welcoming? I send the tiger image, add: *Apartment 311.*

Justin: *I'll bring dinner.*

I blink. He's bringing dinner? After two days of silence? My pulse rises with a turbulent mix of relief and anxiety. Putting the book down, I head to the balcony. Tai Chi will calm me down. Breathing deeply, I work through the moves, and just as I'm bowing to the setting sun to conclude the session, I hear a rap on the door. Wiping my clammy hands down my cargo pants, I go to open it.

"Hi Justin." I smile, and he gives me a tentative return one. He looks … nervous. I glance at the paper bag he's holding, from which wafts the tantalising aroma of Chinese food. "Did you make the team? Are we celebrating?" Belatedly, I stand aside. "Come in."

"Thanks." Stepping in, he kicks off his shoes. "They haven't announced the team yet. On the benchtop?" He holds up the paper bag.

I nod, close the door, follow him to the kitchen. So, this visit isn't about the tryout. He puts the bag down, cracks his knuckles and looks at me, uncertainty etched all over his face. What happened to confident, unflappable coach Justin? This Justin looks shaken, lost, and is trying to hide it. I feel like I'm floundering in murky water, way out of my depth.

I should ask him how the tryout went, but instead my lips blurt, "Are you okay?"

Next thing, he's folding me against his chest, hugging me tight and resting his cheek on my hair. Heart pounding, I burrow into him and clasp my arms around his lower back, feeling the strength and power in his taut muscles. Seems we both need this. Time slows as we stand there, holding each other. After a while, Justin's fingers tickle my neck as he nudges my hair back over my shoulder, then buries his lips and face in my neck. My skin buzzes with his mumbled, "I missed you."

The feel of his lips on my skin is incredibly sexy. My neck grows warm, and a corresponding warmth penetrates my lower abdomen, spreading downwards. I close my eyes. *Yes, come on down there. Wake up. I might need you.* A shudder ripples down Justin. Kind of like what I felt when he was holding me on the whale-watching tour, but this one's even deeper. If that's possible. A stab of anxiety spoils the moment. This hidden intensity … there has to be something he's not telling me.

I lift my face from his shirt. "Justin." That came out strangled, broken. "Justin." Better, firmer. I try to lean back so I can see his face. Reluctantly, he relaxes his hold and looks into my eyes. "Has something happened?"

His eyes go pitch black, like he's pulling a shutter down over them, and he starts to shake his head. Without thinking, I reach up and place my palm along his cheek, insisting he look at me. Two can play at the super-perceptive game. "What's wrong?" After a beat, I add, "Tiger."

"Okay, then. Sprung." Wrinkles of tension spread across his forehead and he tries to smile, but fails. "I want to ask you about something, and …" He draws in a breath, his frown deepening, "I'd value your advice on something else."

"Okay." I'm not really any wiser, and my heart is fluttering like a zillion butterflies trying to escape a cage. What does he want to ask? Is it about my health? A flash goes off in my brain. Natalie. When I told her I wouldn't be at paddling on Thursday she pried out of me about going to Canberra for health reasons. Did she tell

Justin? Is *that* why he's here? No, no, no. I wanted to get my results first. Celebrate, hopefully, not make him worry. Now I'm as reluctant to speak as he is. "Should we eat first?"

I collect bowls and a bottle of fizzy apple juice while Justin takes the bag to the dining table and extracts three containers and two pairs of chopsticks. Coach Justin is back as he deftly serves me fried rice and a variety of dumplings. Seated opposite him, I pick at a dumpling. Better get this over with. "Ask away," I say as brightly as possible, waiting while he chews his dumpling and then puts his chopsticks down in a neat line by his bowl.

He scrubs a hand across his face, "Hayley, I … Natalie told me you have health checks in Canberra?" He clasps his hands together so tightly his knuckles are turning white. "Is it … is it… oh man. I'm worried. For you." His eyes beg me to tell him.

I want to make this lighter, easier, but my courage fails me. Curse Natalie. "This month is one year after I finished all my treatment." Okay, that wasn't so hard. "I'm in the higher risk category, so I have to undergo regular monitoring. Blood tests and a physical check-up every six months, plus full scans every twelve months. For at least three years." I stop. Let him ask.

"So, this is routine?" He looks so relieved at my nod. Then he frowns and fiddles with a chopstick, deliberating whether to ask me more. He goes still and his eyes latch onto mine. "Wait. You said higher risk. So … it had metastasised?"

I swallow hard. "Yes. They took all the lymph nodes in my left arm." I swallow harder, my pulse beating so fast in my throat I can barely force the words out, but I have to do this. Now. I owe it to him. "I … I didn't know how to tell you. Didn't want you to worry. I was going to explain everything — once I had the results. Sorry."

He reaches across the table for my hand. "I *am* worried. This is a lot for you to go through. What scans will you have? Is someone going to go with you?"

I blink back burning tears. He's so sweet, so thoughtful. I need to trust him; he's not like Jonathan. At all. Jonathan ran away, but Justin is running — correction, paddling — right at this. "Mammogram and blood test tomorrow. PET full body scan Wednesday morning, then I see the oncologist for the results on Thursday." There. Full admission. He isn't moving, is he shocked?

Blowing out a tense breath, I add, "My dad's coming from Melbourne for a few days, so he'll be there for me." Brushing at a tear that's got away, I murmur, "But I'm glad you're here now. I was getting pretty wound up."

Justin squeezes my hand fiercely, somehow looking pleased and overcome at the same time. "Can you text or ring me each day?"

"Yes, coach, sir," I say and snap a salute with my free hand.

Laughing, he releases my hand. "The coach says you should eat your dinner. You'll need your strength." He waves a chopstick at me. "You eat, and I'll tell you about the tryout."

Absorbed by his explanation of all the tests he had to do — what the hell are jump-squats — I manage to wade through my dumplings and rice. He makes me laugh with his animated description of how he imagined he was a tiger in the solo paddle test, miming a super high inside arm, and pouncing down with a ferocious growl.

"So glad I could help!" I feel lighter, almost dizzy, such a massive burden has been taken off my shoulders. He knows everything; and he's still here. For me. Wait. Did he say he wanted my advice on something?

I wipe my mouth. "Did you say there was something else you wanted to talk about?" Instantly, the life goes out of his face and I wish I hadn't asked. Should I say don't worry, it doesn't matter? No. Taking in the way his shoulders have tensed and the sorrow emanating from him, whatever it is, it's important. *Be tough, Hayley. Honesty goes both ways.* But help him, like he's helping me.

Standing, I say, "Let's sit on the lounge. I'll make green tea."

I cross to the sliding door and open it to let the sound of the surf in. An evening breeze wafts in, carrying the last cries of the birds before they settle for the night. The swans on the inlet are making their reedy piping noise, and a few plovers are screeching into the darkening sky.

Justin obligingly carries the dishes to the sink, then I motion for him to sit while I fill a teapot, choose mugs and search for biscuits. No luck there, but I find a small block of dark chocolate.

Perching on the other end of the sofa from him, I pass him his mug. Drawing my legs up onto the sofa, I twist to face him and say softly, "Your turn." Then I hold my breath, praying his revelation isn't going to be insurmountable. For him. For us.

Justin takes a few sips of tea, then puts his mug on the coffee table in a slow, deliberate movement. His fingers are shaking. He cracks his knuckles, winces at my wince, then straightens his spine. "After the tryout, I went to Sydney to see my family."

Relief trickles into me. So, that's why I didn't hear from him. He was busy with his family. "You don't look happy about it," I prod because he's now staring vacantly out through the sliding door.

Still gazing out the door, he says, "My father is a strong and dominant man. In China, family is everything. It is an unbreakable bond, an unbreakable duty." He swivels to look at me properly. "On this visit, Father made it clear he wants me to work in the family business, like my brother Ethan does."

I frown when he stops there, his faraway expression suggesting he's considering how much more to say. Is this another one of his massive understatements? Sure feels like it. "And you don't want to?" I probe. He shakes his head, his expression so broken I feel tears prickling the back of my eyes.

"I like it here." He waves a hand at the view outside. "I love Narooma. Enjoy my work. Like the people." He gazes at me. "And the Clear Water Dragons are just starting to get somewhere." A shy half-smile. "Partly due to one new paddler, who doesn't realise how special she is. She exudes energy and light." His voice becomes gruff, deep. "I want to stay with her, too. Father's timing is … the worst possible."

So many emotions tumble through me I can't speak. I'm delighted, humbled, honoured … and horrified. How can his father do this to him? Everyone down here adores Justin! Surely, his family can't just rip him away? "Can you say no?" I eventually squeak out.

Justin shakes his head and reaches a hand towards me. Taking it, I slide closer to him, put an arm around the back of his neck. Love feeling his warm breath easing past my cheek. His smile turns wry. "No, but I may have done something incredibly stupid." He starts playing with my fingers. "Father had business documents, contracts, ready for me to sign … and then I got Natalie's text about your trip for health reasons. She was pretty freaked out … so I freaked out too."

I'm holding my breath. Oh my God. What did he do? I squeeze his fingers. "Tell me."

He grimaces. "I got in my car and drove away. Left Father sitting there."

A sheet of cold washes down my back as if someone has thrown a bucket of icy water over me. *He did that because of me?* My chest implodes. *Oh my God, oh my God.* My mind is running in a panicked loop. He can't do that because of me. "Justin … shit. What will your father do?"

Justin gives me a sheepish look. "Father is furious. As is my brother. I've turned my phone off. I don't know what Father will do."

"Will he come here? To get you?" I feel like frozen fingers are jabbing into me all over.

Shaking his head, Justin says, "No. That would be beneath him. Possibly, he will disown me." He shrugs. "That would be easiest all round. He can give everything to Ethan. I don't mind." A frown follows this statement. "But that would wound Mother incredibly. And be *massive* loss of honour for my family. I would be forever known as the bad son." He hangs his head.

Unable to think of anything to say, I snuggle closer to him and rest my head on his broad chest, listen to the erratic thumping of his heart. His arms wrap around me, his lips brush my hair. We are such a pair — neither of us in control of our future, our destiny. Both of us trying to dodge unwelcome events. "Well," I murmur, "*that* sure has taken my mind off my scans. I'm not sure who's in the worst trouble. Maybe we could just paddle away into the sunset?"

Justin crooks a finger under my chin and tips my face up, his eyes filled with passion. "Nice idea, but we must both face our dragons." He presses his mouth over mine, and I lean into him.

The kiss deepens and I feel Justin's fingers creep up the back of my head and pull me closer. I am melting into him. His tongue gently probes at my lips until I part them so he can slide it into my mouth. The tip of his tongue moves gently, exploring, and heat flames across my cheeks and scorches down my neck. *Holy hell. No-one has ever kissed me like this.* I'm going to start sweating any second. I lift my tongue to caress the base of his tongue and he grunts, pulls me closer again.

I'm not sure I can take much more, my body is giving me mixed signals … my nipples are throbbing uncomfortably, my belly is on fire, and between my legs is prickling, but dryly, painfully. *Too fast. We're moving too fast.* My heartbeat stutters. *Stop.* In case my body can't deliver. With a shiver, I try to pull back. Justin's mouth follows mine, and I tense up.

His warm mouth leaves mine, and he peers at me with desire and concern in his beautiful dark eyes. "Too intense?" he murmurs.

I nod and try to smile but embarrassment keeps my lips and cheeks stiff. "Nice, but intense." *Come on Hayles, reassure him. Lighten up.* "Might need a few more drills first?"

"Good plan." He plays with my fingers again, looking down. Is he disappointed? I can't tell.

An awkward silence stretches, and I realise it's fully dark. My lips crimp, suppressing a yawn. Big day tomorrow, I should go to bed. How do I broach this? My heart flutters with anxiety. I need to sleep, but I also don't really want him to go. Would I sleep, or lie awake tossing and turning?

"Hayley," Justin tips my chin up with his finger. I could drown in the depths of his eyes. "You should rest. But ..." He lowers his jet-black eyelashes. "... I'd like to stay, until you are asleep."

My heart feels like a disoriented frog, leaping around all over the place. What does he mean? I can only stare at him.

He gives me a push. "Go get ready for bed. I'll tidy up. What time do you need to get away tomorrow?"

"By 7.30," I manage to say, my mind still pondering his words. "So up at 6.30." I don't understand what he intends, but I'm not game enough to ask. Don't want to ruin this. *Trust him. Maybe he just needs company tonight too.* I push up off the sofa and head to the bathroom.

Ten minutes later, teeth clean, face tinglingly fresh and in my pyjamas, I slide under the doona. Then get up to open the curtains and window, letting the sound of the surf in and allowing pale moonlight to wash over the bed, before sliding back under the warm covers. I can hear Justin clattering around in the kitchen, hear the screen door sliding closed, the click of the light being turned off.

Then he glides into the bedroom, a ninja in the gloom, pauses at the foot of the bed then crawls on from the window side and wriggles up on top of the cover, props himself up on an elbow and gazes down at me, shadows playing across his features. "Close your eyes," he whispers, his lips brushing ever so faintly across my forehead.

I lower my eyelashes, peeking at him subtly. The arm he's not propped on swings over, and his thumb lightly traces my eyebrow. Oh man, that is so nice. My heart rate lowers a notch. He traces both eyebrows, brushes stray hairs back away from my temples, then slides his thumb over my eyelids, which are growing heavy. Sadness wells in my breast. Mum used to do this when I was sick as a child. It always calmed me, made me feel better. A tear seeps out and Justin's onto it, gently brushing it away.

"How can you be so perfect?" I mumble, letting darkness take me.

CHAPTER FIFTEEN
Tests

I prise my sluggish eyelids open. Silvery dawn light is fingering the windowsill. Did I sleep right through? Wow. The bed feels unusually heavy, and I glance to my right. *Oh my. Justin's still here. He stayed.* His face is so close, his black hair delightfully tousled. I lift my head. He's fast asleep, fully clothed, on top of the covers. Tilting my body sideways, I study his face and my heart swells painfully. *Admit it, Hayles, you have so fallen for this man. How did this happen so fast?*

His brow is furrowed above the bridge of his nose. Is he worrying about his family situation? That sounds like such a mess. And I bet there's more to it than he's said. There must be for him to simply bolt like that. I reach over and press my thumb to the furrows, wanting to smooth them away.

Justin's eyes fling open and he jerks backwards with a gasp. And tumbles clean off the bed, disappearing down the narrow gap between the bed and the wall. There's a thump as he hits the floor. Oh my God! I scramble to the edge and peer down at him. He looks pretty wedged, his hair all mussed and his face peering up at me.

"You alright there, Tiger?" I can't help but grin.

"Meow!" he replies. "Might be stuck. Meow!"

Laughing, I stretch a crooked elbow down for him to hang onto and lever him up.

Standing up, he brushes a hand down his legs and fluff floats up. "Might need to dust a bit more, Hayley."

"Oops." That's embarrassing.

He wriggles out sideways from behind the bed. "What time is it?" Without waiting for an answer, he heads to the door. "I'll put the kettle on."

Assuming that's his tactful way of leaving me to get dressed, I race into the shower. The scan and hospital people prefer clean patients. Just in time, I stop the roll-on deodorant from connecting with my armpit. Clean and perfume-free patients. I twist my hair back into a ponytail and rinse out my mouth. In case Justin plans a kiss.

In the kitchen, Justin is gulping down a mug of green tea. "I need to go home and get ready. I have an early physio client."

When he puts down the mug, I go to him and give him a big hug. "Thank you. For coming over. For dinner. For staying." I bite back, 'for being so perfect'.

Placing his hands on my shoulders, he plants a kiss on my forehead. "Good luck. Keep being strong." Gently, he caresses my lips with his. "Thanks for listening to me."

"I'd like to know more when I get back." I tilt my head. "You'll be here? You won't be whisked away by then?"

His face melts with tenderness. "I'll be here. Call or text me. Daily. Coach's orders."

My lips quirking, I say, "Yes, coach. Er …your phone will be on?"

"Funny." He kisses my nose. "But good point." Then he moves away, slips his shoes on and is gone, with a last waggle of fingers around the edge of the door.

For a few heartbeats I stand staring at the door. Am I dreaming? He — this — is way too good to be true. What can go wrong? Foreboding slinks over me. *My tests. His family.* The next few days will be revealing.

~

There's little traffic and I make it to Canberra in good time for the first set of tests. Before I get out of my car, I force myself to finish the whole bottle of water. They have enough trouble finding a vein to take blood from even when I'm fully hydrated. *Alright, let's do this.*

The pathology centre is almost empty, only one person before me. I hand my form to the pleasant-looking red-haired woman. Then the drill starts. Use my right arm because the left arm has no lymph nodes — no needles, no cuts, no blood pressure cuffs or tourniquets. Better hope I never need surgery on that arm. Of course, the veins in my right arm don't cooperate until her third attempt. Too scarred from the intravenous chemo last year. She's embarrassed, and I reassure her, saying, "Never mind, I'm used to it." I leave with a stepping-stone trail of small round plasters up my arm.

The imaging place is busier, and by the time my name is called I have a headache forming. Maybe I should have eaten more, despite my churning stomach. The sonographer takes me into a dimly lit, quiet room, just the hum of the machine.

"Slip the gown off," she instructs, "and stand close to the machine."

I try to breathe normally while she prods me closer, then nudges and pulls my right breast onto the slab. Her fingers are cold. I wince when the machine squeezes my breast until it looks like a pancake.

"Don't move."

I hold my breath while the machine whirrs and clicks. *Another year until you have to do this again. You can do it.* The pressure eases and I draw in a breath.

"Now the left," says the sonographer briskly. She tries to grasp a handful. "Oh my. They took a lot, didn't they? Sorry, dear, this is going to be uncomfortable."

Uncomfortable doesn't begin to describe it. My eyes are watering by the time she has nudged and prodded my scarred, crooked half-breast onto the plate. I look away. Two eleven-centimetre scars, one running from the nipple to under my armpit, pulling the nipple outwards, and another large curve running all the way under the armpit. How will Justin react when he sees the extent of this? I can't imagine him wanting to fondle and kiss this mess. A tear escapes and, pinned as I am, I can't prevent it from trickling down my cheek.

"You alright, love?" asks the sonographer. "Sorry, I'll be as quick as I can."

The machine whirrs and clicks. A few times. This side seems to be taking longer. So much for being quicker. I wriggle my toes to distract myself from the discomfort and, eventually, the pressure releases.

"Put the gown on and take a seat. I'll check the images with the doctor." The door clicks closed behind her.

I plonk onto the chair and pull the gown around my shoulders. My left breast and nipple are throbbing mercilessly. I gently massage it. The wellness retreat said we need to learn to accept and love our new selves. Easier said than done. I loathe being uneven, but a reconstruction seems risky. Less tissue, less opportunity for a recurrence. Maybe in another year or so … if everything remains okay.

The door flings open and the sonographer marches in. "So sorry, love. The doctor wants another image." She's not quite meeting my eyes.

Cold flushes down my body. "Another image?" I croak.

"More side-on, where your scarring is. Sorry, I know this is unpleasant."

I endure, panic swirling in my stomach and my head pounding. *Keep cool. Better they are thorough,* I tell myself. *But why an extra image?* With effort, I refrain from whimpering as the machine tries to squeeze the last ounce of life out of my battered breast. I could so use a Justin hug right now. Then I shake my head. He'd be horrified.

Thirty minutes and several hundred dollars later, I'm sitting in my car eating a Kit Kat. Rob would be pleased. For a moment, I think of my workmates and David, my boss. Maybe I could drop in while I'm up here. Two months of leave left … will this be long enough? Justin's handsome face looms in my mind and I swallow. Maybe not … but maybe yes. What if his family force him back to Sydney? Would I follow him? More the point, would he ask? Whoa! Bit soon to be thinking along these lines.

Better text Justin before I get chatting to Dad. I type: *round 1 and 2 down* and add a horrified face emoji. He sends back a thumbs-up emoji. My phone pings again, with an image of a lollipop and a heart. Smiling, I send back a tiger and a heart. Trauma for the day over, my next stop is to check in at The Hyatt, have a quick swim then go to the airport.

~

The ends of my hair are still damp as I hover in the arrivals area scanning for Dad. There. Of course he's first off the plane, striding determinedly ahead of the other passengers, a large khaki carry-on bag in his hand. I wait until his eyes latch onto me. His face lights up above his trim, grey beard and he veers towards me. Searing blue eyes peer at me before he drops his bag and crushes me to him.

"Dad." I wriggle. "Can't breathe."

"Sorry, kiddo. Good to see you." He holds me at arm's length and does a face and body scan worthy of the archaeologist he is. "The sea air suits you."

"I can't wait to tell you about it," I say around a broad smile. "You look fitter than ever."

"Lots of hiking." He picks up his bag. "Where's your car?"

"The usual trek away. Good job you're fit." I fall into step beside him as he seems to have remembered the way to the carpark. "The room is nice, thanks. As is the pool."

"My treat. Let's get you through these pesky scans."

In another hour, Dad's checked in and we're seated at a table with a crisp white tablecloth in The Hyatt restaurant. Soft mood music is playing in the background and there are carnations in a vase and a scented candle flickering in front of me. I sip at the rose prosecco Dad insisted I have 'to take the edge off'. He is in good humour, regaling me with tales of his latest dig down in Tasmania and a detailed description of the rugged mountain they had to hike over to get there. Warmth rushes into my chest. It's so good to see him fit and happy. Five years since Mum died, and it has taken both of us a while.

"So, did you find anything to justify this epic hike to get there?" I ask.

Dad laughs. "Two shards of pottery from a colonial era vase and a bent and rusted colonial kitchen knife. Veritable treasure." He lifts his glass of white wine in a mock toast.

I clink my glass against his. "Better luck next time. Which is when?"

"Week after next." He takes a swig of wine. "Some remote town way out of Adelaide." He puts his glass down. "Enough about me. How did today go?"

Wincing, I fiddle with my glass stem. "Not great. They took extra images, which has made me nervous."

"Left side?" His smile fades and his brows furrow at my nod. "Could be scarring … what's the test you do tomorrow? Will that shed light on it?"

"I guess so." I shrug. "It's called a PET scan. I haven't had one before, but it's supposedly the most granular whole-body scan they can do." I swallow. "Like they expect to find something." My voice drops. "Sometimes I wonder if it's better to just get it all over with. This persistent dark cloud … is difficult."

Dad reaches across the table and grabs my fingers. "Chin up, Hayley. That's my girl. Come on, you can do this. You're supremely fit and determined enough to crack a sub-three-hour marathon — twice. Muster that Banks' drive and courage of yours and redirect it. If they find nothing on the *best* scan they got that'll be excellent news. Be positive."

I smile wanly, knowing he's right, but some days are harder than others. Looming results do not help. Our meals arrive, salmon and mash for me and steak with the works for Dad. My stomach rumbles eagerly.

"Tell me about your sea change." Dad waves a forkful of pink steak at me. "You mentioned you went in a boat?"

"Two, actually." In between mouthfuls of divine-tasting salmon, I tell him about the whale-watching tour, and about being conscripted into a dragon boat on my first day there. Dad laughs and wipes his eyes when I tell the story about Justin dropping lollipops all over the path and then just giving me a paddle and telling me to get in the boat.

"He sounds quite a character!" says Dad. "But you enjoy this paddling?"

I scoop up the last of the béarnaise sauce with a forkful of mash. "It's surprisingly good for you, a whole-body workout." I eat the forkful then flex my right arm muscles and Dad raises an eyebrow. "And it gave me instant friends. The other paddlers are really nice." I toy with the remaining mound of mash. Should I tell Dad about Justin?

Dad puts his knife and fork together neatly on his empty plate and gives me his best Dad look. "This coach, he looks after you? Does he know about your … left arm?" He sits back. "Ah. You're blushing, my girl. My honed archaeology skills are buzzing, telling me there's more to this paddling than meets the eye. You like him?"

Abandoning the last of my mash, I nod. "Justin is kind, he's a physio, owns his own practice, and he's the head coach and leader of the club." I swallow. "He seems to like me too … he's the one that took me whale watching." I drum my fingers on the table. "He's an awesome paddler, and he offered to train me up. Thinks I have potential."

"Now that does not surprise me," says Dad. "You're good at anything you turn your mind to. Always have been, even way back when you were a toddler. Woe betide your mum and me if we told you that you couldn't do something!" He leans forward. "How do you feel about this?"

I shiver. "It's all so fast... good … nervous … anxious. Is it fair when I …" I can't say it and clench my hands in my lap to stop from screaming.

Dad drains his wine glass and gives me a serious look. "Ah. This is serious. Already. I'd better come and meet this Justin." He strokes the end of his beard. "What Jonathan did to you was wrong, plain wrong. Although, I confess, I was never certain about him. Always seemed a bit too self-focused to my eye." His eyes crinkle with a smile. "But marathoning is a solo, self-focused sport. If Justin is a coach of a team sport, that's a different ball game. Or boat game, in this case."

Dad always was perceptive, and that is an excellent point. I crunch my fingers together in my lap. "Another key difference. Jonathan was fair and blond; Justin is tanned and dark. He's Chinese."

"I see." Dad's eyebrows lift comically. "Well, that kind of fits. You've always loved Asian culture."

Relief washes into me. I thought the cross-cultural aspect would be fine, and it is. "Thanks, Dad."

"As long as he makes you happy, Hayles." His smile is wistful. "I wish your mother was still here to meet him too."

"Me too," I say softly, a dull thud reverberating through my chest.

But I just know she would have liked Justin.

CHAPTER SIXTEEN

Brothers

I race into my physio practice just before eight, and find Simone already established behind the reception desk and Gerald in the waiting room with Geoff, one of the aged care workers.

Simone beckons. "I tried to ring you. Is your phone off? Gerald's had a fall so I had to slot him in early."

I scrub at my hair. "Thanks, that's fine. Give me a minute or two and send him in."

No sooner am I logged on and organised than Geoff brings in a hobbling Gerald and helps me sit him on the table. Hastily scrambling my act together, I peer at Gerald, noting the bump on his temple and bruising on his arms. "What have you done, Gerald? Been for a tumble?"

Gerald nods glumly. "Fell down me stairs. Missed the top step."

"When? Have you seen a doctor? Nothing broken?" I gingerly lift his right arm and he winces.

Geoff speaks up. "He fell on Sunday. The hospital did X-rays and he's fine, just bruised ribs and sundry bumps and lumps."

"Gee, Gerald," I say. "Lucky you're so tough from all that swimming! Let me move a few things around to unstiffen you. But you must tell me if anything hurts, okay?"

I treat Gerald carefully, relieved to find he's essentially okay, just stiff and sore. He's one of my favourite clients; so cheerful and determined to keep going, no matter what. Straightening up, I say, "There you are, Gerald. Take it easy, and try to stay upright!"

With a glum look, Gerald mumbles, "Can I go swimming?"

"Swimming?" I repeat. "Well, put your arms up and take a deep breath for me."

"Ouch! Can't." Gerald looks even glummer.

"Pretty difficult to swim when you can't breathe properly due to bruised ribs." I pat Gerald's shoulder, knowing how much his daily swim means to him. "How about some water-walking for the next week? The sea water will still be good for you." His face brightens and I squeeze his bony shoulder. "Make sure you take someone with you in case you stumble or the current's stronger than you think. Okay?"

Gerald grabs both of my hands. "Thanks, Justin. You're a lifesaver. I'll do that."

My throat tightens. How could I possibly walk away from my clients and paddlers? They're all special to me. I feel melancholy building. Father can't do this to me. I can't let him. Speechless, I grip Gerald's hands back then help him off the table. Geoff shuffles Gerald out, promising to make a follow-up appointment next week.

Plonking onto my desk chair, I check my schedule. Busy all day. Good, that will keep my mind off what's happening to Hayley. I swivel the chair from side to side. I don't suppose I'll hear from her until late afternoon. My computer diary blinks and a vacant square opens up. My 4.30 client has just cancelled. Wait. It's Tuesday … if I go home at lunchtime and get my car and paddling gear I could make the 5.30 paddle at Moruya, one of their more intense sessions.

I pull my phone out of my pocket and turn it on so I can send a text to the coach for Moruya, check whether there's space in the boat. It buzzes like an angry bee in a bottle with all the missed messages coming in. Crap. I skim the list. Six missed calls from Ethan, then an irate text: *Call me!* Nothing new from Father since his two hang-up calls yesterday. Unease swirls. He won't give up that easy. He'll be forming some plan. A new noose. There are two messages from Natalie asking if Hayley is okay, and three from Simone about slotting Gerald in.

My phone pings in my hand and I blink. Talk about timing, it's a message from Grant: *Congrats Justin. Eight of us are in too. Can you train with us tonight?* Okay, then. The Southern Region Dragons team has been announced. I text back: *Congrats to you too. I'll be there tonight. Thx.* My mood lifts. A positive for the day, and a hard paddle is just what I need.

With a constant stream of clients, it's lunchtime before I know it. I cycle home, pack my paddling gear in the car, then make a mug of tea and a sandwich to eat on the porch. Another text arrives from Natalie. Chewing slowly, I consider it. Not my place to tell her what's going on with Hayley, but she's justifiably concerned and being a good buddy. What to do? I send back: *Hayley ok. Will tell her you asked. BTW I made the regional team.* A mouthful of sandwich later my phone pings. *Thx and no surprise there, Tiger.* I groan. I can see I'm going to have a hard time shaking this nickname. Might have to resort to growling more often.

The afternoon blurs by, then I'm dressed for paddling and in the car heading to Moruya, wondering who the eight paddlers are that made the team. I haven't even had a chance to check the formal announcement. By the time I pull up in the carpark next to the boat shed, the paddlers have got the boat out ready and are starting their on-land warm-up. My phone pings just as I'm slipping it into the glove box and, heart in mouth, I scan it. Hayley: *round 1 and 2 done. Horrified face emoji.* I send back a thumbs-up emoji, then tap the phone on my knee. That feels woefully inadequate, but what can I say? My pulse skittering, I send a lollipop and a heart emoji. Is that too much?

I change my shoes for my paddling ones, and my phone pings again. My eyes water as I stare at the emoji of a tiger and a red heart. Swallowing my tumble of emotions, I hurry to join in the warm-up. The coach nods a welcome. Five minutes later, pleasantly warm, we're waiting to be assigned seats.

"Right," says Emma, the seventy-year-old head coach, wiry and fit as ever. Everyone calls her Em, like in the Bond movies, and she even reminds me of Judy Dench. "I'm going to seat the regional paddlers in the front half of the boat so I can watch how you work together." She rapidly assigns seats. "Justin and Grant, take bench four, Justin on the right."

Soon, the boat is sliding backwards fast away from the boat ramp and turning to face upriver. Moruya Bridge looms high up ahead, the evening traffic crawling across it, the hills and setting sun spectacular beyond it.

"Nice evening," mutters Grant.

I nod and flex my fingers, anticipation rising. This will be a solid session. If only the Clear Water Dragons could reach this club's level of capability, but it would take a year or so and a load more effort and focus. But they surprised me at the regatta, maybe I should put it to them.

"Paddles up. Go!" calls Em and we're away.

Time passes quickly as we warm up, swap sides, and move into a pyramid of alternating sixty per cent and eighty per cent effort all the way up to a hundred strokes and back down, on both sides. My troubles melt away as I concentrate on matching my timing and power to the strokes. In the second half we focus on strength work, lots of the five strokes backwards then fifteen forwards drill, and then move into a series of race starts. I recall my image of coiling like a tiger and pouncing, enjoying the massive bubbles of water surging back from my blade. The paddler behind me swears under his breath. Did he catch his paddle on my wash?

The sun has almost set when we bring the boat in, clean her and put her away. Em calls the paddlers to gather around.

"Good work, everyone," she says briskly. "The boat felt good." Her gaze lands on me. "Can you make this session every week?" At my nod, she continues, "Right, Tuesday will be our main training then. I'll form a regional subgroup in the schedule. There'll also be longer sessions on a few Sundays so the other paddlers from Nowra, Illawarra and Merimbula can join us." She puts her hands on her hips. "And in case you're wondering, you're stuck with me as team coach."

The Moruya paddlers clap and catcall and I join in, pleased. Em coached the team last year and we came home with several medals.

"Right. Dinner?" asks Em. "Where are we going?"

They're going to dinner? Lucky my work clothes are in the car. I might as well join them, more distraction from thinking about Hayley. Or my family. The team is in high spirits, jokes and friendly banter flying as we devour a well-earned dinner at the nearby hotel restaurant. Movement to my right catches my attention.

Em wedges a chair in next to me. "So, what's going on with your Narooma club? Are you doing regattas with them or can we still snag you for our team?"

I turn my chair on an angle to talk more comfortably. Good question. I shrug. "They enjoyed their first regatta." I think of their shining faces and the special banner, and I realise they will want to compete again. "So, I'm probably taken for the next few Canberra regattas." At Em's frown, I add, "But if you're travelling to any other regattas, I'd love to paddle with you."

"Fair enough," she says, although I detect disappointment. She takes a breath. "Another question. The backwards and forwards drill … how the hell did you pull so much water? What did you do differently?"

I feel heat rising in my cheeks. "Er … I used visualisation."

She flaps a hand, her blue-grey eyes intense. "Speak."

No way I'm telling her I was pretending to be a tiger! I shuffle on my chair. "I imagined I was coiled, then springing up high and pouncing on the water."

Her lips press together like she's trying not to smile. "Simple but effective. Gave you excellent height and power. Next week, I want you to show the others."

"Okay." An idea occurs. "Actually, can I ask you something?"

"Shoot." I get the full-on Em focus.

I feel awkward, all bumbling and shy. "We have a new paddler … I think she's got potential. Can I bring her to a Tuesday session? If you have a space?"

"How much potential?" Em's eyes narrow.

"She's fit, an ex-marathon runner. Determined, and took to paddling like she's been doing it all her life." I shrug. "Don't know how far she could go. Possibly regional level."

"Okay. Bring her. Add plus one when you book in." Em grins. "If she's that good we'll pinch her." She pats my shoulder and moves her chair to slide in beside her next victim.

I exhale slowly. Will Hayley agree to train this hard? Should I give her more time? Despair trickles into my chest. Please let her scans be clear. My ears are buzzing insistently. Am I that anxious?

"Is that your phone?" Grant asks.

Shit. Feeling stupid, I snatch my phone out of my pocket. *Ethan.* Pressing answer, I excuse myself to find a quiet corner.

"Justin!" Ethan sounds so relieved. For a nano-instant. "Where are you? What's going on?"

"In Moruya, been paddling with the regional team."

"Funny, bro. Not what I meant," says Ethan drily. "Father's ready to execute you. What *are* you playing at?"

Sadness floods me. How can I make him understand? Can I make *anyone* understand? "I like my life here," I say slowly.

"What? Say again. What's that racket in the background?"

"Hang on." Sighing, I leave the hotel and head to my car, get in. "Is that better? I said, I like my life here." My pulse rises in the ensuing pause. I can hear Ethan breathing.

After what feels like an eternity, Ethan says, all choked up, "God, Justin. *Jun Jie. Oldest* son. This is a mess. You can't just run away. Father is furious, Mother is devastated, and Father's cousin is insisting he'll only invest if you're on board." His breath catches. "You know the racing stables ordered $50,000 worth of equipment after your demonstration?" His voice breaks. "We could so do this, *together*. Make Father proud. Make it *our* success."

He stops and I worry that he's actually crying. My heart shrieks like it's being ripped in two. Shame flushes over me, from head to toe, leaving a burning, tingling sensation. How can I let my brother down like this? I love Ethan. I want him to be happy.

"Say something," pleads Ethan, sniffing. He is crying.

My eyes are burning, but I'm paralysed. Thoughts and words are rocketing through me and I can't grasp any of them. Hayley's smile and the way she tips her chin up when she's determined keep flashing into my mind. I can't let Ethan down. And I can't let Hayley down. Can't leave her. This Tiger is broken. Ripped in half. I brush at the tear sliding down my cheek.

"Justin." Ethan sounds shattered. "Please. Say something."

"Brother," I croak. "I love you. I'd do anything for you." I hear Meatloaf's 'Bat out of hell' in my head. Come on, Justin. Coach mode. Big Brother-mode. There has to be a way forward. I sit up straighter, grip the phone to my ear. "Okay, look, let's work on it. You and me. See if we can find a way forward."

"How?" wails Ethan. "Father wants answers and contracts signed now!"

A surge of rage ousts my shame. "He'll have to wait," I snap, then nearly drop my phone in fright. Shit. What am I saying? Another surge of rage. "These are big decisions. *You* want Hong Kong, I don't." An insight. "You want Li Na too? Right?"

"Yes," says Ethan. "But how can I, *older* brother?" I hear anger creeping into his voice.

"Listen," I say quickly. "I might have found someone too … but it's early days."

"Serious?" Ethan says, now hopeful. "Was that the mysterious crisis you panicked about? Can you at least tell Father that?"

"Not really," I say slowly.

"What do you mean 'not really'?" Ethan demands, then gasps. "Oh God. She's not Chinese, is she? You're such an idiot! Are you *deliberately* goading Father?"

I hear his unsaid wail loud and clear: *Why can't you just be the dutiful older son? You're ruining everything.* I hang my head, my hand with the phone dropping into my lap, Ethan's squawking fading into background noise. Maybe I should just jump off the Bar. Let the turbulent sea take me. There's no way out of this. Then Ethan will be oldest son. He can take over the empire, do whatever he wants.

A rap on the car window makes me jump so high I drop the phone into the car footwell.

"You alright?" Grant peers through the car window. "You left ages ago."

Mouth dry, I half wind down the window. "Yes. Sorry. A family matter." I dredge up a smile. "See you next Tuesday."

"Okay. Train hard." Grant taps the car roof and walks away.

My breathing ragged, I fumble in the dark for my phone, my fingers finally snagging it under the brake pedal. The screen is dark.

Ethan has hung up. For a minute I sit looking out the windscreen, watching the river ripple darkly past a hundred metres away. Think of jumping into the sea, letting its cold embrace wash all my troubles away.

'You will be here, won't you?' I recall Hayley's words, the subtle anxiety in her face. Was that truly only this morning? With numb fingers, I call up her texts. Run my thumb over the tiger and heart emoji. If she's brave enough to face her fears, to go forward and find a new life for herself, then surely, I can hang in and sort my mess out.

There has to be a way.

CHAPTER SEVENTEEN
Shadows

Five in the morning. I groan. Might as well get up than keep tossing and turning. No breakfast allowed before the PET scan, only water. Lots of, to help spread the radioactive dye they'll pump in. Assuming they can find a vein for the cannula. Sighing, I slide out of the crisp hotel sheets and patter into the shower. Taking my time, I wash my hair and stand with the hot water running down my back. Try to imagine the water washing away any nasty cells, leaving my body cleansed and healthy. No good. I see shadows lurking deep in my left breast.

Once dressed, I open the curtains and do my Tai Chi moves looking out at the garden. I think of the rolling ocean view from my apartment. It feels like home. Wow. Already? Or is that because of Justin? My eyes immediately prickle. How can I tell Justin there's a shadow? A doubt. A thundercloud hanging above me. He should choose someone else. Okay, Hayley, pull yourself together. You can't turn up for the scan in tears. Get on with it.

A rattling noise intrudes outside in the hall; Dad's breakfast being delivered. I roll my ankles around and shake my arms and hands out, gathering energy. Brave face, Hayles, or Dad will stress. I fill my water bottle and slip outside to amble around the hotel garden. Focus on the here and now. *Breathe in for four, out for four, take a swig of water.* As I walk, I brush my fingertips across the silky petals of the slowly unfurling flowers. Wan dawn light casts a faint glow over the white and yellow petals. New day. New life. "It will be alright, it will be alright," I murmur over and over like a mantra. I found dragon boating. I met Justin. It can't be my time yet. Got things to do. I finish the water bottle and head back inside.

Dad is standing outside my room door, hand raised to knock. "There you are. Been for a walk?"

"Yep. Had to do something to take my mind off no breakfast," I quip and lift a palm. "Don't tell me what you had. I'm sure it was delicious."

Dad gives me a look, like he can see through the bubbly façade. "You drunk enough water? Ready to go?"

"Just grab my things. And a book."

Twenty minutes later, Dad's dropped me off and I'm winding my way down the hospital corridors, following the blue line then the yellow line, until I reach diagnostic imaging. I've only read three pages when I'm called. One good outcome of Covid is that the hospital runs close to time as they don't want patients bunching up in waiting rooms. I recognise the male nurse from when I was here having my surgery.

"Hi Hayley," he says. "You look fit. Still running?"

How can he possibly remember that, remember me, out of the thousands of patients he must see? "Not so much, but I've taken up dragon boating."

He arches a silver eyebrow. "You trying to make my job harder? All those muscles in your arms."

Smiling, I follow him into a side room and take my seat in the big yellow chair. Answer all the questions about my name, date of birth, have I drunk two litres this morning.

"Okay, show us your muscles," he says.

I hold out my right arm and try to breathe deeply while he prods up and down the veins. I wish I could remember his name, he's so kind and professional. He puts the tourniquet on, bumps a vein a few times and gets his needle ready. Closing my eyes, I think of flowing rivers running through my arm. A brief sting.

"Got it," he says, looking pleased. "You should do more of this dragon boating. I had you pegged as trouble." He tapes a cannula to my arm, and pushes in some fluid. "I'll get you a heated blanket. You need to sit here quietly. No reading," he adds when I reach for my book. "Have a snooze. For this scan we want all your body and mind functions shut down. We're looking for unwanted activity, right."

I drop the book on the floor beside my bag and lean back. The warm blanket is delightful and I snuggle under it. No brain activity … so I shouldn't think of Justin?

In no time, an hour has apparently passed and I'm being shaken awake by a female nurse. "Hayley. Come through for the scan now."

I follow her into another, dimmer side room with no windows and a heavy-duty door. I can't see any scan equipment, just another large chair. I climb into this and the nurse gives me a fresh heated blanket. Coming to my side, she clips a long hose that reminds me of a narrow snake into the end of the cannula. The far end of the hose disappears through a tiny hole in the wall.

"Once you're settled, you'll hear a beep and some yellow liquid will come down this small pipe and into you. This is the radioactive dye." She rests a hand on my arm and smiles. "It doesn't sting or anything. Just keep lying as still and inactive as possible. It takes a few minutes to spread, then we'll run the scan. Takes about forty minutes." She hands me a buzzer. "Any troubles, press this. We'll be on the other side of the wall."

She leaves and the door thuds shut. Swallowing, I try to relax and close my eyes. Surely, all this dye and stuff isn't good for you? It's so potent the staff are outside the room! A beep sounds and my pulse races. *Keep calm. Has to be done to get answers.* I roll my head slightly to relax my neck, then visualise I'm walking barefoot along the sand at Bar Beach, Justin by my side. I can almost hear the waves hissing on the sand and receding.

The door flings open. "Good girl, well done," says the nurse. "Come and take a chair outside and I'll take the cannula out and get you a sandwich."

Sleepily, I follow her out and plonk into the hard chair by a low table. These scans are exhausting. Cannula removed, I gratefully drink the apple juice and eat half the tuna sandwich. Dad promised a slap-up lunch. I text him to say I'll be ready in five.

Despite Dad's best efforts, the day passes slowly. I fade in and out of being present and stressing about the scan results. One o'clock tomorrow seems so far away. We stroll around the Botanic Gardens, have an organic lunch there, then wander around the National Gallery of Art. Dad chatters away, but I can tell he's monitoring me closely, his brows pinched in a slight frown. I'm so glad he's here.

It's almost five o'clock when we exit the gallery. Dad puts a hand on my arm. "You want to go back to the hotel for a swim? You look like you could use one." He pauses. "Followed by room service and a movie night in?"

"Sounds perfect." I summon a smile. A swim and spa would be excellent. Dad insists on driving, muttering about not needing an accident on top of everything else. Meekly, I climb into the passenger seat. He's right. I haven't felt this spaced out since the original diagnosis. If anything, this is way worse. A recurrence this soon would be a total game-changer. Recurrences are often incurable.

Unstoppable. Note to self: Make sure I have company for all future monitoring scans.

I plough up and down the hotel pool for thirty minutes, then soak in the spa. Okay, now I feel better enough to text Justin. Back in my room, I dry my hair then sit on the end of the bed and retrieve my phone. Disappointment shivers through me when I see no text from Justin. Maybe he's trying to give me space … Anxiety pings through me. No, wait. He asked me to text or call every day. I should prepare him for possible bad news. Another bolt of anxiety zips through me. That is *not* something to convey in a text. Heart thudding and mouth dry, I press the call button.

"Hayley!" Justin answers on the first ring. "Finished all the tests?"

"Yep." Oh crap. What do I say next? "No news until tomorrow … but they took a lot of images." My voice falters. He'll work it out. I hold my breath, realising how important his next reaction is to me. If he says the deflective response of, 'It will be okay,' I'm likely to hang up.

"Oh. Does this mean they're worried about something?"

"Maybe," I admit, relief gushing through me that he's not dismissive. "There might be something back in the original site."

"Man, that's tough," he says softly. "What do *you* think? Can you feel anything?"

"Actually, no," I reply slowly. "It feels the same to me."

"Okay, then." Justin sounds happier. "Wait and see then. As a competitive marathoner, and now paddler, you know your body."

Speechless, I stare at my phone. That's what the counsellors at the wellness retreat said. Fit people tend to know. They also said we're often naughty about overriding feelings of being unwell and keeping going. Guilty, as charged. It wasn't until I nearly passed out after a race that I went to my doctor, and she found the lump.

"Earth to Hayley? Are you still there?" says Justin.

"Thanks, coach. Good point. I will not panic. Yet."

I hear Justin's smile around his response. "Good. Don't panic until you have to. I have news, I made the regional team." He talks about the team and how he went training at Moruya, cheering me up. Then he tells me I'm in deep trouble for calling him Tiger, and even the head coach at Moruya noticed his pouncing at the water.

I laugh aloud at that.

"Okay, you'd better rest," he says.

"Yes, coach," I say brightly. "Actually, my dad's waiting for me with dinner and a movie."

"Goodnight, Hayley. Try to get some sleep." Then he's gone.

Dad has selected 'The Lost City' for our movie. Good choice with its archaeological theme and he knows Sandra Bullock is one of my favourite actors. Watching Daniel Radcliffe as the villain had me in stitches. Clever casting.

Soon I'm snuggling under the sheets, yawning. *Do not panic, coach's orders.* As my mind slips towards sleep, it occurs to me that Justin didn't mention anything about his family situation. He was too busy cheering me up. Kind, caring Justin, looking after his physio clients, coaching and being sweep for the club, and now looking out for me … but who looks after Justin? My heart skips a beat. Could that be me? Could I somehow help him?

～

The sound of the breakfast trolley wakes me. I go grab my tray and eye the croissants and bowl of fresh fruit with yoghurt. I imagine Justin telling me to eat, and slowly work my way through it. Then I don my walking gear. Dad wants to walk a lap of the lake. I'm onto his plan of piling on activity until it's time to go to the hospital.

Half an hour later, having wound our way through the early morning joggers and boot campers, we're striding across Commonwealth Avenue Bridge, and I realise I can show him where the dragon boats are kept here. I take him to Grevillea Park, showing him the boats along the shore and explaining this is where the regatta was held. After a while I think I sound like Justin, babbling on about boats and drills and training. I say so and Dad laughs.

"I'm enjoying it, kiddo. You've always been full-on in anything you do. First the horse-riding with your mum and then the running." Dad plants a kiss on my cheek. "I've always admired your focus." His eyebrows kind of waggle. "But I'm glad we stopped short of buying you your own horse. Now *that* would have been expensive."

I punch his arm lightly. "I remember sulking every Christmas when my stocking didn't contain a pony." We fall silent for a few minutes, and I know we're both thinking of Mum. Taken from us too soon. Inexplicable complications from pneumonia after getting soaked on a camping trip with Dad. She adored horses, loved the discipline and training for dressage competitions. Won so many championships. It was heartbreaking, selling her beautiful, dappled warmblood mare after she died, but neither Dad nor I could bear to even look at the horse.

Dad clears his throat. "Have you been riding … at all?"

I shake my head. No, it didn't seem right to go without Mum. Dad silently pats my shoulder, and we head back towards the hotel.

An hour later, Dad drops me off at the entrance to The Cancer Clinic, suggesting I buy him a cappuccino while he finds a car park. I go in the wide glass doors, sanitise my hands and walk towards the lounge and café area. A group of women are hovering around one of the coffee tables and plush sofas. I feel a jolt of recognition: aren't they paddlers? The uniform seems familiar. I read the team name on their shirts: Dragons Abreast Canberra — GoAnna. My heart races. Didn't Alexa mention them? These are the survivor paddlers. I hover, debating whether to go over. A tall, strong paddler looks up, sees me and smiles.

Encouraged, I approach. "Hi. Are you paddlers?"

"Sure are," says the tall woman, who reminds me of Natalie,

the same no-nonsense air. "Would you like to join us?"

I'm not sure whether she means now or to paddle. "Er … maybe. I'm living at the coast at the moment, but I do paddle."

Next thing, I'm pulled down onto a sofa and all five women are plying me with questions. How long have I been paddling? Where do I live? Do I come up to Canberra often? Do I do regattas? They rattle off their names, which I promptly forget. Their energy is making me dizzy.

"Here she comes!" one of them exclaims and they all stand up and face another paddler, who has just stepped out of the lift.

The paddler approaches, wiping her eyes with a tissue. When she stops, she beams and says, "Ten years clear! Yay! I'm officially in remission!"

She's immediately engulfed by the others, laughing and slapping her back and doing high-fives. I'm overwhelmed by their caring and camaraderie. Alexa is right: I should join them. Can I paddle with the Clear Water Dragons and their club, though?

The tall woman remembers I'm there and takes me aside. "I'm the club coordinator, Jeannie. Tell me your phone number and I'll send you some details. You can join us as a dual membership if you like, and train with us when you're up here. Or be in our team for pink paddler events." She keys my number into her phone. "I'll text you later."

"Hayley," Dad calls from where's he's standing by the lift and points at his watch.

"Thank you," I say. "I've got to go to my appointment."

"Good luck," says Jeannie sincerely. "Do text me back. There's lots happening that you could join in, if you want to."

"Thank you so much." I wave at the other paddlers and follow Dad into the lift. My surge of optimism fades as we step out into medical oncology with its familiar muted colours, faint hospital smell and subdued people waiting. I check in and we take a seat.

Dad pats my knee, his face looking gaunt and tight. I explain who the women were and he nods.

"Well, that was a good chance encounter. And didn't they all look so strong?" he says quietly.

I nod, realising how right he is. They all look amazing. Vibrant. Powerful. Such a long way from some of the other patients I see around us, who are in the chemotherapy treatment phase. My stomach churns with anxiety. Will I soon become like them again? Pale, no hair, no strength?

"Hayley?" I spring up, Dad in tow, follow the oncologist into the consulting room and take my seat by her desk. Dad quietly composes himself on the extra chair. We wait while she calls up images and reports on her computer.

"How do you feel?" she asks, turning to me. "Do you have any symptoms? Anything worrying you?"

"Okay," I say, dry-mouthed, with a shrug. "Not really, I haven't noticed anything. I'm staying by the sea and trying to get fitter again."

She smiles. "That sounds nice, you do look tanned and fitter." Her face grows serious. "Your blood test results are good, very good, and everything looks fine, except for a slight shadow below your surgery site." She points to the image on her screen. "See here? This denser, darker area? We can't actually tell what that is. If I look at your post-surgery scan, there's a shadow there then too, so it's quite possible it's scar tissue and retained fluid."

My heart skitters with a mix of anxiety and hope. Then she calls up the PET image of my whole body, with bits lit up green, yellow and orange.

"The PET scan is clear everywhere else, no sign of any activity or hot spots anywhere, which is very good news." Her finger drifts to the area of the left breast. "There's an orange area here, same as on the mammogram, showing blood flow and mild activity."

She tilts her head, considering me. "It's possible this is ongoing re-modelling after the surgery. I suspect this will turn out to be a red herring, but I'm going to suggest a blood test, breast ultrasound and follow-up appointment in three months, to be sure."

"Three months?" I gape at her, mind whirring. This will be hanging over my head for three whole months? Dad clears his throat but doesn't speak.

The doctor looks at her screen then back at me. "Where are we now? Mid-October … tell you what… let's do the ultrasound and appointment in mid-December so you know before Christmas and we can catch other specialists if we need to. Two months will be enough time to detect any further changes."

I nod and blink back tears. She's being so thoughtful. I twist my fingers in my lap while she writes out the blood test form then passes it to me.

"It's better if you do this at pathology here as I get the results straightaway, but you could do it down the coast if you like. The imaging staff will ring you to book in the scan. Now hop up on the bed and let me examine you."

I comply and swallow nervously while she listens to my heart and chest and then has a good feel under my armpits, along my neck and shoulders, around my tummy and spends a lot of time checking each breast.

"Nothing sore?" she asks, and I shake my head. "Okay, slip your top back on. I can't feel any raised glands or a lump so I think we're probably looking at scar tissue, but we'll make sure."

"Thank you," I say, trying to raise a smile.

We head back towards the waiting room and I lift each foot feeling as if I'm on the moon and there's no gravity. Dad takes my elbow and steers me to reception to sign for the Medicare assignment of fees and to book in the next appointment, just eight days before Christmas.

When we're back downstairs, Dad hands me a Cherry Ripe. "You need some sugar, kiddo. Let's go find a nice cup of tea somewhere."

He ends up taking me back to The Hyatt, finds a window table looking out onto the gardens and orders a slap-up afternoon tea with the works. It feels like midnight, not three in the afternoon. I sip at my black Earl Grey tea and eye the sugary morsels with a renewed sense of dismay. *Cancer likes sugar, cancer likes sugar...* I choose a fruit flan, which seems the lesser of the evils and somehow squeeze that into my queasy stomach.

Dad eyes me over the rim of his steaming teacup. "Kiddo, this is not a death sentence. Your doctor knows her stuff and is just being thorough. Keep doing what you're doing. You look good. You look well. Being by the sea suits you."

I nod. Maybe I'll feel better back by the sea and the beach. In the boat. Being with Justin. But how long can I stay there without any work? I inhale the fragrant aroma and then take a sip of my tea. Is there any chance my boss would let me work part-time from home? My main role is analysing data and preparing reports, so it *could* work. If I invest in a decent laptop.

"I can see the cogs whirring," says Dad. "What are you thinking?" When I tell him, he nods. "If you're enjoying it there, this sounds a good plan. And you know I'd help you out if needs be. I'd like to visit you down there soon. Check out the area." He puts his cup down. "And meet Justin. I sense he's important." His face and tone soften. "You should stay there to give that some time too."

My cheeks flaming, I gulp down some tea.

CHAPTER EIGHTEEN
Conundrums

Thursday is the slowest day ever. I log off, fatigue etching down my neck and shoulders. Did any of my clients notice my lapses in concentration? None of them said anything. It's time for paddling and still no word from Hayley. I scrub my hands over my face. Vigorously. What will I say if anyone asks where Hayley is? How about that she's in Canberra, with her father? That won't fool Natalie. Sighing, I change into my paddling gear, lock up the physio practice and head round the back of the building to my bike.

As I chain my bike to the tree by the boat shed, I realise it's been two whole days and there's no word from Ethan. *Man up, Justin. As the older brother you'll have to reach out to him.* But what can I say? I need to find something constructive. Some way forward. My arms feel heavy, for the first time in history not relishing the pending training. *Snap out of it.* I straighten my shoulders and swing my paddle as I head to the boat shed.

"Yo, regional Tiger," says Giulio, slapping me on the back, a broad grin across his Romanesque face.

"And our father Tony says yes," adds Gianni, with a matching broad grin.

That stops me dead. "'Yes' to what?" I blink at the beaming brothers.

"To sponsoring the team and club. Make a list of what we need, how much it would cost, and I'll give it to him," explains Gianni.

"How about matching team paddles?" Giulio says enthusiastically. "Most international teams have those."

"With team towels and paddle bags," says Sandi, catching onto the conversation as she slips by me into the shed.

"Can we have team jackets?" asks Natalie, nudging me in the ribs. "We could add a tiger somewhere."

I hold my hands up. "Okay, okay! Thanks, boys. I wasn't being serious when I said it, but this is wonderful and most generous of your family. Let's talk it through as a team and come up with a list after training." Energy zings into me; team paddles would be awesome. "Let's see how keen you are after we do some 500-metre race practice, ready for the next regatta."

The boys laugh. "Too easy," says Giulio.

I turn to look at the board where Sandi is busy assigning seats and my eyebrow raises at the number of names. Apart from Hayley, everyone I talked into the first regatta is here. Unbelievable.

"Sweep or paddle?" asks Sandi.

I choose to sweep. "We need to do different drills for five hundreds."

The session passes quickly. The younger paddlers are in good form, cracking jokes and lapping up the pyramids of up to fifty stokes and back down as well as my calls for periodic lifts during a solid ten-minute paddle. A few of the regular, older paddlers look less happy, and I make a mental note to chat with them and Sandi, to find out how much training they're prepared to give a go. We don't want to lose any of them, and although we do have a ten-person boat as well as *Ming II*, we don't have enough members to have a regatta crew and a more fitness-focused crew.

We put the boat away and gather for our drinks and nibbles. I surreptitiously check my phone: still nothing from Hayley. My throat tightening, I look up to see Natalie making a beeline for me.

"So, how is Hayley?" She plunges right in.

Trying to keep my face relaxed, I say softly, "She's still in Canberra. Her father is visiting."

Natalie frowns. "I'm sure she said a health appointment."

I touch Natalie's elbow. "I need to let her tell you about that. Don't worry, she'll be at paddling on Saturday." I clamp my mouth shut to stop myself from saying more at Natalie's level and entirely disillusioned gaze.

When I don't give in and elaborate, she shrugs and takes a swig from her glass of wine. "Fine. You better sit me next to Hayley so I can prise it out of her."

Wincing, I nod. Tell myself to stay out of it, but warn Hayley. If I see her. My fingers itch to check my phone again and a shiver crosses my nape. Why hasn't she called? Did she get bad news? Not feeling like more chit-chat, I excuse myself and cycle home. I go through the motions of eating dinner, planning out drills for Saturday's training, and at 9 pm give in and text Hayley. *Are you okay?*

Five minutes later, her reply arrives: *Sorry. Tough day. Sort of okay. Last evening with Dad so will tell you tomorrow. Tiger emoji.*

Not at all reassured, I type: *What time will you be back? Dinner?* I hold my breath until her reply arrives. I so want to see her, know she's okay.

Dinner be nice. Takeaway? Dad's plane 2 pm so won't be back til close to 6. Will text when home.

Feeling a smidgeon better, I send: *Okay. Mystery dinner at 7. Sleep well. Heart emoji.*

She sends back a tiger and a heart emoji and my heart lifts. Wait. I re-read her previous text. It definitely said *when home.* My heart skips several beats. If only Narooma would become her home — her forever home.

Then I remember Father's plan: but will I be here?

~

I wouldn't have thought it possible, but Friday passes even more slowly than Thursday. Halfway through my cycle home from work, light drizzle sprinkles my face and a cool breeze springs up. As if I need more gloom. I'm a mess, and I can't even begin to imagine how Hayley must feel if she got bad news. How can she stand it? My arms are all but shaking with the need to hold her, to find out if she's okay.

Right on 6 o'clock her text arrives that she's home. I take a hot shower then dress in smart jeans and my favourite royal-blue polo top. Add the bomber jacket Hayley seems to love. Will she let me stay the night again? Feeling optimistic, and at the same time foolish, I pack a bag with paddling gear and casual clothes for tomorrow, and load my paddle in the car boot. On the way, I stop at the Japanese café and collect a variety of sushi and some tempura prawns and vegetables.

I'm about to knock on her apartment door for the third time when Hayley springs the door open. She's wearing yoga-style billowy pants and a comfy loose-sleeved top. Her smile is kind of nervous.

"Sorry. I was on the balcony doing my Tai Chi."

I step in and hesitate. It doesn't feel right to kiss her straight off, she looks distracted. I hold up the bag of food. "I hope you like Japanese. Do you need to finish your Tai Chi?"

Her smile widens. "Maybe … but is that tempura I smell?"

Okay, then. Pleased, I nod and carry the bag to her small table and start lifting out containers while Hayley collects plates and glasses. I hang my jacket over the back of the chair I sat in last time, then stand there observing her across the table. She's watching me with that fragile, lost look she had the first day I saw her standing there mutely holding out my dropped lollipops.

In three strides, I'm around the table and placing my hands on her shoulders, peering into her face, seeing pain and turbulence in her gorgeous hazel eyes. "Tell me."

Her chest heaves with a deep breath and the tip of her tongue darts over her rosebud lips. "It could be nothing," she whispers, "but there's a shadow."

Throat tight, I gently caress her hair, trace my right thumb over the freckles running over her nose, feel her subtly lean into my touch. My heart aching, I force the question out. "What does this mean?"

"More tests in two months." Her shoulder trembles under my left hand. "Doctor thinks it's probably just scar tissue and fluid, but wants to be sure."

I brush my lips over her forehead while I think. Scar tissue. That sounds more promising. "So, it's where your surgery was?" I tilt her chin up so I can look deep into her eyes. "Everywhere else is clear?" Hope rises at her nod and my physio brain leaps into action. "Okay, then, that must be good to know. Scar tissue can take ages to settle. It will be an anxious two months … but we can work on it. I can treat scar tissue... if you'll let me."

"Really?" Hope flickers in her eyes and her chin tips higher in the familiar sign of determination kicking in.

"Really," I confirm. "And paddling will help. The more you move the scarring, the better."

Her arms steal around my waist and she buries her face in my chest, her words buzzing against my shirt. "Thanks, coach."

I crush her to me and inhale the cherry blossom scent of her hair. Try, and fail, to control my own turbulence. I do not want to lose her. Even though it's only been a month. My legs feel adrift, like I'm floating in a wild current. I've never felt like this, never been so overwhelmed. Truth is, I'm as lost as she is.

"Justin," gasps Hayley. "Need to breathe."

Relaxing my stranglehold, I grin, embarrassed.

Hayley punches my arm lightly. "God forbid you get any stronger, Tiger."

Okay, she's back to bantering. I'm in awe of how fast she can swing her resilience back in. "I'd better train you up too, then. Which reminds me, I have news, but let's eat."

Over dinner I tell her about the sponsorship from the brothers' father Tony and his restaurant. She adores the idea of team paddles, insisting they have a fierce clear crystal dragon on. Then I tell her about the invitation to train with the Moruya club and the regional team on Tuesdays.

Face grim, she pushes a grain of rice around her plate with a chopstick. "Sounds good in principle, but what if I *am* sick?"

Putting my chopsticks down, I say gently, "Then you only train as often and as hard as you want to. It's up to you. But if you feel okay … then I think that'd be a good sign." My heart is pounding against my breastbone. Man, I didn't appreciate how deeply this uncertainty about her health is affecting her. She's reluctant to plan anything not short term. I resist the urge to drag my hand through my hair, manage to choke out, "Go forward, Hayles. Keep going forward."

She crushes the grain of rice with the end of her chopstick. "Yes, coach. Forward." Standing, she waves a hand at the sofa. "Let's sit there."

I follow her to the sofa and obey her prompt to sit where I sat last time, wait while she settles cross-legged, facing me. My pulse skips several beats. Her expression is serious, focused. Is she going to tell me we can only be friends? Does this not planning anything include me? The sushi lurks like a lead weight in my stomach.

Reaching forward, she takes my hand and plays with my fingers, blows a wisp of hair away from her mouth. "Justin … this is so hard … and I'm sorry. I'm all over the place." She smiles shyly. "I love being with you. I want to be with you, but it will take me a bit of time."

I open my mouth to say this is okay with me, but she shushes me.

"I'm trying to share, to be honest about my situation … but I'd like to, no, I *need* to, know more about you. Your family." She gives me such an intent look my mouth runs dry. "You're wonderful, so caring, always looking out for people … but what about you? What do *you* need?"

I feel like I'm drowning in her wide, serious, hazel eyes. No-one has ever asked me this. Where do I start? Do I even know what I need? My stomach does a triple roll, the sushi tumbling heavily. I want to scrub at my face but she's still playing with my fingers. *Come on, man up and speak, or you'll lose her.* Terror forces the words out.

"I … I want my family to leave me alone." At her arched eyebrow, I say, "No, that didn't come out right. I want my family to respect my life here, to allow me to choose my life." I bite down, 'choose who I marry'. Too much too soon.

"You think they don't?" asks Hayley. "How?"

"Father wants me to work in his business, like my brother Ethan does."

Hayley looks pensive. "You mentioned that. So, how did you come to be here, in Narooma, with your own business? What has changed now?"

I squirm on the sofa, and swing my legs up to sit cross-legged facing her. Think back, and choose the key points. "Father reluctantly let me study to be a physio because it is linked, relevant to his business, which is designing and selling medical equipment."

"Okay. Makes sense." Hayley nods.

"But then I realised I *liked* being a physio. Didn't want to work in sales, exports and product design."

Hayley smiles. "I can guess, but tell me why you like begin a physio?"

I crack my knuckles. Such an astute question. Digging deep, I think about it. "I like helping people. Being with people, making their daily lives a little better. Helping the injured recover, get back to what they love doing … I love analysing their bodies, sussing out what's wrong, piecing it together and devising a rehab plan." Astounded, I stop and stare at her smiling face.

Hayley spreads her palms open. "This is you; this is the Justin I see." She frowns. "But your father doesn't?"

I shake my head. "No …" I begin slowly, "back then, when I graduated, we argued and I left. Stormed out because he wouldn't listen. At all." A flush of shame heats my cheeks. Bad son. "We didn't speak for nearly a year, but then Mother reached out to me and we have an uneasy family truce."

Pausing, I think of the fleeting look of admiration on Father's face after I treated the racehorse. He saw my skill then. "But on my visit this week he *possibly* saw my true skills." When Hayley flaps a hand at me, I elaborate, telling her about Father's plan to expand into the Hong Kong horse racing industry and how he wants me to demonstrate the equine products while Ethan manages the sales. She asks several questions about the products and I'm amazed how quickly she understands their purpose and value. As if she already knows.

"One last question," she says, peering into my face. "Did you enjoy working with the racehorse? Helping the trainer see how the colt could be made more comfortable and run faster?"

"Yes," I reply without even thinking about it. "Why would a horse want to run in pain? Father's product is actually good." Surprised, I falter to a stop. We sit in silence, and I listen to the waves breaking on the sand outside, the breeze rustling the leaves in the trees, waiting to hear what she says next. She's so smart, so analytical. What will she think of that I haven't? I crack my knuckles twice: I've been too busy freaking out to reason it through.

Reaching over, Hayley grips both of my hands in hers. "Is there any reason why you can't do both?"

"What? Do both?" I stare, confused. How can I do both? Disappointment surges through me: I can't be here *and* in Hong Kong.

"Well, it seems your skill is the demonstration aspect, working with the horses and gaining the respect and trust of the humans involved, the trainers and owners. I totally see why your father wants *you* to do that. But could your brother manage the rest of it? How many demonstrations do you need to do?"

My heart is thudding so loudly I can't hear myself think. Is she suggesting I fly to Hong Kong for just the demonstrations then come home? *Could* that work? Would Father ever agree? Hope rises: Ethan would because it gives him control. He'd side with me to argue the case. The family honour would be saved because I would be involved, even if intermittently. "You're a genius!" I croak and fling myself at her.

We fall back onto the sofa arm, our legs entangled, and I smother her face with kisses while she squirms and giggles beneath me. I find her mouth and kiss her long and hard, her return passion filling me with elation. Nuzzling her neck, I become aware of the soft swell of her breast showing above the lip of her top, the cute freckles adorning the skin there, like on her nose. Ooh, can I kiss down there too? Desire floods my body and heat flushes between us. My cock swells, pressing into her leg.

Hayley murmurs, "Settle down, Tiger." She kisses the top of my head. "It's been a tough couple of days." She tugs on the hair at the back of my head, lifting it until I'm looking into her eyes. A faint frown draws her elegant eyebrows together. "Not quite ready."

My desire ebbs and I brush my lips across her forehead, decide to use her tactic of banter to defuse the moment. "Besides, we have paddling in the morning and who knows what drills mean coach has planned?" I ease down beside her to a less intense hug and kiss her hair. "And I'm drained from the interrogation. What exactly is your job in Canberra? FBI equivalent?"

Laughing, Hayley strokes my cheek. "That'd be cool, but I'm a lowly evaluation expert who analyses data and writes about what it means. I didn't realise the skill could be so useful. Glad I could help."

"I have to convince Father, but it's worth a shot." I run my fingers through her wavy, silky hair and sadness thrums in my chest. That's not the only thing I'm going to need to convince Father about — and there's no compromise solution I can draw out of a hat to convince him re Hayley.

But if I help Ethan, will he help me?

CHAPTER NINETEEN
Compromises

I could tell Justin didn't want to leave, was disappointed I didn't ask him to stay, but I'm exhausted, limbs as heavy as if they're full of post-race lactic acid. And I need space. Sleep eluding me, I stare at the ceiling, an eerie luminous white in the muted moonlight. There's too much happening. Some of it good, some not so much. My right hand wanders to my left breast, my fingers nudging along the ridge of scar. *Could* the shadow be knotty scar tissue and retained fluid? God, I hope so. Two whole months until I know. Sixty-two days. Will every check-up be like this? Every Goddamn year? A tsunami of fatigue crashes over me.

'*Go forward, Hayley*'. I see Justin choking out the words. He's upset too, and doing his best to hide it. A tremble travels from my nape to my toes. Justin. Adorable, handsome, strong, funny, caring and intense Justin. Who seems entirely serious about me. So fast. What am I going to do? How much longer will he hold off on wanting sex? You mean asking, Hayles, you know he already wants you. Do I want him? Hell, yes. With every fibre of my being — except perhaps the parts that matter. My limbs tremble at the mere thought of his magnificently sculpted body lying over mine … but what if I *can't*? What if everything is still too dry, too sensitive to make sex possible? The stupid Tamoxifen isn't helping, and I have four more years of taking that. I ignore the tear seeping from my eye. How can I possibly explain this to him?

A tear seeps from my other eye. What if Justin wants children? I'm terrified of getting pregnant, of elevating my hormone levels. Wouldn't that be a magnet for a recurrence? I bawled my eyes out when the Olympic medal marathoner Kerryn McCann died only months after giving birth to her daughter because she refused treatment during her pregnancy. So unfair. Breast cancer doesn't discriminate. Why would I fare any better? Oh God, I don't even take the pill any more for fear of hormones. How would I even avoid getting pregnant?

I have to tell Justin this. I know I do, but it seems so heavy. Could spoil everything. A yawn escapes. I'm so tired. Wrung out. How on earth will I paddle tomorrow? *Brave face, Hayles. Snap out of it. Lift those arms high and move that scar tissue. Coach's orders.*

My mind drifts to the pink paddlers I met at The Cancer Clinic. I think of their vibrancy, strength and camaraderie. Jeannie texted as promised, inviting me to be a secondary member with them. Seems there's a survivor paddlers' regatta in December — in Melbourne, I could see Dad — would I like to go? Swallowing, I scrunch my toes. I'd love to go. Sounds fun, and would be so good to meet more survivors. Good plan, something to aim for. Should I ask Justin? I relax then scrunch my toes again. No, I should do this for me, join the club, race with them too. Then if I end up back in Canberra, if things don't work out here … I'll have a club. Have support. I think of how Rob and David's nickname for me is 'Plan B'. They claim I always have a Plan B for my projects, ready to go if something goes pear-shaped in Plan A. So, Plan B … text Jeannie and sign up to the club and the pink regatta. Tell Justin later.

~

I'm in a deep sleep when my alarm goes off. Groaning, I tumble out of bed and head to the shower to wake up properly. I have to jog to the boat shed and get there just as the others are pushing the boat out the back of the shed. Wow, everyone is here! Is there even a seat for me?

Sandi spies me. "Oh good, you're here. Bench three with Natalie. Snap to it."

I run down the side of the shed and help bring the boat into the shallow, sandy area we usually board from. Crap. I haven't got a paddle. I spin around to run up to the shed and almost slam into Justin, standing behind me.

He hands me his special paddle, his coach face on. "I don't want you going back to a heavy wooden paddle. Keep this one until you get your own. We'll be training hard today."

"Thanks," I gasp, taking it. Then tip my chin up, my lips twitching. "Good morning, coach. Sorry I'm late."

Justin opens and shuts his mouth, but his eyes crinkle with a hint of a smile before he steps away and starts giving orders to the others.

So, mean coach today. I hope I'm up to it. I nod and greet the others as they pile into the back rows of the boat, and smile at Natalie as we settle onto bench three.

"You okay?" she murmurs, peering at me.

"Tell you after," I murmur back, then take a deep breath; she deserves better. "You got time to go for a coffee?"

"I'd like that." She bumps my shoulder with hers.

"Paddles back!" yells Justin, in full coach mode.

By halfway through the session, I am seriously doubting the wisdom of even considering going to the Tuesday regional training with Justin. Admittedly, it's been a stressful week, but my arms and legs are burning. If Justin asks for a race start next, I might just jump overboard.

"Stop the boat, swap sides," calls Justin. "Have a drink."

Natalie takes a long swig from her water bottle, then nudges me. "I have a better idea. This has been such a workout, how about coming to lunch at my place? Then we can get cleaned up first."

I slick sweat from the back of my neck and shake moisture from the ends of my hair. "That would be lovely."

"I hope you like dogs." Natalie grins. "Exchange numbers after and I'll text you the address." She waves a hand towards the hilly, rural edge of Narooma. "We live on a property, over there."

"Bench three, are you swapping?" chastises Justin.

Giggling, we hurriedly swap sides. Buoyed by the thought of seeing Natalie's place, I make it through the rest of the session, even the dreaded race start practice. But by the time Justin turns the boat for the shed, I'm hanging out to go home and use the spa bath.

When we're all out of the boat, Justin gathers us in a circle and Sandi stands beside him. He rummages in his pocket, pulls out a handful of lollipops and passes them to Sandi to hand out. "Everyone gets a lollipop today. You did really well in what was a hard session for us. How is everyone feeling? Any issues? Comments?"

Andrew flaps a hand. "How many sessions like this do we need to do before the regatta?'

"Good question." Justin nods at him. "It's only three weeks to the regatta. It would be good to have another two sessions like this, and paddle as usual the other days." He grins at Giulio. "We're not international paddlers, we just need to be a bit fitter, bit more confident. There's a whole season of regattas ahead, we have time to slowly build fitness and strength."

"And we want you to enjoy it," adds Sandi, stepping back beside Justin. "If it gets too much for anyone, come and tell us. Seriously."

Justin looks at Andrew. "Okay?" Andrew doesn't look delighted but he nods.

Beside me, Natalie sighs. No-one else says anything, so Natalie and I exchange numbers. "My place is about fifteen minutes from here," she says. "Dress casual, and no need to bring anything."

"Thanks. See you soon." I look up to find Justin watching us. Retrieving my gear slowly, I hover as he gets his bike ready so we can set off along the bike path together.

"You okay after that?" he asks, peering at me from under his helmet rim.

"I'm tired, but it was a good session." I look closely at him. With the mid-morning light fully on his face, I notice the dark rims forming under his eyes and feel bad. He has enough going on without my issues. Maybe it will help if he knows I'm going to tell Natalie too. "Hey, I'm going to lunch at Natalie's. I'll tell her about my scans, but can we keep it to just the two of you? For a while, anyway."

He stops cycling slowly, gets off his bike and walks beside me. "Of course. Natalie's a good person. A good buddy." He looks sideways at me. "You can tell her about us if you want to. She's no doubt guessed anyway."

I breathe out, a weight lifted, suspecting she was going to ask me. "Okay. Thanks." We walk in an awkward silence for a way; for once he isn't chatty. I can see the slate-blue roof of the Wharf apartments looming up ahead. Does he expect we'll have dinner together? I can't read the bland look on his face. Is he unsure why I sent him home last night? Is he hurt? Should I ask about tonight? My mouth feels dry. Am I up to company? To be honest, I'm not sure. We arrive at the entry to my apartment block.

Turning to him, I place a palm along his cheek. "I'm not sure what time I'll be back from Nat's."

He turns his face to kiss my palm. "It's okay, Hayley. Take your time at Natalie's. We've both got a lot happening." He leans in to kiss me and the rim of his helmet jabs into my forehead.

"Ouch!" I rub my forehead, then giggle. "Angle your face sideways …" I lean in and kiss him properly, hoping he'll understand we are okay, we're both just tired.

When he pulls back, he's smiling. "How about a day trip tomorrow?"

"Where?"

"A *mystery* day trip," he corrects.

"Yes, as long as you let me pay for something." I try to look stern.

"Maybe." He shrugs and slings his leg over his bike. "I'll pick you up at nine."

I watch him turn his bike and cycle up the hill, his calf muscles bulging.

~

One delicious spa bath and an hour later, I'm driving along Rainforest Parkway ogling the beautiful properties. I wouldn't mind living here! Neat small rural residential blocks with mainly gorgeous houses, and plenty of space between them. Natalie's house is at the far end, and I park at her property gate and text I'm here, as instructed.

Natalie soon appears, with a bunch of dogs cavorting around her ankles. "Leave your car there," she says, "and come to the gate. Be prepared to slip through fast, one of these is related to Houdini."

Amused, I comply and she slams the gate shut just as the black Labrador tries to stick its head through the gap. I look at the motley collection. "Are these all yours?"

"God, no," she says, grinning. "My business is dog-minding. Only these two wee adorables are mine." She points to two similar small grey dogs with boxy faces, reminding me a bit of the Scottish

Terrier that used to be on the tissue boxes. "Meet Zoe and Bingo."

I crouch and put my hand out and the two grey dogs sniff my fingers and wag their tails. "What breed are they?"

"Miniature Schnauzers. Renowned for their good temperament, and the cuteness factor is off the scale." Natalie wags a finger at the dogs. "Although you do have your moments, don't you, my sweets?"

The two dogs kink their heads at her, looking like butter wouldn't melt in their mouths and I laugh. "Gorgeous."

Natalie gives me a quick walk around the three-acre property, which has ample lawn for the dogs to play on and an impressive array of fruit trees and vegetable beds, all immaculately fenced and netted. "David's terrain," says Nat. "We grow as much as we can of our own fruit and veg."

The sun goes behind a cloud and I shiver. "Come on, lunch is ready," says Natalie, explaining that she and David designed their house, which is passive solar.

Near the back door are several large urns with trickling water and I glimpse a flash of a goldfish. "Your place is stunning. I'm envious. When I was growing up, I wanted to live on a farm and have my own horse."

Natalie slides a sly look my way. "Well, if you stay down here maybe you can become a neighbour."

"As if I could afford this!" I exclaim automatically.

"You and a partner could…" says Natalie suggestively. "Who do I know that could possibly be suitable? Gee, I'll have to think about that."

"Very funny," I reply. "I agree to be interrogated over lunch."

"Excellent." Natalie rubs her hands together. "I was planning to bribe you with food, and, of course, the ferocious beasts might not let you leave unless you answer all questions satisfactorily!" On cue, Zoe barks at her tone.

Smiling, I shake her husband David's hand. He seems nice, a studious, quiet chap. As they serve lunch, I observe how comfortable and relaxed they are with each other. The lasagne and salad are delicious, and I force myself to eat slowly as my body declares how ravenous it is. I decline the wine they offer, explaining that drinking during the day gives me a headache. "Don't worry, I'll spill," I assure Nat, who looks disappointed. "You don't need to get me drunk."

She splashes Rosé into her glass then lifts it at me. "Okay, spill. Health appointment?"

Her face drops as I tell her, and David manages to quietly slip out of the room, probably feeling this is women's talk. When I falter to silence, Natalie wipes an eye. "So, two months until you find out?"

I nod.

"How can you stand it?" she asks. "I didn't even think anyone as young as you could get breast cancer. I'm fifty, and I've only just been offered my free mammograms."

"It is rare," I admit. "Only about four per cent of us are under thirty." I shrug. "I didn't even have any risk factors; it just happened."

She reaches over and squeezes my hand. "I'm so sorry. Is that why you came to Narooma? To recover? What do you do usually?"

I fill her in, delighted to find out in return that she and David are former public servants from Canberra, who worked in a science field. We chat about data and evaluation techniques for a while.

"Do you miss it?" she asks.

"Not yet," I say, fiddling with my napkin. "I like it here, but I'll need to find a job if I want to stay longer."

Natalie sips her wine, then gives me one of her laser looks over the rim of the glass. "I can think of at least one other person who would like you to stay."

"Good segue," I say, my cheeks heating. "And yes, Justin and I are seeing each other."

"Good," says Natalie, with an even more intense look. "I hope you like him as much as he obviously likes you."

I use my napkin to fan my cheeks. "Maybe." I laser-look her back. "How can you tell he likes me?"

Rolling her eyes, Natalie laughs. "From the minute you arrived our professional, competent coach has been all fingers and thumbs, dropping stuff, banging into things, totally distracted. Plus, he's always watching you." She leans on her elbows and rests her chin on her hands. "Seriously, though, I've never seen him look so … *vulnerable*. He's always been fun but kind of closed-off. You're good for him."

My heart gives a strangled pang. "Can I ask, how long have you known Justin? Why is he single?" I'm holding my breath: what can I possibly have missed about him? What am I not seeing?

"Good question," says Natalie. "Let me see … I joined the club eleven years ago, when we moved here, and Sandi was in charge with an older chap, who left a while back. Justin … appeared maybe nine or ten years ago? He bought the physio practice and immediately lobbed into the club."

My eyebrows go up. "So, he already paddled?"

"Oh yes. He was already a regional level paddler, way outclassed all of us put together! But fortunately, he and Sandi get on and they've made it work, managing the club together." Natalie's focus drifts for a moment. "I vaguely recall him saying his family were paddlers. I think they're in Sydney, but now that you're asking, I realise just how little I know about him."

"That's what I'm worried about," I murmur before I can stop myself. "Why does nobody know him? The *real* him? What is he not telling anyone?"

Natalie's blue eyes latch onto mine. "Well, if anyone can find out, it's you." She thinks for a minute. "I find it impossible to imagine it's anything sinister, he's such a good person. Maybe it's a cultural thing?"

I sit back in my chair. His family and his cultural background … Nat could be on to something, but I can't tell her what Justin confided in me about his fight with his father. Not when I had to dredge that out of him, and he's in such pain about it. Why would this make him still single, though?

Natalie is watching my face carefully. "For what it's worth," she says slowly, "I've never seen him with any other women, he treats everyone with the same good humour, respect and care. But around you, he's different. He's lighter, softer, funnier, also more ambitious, we're going to regattas for God's sake … he's in love, bench buddy."

I hear her unspoken question: *what are you going to do about it?* Miserably, I say, "And I am … broken... a risk."

"Oh, Hayley," Natalie chokes out. "You're not broken, far from it. I can barely keep up with you! Anyway, don't you need to let Justin decide? He knows, right? He's a smart man. If you want him, if you love him, then *you* choose to be with him — and let *him* choose whether he wants to be with you, honey. You can't decide that for him."

"Thanks." I rummage for a tissue and blow my nose loudly. A squall of wind hits the floor-to-ceiling windows, bringing a spattering of rain. I can see David tinkering by one of the vegetable gardens, three of the dogs milling around his legs. Before any tears can fall, I say, "Do you think we should let David back in now?"

Natalie laughs. "Absolutely. All questions have been answered, and I'll even tame the beasts when you go."

CHAPTER TWENTY

Mystery Tour

Ipull up outside Hayley's apartment right on nine and text her that I'm here. She hurries out of the entry, runs to my car in the sprinkling rain and hops in.

"Morning, coach," she says brightly, looking less drawn than she did yesterday. She clips her seat belt in. "So, do I need to wear a blindfold or are you going to put a sack over my head?"

It takes me a few seconds to make the connection to the mystery outing. Putting on my most serious face, I say, "I forgot the sack. I suppose I could put my jacket over your head." I pull away from the kerb, and indicate to turn onto the highway and head up the hill.

"If you mean the one with the gorgeous dragon on, let's do it." She gives me an impish grin. "But you won't get it back."

"Is that so?" I arch an eyebrow at her. "In that case, given that you're unfamiliar with the terrain, I'll let the sack part go."

"Nice. Good to know I'm with the good coach today, not the mean one."

Focusing on the road, I ask, "How did you pull up after yesterday's harder session? Good coach wants to know."

She grimaces. "It was tough, and it's been a big week. I admit I needed my spa bath after, and Natalie plied me with lasagne and lots of carbs. I feel okay today, though." Twisting in her seat, she studies my face. "I can see why you chose those drills. We could do with more endurance and more strength."

"Five-hundred metre races are hard. You're paddling fast for about five minutes."

"Kind of like a middle-distance track run," says Hayley. "Right on your anaerobic threshold the entire way. I hated those; give me ten kilometres or a marathon any day."

My fingers grip the steering wheel. She knows so much more about training than she's let on! It'll be nice to have someone to talk the more scientific aspects with. Out of the corner of my eye, I watch her peering out the window, open curiosity on her face as we drive past the main shopping centre and exit Narooma.

"We're going south?" she asks. "Cool."

"Have you been this way before?"

She taps her fingers on her knee. "Is Eden this way? I went there once when I was crewing for Jona- someone for the Coast to Kosciusko race. It starts in Eden."

"Is that a bike race?"

Smiling, Hayley shakes her head. "No, it's an endurance run of 246 kilometres, mainly uphill. It takes the winners nearly 24 hours."

I nearly swerve off the road as I gape at her. "They run without stopping?"

"Yep. That's why they need a crew, to keep passing them drinks and food, dry tops and so on."

"Oh man. Did you ever do it?"

"No … I wanted to, but then I got sick."

Reaching over, I pat her knee, a shiver running through me

when she brushes her fingers over mine. "I think paddling might be better for you, more overall strength and less risk of injury."

"True." She sits straighter, "Okay, let's do twenty questions."

"Like an IQ test?"

"No, I already know you're smart," she says smugly. "Like, what's your favourite colour?"

"My favourite colour?" Why does she want to know that?

"Okay," she rolls her eyes. "Maybe not so smart. Not a hard question."

"Royal blue, but I also like gold." I glance at her. "And yours?"

"Jade, or a kind of misty green."

"That would suit your eyes." I swallow, thinking of just how good she looked in the jade top on our first dinner.

By the time we're nearing Bega, she's dragged out of me that my favourite food is Peking Duck, my favourite animal is a water dragon, I don't read books unless I want to learn about a topic, I love summer best, I like music without words, and my favourite fruit is a feijoa. And I discover that she loves autumn, sushi, horses, reads fantasy, likes happy music, and her favourite movie is *Unstoppable*.

"Where are we going?" she asks next.

"Mer- whoa! Sneaky. Not telling you. Nice try."

She shrugs. "Okay. What do you want most in life, then?"

My hands tense around the steering wheel, and my chest squeezes. How can I answer that? A sideways glance tells me she's deadly serious. She wants to know. "Big question." I stall for time. Thinking hard, I try to select something from the emotions whirring through me. The answer arrives. Oh man. She has a knack for interrogation … can I tell her what I truly want? Swallowing my doubts and reluctance, I flex my fingers and say, "I love my life, love what I do, but it would be even better with someone to share it." The next part tumbles out. "Someone who *sees* me, gets me. Doesn't expect me to be or do something else." I clamp my mouth shut.

Whoa. Said way too much already. I can't look at Hayley.

Her hand creeps onto my knee. "Me too," she says softly. "And I hope to be around long enough to enjoy it with him."

I reach over and grip her hand, driving one-handed for a bit and wishing we were there already so I didn't have to keep concentrating on the road. Should I pull over? We pass a road sign listing the towns ahead. Still twenty kilometres to go. Raindrops splat against the windscreen.

"Ah hah. Does Mer-whoa stand for Merimbula?" asks Hayley. "What's there?"

"That's for me to know and you to find out," I say. "And no, it doesn't matter that it's raining."

When we take the last few turns, I tell her to close her eyes so she can't read the signs. I drive up the last hill, and pull up in the carpark outside the Aquarium and Wharf Restaurant. "Okay. Open your eyes."

"An aquarium? Oh wow!" She sounds thrilled. "I *love* watching fish."

"No whales here, but the exhibits are good and the restaurant is fabulous." I get out and run around to open the door for her, holding my jacket over her head. We jog to the entrance and dash inside.

Hayley elbows me in the ribs so hard I stop to catch my breath while she marches to the admission counter. "I'm paying."

I hold my hands up in surrender, taking a cautious breath. Man, that was some elbow. Remind me not to piss her off.

Handing me my ticket, Hayley says, her eyes shining, "The fish feeding is at 11.30. Have you been here before?"

"Once. A few years ago." I take her hand and lead her down the stairs and through the ajar door to the exhibit area. The lighting is muted, as if you are in a massive underwater cavern. The walls are all adorned with large tanks filled with myriad fish and other aquatic creatures, and charts on the wall above to describe them. There are two rows of chairs in front of the largest tank.

Hayley heads to the first exhibit, pulling me with her. We're early enough to beat the crowds, even on a rainy Sunday. I'm soon absorbed by the swift-changing expressions that fly across her face. Barely noticing the fish, I watch the way her hazel eyes widen and narrow, the way her cute freckles scrunch together and then slide apart with her frowns and smiles.

"Seahorses!" she exclaims, her fingers pinching mine. "My favourite."

Standing behind her, I wrap my arms around her and rest my cheek on her hair while we observe the tank of majestic seahorses. It takes a while to find them all, they're so well camouflaged in the wavy seaweed. Hayley murmurs about the teeny baby ones, hatched only last week according to the display sign. I kiss her hair, glad to have brought her a moment of joy. The tiny blips are cute as they float around near a seahorse that could be the parent. Does Hayley want to have children? I bite my lip. Do *I* want to have children? I inhale the scent of her hair, considering. With Hayley … maybe. But it doesn't feel like a deal-breaker. I hadn't thought about it before.

"You right there, Tiger? You'll suffocate if you get hair up your nose," warns Hayley, twisting in my arms and tilting her mouth up.

I plant my mouth over hers, revelling in the taste of her, the romantic mood of the dimly lit cavern. A bunch of kids squeeze past, giggling, and one of them mutters, "Get a room." I feel Hayley's lips quirk into a smile, and she kisses me harder.

A chime sounds. It must be fish feeding time. I turn her around so we're facing the largest tank and a chap in a kind of uniform beckons us over. We take seats, along with a dozen or so others. The fish are circling behind the chap as he explains the species in the tank, that they can see us all seated so they know they're going to be fed. Another staff member disappears out a door, apparently headed to an external platform. Suddenly, food plummets into the top of the tank and the fish, biggest ones first, dart in to snatch morsels.

Hayley asks a series of questions and the chap seems delighted to have an active audience, glee on his face as he answers. Amused, I listen as Hayley extracts fascinating facts that he might not have usually shared. Who would have thought that Gropers are born female and one changes gender to become the male in a shoal? When the next male dies, another female changes gender.

The feeding over, we wander from tank to tank, my arm around her shoulder.

"I like those." Hayley points to a boxy yellow fish with a white face. "They look kind."

I watch the yellow fish for a moment, trying to fathom why she thinks it looks kind, and give up. "Would you like fish for lunch?"

Hayley screws up her nose. "Bad coach!"

Grinning, I say, "In the restaurant. I booked a table for midday."

"Oh." She tips her chin up. "In that case … but I might not have fish. It seems disrespectful."

I kiss her scrunched nose, unsure whether she's joking. "I assume they have bread. Will that do?"

Hayley insists we watch the seahorses again for a while, then I lead her to the restaurant, pleased when the waitress takes us to a table by the window overlooking the small, sheltered Merimbula beach. Shame it's not sunny, but the view is still great.

"Is this their equivalent of Bar Beach?" asks Hayley. "It's nice, but I prefer ours, it's more natural, no houses overlooking it."

Fixing my gaze on the menu, I ease in a subtle breath to steady my pulse. She *really* likes Narooma. *Focus, Justin. You have decisions to make. Big ones. Impossible ones.*

"Okay, I surrender." Hayley looks at me over her menu. "I can't go past the grilled scallops. At least they don't look like a fish."

"I see. What happened to adhering to your principles?"

"Flexibility is a virtue too," says Hayley, her expression prim.

I burst out laughing. "Sounds like you've got it all covered."

A mischievous glint in her eyes, she waves a finger at me, "Wait until you see what else I have covered."

"Like what?" Worried, I fumble my menu and almost knock my glass of water over.

"When the food comes, I'll tell you. My fee is dessert or chocolate."

I sit back. "I might need to know what's covered first, so I can assess its value."

She just grins, then the waitress returns and she orders. By the time we're halfway through our meal, I can't taste my pasta anymore, I'm so curious. But I know she's waiting for me to prod her; can see it in her suppressed smiles. The dimples of mischief in her cheeks.

"So," she says eventually, "given how busy you are, and I'm not working, I decided to do some research."

I swallow my mouthful carefully, intrigued as she bends down, picks up her compact shoulder-bag, and pulls out a few sheets of folded paper. Placing these on the table, she smooths her hand over them.

"Sorry, the notes are handwritten because I don't have access to a printer. But I can email my typed notes if you like."

I put down my knife and fork. What has she done? Now she's regarding me with a serious, but kind face.

"How much do you know about your father's proposal for Hong Kong?"

She wants to talk about *that*? Dizziness flushes through me and I shake my head. "It's to sell equine recovery products to the racehorse industry." But I already told her that.

"Yes," she says patiently, "but how much do you know about *exactly* what your father wants you, and your brother, to *do*?"

"He didn't say …" I trail off as shame floods me. I didn't give him the chance. Nor Ethan. I ran. My insides howling, I scrub a hand over my face. I'm no better than Father is! I'm not listening to him either.

"Justin," Hayley's voice is gentle, concerned, and she passes me the sheets of paper. "His plan mightn't be as bad as you think. Do you know there are only 1300 racehorses in the whole of Hong Kong? And they're all stabled at three racecourses. I can't see how what he wants you to do is full-time."

My vision blurring, I take the sheets of paper. Unable to focus on the words, I listen to her voice, relying on it to anchor me.

"The industry there is a multi-billion dollar one, but it's highly regulated. Amazingly so. The horses are all kept at Happy Valley, Sha Tin and Conghua racecourses, and there are only twenty-two trainers registered, with up to sixty horses each, seventy horses maximum if they race at all three courses. Your demonstrations to the trainers could be done in a week or two, if that's all your father wants you to do."

I force my gaze to meet hers. "I'm an idiot."

Hayley tilts her head. "Not to me, but I think you might have panicked, Tiger."

That's putting it mildly. I groan, thinking of Ethan running after me in his socks as I drove away. I don't seem able to think straight, can't manage to connect the ideas. Maybe I'm still panicking. "What do you think I should do?"

"I don't know anything about your family … but from the little you've said, could you talk with your brother? Find out *properly* before you approach your father." She looks sad. "Have you tried ringing your brother? Has he called you?"

"He did," I mumble, horror and guilt burning me that I haven't called Ethan back. I'm a coward and an idiot. "It didn't go well." Squirming, I put down the sheets of paper. I can't tell her we ended up arguing about *her*. I'm no way ready for that battle. Head bowed, I sit with my hands in my lap.

Hayley is silent for a minute, then she says, "Okay, Tiger. It's stopped raining. Let's go for a walk so you can buy me chocolates." She stands and goes to the counter.

My legs feeling far way, I sit there, presuming she's paying for lunch, then see her duck to the toilets. *Rally, man. She's amazing, and she's probably right. She's given you a way forward.* Looking up, I spy the souvenirs near the counter. Resolve energising my legs, I stride over and scan the products. *There.* A snow globe with two of the yellow box fish swimming among bubbles and silver glitter. The serving girl only just wraps it in time before Hayley reappears.

I hurriedly put my hand behind my back and she arches an eyebrow at me. "Not chocolates," I say firmly. "We have to walk for those."

I move the car to the beach car park, and we kick off our shoes and stroll along the beach, jackets on against the drizzle. Hayley rattles off more facts about the Hong Kong racing industry until I don't know how she can possibly remember them all. Eventually, I say, "Enough research! You've earned a massive box of chocolates already. Milk or dark?"

"You choose," she says playfully. "See if you get it right."

"If I get it wrong, do I have to buy another box?"

"Yep. And *you* have to eat the wrong box."

"Hard bargain," I murmur, thinking I should choose a mixed box. Heavier drops spatter my face. "You want to head home?"

"Good plan," says Hayley, leaning in to kiss me. "Loved the mystery tour."

～

As I'm passing the Bega turnoff, I realise I'm talking to myself. Hayley is slumped against the window, sound asleep. I turn the car heating up a notch and take a few seconds to observe her face. She looks relaxed, happy. Good, I've taken her mind off her health for a while. She doesn't wake until I'm entering Narooma.

"Better?" I ask gently.

Yawning, she pushes upright and nods. "Sorry. Must've needed that."

I park in a visitor spot outside her apartment and before she can say anything, turn to her. "Can I come up, just for a while? I've brought my mobile TENS machine and would like to give your scar a treatment."

Her mouth drops open.

"You could come to the physio practice, but I can treat you here. It'll be more comfortable." When she doesn't say anything, just gapes at me, I add, "Two months, Hayley. Let's get rid of that fluid and shadow."

"You think you can?" she whispers.

"If it is just scarring and fluid, yes." I don't say the obvious about if it isn't.

She swallows. "Okay. Let's give it a go."

I grab two boxes from the boot, then follow her to her apartment, and agree to a cup of tea first. I get her shyness. Given the location of the scar, this will be intimate despite my best physio approach. Sipping my tea, I send my body instructions to behave; which is becoming increasingly harder. Man, I'd love to see her body, caress it all over … but she's not ready. *Take it easy, Tiger,* I imagine I hear her voice in my head.

Tea finished, I pick up the TENS machine box and pull it out, checking if there is a power point close enough to her sofa. There is, so I plug it in and place the machine on the coffee table. "Grab a towel, then come lie on the sofa."

Hayley gives me a startled rabbit look, but disappears into her bedroom. A minute later, she's back, with a towel, and she's changed into looser clothes.

"Left side? You'll need to lie with your head here, facing the back of the sofa, left side up." After she's positioned herself, I squeeze her shoulder reassuringly. "Take a few deep breaths, just relax. Then prop your left arm above your head. This won't hurt. Promise."

She complies, and I sit on the coffee table, lean over to stroke her hair away from her face. "Adjust your top so I can see the scar, and keep yourself covered and warm with the towel so you're comfortable. Is your arm going to be okay like that for twenty minutes?"

"Yes, coach, sir," she says, wriggling around and slipping her top down over her left shoulder, exposing her arm, armpit and the edge of her breast. Putting her arm back up, she mumbles, "Here okay?"

"Perfect," I reply, drawing in a steady breath. Oh man, there are *two* massive scars. One in a large curve under her armpit, and another one stretching from what I guess is her nipple, concealed by the towel, to almost meet the other one in the hollow of her armpit. It's an effort to keep my voice even. "What's the curve scar for?"

"Lymph nodes," mutters Hayley. "They found cancer in five, so they took out about twenty or so."

That's well and truly metastasised. Suddenly I remember the haggard face of a client from years ago whose cancer had metastasised. Recall her saying she was terrified of the little atom bombs circling, just choosing a spot to land and take root. She died a few months later. My fingers tremble as I pick up the TENS machine. "The machine will feel a little cold at first, then you'll feel a tingling, electrical sensation. This sends a teeny current into the tissue, stimulating it to heal. Tell me if you want me to stop. Any time."

"Okay." Hayley closes her eyes, and her chest moves in a deep breath.

Leaning forward, I choose to begin at the top end of the curved scar. It must be 11 or 12 centimetres long, and it takes a while for me to move the TENS module down, bit by bit, holding it for almost a minute in each spot. My right arm is tiring by the time I reach the bottom of it and I sit back to take a breather. "How does that feel?"

"Nice, actually," murmurs Hayley. "It feels good to be doing something proactive, positive."

"Okay, then. Glad to help." I hadn't thought about the psychology of this. "Ready for phase two?"

"Yes, coach." Hayley's words slur around her smile.

Focusing, I work my way along the straight scar, another eleven centimetres or so. My chest grows tight as I approach her nipple, and I release the breath I was unconsciously holding. There's no reaction from Hayley, and when I glance up, I see she's fallen asleep again. Man, this week has taken a toll on her. I diligently adhere to only the scar tissue I can see, but then her hand holding the towel relaxes and it slips down, revealing her nipple. The scar goes right to the centre of the areola and base of the nipple, pulling it taut sideways, and it's inverted. That *must* be uncomfortable, and it isn't pretty. No wonder she's shy about us going further.

I nudge the towel back up, in case she wakes, and sit for a minute, pondering. I have a bottle of pure Vitamin E oil in the box. But if I start rubbing it in and she wakes … She looks deeply asleep; I'll make it quick. I put the machine down, rub my hands together to warm them, and grab the bottle of oil.

Dabbing a liberal amount on my fingertips, I gently massage along the ridge of the straight scar. This one needs it most. Her skin is silky soft, and I can see freckles cascading down her chest to below the line of the towel. God, she's pretty. Blood rushes to my groin. *Focus, Justin. Hurry up.* About three centimetres away from the nipple the scar is bulkier, harder and kind of elevated. I bet this is where the fluid is. The cursed shadow. I work my fingers in circles over the thickest part, increasing the pressure slightly when she doesn't stir. Maybe I should leave the oil with her, tell her how to do this.

Her eyelashes flutter, and I pause. She doesn't move further, so I work my way back outwards along the scar, gently stretching it away from the nipple, then sit up, my lower back aching. She'll get a cramp if she keeps her arm above her head like that for too much longer, so I ease it down, placing it across her chest. Hayley mumbles something and snuggles under the towel. After a minute, I stand, use her toilet and then find a cupboard that contains linen. There's a woolly throw rug on the top shelf and I take this back to drape over her, tuck it in around her shoulders and smooth a strand of hair back from her face.

What to do? She looks so slim and vulnerable, asleep like that. *Keep fighting, Hayley.* My eyes burn and I pinch the bridge of my nose. *Keep it together, man.* I head out onto her balcony. The rain has stopped and a gloomy dusk is falling; the air is moist and clingy. It seems wrong to just go home and leave her. Pulling the door closed, I sit on one of the chairs, looking out to sea and ignoring the damp seeping into my trousers.

Pulling my phone out of my pocket I turn it over and over in my hands. Do it. Do it now. Before I lose my courage. I text Ethan: *Can you talk?*

Give me 5, comes straight back. I sit listening to the surf until he sends *okay.*

"Sorry," I blurt as soon as he picks up. "Sorry, brother."

"What the hell, Justin? What is going on with you?" He sounds angry, then he grunts and says, "Wait. Let's start again. I'm sorry too. Speak."

"Are you alone?"

"I'm at their place for dinner so I'm hiding in the back garden."

I hesitate, pulse racing. Where to start? I should have thought this through! Swallowing, I say quietly, "Sorry I raced off. I might have panicked … about a few things."

A heavy sigh comes down the phone. "I don't get it. You and Father … you don't listen to each other. You're determined to goad each other. Why?"

Stunned, I sit rigid, pushing down my hurt. This is the second time today I've been told I don't listen. Can that be right? Where Father is involved … I open my mouth to snap that he didn't listen to me first, was always pitting me against Ethan, then realise how pathetic that sounds. *Crap.* I'm as mulish as Father is. Go figure.

"Are you still there?" asks Ethan.

I croak out, "I can't help it, it just keeps happening. But I see now that I could listen more. Will you talk to me? Tell me what's happening?"

"You'll listen to *me*?" Ethan sounds incredulous. "That would be a first."

Shame burns my cheeks. "Yes, brother. I want us to be friends. I need you."

"Huh," huffs Ethan. "If you hang up on me, I'm never talking to you again. Listen hard. Father is furious with you, but he's also shaken. I overheard him and Ma arguing. She's afraid you'll be lost from the family forever and, believe it or not, he doesn't want that either but he's too stubborn to tell you this. You need to get your act together. Real soon." He chokes up. "Why can't you work with me on this? Make everyone happy?" He stops to blow his nose and guilt flames from my head to my toes.

"My fault. I possibly thought the plan is bigger than it is. What exactly does Father want us to do?"

"He wants me to stay in Hong Kong for a month or two, set up an office there, manage initial sales, and his cousin will pay for two staff. He wants you to go over for a week at the start to do all the demonstrations to the trainers, then another week later to train the grooms in how to use the products." Ethan sniffs. "You are impressive at that, bro, even Father can see it."

I lean against the damp chair back and close my eyes, nausea surging. If only I had listened. "Okay," I mumble.

"Okay what?" snaps Ethan.

"I can do that." There's a loud clatter, and I guess that Ethan has dropped his phone. I hear him cursing, then hear his breathing.

"Did you just say yes?"

"I did, for *this* project. It doesn't mean I'm in for anything else. But I promise to try harder to listen in future."

"Can I tell Father? Or do you want to?"

"Give me a day to think about that?"

"A day, Justin. *One* day."

"Got it. Talk tomorrow night."

CHAPTER TWENTY-ONE
Awakening

When I wake, it is fully light. Stretching out in the bed, I think about yesterday. The mystery tour was fabulous. Justin is so kind, so thoughtful. Gently, I probe along the straight scar, a lump forming in my throat, thinking of Justin's warm fingers deftly massaging it. My groin tingles. I pretended to be asleep so he could keep working, but when I next stirred it was midnight, pitch dark and I was alone, still tucked in on the sofa.

Getting up, I pad out to the kitchen and blink at the items on the benchtop. There's a box, a wrapped thing perched on top of it and a scrawled note: *Had to go. You can borrow the hand-held massage machine for a bit, use it daily. Memento from the mystery tour. Chocs on way. Talk later. J.* Followed by a striped blob that I suppose is his impression of a tiger. An artist, he is not.

I unwrap the memento and blink harder. Two yellow butter-fly fish in a snow globe. Way more romantic than a red lollipop. Hugging it to my throbbing chest, I struggle to think of a time when Jonathan did anything as sweet as this. Not once, over the four years we were together. I put the globe on the coffee table, where the sunlight will catch it.

After Tai Chi and my fruit breakfast, I carry the box to the coffee table, along with my mug of coffee. The image on the top of the box has Zhao Medical Enterprises in a bold, Oriental-style script, and a logo of a human shape, arms out wide and legs apart, with a faded image of a dragon roaring behind it. Zhao … sounds familiar. My breath catches. Is that Justin's surname? Grabbing my phone, I open the TeamApp for the club, check the list of paddlers registered for the next paddle. *Justin Zhao.* Excitement bubbles: this is one of his family business products.

Curious, I take hold of the lid, blow off some dust, and open it. *Oh my God.* It's positively phallic. A long cylindrical machine with a rounded snub nose with slits in, and a shaft heading to the power end with buttons on. There's a charger, so it must be battery driven. I prise out the instructions, which explain it is a cyclonic vibration therapy, or CVT product, that sends electrical impulses deep enough to stimulate bone health, and can be used anywhere on the body. Anywhere... *Hayley, keep your mind on the job, this is not a sex toy.*

No time like the present. The sun is sending bold sunlight into my lounge, warming my legs and feet, and the sea has resumed its glittering azure. I take a swig of coffee then press the power symbol, hoping the thing is charged. It buzzes to life in my hands, and I press the intensity dial to three, the midpoint. Leaning back, I rest it against my left breast, aligning it with the scar. It sends shockwaves through my thin pyjamas. Man, this thing packs a punch. I think of how Justin kind of stretched the scar tissue away from my nipple and try to mimic this with the machine.

After a few minutes, my whole breast, what's left of it, is tingling and humming. Even my right nipple is becoming *aware*, standing up and telling me it wants attention too. I circle the nozzle over the right nipple and gasp when warmth radiates out from the nipple and I swear my labia just twitched. I'm sure this is not what Justin intended … but the possibilities are zinging around in my mind.

I slide to lying on my back on the sofa, with my feet up and knees bent. Brief panic thrums: what if it doesn't work? *Be brave, only one way to find out.* Better to find out with this machine than with Justin. The machine can't be disappointed.

Swallowing deeply, I press the machine to my leg, near the crease to my pelvic area. Vibrations tingle through my skin, penetrating deep, pleasantly jiggling muscles and tendons. Ooh... no hardship using this. Crooking my leg outwards, I take a deep breath. Come on, let this thing send healing into me. Moving the device higher, I close my eyes, lapping up the relaxation. The sun is cosy on my legs. This is bliss. Waves of vibration seep into my groin. I nudge the device higher, placing it on the silky pyjama pants covering my crotch.

Oh my. Vibrations ripple across my groin and spread tinglingly until delightful warmth oozes over my lower belly, an awareness blossoming in my labia and clit. *Go on, try it.* I push the device onto my crotch, gasping when pleasure pulses into my folds. Deep vibration healing … the medical team failed to mention this option! This could be a miracle for more than my scars if I can coax a response here, raise a lick of moisture.

The machine clicks off.

Damn. Sitting up, I peer at the dials. Oh. The fifteen minutes is up. Already. I press the power button and the machine obligingly vibrates to life. Phew. I dislodge my pyjama pants and lay back. Swallow. *Go, girl. Get something happening so if Justin makes a move* … Licking my lips and closing my eyes, I place the device full length along my folds. Delicious energy spreads tingling pleasure. Oh, yes.

I imagine Justin's fingers stroking me, teasing my clit, exploring my opening … My clit swells. I visualise his sculpted, athletic body on top of me, broad arms wrapping me tight, handsome face close to mine, his tongue probing into my mouth. My nipples tingle, even the scarred one, and my clit throbs insistently. Is that me moaning? Using my free hand, I gently stoke my labia, just below the machine nozzle. My fingers slip on slick moisture. *Yes. Finally!*

Waves of pleasure roll upwards and putting the nozzle on my clit and gently stroking my entry, I feel the hint of an orgasm building. My whole body is tensing, shrieking *come on!* I wonder what Justin's penis looks like. Surely, it would be powerful, muscled, like the rest of him. I arch, imagining him pressing into me, his so handsome face smiling, loving me … Unbelievably, contractions shake me and I climax, the area tugging, yearning for Justin's presence. A warm, happy tear slides down my cheek. Well, that was a start. A kind of medium one. Needs more practice, but feels promising.

I *can* still do this. I *want* to do this. With Justin.

Sitting up, I gulp down my cold coffee. Check my phone. It's only nine. For the first time since arriving here, I'm restless, and feel like I need more to do. Maybe I could email Noel to see if there's a way I can work from out of the office in some modest capacity? Got nothing to lose, really.

I search through my contacts until I find his email address and send: *Hi Noel. Things are going well down here and I'm feeling a lot better. The sea air is working wonders. I'm wondering if there's a way I could work casually from down here? Let me know if you'd like me to call you or drop in next time I'm in Canberra. Thanks. Hayley.*

My gaze lands at the beginning of my list on Akiko's mobile number. I really like her, she's smart and funny. Perhaps we could go for a run or have lunch again? I text her, asking if she'd like to do either.

After making a fresh mug of coffee, I return to the sofa with my tablet, a notebook and a pen. Tapping the pen on the table, I consider. Talking about his family is really hard for Justin, like dredging blood from the proverbial stone. He seems almost … traumatised. But in every other way he comes across as confident, controlled, relaxed, caring and funny. Why is it so different with his family? He seems scared of his father, and angry. If you can apply the words angry and Justin in the same sentence. Is bitter a better word? I fire up my tablet, type 'Zhao Medical Enterprises' into my search engine and sit holding my breath.

Whoa! A zillion references and articles spring up. Facts first, Hayles. I go to the official business website.

Zhao Medical Enterprises was established by Chaoxiang Zhao, who arrived from Beijing under the Australian Government's Business Skills visa class in 2004. Zhao brought a wealth of expertise with him, based on lifelong experience as an elite sportsman and working in the field of rehabilitation and re- covery with athletes in China. The company designs, produces and distributes medical equipment to support rehabilitation, injury prevention and rapid recovery from strenuous compe- tition. The products have also proven beneficial for prolonging circulation and joint mobility in the aged. The Zhao range of products are used worldwide, in a range of contexts.

Intrigued, I click on the 'Products' tab. And gasp at the array of products and their prices. The hand-held machine Justin so ca- sually lent me retails for $2,200! There's a back massage flat pad for $3,600, an assortment of massage chairs and even beds with in-built massage equipment for much higher price tags. A segment explains about cyclonic vibration therapy and how it was discovered by miners leaning on vibrating mineshaft belts back in the 1800s. The story is supported by several full body scan images showing before and after use levels of blood flow and circulation.

Below photos of technicians working in pristine, high-tech laboratories, there are photos of Zhao consultants working with athletes, businesspeople and the elderly — all followed by glowing testimonials from hospitals, physios, sports clubs, elite athletes and retirement villages. I sip at my coffee. This is massive. The family must be *incredibly* wealthy. Yet Justin is a physio in a small seaside town with a population of 7,000, paddles with the local club, drives a modest car and never even hints at having money. From the brief glimpse I had from the outside, his cottage looks quaint and somewhat old-fashioned — Why on earth would he walk away from his family and such success?

I go back to my search results and skim through the list of media articles, looking for one that says more about his family. There. One in the *Australian Financial Review*, dated 2018, shows a photo of his father. I carefully mouth the pronunciation spelled out after his name — 'Chow-Shyang' — and eye the headshot. Okay, I see a resemblance to Justin, but his father is serious, the cheekbones are sharp and angled, the eyes kind of flat. The crew cut doesn't help. Justin's father does not look like someone to cross or mess with.

The article describes how Zhao migrated with his wife and two sons, Jun Jie and Yichen, in 2004. Whoa! So, Justin's real name is Jun Jie, pronounced Chuyn-Hee-e? I bet absolutely *nobody* down here knows that! The article describes how the father and two brothers were highly regarded in Beijing as elite paddlers, the father making several national teams and the boys competing fiercely in junior national teams. Okay, at least they are all interested in sport and are fit. The article states the Zhao products are highly regarded in China, and Zhao's visa application was a 'shoe-in' with the company bringing more than 300 million dollars in capital, and promising to employ 100 Australians within two years.

Trembling, I sit back. What have I landed myself into? I feel like I've been dropped into a mystery novel where nothing is as it seems and the unsuspecting lead character gets duped. But everything in me says Justin is genuine. Is he embarrassed about his background and wealth? Does he want people to respect and like him simply for who he is? I crick my neck. That, I could understand. No pretensions. He was overwhelmed by the club banner we made, he wasn't faking that, and seems thrilled by Gianni and Giulio's family offering sponsorship. When the reality is he could purchase absolutely everything we asked for — and even a new boat, or a fleet of them — with a snap of his fingers! Nausea shivers through me. What am I going to do? How will I keep a straight face when I see him?

My phone pings and, dazed, I peer at the screen.

Akiko: *Lovely. How about a run tomorrow then brunch? Meet at the pool at 9am after I drop Miki?*

Me: *Awesome. See you tomorrow.*

I skim through more search results, looking for more recent articles. I find a few confirming the company has fulfilled its visa promise, employing 150 people by 2010, and entering the export market to expand beyond China and Australia. Concern mounting, I find no further references to Zhao's family. There are a couple of mentions of Yichen accompanying his father on business trips, but no photos. Justin, or Jun Jie, to all intents and purposes, does not exist.

A fresh wave of nausea shivers through me. *Does this matter? Does this matter?* My heart pounding at my breastbone, I stare out at the glittering ocean. Does it matter to me if he — we — have no connection to his family? I recall how Justin squirmed when I asked him on the drive yesterday about what he wanted in life. What did he say? Someone to share his life … 'Someone who *sees* me, *gets* me. Doesn't expect me to be or do something else'. I'm sure that's *exactly* what he said. If I close my eyes, I can hear him saying it, see the way he clamped his mouth shut afterwards and his knuckles went white gripping the steering wheel.

Getting up, I pace around the lounge room. Does he feel his family doesn't see him, doesn't respect him? The references to the three of them being national level paddlers, in *China*, the origin of dragon boating … has Justin walked away from that too? Is he tired of the competition? Tired of the comparison? I stop and face the sea. But he still made the regional team. The fierce competitive spark is there, but contained.

I play with the ends of my hair, twisting it this way and that. Do *I* see him? Do *I* get him? Is that why he likes me? *Maybe, but it's more than that,* my heart insists. *You know he just likes you.* True, *he* sees *me* — as far as I have let him. Resuming pacing, I swing my arms. *Think, Hayles, think.* This whole relationship is moving way too fast, but is that because we need each other? *Really* need each other? We both need someone caring, bold, not afraid to face the hurdles. We connect, we fit. We do *see* each other. But there's still more to both of us, we both have more truths to share, more opening up to coax. We need more time, deeper trust.

Staring down at my bare feet, I notice my silk pyjama trousers. Critical thinking is best done on the move; time to get dressed and go for a long walk. After dressing, I retrieve my phone and see I have new messages.

Noel: *Glad you are feeling better. I have an idea, will talk to the Div Head and get back to you.*

Okay, being able to work casually would give me the funds to stay here longer, give things, us, a chance. Fingers crossed the division head likes Noel's idea, whatever it is.

Justin: *Can I drop by later? Bring dinner?*

I tap my phone against my thigh, my pulse racing. Better to keep talking, sooner rather than later. I send back: *Yes, but I'm cooking. Aim for 6.30?*

Justin: *Super … I think!*

Smiling, I send: *Tigers eat raw meat, right?*

He sends a horrified face emoji and I laugh.

CHAPTER TWENTY-TWO
Stepping Stones

If I stare at the boxes of chocolates in the IGA any harder, I'll go cross-eyed. Milk or dark or cheat and buy a mixed box? *Guess, Justin, guess.* Hayley doesn't like sugar much and is focused on healthy options, which makes total sense given her past as a runner and now as a survivor. It *has* to be dark chocolate. Go with it. I choose a large box of Cadbury's dark chocolates with an assortment of cream and nut centres. Then I go to the liquor section and select a bottle of quality Tasmanian cider. I'm going to need a drink before I ask for her advice on speaking with Father.

Ten minutes later, I knock at her door and when she holds it ajar my mouth drops open. She looks gorgeous in billowy grey pants and she's wearing another jade top which leaves her slim, muscled arms bare and is slung low in soft folds across the top of her breasts. Tongue-tied, I thrust the wrapped box of chocolates and bottle at her. A tangy, meaty aroma teases my nostrils. "Smells great."

"I relented and decided to cook the meat. Beef teriyaki with rice and an Asian salad." She carries the cider to the dining table and stands eying the wrapped box. "Okay, I'm officially curious.

Let's see if you got it right."

Holding my breath, I watch her slender fingers deftly undo the orange ribbon then prise away the tissue paper. Her lips curve in a delightful smile. "Damn. Looks like I'll have to eat these after all. Good job, Tiger." She tilts her head. "Thank you."

Stepping closer, I kiss her lips. "You earned them. The reward for good work is always–"

"–more work," she interrupts me.

"After dinner, if your FBI mind is still available."

"I'm sure a chocolate or two will help boot it up." She flaps a hand at the table. "Dinner's ready."

The teriyaki is delicious, despite her protestation that it's only a packet-mix sauce. Hayley chats animatedly about the things she saw on a long walk today, and I tell her about a couple of my clients.

Putting down her chopsticks, she rests her elbows on the table, places her chin on her hands and fixes her hazel eyes on mine. "I made a paddling decision I'd like to share."

My heart thumps wildly. Don't tell me she's giving up paddling?

"Did I tell you that when I was at the hospital, I met some Dragons Abreast Canberra paddlers?" At my mute shake of a head, she says, "Anyway, they invited me to sign up with them as a secondary club." She swallows. "And I have, so I can paddle in survivor races."

"Okay." I exhale slowly. "So, you can do both? Paddle with us and with them?" I now recall that most of the major regattas have BCS category races, just a couple. I've never paid that much attention.

"Yep." The green glints in Hayley's eyes are vivid against the brown. "Not at the Canberra regattas, I have to choose one club there apparently, but at other events I can paddle with Clear Water Dragons and join DA Canberra for any survivor races." Her gaze deepens, the glints in her eyes glowing a striking emerald. "There's a particular event I'd like to mention … it's on the first weekend in December and is a breast cancer survivors-only regatta on the Saturday and a social paddle on the Sunday, at Docklands in Melbourne."

"Okay, sounds good." I assume she's telling me she wants to go to this.

She flexes her fingers beneath her chin. "Will you come with me?"

Oh man. My heart soars. "I'd love to, Hayley. Do they need volunteers to help with boat loading and marshalling? I could do that."

Hayley beams at me. "Probably, and there's a supporters' race so you could paddle in that. If you want to." When I open my mouth, she rushes on. "Wait, there's more." Her eyes are shining. "There's a gala dinner and ball, with keynote speakers and dancing … at the Marvel Stadium."

I choke as I swallow air by mistake. "The Marvel Stadium! How big is this event?"

Hayley shrugs, "I don't know, never been to one. But it's a full day of racing and the DAC Coordinator said they're expecting four hundred paddlers." She tilts her head in the way I know precedes something important. "My dad lives in Melbourne … you could meet him."

This is too much. Racing around the table, I pull her to her feet and into my arms. I can't hug her tight enough, nor plant enough kisses in her hair. *She wants me to meet her dad. She wants a weekend away with me.* My heart is singing. Heat flushes down me at the thought of dancing close with Hayley in a dress … I seek her lips and crash mine onto them.

Just as the heat is getting too much, Hayley pulls back and murmurs, "I take it you like this idea?"

"I wish it was December already," I murmur, my voice husky.

"Great." Her cheeks flush a deep rose. "I'll register us both. Oh, and we'll need to join Dragons Abreast Australia, but that's a charity and it's only $35 a year." Her lips twitch. "Can you join up? Or, you can tell me your birthday and address, Tiger, so I can sign you up."

"I'll do it," I reply. "But the relevant date is 1 January."

Her eyebrows tilt comically. "You were born on New Years' Day? Is that an omen in China?"

I shake my head. "Our Lunar New Year is early February. We should go to the Lunar New Year regatta too, it's in Darling Harbour, is major and a lot of fun." Reaching up to caress her cheek, I say, "Would you like to fire up those FBI neurons now?"

"Yes, coach, sir," she snaps me a salute. "I'll make some tea to help wash the chocolate down."

I plonk onto the sofa and crack my knuckles. Where do I start? What exactly do I need to discuss? Sighing, I realise this is the trouble. Where Father is concerned, I *never* know where to start, it's like there's an invisible wall that bounces me back, stopping me from looking at things closely.

With a soft swish and rustle of clothes, Hayley puts a mug of green tea before me, places another mug for herself, then retrieves the chocolates and sits next to me. She offers me first choice and my stomach churns. I choose an orange cream, but put it on the table beside my mug, noting her well-disguised frown.

She chooses a lavender cream, munches on it delicately and takes a sip of tea before twisting to fix me in what I can only interpret as a forensic gaze. "Okay, Tiger. Spill."

I crack my knuckles, and she reaches over to take my hand so I can't do it again. Now I can't scrub at my face either. Swallowing, I open with, "I rang Ethan last night."

"That's good." She looks pleased. "How did it go?"

My insides squirming, I hold her gaze. "You were right, the Hong Kong business probably isn't a full-time job so I told Ethan I would do it. Just this one."

Squeezing my fingers, Hayley smiles. "Good job, Tiger. Is your brother pleased?"

I nod. *Come on, spit it out.* "But he asked me to tell him, *today*, whether he could tell Father or whether I wanted to." My throat clamps closed.

Hayley peers into my eyes searchingly. Then surprises me. "What does your gut say?"

"Huh? What happened to the FBI analysis?"

Shrugging, Hayley says, "We could do that, but often the gut, especially in women," she adds with a sly smile, "is more powerful." She gently plays with my fingers, her contact calming. "I can tell from your face that you don't want to ring your father. Why not?"

I open and close my mouth a few times. She's right. Again. I *don't* want to talk to Father. Not yet.

"Justin," Hayley's voice wavers. "You're going to need to go deeper to resolve this. I can only listen, and try to ask questions that might help. What could go wrong if you ring your father?"

Okay, that's easier. "I could get roped into doing more than I want to, set up an expectation that I'll work in the family business from here forward." My eyes feel hot and dry. Man, this is hard. "In China, family is *paramount*. I'm failing my family now, bad oldest son, worst ever, but there seems to be no middle path."

"I see," Hayley says uncertainly. "Even though you live here now, not in China?"

It feels as if a load of weights has been stacked onto my shoulders. "Yes. Father's family is … traditional. It's not easy to redefine the family expectations."

"Okay, let's put that aside for a minute, focus on the immediate matter. For the Hong Kong task, does your father just expect you to go and do the work or is he going to employ you in an official capacity?"

I think of the piles of documents Father had set out on the

coffee table ready for Ethan and me to sign. "He had contracts drawn up … but I didn't look at it."

Hayley reaches for a chocolate, choosing one at random, and chews for a moment. Then her eyes snap to my face. "He was expecting you to read and sign then and there? Both of you?"

As I nod, I begin to follow her logic. "Yes. Maybe that's partly why I freaked out …"

Her fingers creeping to take another chocolate, Hayley says, "Okay. So, this is a business arrangement, in which case the parties should all be allowed time to peruse the contract details, negotiate terms, request any alterations they see fit, seek legal advice if necessary … and then sign. Or choose not to. You have no idea what the conditions are?"

I stare at her. How can she possibly know all this? I feel like an incompetent idiot. Is this the key, to view interactions with Father as professional business deals?

"What?" She shrugs. "I'm a project manager. At work, I negotiate contracts with evaluation and research providers. These are standard protocols." She squeezes my fingers. "Maybe your next step is to ask for a copy of the contract. Which you could ask Ethan to send, *before* you speak to your father. First rule of negotiation, Tiger, know your ground, know your parameters, prepare a fallback option but also have a no-go zone."

For what feels like an eternity, I'm speechless. Eventually, I find my voice. "That is an excellent plan, Miss Hayley Banks. You're so smart. I see now that FBI stands for Forensic Banks' Intellect … I'll get you a hat."

"Very funny, and yes, I'd love a hat," says Hayley. "My parents are, and were, smart too. It's in the Banks genes. My father is an archaeologist." Nudging the box towards me, she says, "Take two chocolates and eat them, you're going to need sugar for my next insight."

The intensity of her furrowed gaze sends a ripple of unease through me. Mesmerised, I snag two chocolates and chew them, my mind darting here and there trying to work out where she's going next. She points to my mug and I obligingly take a sip of tea. Crossing her legs in front of her, she adopts a yoga-style pose and looks deep into my eyes.

"Justin … I googled Zhao Medical Enterprises."

My heart stutters, nearly stops and I close my eyes. Shit! I *soo* should have anticipated she'd do that. A groan escapes, and the chocolates become tiny leaden lumps in my stomach. *She knows.* Are we over before we even got started? Wait, no she asked me to go to the survivor regatta with her. My heart resumes beating with stressed thumps. Miserable, I force my gaze to meet hers. "And?"

"Well," she says evenly, her eyebrows tugging in a frown, "first, I can see that your father is highly successful and powerful … a force to be reckoned with. I think I get some of your anxiety. What the family does and what you do…" She spreads her hands wide apart. "Second," she smiles briefly, "I'd like to know how to pronounce your real name. Properly."

My mouth is so dry I can barely form the words. "You're okay with it? And that I didn't tell you?"

Her slim shoulders lift in a shrug. "I suspect you haven't told *anyone*, yet you gave me enough hints so I figured you wanted me to work it out. Besides, you're still you, the sweet bumbling coach I met who showers lollipops on the bike path. I'd like to understand more, but," she blows at a wisp of hair, "this is complex, has layers on layers … worst thing we could do is rush it."

I bite my tongue, the taste of iron crawling between my teeth. Oh man. My ribs feel like they're strangling my lungs and heart. I'm being so unfair. Hayley's sincere, so honest, so adorable, so brave and I'm hiding something else she deserves to know. The most critical thing. She's planning to introduce me to her father … and I can't even tell my family about her. The wave of nausea is so strong I fear I might actually vomit.

"Justin?" Hayley edges across the sofa and puts her arms around my neck. "Tiger?"

Crushing her against me, I croak, "I don't deserve you."

"Okay," she mumbles into my polo shirt, "I think the FBI neurons have stalled. Now I'm confused."

My phone buzzes on her coffee table. A one-eyed peek shows the caller ID: Ethan. "My brother. I'd better ring him."

Hayley sniffs and sits back. "Yes. Get the contract?"

I kiss her forehead. "I will. I'd better go home to call him. Could be a longish call." Stroking her hair, I ask, "Are you still interested in going to the regional training at Moruya tomorrow? Pick you up at 4.30?"

"You sure I'm up to it?" Now the brown flecks in her eyes are stronger, reflecting concern.

I travel my eyes over her face and shoulders. "I reckon, only nine of us are going to regionals, the others are regular regatta paddlers. We could go to the Thai place for dinner after if you like."

She squares her shoulders and lifts her chin. "Okay." Leaning in, she gives me what feels like a bittersweet kiss, and murmurs, "Good luck with your brother." When I start to stand, she puts a hand on my shoulder. "Wait. The second thing. How do you say your name?"

I read in her eyes how important this is to her. As much as I might want to leave my Chinese past aside, she seems determined to connect me back to it. "Jun Jie. You say it Chuyn-Hee-e, more with a ch and hie sound."

"Chuyn Jee. Okay, that's quite difficult. Choon Heee. Is that better?"

"Kind of." I grin. "Justin is much easier."

She shakes her head, sits taller and says, "Chuyn Hee-e. Think

I got it. What does it mean?"

My eyebrows rise. "Okay, impressive. But please don't call me that in public."

She flaps a hand. "I know that. So, what does it mean?"

I feel a burn spread along my cheekbones. "Outstanding."

Silence hangs between us for a few heartbeats. Then Hayley laughs. "That's priceless, and so true." She kisses me. "My outstanding Oriental warrior."

My heart does several somersaults, chased by worry that she'll add this to my nickname to call me Outstanding Tiger. The way the dimples in her cheek are forming I'm sure she's thinking of it.

"How about you call me 'Laohu' instead? That's Chinese for Tiger."

"Laohu ..." She tilts her head. "I like it."

Inspired, I kiss her forehead. "And you are my Mu Laohu, my Tigress." My phone buzzes. "I'd better go, or Ethan will think I've bailed on him."

I pause with my hand on the door handle. "Thanks for dinner, for everything. See you tomorrow."

Her bright smile hits my gut like a bolt of dread. Oh man. How the hell am I going to make all this right?

CHAPTER TWENTY-THREE
Running Hard

Akiko is already at the pool, leaning forward with her hands on the grass doing an impressive double calf and Achilles stretch, her long dark ponytail flopped forward over her shoulder.

I jog over. "Hi."

Bouncing upright, Akiko beams at me with gleaming neat teeth. "Ohayoo! It's a nice morning for a run." The cherry blossom tank top accentuates her beauty and shows off her lean, muscled arms. "How far do you want to run?"

That is a good question, and I hesitate, curbing my instinctive reply of 'ten or twelve k'. I'm not sure how fast she is and whether my new, limited body will be able to keep up. "About 8k?"

"Okay. Do you need to stretch first?"

I shake my head. "I've been doing Tai Chi." I wave a hand at the water. "Great view from my balcony for that."

"You must teach me," says Akiko, fiddling with her watch to turn it on.

I hastily press 'run mode' on my Garmin and draw alongside

as she starts to jog towards the bike path, and turns left.

"That's a good distance," says Akiko. "We can take a drink breather at the lookout. Might even see a whale."

"Still?" Hope gushes. I'd love to see another whale, although I have seen what I think are spurts of spume out to sea.

"It's the very end of the season, but if the wind picks up as predicted, it's possible."

We cruise along in a brisk but even cadence and I glance at my watch. We're doing 5'20" kilometre pace. That *should* be sustainable. My chest feels subtly and annoyingly tight, my legs awkward, clunky, but if I press on that might ease. I nudge down the bitter thought about how easy 4'20" kilometre pace used to feel.

"Pace good?" Akiko flicks me a glance, her long legs floating over the ground.

"So far," I say. "I need to get back into proper training." I try lifting my chest and opening my rib cage more. Better.

I end up settling into a rhythm, listening to Akiko's happy chatter about how Miki is doing at school, a new species of fish she saw when diving last week, and Kraig's plans to try to organise a picnic tour. The bike path is well designed with broad grass verges and coastal shrubbery. It hugs the shoreline with some short but testing pinches over wee headlands that provide great views out to sea. On our left there is an eclectic mix of impressive real estate that I guess must fetch well over a million dollars apiece.

"This bike path goes all the way to Dalmeny and Lake Mummaga," explains Akiko. "It's thirteen kilometres long."

"Nice!" I glance sideways; she still looks like she's floating. "Have you ever run all the way along?"

"Once." She grins. "But I had to walk half the way back. Kraig said I was nuts, said he thought he'd have to come get me."

Busy laughing, I lose my pace and have to catch up. Akiko abruptly takes a right-hand turn to a whale lookout, a curved, polished wood platform that hangs out almost over the sea, with rocks directly below.

"Drink break," she says, walking to lean on the railing and peering out to sea.

I pause my watch, observing we've done 4.5 kilometres in 22 minutes, so we sped up marginally. Encouraged, I pull my drink bottle out of my Flip Belt and take a few mouthfuls as I join her at the railing. A breeze chases over my nape, a cool tinge despite the warm sun. As we watch the water, I see white crests forming further out. It will be windy.

A few cars pull into the small carpark and two elderly couples saunter down, binoculars hanging around their necks.

Akiko flashes me a grin. "Whale coming. A local alert's gone out." She moves to the railing facing north and peers intently at the water.

Taking the opportunity to stretch the back of my legs, I look where she's focused. And grab her arm as a sleek grey back rises above the water and submerges. I can't believe it. I rub my eyes as another grey curve arches beside it.

"There's a current that brings them in close to this point," says Akiko in her tour-guide voice. "Whoever put this platform here knew exactly what they were doing."

A lump in my throat, I watch as a mother whale and calf glide towards us, elegantly rising and sinking, the mother blowing huffs of water. We crane over the railing as the pair pass by, less than a hundred metres away, heading south.

"Lucky day," murmurs Akiko. "Do something important this day."

My mind immediately leaps to Justin, and going to the Moruya training with him. That counts as important. A shiver hustles across my neck.

"Time to head back?"

I nod and press 'resume' on my watch. Akiko chatters all the way back, seemingly not needing to draw breath, and it feels like I've only blinked a few times when we jog onto the grass in front of the holiday cabins on the Narooma foreshore.

"The Ice-creamery again?" asks Akiko.

"Great," I say, realising she's intending to head there now. Lucky I brought my phone and credit card. "My shout," I call as we hurry cross the road and select an outside table in the sunshine.

"Doomo." Akiko bows with clasped hands.

I place our order, then sit opposite her, my legs pleasantly fatigued.

"So," says Akiko, leaning forward conspiratorially. "You and Justin?"

Warmed by her enthusiasm, I tell her we are seeing each other, it's progressing slowly.

"Slow is good," says Akiko looking older than she is, and wise. Then she snaps her fingers, startling me. "With me and Kraig it was instant, we both *knew* from the moment of the dropped ice-cream, but given our past tragedies, and me being extra cautious for Miki's sake, we took it slowly." She gives me a wicked grin and rolls her eyes. "At times was *very* difficult as the body was more enthusiastic! Impatient, even."

I smile, warmth creeping across my cheeks. "I feel the same way…" Can I confide in her? I regard her seriously. She's not a paddler, a good thing, but she does know Justin, another good thing. The waitress arrives with our coffees and food, affording me another minute to consider. I conclude this is not a conversation to be held with my dad, and Akiko is my best choice. Her eyes are bright as a bird's while she waits for me to speak.

Stirring the froth of my cappuccino, I speak softly. "My trouble is my body might *not* be enthusiastic. When it comes to it."

Akiko gapes at me. "But you desire Justin?" Dimples form in

her cheeks. "He is most perfect, but don't tell Kraig I said that."

I nod. "My heart and mind are keen, impatient even, as you put it, but my body is damaged." Her frown tells me she's not following; I'll have to spell it out. "My treatment, the chemotherapy, the radiation, it is intensive and it affects *everything*." I swirl my spoon faster in the mug. "My heart and lungs feel like there's an invisible but rigid ceiling that wasn't there before … and my female parts are dry and overly sensitive." I stop, my chest tightening. The hormone-suppressant medication I'm supposed to take for another four years isn't helping. "My recent pap smear was torture." I struggle to keep my voice steady. "I'm worried that if we try … I won't be able to."

Tears glint in Akiko's eyes as she reaches over to pat my hand. "Oh, Hayley. So sorry." She sniffs. "I've never met anyone so young with this. Is there something you can take to help?"

"Maybe, but I'm reluctant to use anything with hormones in. My risk of recurrence is already … significant." I blink rapidly, not able to tell her about the shadow too.

Akiko drums her fingertips on the table. "There must be a cream with no hormones … but I don't know." Her eyebrows furrow then fly apart and she gasps. "Hormones! You need them for … what if … can you have children?"

"That's another thing." Misery swirls in my chest. "I'm thirty-four, not too late, but I don't have periods, they may or may not return, and I'd have to wait another year or two from my treatment. At least." I summon a wavery smile. "But I did preserve some eggs before my chemo. I wasn't going to because I was so dejected after my boyfriend left me, I couldn't see the point, but my dad talked me into it. Insisted my mum would be cross if I didn't keep that option open."

Akiko's weird expression makes me think she's working hard to keep from showing her horror and dismay. "You harvested eggs? Like IVF?"

"Yes. My chemo was delayed while we induced ovulation and the eggs were collected." I brush the back of my hand across my eyes. It was yet another sterile and unpleasant experience in the mix. "Dad insisted on paying the gap expense, said he didn't want me worrying about it."

"Your dad sounds kind." Akiko's smile fades. "Justin doesn't know this?"

A massive internal wail building, I shake my head. "Not yet. A big thing to drop on him, and I don't even know if he wants children." I bite my lip. "I don't know whether *I* want children now."

"Eat, while I talk." She points at my congealing tempura. "We have concerns about a baby in common, but for different reasons."

I pop half a prawn into my mouth and my body approves, telling me food is good just now.

"Miki is now eight, and I'm thirty-four, like you. Kraig is thirty-six, so I've been wondering whether we could have a child. Soon. But Kraig's first wife nearly died when their unborn baby died at twenty-one weeks and she had to have a false labour to expel the body."

My turn to smooth my face and suppress my horror. "Oh my God! That is awful." My pulse hammers: what if my treatment leads to such a thing happening to me?

"They were devastated, and the marriage did not survive. Lucky for me," she smiles wryly, "as I now have Kraig. We are so good together, and he and Miki adore each other. I'd love to have a baby with Kraig, but if I mention it, he shies away. He is afraid in case it happens again." She pauses and sips at her coffee.

"I don't know what to say," I say truthfully. Stunned, I realise my natural reaction is to side with Kraig. I get his fear. Instantly. Viscerally. Why risk it when what you have is so good? His reaction is aligned with how I feel. I was vaguely interested in having children, and now I'm far less sure. At the moment, I'm focused on just still being here. But the distress that Akiko is failing to hide tears at me. She wants Kraig's child, and there are two of them in the marriage.

"How much do you want his child?" I whisper.

"Some days, it is all I can think about," she admits. "My body clock is ticking, and I didn't have any problems having Miki, so it easy for me to be confident." She swallows. "On the other hand, I know the grief of being left behind. I thought I'd never recover when Satoru died so unexpectedly. If I didn't have Miki…"

She shrugs so non-committedly my heart races. Is she saying she would have suicided? I swallow hard. This is a waaay deeper conversation than I was expecting, but welcome as our issues are of a similar magnitude. "So, because you wouldn't want to put Kraig through that misery, you understand his fear," I finish for her. Reflecting, I add, "Me too, I'm afraid to be with Justin and to then leave him behind … and still young. My mother died, unexpectedly, at fifty-two and my father and I were so bereft and adrift. I honestly thought he wasn't going to make it for a year or so." An insight arrives, based on what Akiko said. "He possibly pulled through for me, an only child."

"You understand well." Akiko gives me a sad smile. "We are sabishii together."

I lean against the chair back and for a long moment we simply look at each other. We are indeed both sabishii, melancholy, no easy solution for either of us. Eventually, I say, "I think we're going to need to run further."

Akiko claps her hands in delight. "Maybe so. Every week. Is Tuesday a good day?"

Smiling, I agree. A gust of wind chases some leaves and bits of paper along the sidewalk and shivers race down my arms, bringing goosebumps. Reluctantly, I stand. "I'll bring a jacket next time. I'd better go and shower."

"Have a good week. See you next Tuesday." Akiko rubs my upper arm briefly, then jogs away, her ponytail bouncing between her shoulders.

Walking briskly back to my apartment, I'm glad to get inside out of the wind. Just as I put my things on the benchtop, my phone rings. I'm tempted to ignore it, but recognise the number as Noel's. Better take it. "Hi, Hayley speaking."

"Hayley, it's Noel. How are you?" he asks, but doesn't wait for an answer. "Look, I had a chat with Neville and he's actually keen to take you on board in a different capacity. Seems he and I have been thinking along the same wavelength for a while now."

Gripping the phone, I head to the sofa and sit in a sunny patch. This sounds promising, although I have no idea what he's talking about. "Okay."

"You know that we've always valued your skill as a clear writer. Your briefs and executive summaries always need less adjustment than those of others. Seems the quality of writing is a concern not limited to my team." I can hear his smile as he draws breath. "Neville and I would like to move you to a divisional resource role to provide the first layer of quality checking on the briefs and evaluation reports. You can work with the writers to fix a lot of things up and save us the time."

"Wow!" My heart races. Such responsibility, but an important and interesting role.

"Basically, this is something you can mainly do offsite, and you could Zoom meet with project writers if needs be. We'd assign you a secure office laptop, and we'd like you to spend a day in the office per month for a catch-up with Neville and me and to debrief on the issues you are encountering in the writing."

"This sounds amazing," I say, excitement building, my mind already leaping to the logistics of how they will choose which reports need review.

"Neville is happy to start you at fifteen hours a week while we do a few test runs and see how it goes, but be prepared that he may ask you to increase to twenty or so hours, depending on the workload."

"That sounds reasonable. What happens if there's not enough work in any given week?"

"We have that covered too. We want you to research best practice evaluation writing and prepare some checklists for our writers, including the research consultants we engage. This is part of the catch-up day." Noel chuckles. "Be warned, you could find yourself giving a few writing workshops. And I know how much you love public speaking!"

"I *knew* there had to be a catch, but okay. Thank you. This sounds amazing. When do you want me to start?"

"The week after next as we need to get the paperwork organised and decide which report you should review first. I'm glad you like the idea. As I said, we'd prefer not to lose you from your job here."

I thank him so profusely I can tell he's getting embarrassed. After we hang up, I blink furiously, my emotions getting the upper hand. I expected my sea change to bring me better health and a break, and instead my whole life is being redesigned. *Spectacularly.* Justin, dragon boating, new friends in Natalie and Akiko, finding other survivor paddlers to get to know, and now this, a related but significant career shift …

My heart gives a massive thump. With money coming in again, I can afford to extend the lease on this apartment. Before someone else nabs it. I blink harder, overwhelmed by how much like home this apartment feels. Love the colours, adore the view and sunlight. It feels like me. Wish I could afford to buy it. *Wait for the next scan results*, my inner voice reminds, not at all subtly.

For a moment I see myself sitting back at my old desk on that blustery September day, considering a break. *Do it, Hayles. Extend the lease. Be positive.* Another flurry of goosebumps reminds me I need to shower and put warmer clothes on.

Soon, armed with another coffee, I ring Dad and tell him about the job possibility.

"That's great news," Dad says enthusiastically. "An excellent use of your writing and analytical ability."

Pausing, I consider briefly and then decide to reveal more. "Justin calls it my FBI neurons."

"FBI?" Dad sounds perplexed.

"Forensic Banks' Intellect."

Dad cracks up. "He sounds like an astute man. When do I get to meet him?"

"That's partly why I'm calling. I've also signed up with a group of survivor paddlers, I'll explain more later, but anyway there's a major regatta in Melbourne on the first weekend in December. Will be you be at home then, not away on a dig?"

"I will make sure I'm home then," Dad says firmly. "Can't miss out on seeing you paddle in a big event. And Justin is coming?"

"That's the plan… keep the weekend free and we can finetune the plan later."

We chat for a few more minutes, until Dad has to go to a meeting. I lie down on the sofa, listening to the wind racing through the trees and the surf crashing. What a day so far. Hard to tell which is more fatigued, my legs or my mind. I give in to sleep.

CHAPTER TWENTY-FOUR
Practice

At 4 pm I check the Moruya TeamApp. It's windy here, but the weather can be different in Moruya, even though it's only forty kilometres away. The session hasn't been cancelled, and maybe the wind will drop with dusk. I guess I'll collect Hayley and we'll go. If it's too choppy and the sweep calls training off, I can take her to dinner. I text her to say I'll see her at 4.30.

I pull up out the front of the apartments, and wait a few minutes before Hayley charges out the door with her gear and backpack. Her hair is braided back. She looks somehow fitter, more determined, like that.

Jumping into the car, she says, "Sorry. I fell asleep. Your text woke me up."

"You okay?" I study her face. "You right to paddle?"

"I hope so." She looks frazzled. "I went for a run with Akiko this morning, which may not have been the best plan. As fun as it was."

I start driving, internally agreeing a run and then a hard paddle may not be the best plan. I hope the river's not too choppy, which will make it even tougher. Maybe I am pushing her too hard. A sideways glance shows me she's sitting straight, her chin tipped up. Then again, I shouldn't underestimate her. "How far did you run?"

"Nearly nine kilometres, and we saw a whale from a lookout on the bike path!" She chatters on about how much fun Akiko is, and what a good runner she is too, and after a while falls silent, looking pensive.

I don't talk for a bit, concentrating on driving as there's more traffic than usual. I catch Hayley studying me, quickly looking out the window if she senses I'm going to look at her. Shifting in my seat, I wonder what she's thinking. Did she and Akiko discuss me? "I can hear the FBI neurons whirring from here," I say lightly.

A smile teases at her lips. "They might be. I was wondering how your chat with Ethan went, but don't want to distract you before your training. And, I have news."

"*More* news already?" My eyebrows arch. "Where are you off to, or what are you doing now, busy person?"

"Actually, this news means I can stay here longer." She stops there, giving me a sly glance.

My heart thuds. This sounds positive. I give it a minute, but she doesn't elaborate. "Fine, I see I have to guess, without any FBI cells to help me. You won the lottery? Or did you give up your job?"

"Close. My boss is giving me a new role so I can work from home … which could be down here."

I hang onto the steering wheel. She wants to stay longer. Dare I hope this is to give us a decent chance? "So, you've seen the light about the superior weather down here? You don't want to have to paddle wearing heated booties?"

"Yup. You nailed it." She looks smug. "And *some* of the scenery down here is worth hanging around for too."

"I see. Like the whales, you mean?"

"Nailed it again," she says, laughing, then twists to look at me, the glint of mischief in her eyes. "There's also a rare tiger down here, which is quite fascinating."

For a moment I'm choked up. Did she just confirm she's staying longer for *me*? For us? Oh, man. Need a response here. "Well, if there's no chance I'm going to get my special paddle back anytime soon let's go online and order you one. Call it an advance Christmas present."

"You don't have to do that." Hayley puts her hand on my knee, looking emotional.

"In my best interests. Besides, I'd like to." I grin. "You choose the pattern on the blade though, I'm not even going to attempt to guess your preference for that."

She leaves her hand on my knee for the rest of the trip. From her distracted expression, I conclude the FBI neurons are working double-time.

When I pull into the car park by the boat shed, the boat is out on the grass, but I see Em and a couple of paddlers are down by the boat ramp studying the river. Touch and go whether we train, which I explain to Hayley. We join the paddlers waiting by the boat and I introduce Hayley, explaining to her which ones are in the regional team. Everyone nods and smiles and Grant gives me an appraising glance. Which I pretend not to see.

Em strides back up to the boat and everyone focuses. "Okay. It's choppy but we'll go out. We'll hug the shore to warm up, stay close to home, and do some strength work. If conditions deteriorate, we'll come in." She hands Grant a piece of paper. "Get paddlers by their benches while I meet Justin's friend." She charges around the tail end of the boat and Hayley promptly licks her lips and stands tall.

"Hi. Hayley, is it?" Em shakes her hand. "I'll put you in row nine so I can observe your form, but welcome." She moves away before Hayley has finished nodding.

"You'll be fine," I murmur. "Em is a top coach, so don't be alarmed as she's bound to chip you for something. Remember to pull your paddle if it gets too much." Grant is beckoning to me. "Relax and enjoy." Oddly reluctant, I leave Hayley and take my position by bench four. Studiously ignoring Grant's mimed question mark in the air.

The session is tough, and guilt eats at me. Although Em runs us with the current as much as possible, it's choppy and gusts of wind whip up extra waves that try to snag my paddle. We only change sides once, Em keen to keep everyone warm and moving. I reach for my drink bottle.

Grant nudges my ribs. "You dark horse. Your girlfriend?"

"Working on it," I grunt, then take a pull from my drink bottle.

"Looks nice. Wish my girlfriend would paddle."

I nod, unable to come up with a suitable response to that. What is it about Hayley that makes people suddenly open up all over the place? I resist the urge to turn around to see how she's going.

"All changed, paddles up!" Em calls above the wind.

We don't paddle as far as usual, but we do several backwards then forwards drills and a number of race starts. I only catch a snatch of Em saying something to Hayley a couple of times, so she must be doing well. I should offer her a massage as a reward. Assuming she's still talking to me.

Em brings the boat in ten minutes early, and we gather around for a cool-down stretch and debrief. "Good job, everyone. If it's choppy at regionals, we'll do the paddle out of the water start. The first few were a bit sluggish, so remember to snap your blades down and deep straight off." She looks at Hayley. "Not bad for a newbie. Keep working on your upper body strength so you can lift your paddle higher when it's rough like this."

I feel my eyebrow lift. From Em, that's high praise. I give Hayley a thumbs-up and she looks thrilled.

We pack the boat away then everyone is scurrying to their cars to get out of the wind. I'm soaked from the spray and chop, and Hayley is shivering. "Get changed in the back seat before we head home." She complies without a murmur, and I stand by the driver's seat, facing away while I strip off my top and yank on a long-sleeve top and track pants. For the end of October, it's cold.

"Do you like Thai?" I ask when we're in the car. "We could grab some from the restaurant here and warm it up at your place."

"Some chilli might warm us up! Can we have fish cakes?"

We grab the food and set off for Narooma. My stomach rumbles at the wafting aromas, although the chilli in the fish cakes and the spicy beef Hayley chose tickles my nostrils, making me want to sneeze. I slide a glance at Hayley. "How was that? Honestly."

"Tough." She grimaces. "My arms ache now. But I'm impressed. They're all strong, even the ones not in the regional team. How come you don't paddle with them all the time?"

I open my mouth then shut it, and think for a minute. "I've considered it, but it's an hour's drive return." Drumming my fingers on the wheel, I add, "Also, this is a bigger, stronger club, more sweeps and coaches, and I feel the Narooma club needs me more. I have the best of both worlds, I can paddle, sweep and coach at home, but I'm welcome up here any time and can join any combined teams." I hesitate a beat. "I enjoy our home club. I've come off an entire childhood of intense training and competing."

"In China?" Hayley twists so she can study my face.

Digging deep, I gather some courage. Time to reveal more. "Yes. Father and Ethan are elite, national level paddlers too, I might have mentioned that. What I didn't say is that Father pitted Ethan and me against each other constantly. For a while, Ethan and I loathed each other." I glance across; she's listening intently. "Then we came to understand that it was more about him than us, and we made our peace with each other. Although every now and then … old habits die hard."

"Such as in this business plan," says Hayley softly. "Oh wow."

"As the oldest son, there is a mass of expectation on me, and Ethan remains fiercely competitive. We love each other, but if he can outdo me, he will. He's as ambitious as Father."

"And you are not ... your dreams are different," Hayley says slowly. "I see now why this is so difficult. But Ethan will work with you?"

"Yes, he's sending the contract, as you suggested, Miss FBI. We decided he will tell Father I have agreed, and let me know what the reaction is." Hayley opens and closes her mouth. "What?"

"Can I ask ... how does your mother fit into all this?"

"Good question. The business empire is Father's realm. Mother manages the home, the social life and keeps the family ties and connections going in China, even though we are here, in Australia." *Manages the home ... and relationships.* My heart hammers at my breastbone. If I want to be with Hayley, *Mother* is the key! I should have seen it before, was too hung up on dodging Father's noose.

"Justin? Whatever the Chinese equivalent of the FBI is, I can see your neurons working so hard I worry you can't drive at the same time."

I shake my head. Nope, can't go there yet. Not without some gleam of hope to offer her. How can I approach Mother? I'll only get one shot at it. Better get it right. "Sorry, must be hungry, think I spaced out for a second." Hayley bestows the disillusioned look I deserve.

A few minutes later, I pull into the parking spaces outside her apartment.

Instead of getting out, Hayley turns to me, fiddling her fingers in her lap. She takes a rushed breath. "Will you stay tonight? And hold me, like you did last time?" The lost look drifts onto her face.

Difficult to speak above my pulse thundering in my ears. "I'd love to. Let me duck home to shower and get work clothes for tomorrow."

She smiles shyly. "I'll get dinner ready. Thanks, Tiger." She grabs her gear and the bag of takeaway.

I watch her race into the apartment entry. Not sure what's going on, but I'm paddling with it.

CHAPTER TWENTY-FIVE
Moving Deeper

I tip the food into bowls and put them in the oven, then shower quickly. Drying off, I find myself reaching for my pyjamas and hesitate. What will Justin think if I'm in my pyjamas? Does it matter, really? I've already asked him to stay, I'm exhausted and this will save getting changed again. Hurrying, I set the table then head to the balcony. Would be good to get my Tai Chi in, although knowing Justin he's in race-mode to get here.

The wind is easing and a bright crescent moon is rising, casting mystical silvery light on the water. I focus on my moves, inhaling deeply to help shift the lactates. My left armpit feels tight. A warning. I sweep down to brush earth and sweep my arms up to peer at the moon. I don't want to wear the pressure stocking but if I do these harder sessions I might have to. Damn.

I move onto 'gathering clouds and dreams', arms in a cradle position and swinging my torso from right to left, ouch my ribs hurt! That backwards-forwards drill has taken a toll. I think of the look on Justin's face when I asked about his mother. Sadness pangs in my chest. He closed down on me, right when he was being more open. I breathe deeply. *Relax, Hayles, you're getting there.* We both have a lot to think about. To work through. I guess the more open and honest I am with him, hopefully he'll respond in kind. I think of my conversation with Akiko. Fair enough, I have a few elephants of my own in the corner. Big African ones.

Justin knocks as I'm winding down with the final move of 'playing with water'. I open the door and his eyebrows virtually lift into his hairline and a grin erupts on his face.

"You didn't say it was a pyjama party!" Now laughing, he eases in the door and peers closely at my top. "Is that Winnie the Pooh?"

"Could be." With Tigger. My cheeks flame.

"Cute." He closes the door and puts his overnight bag near the sofa.

When I put the bowls of food on the table, he magically produces a bottle of cider.

"Thought you might need this to aid in muscle recovery." He tilts his head. "I also brought the Vitamin E oil. You deserve a massage."

Cheeks now burning, I murmur, "Sounds wonderful."

As we eat, he asks me about my new job role and what kind of projects I'm likely to work on. I prattle on, watching him sniff at the beef dish then pile some onto his rice. He takes a large mouthful and starts coughing. "Too spicy?"

Justin fans his mouth with a hand, still spluttering, and a couple of tears slide from his eyes. "What's this dish called so I don't order it again?"

Oh my God. I crack up and can't get the dish name out.

"Not that funny," says Justin, taking a swig of cider.

Between giggles, I gasp, "Crying Tiger."

"Ha ha. And the dish?"

Giggling harder, I choke out, "Name of the dish. Crying Tiger."

"You did this on purpose!" He waves a chopstick at me menacingly.

Shaking my head vigorously, I say, "No. I like chilli, but I'm guessing you don't?"

He stops waving the chopstick and uses it to nudge the beef slices to the side of his plate. "Not a huge fan."

I push the fish dish across the table. "Here. I'll finish the beef. Seems Tigresses are made of stronger stuff."

"Their stomachs are, anyway."

When he's happily eating the fish I ask, "Where do you think we should stay when we go to Melbourne?"

"Choose somewhere within walking distance of the regatta and functions," he says earnestly. "With a pool, for your recovery. A big event like this could run late and you don't want to be dealing with transport too."

"Good idea." I can see he's restraining himself from taking over and offering to book a place. Good, because I'm not going to let him do it. This is my regatta and I intend to pay for the accommodation. "Are you able to take a couple of days off work so we could stay with my dad for a night or two?"

He drops a chopstick and gapes at me. "Before or after?"

"After would be nice."

He opens up his phone calendar and his fingers fly over the keys. "Okay. I've blocked out until the Thursday after so we can come back Wednesday."

It crashes over me that, including the driving, I'll be spending six whole days with Justin. *Six days.* I put down my chopsticks to disguise my trembling fingers.

He looks up. "You alright?"

"I … this is massive."

"It's going to be awesome," he says, before running a hand through his hair and adding, "although keeping up with these survivor paddlers when they get out of the boat could be a challenge! I've heard they love to dance. And they've chosen the Marvel Stadium for their ball."

I laugh. "I'd better keep running with Akiko to strengthen my dancing legs!"

Justin stands and starts clearing the dishes. "Mu Laohu, clean teeth and report to the sofa."

"Yes, coach, sir." I head to the bathroom as ordered, and then set my aromatherapy infuser going in the bedroom with the usual sleep blend. Nerves shiver through my stomach. Am I ready for this? I peek out at the moon for inspiration. God, I want us, this, to work. Swallowing hard, I patter back to the lounge room. Justin is sitting on the coffee table, the bottle of oil beside him.

Patting the sofa, he says, "Left side up. You know the drill."

"You sure you're not too tired?" He shakes his head. "Thanks. I'll try not to fall asleep on you." He simply pats the sofa and I get into position, slipping my left arm through my sleeve so he can access my armpit and adjust the sports towel across my breasts.

Justin gently grasps my hand and wrist and stretches the left arm up straight. I wince as the armpit pulls tight. He probes down the arm with questing fingers and pauses when he finds the tight bands. "Relax," he murmurs, "I've got your arm."

Closing my eyes, I focus on the sensations as he deftly strokes up and then down the lymphatic system and the tightness eases, as if by magic. I must be the luckiest survivor alive to have my own personal physio. And one so skilled. I drift into thoughts of the regatta and being in Melbourne, revelling in the assured touch of his fingers as he loosens the muscles around the rotator cuff and up along my shoulder into the base of my neck. Divine.

I feel him lowering my arm across my chest, smell the Vitamin E oil, then his fingers are deftly working along the curved scar. Soon, he's proceeding along the straight scar, heading to my nipple.

He pauses at the lumpy spot, massaging in circles, one way then the other, then smoothing back away from the nipple, stretching the scar.

"You know, this feels softer and smaller already," he murmurs.

Hope flushes through me and I squeeze my eyes shut. *Please let him be right.* Let it be fluid. Nothing more. Then I'll be free from scans and worry for another year. A whole year. A luxury. What can Justin and I do in a year? I so want a year, no, many more years, with Justin. *Come on, Hayles, rally, fight. I can do this. Especially with such a tiger in my corner.* I jump when Justin's lips brush my ear.

"Time for bed. Do I need to carry you?"

"Tempting." Yawning, I struggle to sit up.

His broad arms around my shoulder and lower back, Justin lifts me to standing. I wriggle my arm back into the sleeve and put my arm around his waist, allowing him to guide me to the bed.

"Mmn. Smells nice in here," he says. "Lavender? I'd better set my alarm or I won't wake up." He tucks me in. "Be right back."

I hear him pottering around turning off lights, brushing his teeth, then he slides into the room in boxer shorts and a loose T-shirt. And lies down on top of the covers on the window side. "I was thinking *under* the covers, Tiger. Can't have you falling off the bed like last time!"

He wriggles under the doona and pulls me to him so my head is resting on his chest and his fingers are stroking my hair. His heartbeat reverberates into my ear, steady, powerful, calming. I feel safe, secure, wanted. I should kiss him but my limbs are floating away.

~

I wake to the steady drum of Justin's heartbeat in my ear and the delicious sensation of a warm thumb tracing my eyebrows, smoothing my forehead. I flutter my eyelashes open and my heart jolts with joy. My dream, waking with Justin's handsome face close to mine, his strong jaw, high cheekbones, dark, almond-shaped eyes below wiry, glossy raven hair. Which is all tousled and spiking up. I itch to scrub my fingers through it to see if it would all stand on end. Is it naturally stiff or does he use a gel?

Tilting my face up, I kiss his jaw, then nibble at it. He wriggles down and presses his lips on mine, faded hints of minty toothpaste with traces of fish and rice and, beneath that, the unique taste of Justin. *How can you taste a man?* my mind asks. *You just can. Get on with it.* I lean more into him, hot trembles running down my ribcage and into my stomach. Maybe lower. Still kissing me, Justin moves his hand down my cheek, neck, caresses my collarbone and, when I don't protest, fumbles lower, slips inside my top to follow the scar line and gently cup my battered left breast. His thumb traces over the nipple and I stiffen on reflex. He pauses, I can feel his question, then I breathe and subtly arch my breast into his hand.

His mouth quirks against mine, he's pleased, and he continues to explore the contour of the breast. I roll a little away from him to give him more access and he takes the opportunity to remove his hand and slide it up inside my top instead, his fingers brushing a tickling trail up my stomach to get back to my breast.

I begin my own exploration, trickling my fingers down his neck, skipping quickly over the sleeve of his top, mercifully short so I can feel the strength in his upper arm, trace the muscle contours and visualise them rippling sinuously as he paddles. In a fluid movement, Justin breaks the kiss and rips his shirt off. I giggle, wondering if he's dropped it onto the floor amid the dust I haven't got to yet. Then I focus on his torso and blink. Oh my God. He could be a super model with broad pecs and sculpted abs like that, unobscured by chest hair. Talk about a walking advertisement for dragon boating …

Swallowing, I run my hand across the flare of his pecs, then walk my fingers down the ridges of his torso, each band of muscle a mountain ridge in its own right. Justin makes a sound like a low growl and wanders his hand across to my fuller right breast. His touch is firmer on this breast, cupping the shape, then rubbing his thumb over the nipple, which immediately stands tall, craving more attention. A warm pulse sets up between the top of my legs.

He tugs at the bottom of my top and at my nod pulls it up, for a moment pinning my arms and smothering my face. I gasp and squirm when he tickles my ribs. "Not fair!" He tickles harder until I reach out blindly and pinch him.

"You tigress!" He grunts and tugs my top off, but he's grinning from ear to ear.

"You'll keep!" I try to snarl at him and he laughs.

"Payback for Crying Tiger," he murmurs, then plants butterfly kisses down my neck, his lips so feather-light I'm still squirming.

So many sensations are churning through my body I'm unsure what to do next. I opt for resuming my trajectory down the perfect ridges of his muscles until I approach his groin. Playing, I walk my fingers along the rim of his boxer shorts, tickling him back, until he's tensing, trying hard not to squirm, and a low moan escapes him. His breath flowing across my shoulder is hotter. I gently swoop my hand down to brush across his erection and he grunts again.

Next thing, Justin eases a warm, muscled leg over mine and heat rockets through me. I can feel his hard penis on my thigh. Did my clit just twitch? Is now *the moment*? My body is waking rapidly to roaring yes; my mind is shrieking warnings. What if it hurts? What if I can't? Should I warn him? I tip fully onto my back, my legs parting without instruction, and Justin slides on top of me. His hard penis is pressing against my labia, hot even through both of our pyjama bottoms. *Tell him! Tell him!* Shrieks my mind.

"Justin," I croak, tapping his shoulder.

He pushes up on his elbows to peer down at me.

I swallow, find courage. "I'm not on any contraception."

Swallow again. "Too many hormones."

His eyebrows quirk into a frown as he struggles to work out what I'm saying.

Bringing my hand up, I press my palm to his cheek. "I want this, *so* want you. Might need more time to sort through the … logistics."

"Okay then." His frown clears and he brushes his lips over mine. "How about we leave our bottoms on?"

It takes me a second, then I grin. "Genius." I press my lips on his and slip the tip of my tongue into his mouth. He needs no further encouragement and lowers himself back onto me, his mouth hard against mine and his penis pushing against me. I wriggle to give him more space, and close my eyes as he rubs rhythmically up and down. My labia and clit lap up his strokes, waves of pleasure building. I arch up a little and Justin moves so the head of his cock is pressing against my clit. Surprisingly, the soft material between us makes this even more arousing.

Growing bolder, I sneak a hand down and wrap it around his shaft, further aroused by his growled, "Hayley." He breaks the kiss, probably a good thing so we can breathe, and nuzzles his lips into the side of my neck. I wrap my other arm around his lower back, feeling the steely power in the movement of his muscles. Oh God.

I can feel a slick patch forming in my pyjamas and my clit is starting to spasm. I grab his lower back harder and arch up against the nub of his cock. It presses just the right spot and pleasure shudders through me in a massive release. Immediately, Justin goes rigid then twitches and groans as he comes. He kisses my neck, then rolls to the side and pulls me onto his chest again. His heartbeat is hammering in my ear.

For several moments we lie there, legs intertwined, comfortable. My heartrate begins to lower, my muscles languid. That was unexpectedly sexy and satisfying. Definitely repeatable.

A horn blasts into the peace. And again.

"Crap!" Justin fumbles under the pillow to grab his phone and turn the alarm off. Rolling back to me, he nudges wisps of hair away from my cheek. "That was … nice."

I arch an eyebrow at him. "*Nice*?"

"Okay, better than nice … surprising. Delightful?"

"Getting there, Tiger." I hesitate but now is as good a moment as any. "There's more I need to tell you about my treatment and how it affects … this side of things."

"Okay." He focuses on my eyes. "Will it wear off?"

Shrugging, I say, "Not sure, much of it hopefully, it's only been a year." I smooth my finger across his faint frown. "There's more I can do to help it along; I just haven't needed to. Until now."

"Okay then." He kisses my finger. "Don't stress, Hayley. We'll work it out." A shiver runs down his arm. "I'm a bit damp … can I use your shower?"

At my nod, he kisses me again then slides out of the bed. Rolling onto my side I stare out the window at the sky. High wispy clouds are scudding by. I watch their uneven shapes stretching and disappearing into a general kind of bleak layer, my elation dissipating with them. How okay is Justin with all my issues? He always says it's fine on the surface, rallies to be supportive.

But what does he truly think and feel?

CHAPTER TWENTY-SIX

Sparks

The alarm blares into my dreams at 4 am. Jumping out of bed, I eye the pitch darkness outside. Simply crazy to drive up on the morning of a regatta. How did I get talked into this? Showering rapidly, I think about the drive up with Justin, Natalie and Sandi. I feel like I'm in the VIP car! If it's too much, I'll go up the day ahead next time. I throw on my uniform and layers above, grab my container of fruit and nuts from the fridge, make a thermos of coffee, grab all my gear and pelt downstairs.

My breath is almost misting as I hover outside, relief filling me when a large 4-wheel-drive pulls up with Sandi at the wheel. I jump in the back with Natalie. "Morning, bench buddy."

Justin turns around in the front passenger seat. "All good? Got everything?"

"Yes, coach!" I grin at him.

The drive to Canberra with buddies is pleasant and I munch on my breakfast, half-listening to Natalie telling tales about the whacky dogs she cared for this week and simultaneously trying to tune in to the strategy talk Justin and Sandi are having. Did I just hear Sandi say she wants Nat and I in row *two* for the third race? I glance at Nat, who gives me a cross-eyed stare back so I guess she heard too.

As the car winds through the bends on the Clyde Mountain everyone falls quiet, letting Sandi concentrate. First light is peeking through the dense treetops and the early birds are calling out to greet the day, forecast to be sunny with light winds. Suppressing a smile, I think of the new paddle Justin let me choose online yesterday. It's almost a pair for his superb paddle with the Hokusai wave, but the dragon is more elegant, looks female, and is a pink-orange, which will go well with the DA Canberra uniform. He's so sweet he put an express order in so I should have it in time for the Pink Paddle Power regatta.

Soon, we're piling out of the car and Sandi tosses the keys to Justin. "You lock up, I'll go find our tent."

The lake foreshore is teeming with paddlers and officials, the boats are lined up ready and most of the tents are already up. Justin smiles when he spies the grand royal-blue Delisiozo marquee, prominent in the first row, with the Clear Water Dragons banner already in place. Unable to resist, I elbow his ribs. "Wait until we go international."

He gives me a wry grin and strides towards the tent. Nat and I scurry after him. There's barely time to go to the loo, swallow some water and warm-up before the first race is marshalling. We're in heat two, and Sandi calls us into a huddle.

"Right. You know the line-up for heat two. I'm sweeping and this will be a brisk but not all-out effort as we have four heats to get through."

Everyone nods and shuffles their feet. Looking at the faces, I realise everyone is a little uncertain about the testing five-hundred metre heats.

"We'll be fine," says Justin. "This is only our second regatta as a crew. Let's put some times on the board and get a good feel for the distance."

"Heat two, marshalling!" yells the Head Marshal and we scramble to line up in our designated lane.

I jog on the spot while our names are checked off and Natalie gives me a dry look. I have to admit, the runs with Akiko are doing me good, my legs feel stronger. Five minutes later, we're in the boat and paddling down to the start.

"Eyes in this boat," reminds Elena in the drummer seat and I hastily stop peering to see who else is in this heat; no DAC colours though, but I guess they only compete in women's races.

Conditions are good, and I bury my blade ready and fix my gaze on Justin's broad back at the front, two benches ahead. Then we're off, trying to power the boat up fast then settling into a long, powerful driving stroke rate. Elena drums loudly, telling us we look fabulous. Sandi calls for a couple of lifts and I try to respond, driving deeper and harder.

"Halfway!" calls Elena. "Keep driving, looking good."

I feel my inside arm drooping and glance up at Justin, noting how he is indeed coiling up and pouncing at the water. *My tiger.* I emulate him, breathing it in and up, pouncing forward, and feel my blade truly grabbing water. A shiver of pleasure runs through me. My body is responding, regaining life.

"What the …" grunts Natalie, but she tries to copy me.

Sandi calls for three more lifts and then yells for us to bring it home, and Elena shrieks encouragement. Justin has upped the rate and we're powering towards the finish buoys. Then we're past.

Elena beams at Justin and Rose. "Wow. I think we beat two boats."

"Good job, everyone," calls Sandi. "Debrief back at the tent."

Natalie screws her eyes up at me. "You're getting stronger. Maybe this distance suits you. Me, I'm stuffed!"

Feeling a twinge of guilt, I pat her arm. "We're a good bench, you and me."

She huffs, but looks pleased.

Soon, we're gathered back at the tent. The team looks happy: Giulio and Gianni are clowning around as usual, Andrew is muttering about whether we can have gin and tonics instead of lollipops, Greg is flexing his biceps at Mara and Chloe, making them laugh.

Sandi claps her hands. "Okay, that went very well. We're going to keep this line-up for heat five, but swap sides. Then Justin will sweep for heats eleven and fourteen." She looks at me. "When he sweeps, Natalie and Hayley will move forward to bench two, behind me and Chloe, Rose and Mara will go to bench three." Her gaze sharpens. "Hayley, keep doing whatever you were doing last race. The rest of you, watch Chloe and Hayley and try to match their power."

I slide my gaze to Justin, who gives me an imperceptible nod. Does he realise I was copying him?

Heat five goes well, although we were fifth in that heat. Sandi tells us we did almost the same time, it was just a stronger heat. The crew relaxes with snacks and drinks. There's a gap to heat eleven, so I decide it's a good time to introduce myself to the other DA Canberra paddlers. Telling Natalie what I'm doing, I go to the loo then approach the GoAnna team tent.

"Hey, Hayley!" Jeannie spies me and beckons. "Everyone, this is our new member, Hayley. She's joining us for the Pink Paddle Power regatta in Melbourne."

I'm pulled into the tent and everyone shakes my hand or grins a welcome. The paddlers rattle off their names, and I reckon I retain about half of them.

One of the sweeps, Susan, muscles in beside me. "Can you train with us at all beforehand?"

"Are you going out next weekend?" I ask, thinking that while

Justin is away at the regionals could be a good time to come up, go in to work on the Friday to see Noel and Neville about my new role, then train with DAC on the Saturday.

"Yes, that would work. We have an extra effort session early, then a standard paddle. You could do both, then join us for breakfast." Jeannie nods.

"Sounds great." I beam at her. Glancing at my watch, I realise I'd better return to my team. "I'll put my name down for those sessions and see you next weekend. Good luck for your next race." I leave with everyone waving cheerfully.

Halfway back to our tent, Sandi comes racing towards me. "Where's Justin?"

"Justin? I don't know."

"You're faster than most of us. Grab your gear ready and go find him. We'll be marshalling any minute." She spins around and marches away.

I stand for a few seconds. Why would Justin be missing? Unease rising, I jog to the tent to grab my paddle and gloves, listening out to hear that heat ten is marshalling. We're next. Crap! Where can he be? The others are all gathering their gear ready. I spy Justin's gloves on his seat and grab them, almost reach for his paddle then remember he's sweeping.

I start by striding briskly along the front of the tents, skimming faces to see if he's talking to another team. A few of the Moruya paddlers wave at me, but he's not with them. My mouth running dry, I run to the foreshore and start jogging along the beach, looking everywhere. My pulse is rising. Something is wrong.

I'm past all the tents and the announcers table, nearing a grassy area by the new boat shed and stop dead, blinking. On the grass are *two* Justins — arguing, by the jerky arm movements and heated voices. Crap. What to do? No choice, I have to get him. Taking a deep breath, I jog closer. Okay, the one on the right is Justin, in team uniform, but the other one, clad in jeans and a polo shirt, almost looks like his twin. My breath catches. *Ethan.* Why would his brother be here? Did Justin know he was coming? I then see a sheaf of papers in Ethan's hands. Oh no.

I jog closer. "Justin!" No response, they're too busy glaring at each other. Another few steps. "Justin! We're marshalling!"

"Why hasn't he made the changes? I'm not–" Justin breaks off his outburst as he becomes aware of my presence and stares at me.

"We're marshalling!" Finding my courage, I stride up to him and hand him his gloves. "We have to go. Now." I can feel his brother's glare burning into me.

Justin runs a hand through his hair, seemingly rooted to the spot. Reaching out, I grab his elbow. "Team's waiting." Justin tenses, and for an awful heartbeat or two I think he's going to jerk his arm away. His face looks different. Contorted. Angry. "Come on, Tiger," I murmur. "Finish this after."

Yanking his gloves on, Justin snaps at Ethan, "Meet me back here after heat fourteen. We'll finish this then." He strides away without a backward glance.

This leaves me facing Ethan. Who looks furious. I swallow.

Disdain on his face, Ethan snarls at me, "*You're* his girl? Oh God."

What the? Tipping my chin up, I glare back at him. "*You're* his brother? Oh no." Spinning around I stride away too, my shoulders rigid. How dare he?

"Father will skin you alive!" Ethan yells.

I walk faster, uncertain whether that was aimed at me or Justin. Then I run, joining the team in our lane just as the marshal starts ticking names off. Justin is closed down, avoiding looking at anyone. Including me. Natalie tugs my elbow and belatedly I remember we're in row two. I inhale deeply. This is going to be a hell of a race unless Justin can recover his equilibrium. What can I do?

As the team marches towards our designated boat, I jog a few steps to reach Justin's side.

"Breathe, Tiger," I murmur so low only he will hear. His stride hitches and I see his chest expand with a deep breath. "Focus. We need you." Then I drop back to wait by Nat as the back of the boat boards. Justin's steps to the back of the boat are jerky, tense, and I fix my gaze on him, willing him to look up at me. He positions the oar and glances up. I meet his eyes and nod, mouthing, "Focus." His half-smile response is reassuring.

As we paddle to the start, I breathe in, enjoying being a bench closer to the front, to the dragon's head. Natalie is muttering under her breath and I guess she's less enthused. Justin is uncharacteristically silent, until he calls instructions to position the boat as we line up. Pushing away the image of him and Ethan arguing, I tighten my hair tie. *Please let him focus. Give us back the Justin we know. And love.*

Elena leans forward while the last boat is gliding into line. "Justin is saying dig extra deep for this start. *Drive* us out of the blocks."

"Okay." Sandi rolls her shoulders. "Got that, pod one? We drive out hard and the rest will follow us."

Anticipation shivers through me. This is going to be more than a time on the board. Does he want to impress his brother?

The horn blares and with a grunt I drive my blade in and lunge it backwards, mirroring Sandi and Chloe. Holy crap! The boat surges forward. My heart pounds and exhilaration courses through me. We are racing! Elena drums loud, yelling, "Go! Go! Go!" We settle into the long, steady rate, but the rate is slightly brisker than the first two heats. I focus to keep my timing, and isolate each stroke into lift, coil, pounce, drive. Justin calls for lifts of ten strokes at what feels like every thirty strokes or so. Water is gurgling past the sides of the boat and sweat trickles down the back of my neck.

At halfway Elena tips forward. "We're up with the other boats! Keep it going! Looking *amazing*!"

Natalie kind of groans and I mutter, "Come on buddy. We got this."

"Lift for twenty!" yells Justin.

My arms start to burn and I'm glad I'm on my stronger side. The finish is going to hurt if we keep this up. *Focus, Hayles. Lift, coil, pounce, drive.*

"Timing!" yells Elena. "Leg drive, leg drive, keep it on."

"Lift for twenty!" yells Justin.

"Power! Power!" calls Elena.

The last hundred metres passes in a blur of dripping sweat, driving with my arms and legs, breathing hard, barely hearing Justin and Elena coaxing every effort out of us.

Finish horns blare close together, then Justin yells, "Let it run."

"Oh my God." Elena's voice is wobbly. "You all looked so different."

"Good job!" calls Justin, sounding like himself again.

Sandi and Chloe turn around and we all give each other a pat.

Justin turns the boat to take us back and says, "Andrew, I'll buy you that gin and tonic myself. In fact, you can all have one."

A giggle ripples down the boat. Relief washes through me, but I'd like to see Justin's face. Ask him what's going on.

Back at the tent, Justin gathers us. "Okay, then." He waves a hand at the banner. "*That* was a Clear Water Dragons' race. We were a whole thirty seconds faster than the other two heats. We were a close third in a strong heat and I'm proud of you all."

"Does it have to hurt so much?" whines Andrew.

"More training," says Justin with a grin and Andrew groans. Everyone else laughs. "Seriously, though, we'll be marshalled for heat fourteen in about five minutes."

That is met with a collective groan and Sandi frowns.

"I don't expect us to repeat that. We're not fit enough." Justin roams his gaze around the paddlers. "We can participate and go at the rate of the earlier heats, sit it out, or just give it a go. What do you want to do?"

The paddlers turn to each other, shrug and discuss whether they're too tired. I catch Justin's eye and arch an eyebrow. *You okay?* He dips his chin, his eyes asking whether I'm okay. I smile briefly. In the end, everyone decides to give it a go, but at the earlier pace.

"Thanks," says Justin. "It's better we don't withdraw, but seriously, aim for eight-five per cent effort. Plenty more races this season."

"Thanks, *good* coach," I quip and everyone laughs.

"So, we're not going international today?" queries Gianni.

"Next regatta," says Justin, smiling. "When we have our new uniforms and team paddles."

Gianni and Giulio high-five each other.

The final race feels more comfortable, although everyone is tiring, enthusiasm waning. I suspect we're slower than earlier, but hey, we finished four heats of five-hundred metres and got to experience what a hard race is like. As we disembark, I realise Sandi and Natalie and I will have to wait while Justin talks with Ethan. Will he tell them or just vanish again? At least this time I know where he'll be.

I hang back until Justin gets off the boat and hold my hand out for his damp gloves. "You going to talk to Ethan while we pack up?"

He drops the gloves into my palm. "Guess I'll have to." Meeting my eyes, he adds, "Sorry. I didn't know he was coming. Thought we'd do this next week at the regionals."

I search his face. Should I offer to go with him? "Do you need any help?"

He cracks his knuckles and sighs. "Thanks, but better I face him alone." His face brightens. "Can you come to collect me after forty minutes and say we have to go?"

"I can do that." I touch his elbow. "Good luck." He gives me a bittersweet smile and walks away on a wide trajectory, one that will take him to the grassy area and not the team tent. Heart thumping, I watch his tense back. Wish I knew what was going on now. Something to do with the contracts? Will he tell me later? Feet heavy, I trudge to the team tent to change and help pack up. It's been a long day already and we still have to drive home.

Sandi reads out our times for the four heats and everyone whoops and cheers. "So, we didn't make any finals, but we did well. Have some lunch and we'll pack up while the finals are running." She sidles up to me. "Justin?"

I swallow hard. "Something unexpected. Think it might be to do with the regionals. He'll be about forty minutes."

Sandi peers at my face. "I see." Her scepticism shines through.

With difficulty, I chat to the others and nibble my way through an egg sandwich. It occurs to me I could get Justin a drink and some lunch. Almost thirty minutes have passed. By the time I get the food it'll be time to rescue him. I stand, pick up Justin's jacket and tell Sandi and Natalie I'm going to go get Justin some lunch given he's missing out.

Ten minutes later, armed with a chai latte, a salad wrap and two slices of carrot cake, I wind my way back to the grassy area, this time walking behind the team tents so no-one will notice me. Breathing deeply, I round the corner of the new boat shed. Justin and Ethan are a bit further over, still facing off but with less heat.

I approach, realising Ethan won't see me until I'm almost on top of him. How to play this? Keep glaring at him or use my defuse strategy? The latter. "Hi!" I announce, jumping myself in response to Ethan's startled leap up and around. He scrambles to grab the sheaf of papers he almost dropped. I nod at him and walk past to hand Justin his jacket, Chai and lunch. "Here. The team's packing up now."

Justin's mouth is open like a goldfish as he takes everything from me. I look into his eyes and give him an impish smile. Then I put the second slice of carrot cake in one hand, turn around and step up to Ethan with my other hand out.

"Hi. I'm Hayley. Do you prefer to be called Ethan or Yichen?" His eyes widen and his eyebrow quirks so reminiscent of Justin that my smile warms of its own accord. "I brought you some cake, sorry, didn't know what you like to drink." Behind me, Justin makes a choking sound.

Ethan limply takes my hand and I shake it firmly, release before he does, and hand him the cake with another sweet smile. He kind of shakes himself and I sense that he is now actually seeing me properly. He looks totally floored. I take a few steps back and wait to see who will do what next. Ethan is staring at me as if I'm an alien species and Justin's lips are pressed tight, perhaps trying not to laugh.

"Thanks, Hayley." Justin lifts the food at me, then looks at Ethan. "Are we almost done? Just that change and I'll sign next week. Promise. And I'll stay the night after so we can all talk." He tilts his head. "Thanks for coming down, and for all your help."

Ethan's expression softens, but his gaze slides to me, concern and curiosity rising on his face. He looks as if he's trying to decide what to say.

Justin thrusts his drink and food at me to hold, then grasps Ethan in a bear hug. I struggle to hear his mumbled, "Don't say anything. She's your path to Li Na. Let it go. We'll talk." He steps back and says to me, "Did you say we're packing up?" Turning back to Ethan, he says, "I'd better go. We came in a shared car." He grins. "See you next week and may the best regional team win."

Ethan gives him an indecipherable look. "In our wake, Bro, in our wake. Okay, see you next week. Call me before." He nods at me, then walks away towards the car park, his posture and stride so like Justin's. I notice he is a little stockier.

Justin is watching him go. I should give him a hug but my hands are full of his lunch. He shrugs his jacket on and I sense him taking a moment before he faces me.

Approaching, he takes my face in his hands and kisses my forehead, mumbling, "Thanks."

"Want to give me the highlights?" I ask, juggling his lunch so he doesn't squash it.

He puts his hands on my shoulders. "Ethan thought it would be good to get the contracts out of the way so we could just race and talk as family next weekend." He frowns. "But Father hadn't made the *one* change I asked for, and Ethan hadn't noticed, so I refused to sign." He kisses my forehead again. "Details later, but I took your comments about this being a business negotiation to heart."

I smile. "Good job, Tiger. Now eat." As he takes his lunch back, I add, "I told Sandi you were at a regional team meeting."

He stares at me, and croaks, "Genius. *More* thanks." His lips crimp in a suppressed grin. "I can't believe you gave Ethan cake!"

I give him my best wide-eyed, sweetest innocent smile. "Seemed like the best thing to do."

His eyebrow arches and shock fleets over his face as he understands I did it on purpose. I decide not to tell him that Ethan was rude to me. Nor Ethan's comment about his father 'skinning you alive'. Whichever of us the 'you' refers to.

We walk back to the tent, Justin virtually inhaling his wrap and drink on the way. I study his face and posture. What did he prevent Ethan from saying? What the hell does 'She's your path to Leena? Lima?' mean? Contracts and imperious family aside, there's something else going on that I don't understand. Some deep undercurrent. A wave of fatigue sweeps down my arms and legs, followed by a subtle nausea.

I so need my spa bath and some time out.

CHAPTER TWENTY-SEVEN
Region us Region

In almost no time, I'm packing to go to the NSW regional regatta in Penrith. I pause from folding clothes. Although I explained to Hayley that I would've invited her to go with me except it was a bit soon for her to meet my family, and I wanted to have the contract matters sorted, the churning in my gut tells me that didn't go over well. She smiled and said she was going to take the opportunity to go to Canberra to see her work boss and have a paddle with DAC. But her gorgeous smile somehow didn't quite reach her eyes.

Since she met Ethan two weeks ago, she's been bright and bubbly, trained hard, but it feels like a subtle distance has developed between us. I can't put my finger on it. At times I catch her studying my face, an indecipherable expression on hers, like she's trying to decide whether to say something. But she doesn't.

Although she disarmed Ethan with a piece of cake, did she perceive his dismay on meeting her? Did he say something to her that I didn't hear? Or did she just read his vibes? I scrub my face with my hands. God, I wish I knew. I feel like I'm losing her. Bad enough worrying about losing her due to her health, but possibly losing her due to something I've done, or *haven't* done, is unbearable. My chest snaps so tight I can barely breathe, and I walk a lap of my bedroom, forcing air in. Maybe what Ethan says about meeting her will shed some light on it. Man, I wish I wasn't going to be away from her for nearly four days.

Better get a move on, I'm due to collect Grant in Moruya in forty minutes to give him a lift to Penrith. The company will be welcome. I collect him on time and we continue north. Grant chatters away, excited about being in the team, even though it's his third time. We agree the tryouts were harder this year, the competition tougher. The traffic is slow heading into Penrith but we make it in time to join the team dinner. Everyone is in good spirits while Em confirms the line-up for each race and tells us with a smile that the weather Gods are inclined to be favourable. We all toast to that.

Back in the shared room, I lie staring at the ceiling. Grant is already snoring lightly, but I can't shut my mind down. Ethan rang to tell me Father has made the contract change — no apology for not doing it the first time — he's accepted my request for a higher daily rate given that I still have the outlays for my physio practice but won't have the income while I'm in Hong Kong. Shame I had to push the point, but I'm amazed Father actually gave in. We should be ready to sign on Sunday. Part of me is pleased I'm doing something for the family; another part frets about where this might lead. I need a positive way back into the family if I want to even mention Hayley's existence, let alone my intentions — I just hope this one is big enough. My mind shies away from contemplating options if it isn't.

It feels as if I haven't slept at all when the alarm goes off, and Grant and I are bolting down toast and a cup of coffee. A short drive to the venue, which is already chaotic with marshals and paddlers everywhere — even six teams generates a lot of activity, and we have numerous heats over various distances to get through. A pleasing number of spectators are gathering along the shore, and there's a row of dragon boat gear stalls plus coffee and food vans.

Em greets us, her eyes bright as a bird's and her movements quick and fluttery. "Strong teams. This is going to be close racing so listen up."

We huddle around her while she rattles off a few additional instructions. In particular, she wants strong, snappy starts to position us to keep up.

"Word is that the team to beat this year is Sydney Metro. Their coach has been pushing them hard." She fixes her eyes on me. "His surname is Zhao too. Any relation?"

"My father." I keep my voice level. "My brother is in that boat too."

Everyone stares at me while Em's mouth drops open. "You never said. Your whole family paddles?"

Uncomfortable, I nod, then figure I might as well be more open. "Father was a national champion in China, before we moved here." Thinking of the information Ethan let slip in our chats I find a grin forming. "His strategy will be a strong, fast start followed by frequent lifts of twenty long, hard then twenty power, especially in the 1,000-metre races."

Em's brows lift. "So, we emulate their boat?"

"Worth a go. We have a strong team too."

Excitement buzzes through the team and Grant claps me on the shoulder. "If this works we'll start calling you 007."

A minute later we're doing a rigorous on-land warm-up, then hurrying to marshal for the first 1,000-metre race. We're in luck, Father's team is in the same heat, two lanes over from us. Em gives me an imperceptible dip of her head.

Tension quivers through me as we wait poised for the hooter. This is a good team, six Auroras and as many state team reps. If we can give Father a run for his money... he's so accustomed to winning. I flex my fingers one last time and breathe in until my ribs creak. The hooter blares and the crew plunge their blades in deep, pulling water hard. It's a super start. I focus, *lift, coil, pounce, drive. Again.* The boat is skimming the water, water gurgling beside the prow and down the sides. Every stroke, our blades are leaving a trail of massive silver-white bubbles. We're moving fast and smooth. Em calls for the first lift and I drive harder. Our timing is great, there's a solid air of determination in the boat. Lift follows lift, and our form doesn't falter: it's one of those races where the universe is aligned, the dragon in the boat sings and we fly the water.

"Bring it home now!" yells Em and we're all driving, driving, from what feels like a long way out.

The hooter blares once, twice, almost simultaneously. A short gap, then four more hoots. Heaving in breaths, I sit up and flex my almost-cramping fingers. Did we do it? I'm sure we were first or second. The two Aurora strokes high-five each other and my pulse skitters.

"Three cheers for the other boats," calls Em. Followed by, "Three cheers for us. Awesome job, team."

Back at the pontoon, we disembark. As I walk along the platform, I become aware that two Sydney paddlers are standing up ahead, a little to one side. Father. Ethan. I swallow. Are they waiting for me? I square my shoulders and put a spring in my stride.

"Jun Jie." Father nods at me. "Good race."

"Father." I half-bow. "Your team too." I smile at Ethan, then hover. Do they wish to say more? I imagine Hayley nudging my elbow, saying *Take the lead, Tiger.* I meet Father's eyes. "Thank you for making the contract change. I'm happy now."

His eyes glitter with what could be interpreted as respect. "Good. We sign tomorrow." I earn a rare half-smile. "Rest assured, your team will be in our wake next race."

My heart skips several beats. We *did* pip them to the line!

"Only if you work for it," I quip, punching Ethan's shoulder lightly.

They move away, leaving me standing there for a few breaths. So unexpected. Yet welcome. A paddler jostles me and I apologise for being in the way and head for my team tent. I almost wish we could go home now and rest on this victory.

The day passes in a blur of racing. The win in the first heat inspires the team and our performance is solid all day, no matter the distance. Despite the effort, the paddlers find the energy to banter and joke. We pipped Father's boat once more, and dogged his boat's tail every other heat we raced against each other. Overall, Sydney Metro win the region vs region championship again, but we're an impressive second. Em is thrilled and insists we all go for a drink before dispersing. I regretfully decline, saying I'm going to my family's house for dinner.

"Shame," says Em. "Maybe we'll go for a drink after training next Tuesday. You'll still come?"

"I expect so. Thanks so much for today. One of the best region vs region comps I've been to."

"It was a good day," Em agrees. "Take care, and see you Tuesday."

Grant gives me a broad grin as I gather up my gear and I leave the tent amid much back-clapping and cheerful farewells. My gear stowed in my car, I sit in the driver seat and take a breath as I pull out my phone. No word from Hayley. Disappointed, I consider. Should I text or call? Be brave. I press the dial sign.

She answers on the third ring. "Hey, Tiger. Did you win?"

"Almost. A close second on combined points for the day."

"So, the silver medals?"

"Yep. It was a good day, hard races. Father's team won, so I'm about to eat humble pie at his house for dinner."

Hayley laughs. "Damn."

"How about you? How was your meeting at work?"

"Good. I've got my first evaluation report to review and we seem to be thinking along the same lines about what's required. Must be recovering, I'm looking forward to working on it. Just imagine."

I smile, even though she can't see it. "That's great. Did you paddle too?"

"Did I paddle! Two-and-a-half hours, all up. The DAC commands are a bit different so it was good to get used to that. Who'd have thought 'easy' means 'stop'? And their race start is seven-seven-seven rather than five-ten-ten. Took me three goes to get that right."

Warmth spreads through my chest; she sounds so happy.

"They seem impressed with my technique and timing, so thanks, best-ever coach. Looks like I'll be in rows two and three for the regatta in Melbourne, even as a newbie. I can't believe it."

"Awesome, Hayley, and well-deserved. You've worked hard." I hesitate. "I miss you."

"Aww, Tiger." She sounds as if she's smiling but I wish I could see her face.

I wait, but she doesn't say she misses me too. My fingers grip the phone. "Hayley …" I choke. What do I need to say? I hope to have good news when I see her, but I can't promise this. "I'm trying," I croak out. "Give me a little more time." My heart gives several agonising beats before she responds.

"I know, Justin." She takes a deep breath. "My glimpse of Ethan showed me the challenge you're facing. I trust you; I know you'll do your best to find a way to make things work. And I miss you, too. When are you back?"

"Probably late Sunday." I reflect. I've been very good at inviting myself to her place, maybe it's time to share more of my life with her. "How about dinner at my place on Monday?"

"Sounds good." She sounds surprised. "Number 22, right?"

"You remembered! Maybe bring those delightful Winnie the Pooh pyjamas…"

"Okay." I can tell she's smiling.

We hang up and I realise my fingers are shaking from holding the phone so tight. I think we're good, but I'm right, something about meeting Ethan rattled her. It wasn't the best scenario, that's for sure. She's not going to be wildly enthusiastic about meeting my family, even if I can arrange it. Okay, then. One step at a time. Sign contract, listen to Father gloat about winning the regatta, talk to Ethan, talk to Mother. I start the car. Let's do this.

~

An hour later, I park in the side lane at the family house. Ethan's Lexus is here, and I release a breath upon seeing no other cars. I half-expected to find Father's cousin and three daughters still here. I've barely opened the boot before Ethan is clapping my shoulder and grabbing my bag.

"Hurry up. Father is keen to celebrate."

I half-jog after him, presuming I'm allowed time for a shower. Mother waves as I pass the kitchen door, and Father steps out of the lounge room.

"Jun Jie. Good racing today."

I bow. "Congratulations. We tried hard."

Father's eyes light up and I wonder whether he's already sampling the rice wine. He's in an uncommonly good mood.

"I'll clean up and be right down." I race up the stairs. As the hot water runs over me, I feel a curious thrill. The vibe is different, almost pleasant … me signing this contract must mean far more to Father than I guessed. Negotiating a clause, and today's racing … maybe this is what he's wanted from me. To stand tall, challenge him, rather than run away. Oh man. Okay, then. I have some standing taller to do yet.

I jog back down the stairs and Ethan beckons me into the lounge room. The contracts are on the coffee table, with glasses of rice wine ready for a toast. I slide onto my chair, then pick up my contract and turn to the pertinent clause. Okay, the daily rate for the trip now reads $1,800 instead of $1,200. I turn the page and check the other trip conditions to make sure Father hasn't subtly introduced an offset, but no, my airfares and accommodation are covered, the meal allowance remains $150 a day and the commission on sales remains at 10 per cent.

I look up to find Father scrutinising me. "Okay. I'm happy." For the next few minutes, the three of us are busy signing and counter-signing each other's contracts. I don't read Ethan's, which is obviously different to mine as he is the sales manager, I just witness their signatures. Father's lawyer will stamp them officially.

Father gathers up the documents and slips them into a briefcase I hadn't noticed nestled against his chair leg. He lifts his glass. "Jun Jie, Yichen, my sons. I am proud to have you work with me in this enterprise."

My throat swells; he sounds like he truly means it. We down our glasses of wine and, for once, I revel in the liquid searing down my throat. This is a big moment, and even Ethan looks choked up. "When do you envisage the demonstration trip?" I ask, kicking myself for not asking earlier. Then it hits me that the lack of logistical discussions must mean they really weren't confident I'd sign. I put my glass back on the table before my fingers start to tremble.

Father gives me a pleased nod. "Second or third week in February would be ideal as that is a lighter racing month. January is too busy, and Ethan will need time to plan."

"Okay. I can do that."

Both of their mouths part in surprise that I agree so readily.

"If the demonstrations go well," says Ethan, leaning forward, enthused now I'm fully on board, "the trip to hand over the products and train the grooms is likely to be late March." He sits back. "Although we'll start to build stock now."

"Okay," I say again. "Just give me as much notice as possible so I can arrange my physio schedule."

Mother sweeps into the room, wearing her favourite crimson Qipao dress, and refills our glasses. "Dinner is ready."

I jump up. "Let me help carry dishes." I follow her to the kitchen inhaling the lotus flower perfume that drifts behind her, and smile widely when she hands me a dish of ginger fish to carry. She's also done baked duck with lychee, another of my favourites. I feel humble that the family is going to so much effort.

Dinner is the most relaxed I remember for a long time. Father insists on reliving every single race of the day, the telling becoming more elaborate with each post-race toast. I only half-empty my glass each time. Everything is going so well; I can't afford to slip up now and say anything I'll regret later.

During dessert, Mother puts a hand on my arm and says softly, "Will you have time to help me with something in the teahouse before you go tomorrow?"

"Of course." I smile at her. My heart thuds at the way Ethan buries his nose in his glass, confirming this is the arranged special opportunity for me to talk to Mother alone.

The conversation drifts back to the logistics for the trip. Ethan is quivering with suppressed excitement and I study his animated face. This is the big opportunity he's been waiting for: to impress Father and prove he is worthy as his successor. Momentarily, I feel sad. Has he even considered doing anything else? But if this is what he wants … I'll help him achieve it.

By 10 o'clock the day is catching up with all of us. Ethan leaves, apparently still able to drive after so many toasts. Luckily, he lives only a few streets away. I help Mother clear the dishes, kiss her cheek and head up to bed. Lying on my back, I try to summarise what I need to say to Mother about Hayley, but my mind is too tired to focus and drifts to dreaming about holding Hayley tight in my arms at my house.

~

I wake early, slip downstairs and head out for a run. It is a glorious morning, dew sparkling on the grass and sunshine glinting on the harbour water. My back and arms are stiff from the exertion of the regatta, and I stop for a while at a small park to do some stretching. Invigorated, I head for home. As I slip off my shoes in the hallway, my nostrils twitch and my mouth waters. Pancakes? I call "Good morning" as I pass the kitchen and race upstairs to shower and change, my stomach rumbling.

When I enter the kitchen, Mother hands me a tray with two plates of pancakes drizzled with lemon and honey, a pot of tea and cups. "We'll take these to the teahouse. I have a new Bonsai to show you."

The house is quiet. "Where's Father?"

Mother bestows a gentle smile on me. "I suggested a round of golf would help shift the effects of too many toasts of wine. Ethan will be by later."

I slip on the sandals ready at the back porch and follow Mother down the shady, winding path to the ornate cedarwood teahouse in the bottom corner of the garden. I carry the tray over the small wooden bridge carefully, observing the running stream and the healthy-looking Koi. The wind chimes murmur as I step onto the polished floorboards and slip off the sandals. Mother sinks into her usual chair, facing back up the garden, and I place the tray in the centre of the low table and put a plate in front of her. I know better than to pour the tea, though. Taking my plate, I sit in my chair and wait while she pours fragrant Jasmine tea.

My stomach instantly goes from wanting to bolt down the pancakes to churning. Where do I start? "Mother–"

She holds up a palm. "Jun. Take tea. Centre yourself."

Chastised, I savour my pancakes and tea, relaxing to the burbling of the water and the melodic wind chimes. Several vividly coloured Koi approach the side of the teahouse, silently begging for food.

Mother shakes her head. "Greedy fish. They will outgrow the pond."

Once we've finished eating, I stack everything back on the tray and wait.

Mother stands and goes to a high bench at the rear of the teahouse. "This is my latest piece. Can you help me move it to the centre, where the light is better, and hold it while I trim the tree?"

The long, oval ceramic pot is heavy and, between us, we shuffle it to the centre. Taking a step back, I admire the work. The Bonsai landscape rises from a small pond at the lower narrow end to a rocky beach, then a mossy slope leading up to an elaborate and colourful Japanese Maple. Mother has artfully placed tiny white pebbles in a narrow, winding path, edged with miniature violets, and under the weeping boughs of the tree is a tiny stone bench with a wizened Chinese sage reading a book.

"This is stunning, Mother. So peaceful."

She gives me a gracious smile and picks up her small clippers. "Now hold the base steady while I trim the branch ends."

I grasp the pot firmly at both ends, understanding this is my time to speak. My chest swirling with sadness and guilt, I say, "I am sorry. I have let you down as oldest son."

Mother's fingers briefly brush mine. "Jun, this mountain is not yours alone to carry on your shoulders. It took three of you to come to this pass."

I study her face, but she is intent on clipping the end of a low-hanging branch. Snip. Her eyes meet mine. "When you were little, you shadowed Chaoxiang whenever he was at home. You worshipped each other and, as first son, you had him to yourself for four years. Then Yichen arrived, and you adored him too."

I swallow, vaguely remembering holding a swaddled Ethan when I was a toddler, and later, teaching him to build houses with bricks. And then how to ride a tricycle.

Mother's fingers brush mine again. "You were a great help to me. I was unwell after his birth and you held and played with Yichen for hours. You taught him so many things." She smiles sadly. "He idolised you, his older brother."

I wait patiently while she studies and snips three more branch ends.

"Then Yichen became old enough to compete with you. Chaoxiang was thrilled; two talented, fierce sons to coax to greatness. He pitted you against each other, making you strive for his affection and praise." She shakes her head slowly, her pinned hair glistening in the dappled light. "I tried to deflect him from this path, but your father did not become the successful man he is without indomitable drive and determination."

My throat tight, I fix my eyes on her face, absorbing each nuance of her expression and words. Is she blaming Father for the rift?

"For years, you and Yichen outran, out-studied and out-paddled each other." Her eyes grow misty. "I saw the moment you changed, Jun. You were fourteen, and I think you realised the competition would cost you Yichen's love. You cleverly tried less, letting him win Junior Paddler of the Year."

I swallow hard. Did I let him win, or did he beat me? I recall Ethan celebrating, and how proud Father was of him. I remember going to my room early, wanting to be by myself.

"You became closed, more self-contained." Mother's words drift into my ears. "Then, a year later, our visas came through and the dynamic was dispersed when we had to focus as a family on establishing ourselves in Australia."

I nod, thinking back to how terrified I was of starting anew in a strange country but also the feeling of relief that things would be different. Except they soon weren't. A bitter taste creeps into my mouth. "I don't seem to be able to please him." I bite back 'but Ethan does'. The competition remains in play. Despite my efforts.

Mother scrutinises a branch as if she hasn't heard me, and my heart thuds dully in my chest. This conversation is not proceeding at all as I anticipated. Finally, she makes an imperceptible snip, puts down the clippers and gestures to the chairs. She leans towards me, and in the rising sunlight I notice the wisps of grey beginning at her temples, the extra lines of wrinkles around her eyes. The subtly drawn look to her face.

"Jun, you are our oldest son and we both love you. He was so proud of how you paddled yesterday, thrilled that it was your team to challenge his so admirably." She gives a wistful smile. "He saw how happy you were with your strong South Coast team and how much they respect you."

She reaches up to adjust the jade pin in her hair, and I understand she is not finished speaking. I study her face; she remains beautiful, even in age. My chest throbs. Is Father really proud of me?

"Although we are not old-old, we are not young any longer and your father begins to plan his succession. Chaoxiang is traditional, you know that, and he would hand his empire to you as oldest son. Except you seem not to want it." I squirm and she flaps a hand to silence me. "He wants you to go to Hong Kong, work in the business briefly, and be sure that you do not want it."

My chest grows so tight white stars swirl before my eyes. I have so misunderstood what was happening. Blinking fast, I realise she is still speaking.

"Yichen senses this and is desperate to prove himself. You and Yichen are clearly brothers, with many admirable qualities, yet you are different. You have a softer, more measured side, whereas Yichen's ambition has been finely honed and he can be … impetuous."

Now I am staring at Mother's face so hard I am not blinking at all. Where is she going with this?

Mother smiles. "Yichen will, of course, have highly trained advisers, but if you truly do not want the empire, Chaoxiang's wish is that you remain loyal brothers and Yichen can come to you if he needs to."

I pinch the bridge of my nose to block my tears. This is so unexpected. The family understands and will honour my wishes. "Of course," I finally say. "He is my best brother. I will always help him." I flap my hand, uncertain what to say next, and eventually croak, "I remain sorry for the heartache I have caused." I bow low in my chair, guilt roaring that I put Mother through this. A shudder travels through me. If Hayley hadn't encouraged me to ask questions … to clarify … I'd have just run, remained closed, and we would not be having this conversation.

"Mother, you are right. I have been closed, determined to build walls around my life. I see this now." I give her a tentative smile. "There is someone new in my life who has also helped me to see this."

"Yichen implied as much," murmurs Mother. "Tell me."

I describe meeting Hayley and persuading her to get in the dragon boat, speak of her resilience, how hard she trains and how smart she is. Pausing, I take a deep breath. "But she is not Chinese." I stop short of adding, 'another source of argument'.

One of Mother's eyebrows arches elegantly. "Chaoxiang will be less than enthused. He hoped Meng Yao or Xin Yi would appeal." For a moment she regards me steadfastly. "You believe she is the one?" When I nod, she says, "And Yichen will choose Li Na."

"Will you and Father at least meet her? See for yourselves?"

Another long minute passes. I clasp my hands together,

resisting the intense urge to crack my knuckles. *Please let her agree. Please let her agree. Let Hayley speak for herself.* My mouth runs dry. I haven't mentioned the breast cancer. Should I? No, this does not define Hayley. Leave it to her to decide if she gets the chance. In the background, I hear a car door slam. Either Father or Ethan is here. We're out of time.

Mother sits taller and gives me a smile, although her eyes reflect worry. "I will propose that you bring Hai-lee — is that how you pronounce it? — to our New Year's Eve dinner and celebrations. I will suggest Yichen invite Li Na."

Relief rages through me and I bow, stammering, "Mother, that's wonderful, thank you." I bow again. "Thank you for explaining ... everything." I feel her fingers brush mine, inhale her perfume.

"I will confer with Chaoxiang and confirm." She stands and smooths her dress, her expression softening. "Then it will be up to you, Jun."

In the background another car door slams and I hear Father yelling something to Ethan. Mother pulls open the drawer to the low table and passes me a small cloth pouch.

"Would you mind feeding the Koi for me?" Then she slides into her sandals and I watch her composed form retreat to the house.

My fingers tremble as I tug open the string to the pouch. I'm exhausted and it's not even mid-morning. Inhaling to centre myself, I pinch out some fish flakes and drop them into the water, watching the Koi churn and squabble to get their share. Is this how Ethan and I have been? Pushing and shoving each other unless I'm absent? *Not your mountain to carry alone ...* Mother's opening words drift into my mind.

I take a few steps along the tea house to sprinkle the next flakes further apart and admire the sleek shapes of the fish as they separate and glide to snatch a flake. I watch a symmetrically marked red-and-white fish nibble at a flake, so different to the gold-and-black one nearby. Apart, their elegance and colours stand out. Will this be Ethan and I once our paths are defined? Our individuality evident? Okay, maybe I won't ask him what happened when he saw Hayley at the regatta. Let it lie. Hope rises. After these Hong Kong trips, the empire will be decided. No more vying and squabbling. And I will be part of my family.

With Hayley by my side, if the dragons will smile on me one more time.

CHAPTER TWENTY-EIGHT
Justin's House

It seems like forever since I saw Justin. He texted late to say he was home safe, and to confirm dinner at his house tonight. Taking my breakfast out to the balcony, I wonder whether his visit to his family went well, or will he be troubled and upset? I absently devour my fruit and yoghurt, staring at the swell of waves passing through the channel of the Bar. It feels like we're going forward, and then I become less certain. I did not take to Ethan, nor he to me, and I suspect Justin's father is even more severe. What a mess. And we still have my follow-up checks to get through.

I'm sure Justin's massage machine is helping — in more ways than he knows about — and the Vitamin E oil massages are not only divine but do seem to be breaking up the scar tissue. On a good day, I'm optimistic the shadow will be reduced, or even gone. I took Akiko's advice and went to the chemist to get some vaginal moisturiser with no hormones in to use daily, and also purchased some spermicide foam. Not foolproof, but usable and better than nothing. I hope. Surely, no periods means my body isn't recovered enough yet? I feel sad; here's me desperately wanting to not get pregnant, possibly ever, and Akiko dreaming about nothing else. Although she says she and Kraig are at least talking it through now.

Breakfast done, I drift back inside and fire up my laptop. I'll do a solid morning on the report Noel sent me, take a break to go to the pool, then put more hours in until it's time to go to Justin's. Opening the evaluation report, I check the topic, the structure, and who the project writer is. She's from a different branch, not someone I've met.

I read through the first ten pages and pause. I can see why Neville and Noel wanted someone else to review this first. Technically, the report is grammatically well written, but the lines of reasoning are not always logical, and I had to read a few paragraphs two or three times and still wasn't sure what the writer intended to say. Too many ideas crammed together and the relationship between them not spelled out. There are other sections where the discussion seems to stop short of clarifying the real-world meaning of the evaluation finding and how it could be addressed.

I read through the rest without marking anything, then Google search 'Best practice evaluation report'. A raft of useful guidelines pops up and I download several and read through them, compiling my own checklist of the top twenty pointers. Now I feel well-enough armed to provide comments and suggestions, and start my second, slower pass.

I break at lunchtime to go and swim 1500 metres, then return to the report. When my eyes become dry and blurry and I feel the onset of a headache, I look up and am surprised to see it is raining, and it's five o'clock. I'm only halfway through the detailed pass, and it's been a solid day. I had no idea reviewing reports and briefs could be so time consuming and required such focus.

My phone pings with a text from Justin: *Raining. Will collect you 6.30 as no parking here.* I text back thanks and close down the report and my laptop. After completing my Tai Chi and stretching,

I change into my favourite top and trousers and pack my overnight bag. What will his house be like? Spartan or homely? I anticipate something ordered, and will it be adorned with Chinese artefacts? How much has he abandoned his other life? Nerves shiver through me: please let me like what I find.

I run through the drizzle and jump into his car. Justin gives me a nervous smile, reminding me this is a big step for him. "You going to show me your medals, Tiger?" I ask.

"Take too long." He grins and flaps a hand dismissively. "I'll show you the house instead."

"Huh. I'd like to see yesterday's medal please. Evidence, and all that."

He laughs. "Okay. You eat all your dinner, no matter how tasteless it is, and I'll show you."

He's already pulling into a narrow driveway. No wonder he doesn't have a bigger car! A bushy hedge brushes the side of the car as he eases it down into a carport. Immediately, I see his house is a weatherboard cottage with an old-fashioned porch and an old blue, wooden door with a stained-glass pane of parrots on gum leaves. He opens the car door for me and grabs my bag. I follow him up the steps and through the door.

Warmth greets me, with the aroma of a sandalwood candle and a hint of ginger and spices. "Smells nice."

Belatedly noticing he's kicked off his shoes, I slip mine off and pad along the polished floorboards after him. The hallway goes past a couple of doors and emerges into a kitchen. The yellowy downlights shine softly on a marble benchtop, more polished floor and a small, neatly set table with the candle burning in the centre.

"Dinner's nearly ready," he says. "Cider?"

"Yes, please." I move to the white sideboard that matches the table and study the array of photos. The first is a very Chinese-looking house in an ornate garden with a backdrop of distant mountains. His family house in China? The second is a close-up of the finish of a dragon boat race. All the paddlers are Chinese, clearly paddling fast and furious by the spray of bubbles and droplets coming from their paddles. I pick it up and peer closely. Is that a young Justin as the stroke in the winning boat?

Arms reach around me to take the photo from my hands, put it down and gently turn me to face him. The intensity in his eyes sends a shiver down my spine, just before he brushes his warm lips over mine, tenderly, lovingly, like our first kiss. He tastes of ginger and chai. I lean into him and he kisses me fully, his tongue running along my top lip. Oh God, there's an immediate tingle between my legs. His arms move to my lower back and press me hard against him. I wonder whether we're going to get to eat dinner; I can feel his desire rising, and matching warmth pooling in my groin.

After a few minutes, he breaks away and nuzzles my neck. "I missed you. So much."

I reach my arms up around the back of his neck. "Felt like you were gone forever." His lips quirk into a smile against my neck. "Show me house, eat dinner, show me medal, Tiger. Then show how much you missed me."

"A hard bargain," he murmurs, "but fair." Taking my hand, he tugs me back into the hallway towards the front of the house.

We turn right into a compact lounge room with a view of the rolling, verdant golf course beyond the white wooden bay windows. There's a medium-sized TV and a simple grey cloth sofa. In front of the sofa is a stunning red Chinese rug with an intricate image of two golden dragons fighting. I blink. Wow. "Love the rug. Did you bring it from China?"

"Thought you might. And yes, it was my childhood bedroom rug."

He tugs my hand again, and I glimpse wooden lattice Oriental-style lamps as we return into the corridor and cross to another room. This is a small study with a couple of bookshelves and a modest desk. More bay windows reveal a clump of trees on the golf course across the road. I pull him to the bookshelves and regard the few books: all physio textbooks and a couple of books about dragon boating. So, he doesn't read unless he wants to learn something. The highest shelf has a row of jade figurines of dragons, fish and small warriors or sages. I guess this is what I expected, simple elegance with a few items of meaning for him.

"One more room, but an important one," he says, leading me back towards the kitchen.

I swallow: the bedroom. Justin takes me into the kitchen and past the table to stand by the full-length lattice doors. The light is fading, but he opens the doors and we step out onto a sheltered, narrow but long porch running the full length of the back of the cottage. Through the misty drizzle I see a large tree with an abundance of purple flowers, a few tall, glossy dark-leaved bushes, a small square of lawn, and to the right is a neat series of large white pots standing on paving. The garden is contained by a high mist-green Colorbond fence with lattice panels along the top. I'm surprised by how private it feels.

Justin moves behind me and puts his arms around me. "A lilac tree, then those are feijoa bushes, a fig tree and my pots of salad, herbs, strawberries, dwarf blueberries and mulberries."

"Looks very ordered. How do you find time to look after it all?"

"The pots make it easier. I spend an hour or two on weekends tending to it."

Before I can reply, he puts an arm around my shoulders and draws me further along the porch to another set of lattice doors. Opening these, he tugs me into the bedroom. The walls are a pale gold above polished floorboards, there's a large futon-style bed with a pale blue quilt and at its base is another Chinese rug, this one royal blue with colourful koi swimming among white lotus leaves. More of the simple, ordered elegance.

"In the morning you'll wake to the chatter of happy birds feasting on the lilac blooms," he murmurs directly into my ear. "The bathroom is through that door on the far side of the bed."

I twist in his arms and put my arms around the back of his neck. "I like it. It's very you."

A smile lights his face and he brushes his lips over mine. "Let's eat." He closes and latches the doors and I follow him back to the kitchen and sit at the chair he indicates.

He places a long ceramic dish in the middle of the table with what looks like foiled fish and baked potato and sweet potato. My mouth waters when he unwraps barramundi coated in ginger, shallots and pepper. After filling our plates, he retrieves a large salad from the fridge. The fish melts in my mouth and I'm impressed. The whole meal is divine and healthy.

We chatter about his region vs region competition for a while, and he magically produces a silver medal from his pocket and passes it to me. I admire the carved fierce dragon on a blue ribbon. Way more interesting than a running medal. "Nice one, Tiger. Who got gold?"

He pauses his forkful of fish. "Father's team, of course. But we made him work for it."

I study his face, the faint frown that appears. *Ask him, get it out of the way.* "How was your visit? Did you sign the contract?" I wait while he chews his mouthful, puts his knife and fork down, takes a few swigs of his cider.

"I owe you a huge thank you." He reaches across the table and takes my hand, playing with my fingers. "Father was surprised and pleased that I negotiated the contract, and he was impressed by the South Coast team. His attitude to me shifted, because *you* pushed me, *you* made me clarify his intentions." He runs his free hand through his hair. "Turns out, this is what he wanted, me to challenge him, not run."

I squeeze his fingers, my eyes burning with tears and my throat tight. This is a ginormous step forward to Justin being whole.

His dark eyes latch onto mine, his expression serious. "There is more good news, but first I need to ask you something."

"Me?" A tremor of trepidation runs through me.

He watches me, apparently struggling to form his question. "When you met Ethan, at the regatta …" His throat moves in a gulp. "Something happened, didn't it?"

My spine stiffens. Damn, he's detected my anxiety since then. I nod.

"I need you to tell me. Please."

I blow out a breath and he grips my hand. Hard. "Well, first Ethan was, I guess … disdainful. He sneered '*You're* his girl? Oh my God.'" I tip my chin up. "So, I replied in kind, '*You're* his brother? Oh no.'"

Justin's lips part and his eyebrows shoot upward.

"Then, when I walked away, he yelled; 'Father will skin you alive.'" I chew my bottom lip. "It freaked me out. But he's your brother, so I tried to get past it, to defuse the incident." I look down, my voice dropping. "And then I heard you tell him not to say anything, which I guessed meant about me, and you said something about me being his path to Lima or something. I was hurt, and I didn't know what to do."

The legs of Justin's chair scrape the floorboards as he hurries around the table and pulls me up against his chest, stroking my hair. "Hayley, I'm so sorry. I wish you'd told me."

I peer up at him. "How could I? You were working so hard to try to fix things."

Justin crushes me against him, kissing my hair, my forehead, my nose, my mouth. Then he tips my chin up and stares into my eyes. "You are strong. Amazing. The 'skin alive' part was meant for me, not you. Ethan had no right. None. He was angry I wouldn't sign the contract. I can see how this has put you off him, though. He has a hard streak."

"I'm more worried about your father," I murmur without thinking. "They won't like me."

Justin's hands clasp my cheeks and he brings his face so close our noses are touching. "There is only one reason they will hesitate … you're not Chinese."

My chest snaps taut. *Shit.* I can't do anything about that. My heart is trying to bolt out of my chest. Is *this* what he's been holding back? Is he saying we can *never* work? My eyes prickle with tears.

"No, don't cry. My good news is my family have agreed to meet you, Mother is arranging it. They *know* you are Australian." He kisses my nose. "Li Na is the Chinese girl Ethan wants to marry, but traditionally I should marry first. That is why you are his path to Li Na."

I blink, trying to follow what he's saying, my mind skittering all over the place. *Wait. What?* Has he told his family he intends to *marry* me? My heart feels like it's ripping in two. What will he do if they say no? My legs are shaking; I need to sit down.

"Hayley." Justin's voice sounds as if it's coming from deep down a cave. "Hayley." He shakes me gently. "Look at me." His fingers lift my chin and I reluctantly meet his troubled almond-shaped eyes.

"You need to trust me. This will not be fast, but they know about you and will invite you to the New Year's Day celebrations at the family house. As my girlfriend. Mother is working on it." He gives me a lop-sided smile. "I will further challenge Father's traditions — you have given me the courage." He kisses my forehead. "My Mu Loahu, my Tigress. After this visit, I'm hopeful we'll find a way forward while keeping the family intact."

I stare into the deep brown pools of his eyes, take in the

planes of his handsome face, the glossy raven-black hair. My heart thuds loudly. Do I love him enough to take on this stress? Stress is not good for cancer … but I encouraged him to reconnect with his family. I briefly consider a life without Justin. Such pain rips through me I gasp.

"Can you say something?" he pleads huskily.

I lick my dry lips. "Okay. Let's try." I melt into him as his lips close over mine, the kiss full of love and passion. Next thing, he dips down, scoops my legs from under me and carries me into his bedroom.

Plonking me on the Koi rug, he grins. "You use the bathroom first. I'll be back soon. Very soon." He rushes back to the kitchen.

I take it we're going to bed. In my pyjamas, teeth clean and spermicide inserted, I slither into his bed and snuggle under the covers. The mattress is firm, how I prefer it. There are a few final clatters from the kitchen before he comes in, pulls gauzy curtains across the lattice doors, dashes into the bathroom and then emerges in his loose top and boxer shorts. He slides under the covers and reaches for me. My heart races as he pulls me close to him. Time to go the final step with him inside me, not outside.

"Comfy enough?" he asks, brushing strands of hair away from my face, leaving a trail of tingling skin in the wake of his fingers.

"Mm. Perfect." I run my fingers through his hair, down the back of his head, and gently knead the taut muscles in his nape.

He grunts and closes his eyes. "Nice, but I haven't shown you how much I missed you yet."

I keep kneading his nape with my right hand and slide my left hand down his shirt and brush it across his crotch, smiling at the instant response. "You choose," I tease.

"No brainer." He creeps his hand up inside my top, running his fingers over my right breast and nipple, then returning to knead it.

I use both hands to tug his shirt off over his head, then work my way down his impressive ridges of muscle, stroking and caressing, listening to his breaths shorten. He slips my top off, then nuzzles into my neck, kneading my breast harder. His breath is hot over my collarbone. His tongue rasps down my neck and I almost squeal. Oh my God. That is erotic. Warmth surges into my labia. He continues to nuzzle and rasp his tongue over my skin, working his way down to lick my nipple. I squirm with desire and focus on sliding my hand into his shorts, exploring his erection. I rub my thumb over the moisture beading at the tip and Justin groans loudly.

He breaks off from my breast and moves his leg over the top of me, probably thinking we're going to please each other externally again. I slide from under him and wriggle out of my pyjama bottom. He removes his shorts so fast I laugh.

Propped up on his elbow, he asks, "I get a condom?"

I kiss his mouth tenderly. "Not tonight, Tiger. Just you and me."

His eyes widen before he kisses me in earnest and moves his leg over me again. His cock is hot and hard against my folds, moving against a pool of moisture. *Yes, body, let's go.* He pushes experimentally at my entry and I feel a twinge of discomfort. Maybe this will go better if I control it. I push his top shoulder, encouraging him to roll onto his back, then straddle him.

"Hayley," he croaks, putting a warm hand across my shoulders and the other across my lower back.

My hair falls forward like a screen as I position myself so I can ease him into me, pausing every centimetre or so to allow my body to adjust, to accept, to prepare. Justin's groans tell me he's enjoying this. The twitches of his cock send thrills of pleasure into me, and my walls contract, pulling him in. I take a slow breath, then ease the last part, until I can feel his balls pressing against me and the nub of his penis touches me deep inside. *Yes. We're there.*

I take another breath then start to move, feeling him arch into me, striving for more closeness. His arms press my buttocks, pulling me tightly on top of him. Opening my eyes, I study his face as we move together, incredible waves of pleasure building, until my whole body is ready to burst with it. Justin gives a powerful surge and his tip presses my sweet spot. Gasping, I shake as contractions wrack me and my body ripples with ecstasy. Justin tenses and then comes with a long, low moan. We are as one, the experience unique, and I feel tears building. This was special.

I ease off Justin and fold down beside him. He kisses my head and pulls me into his chest.

"Hayley," he kisses my head again, "that was … indescribable."

I smile into his chest, no smart reply coming to mind. My limbs are loose, at peace, and my heart is full.

CHAPTER TWENTY-NINE
Pink Paddle Power!

Five days before the pink regatta, Justin presented my new paddle to me with a flourish. I fingered the blade in wonder, the image more beautiful in real life than the website depiction. Of course, he neglected to tell me that he'd also ordered a paddle case with pink trim, a pink blade guard, pink gloves and, even more amazing, a grip bench seat with a similar-style pink dragon on it. Then he got distressed when I cried because I was so overwhelmed.

My one practice session with the paddle went well and by the end of the hour I was totally in love with the look and feel of it. Even Natalie got tearful, saying it was 'so you' and wiping her eyes commented that she felt like a bit-part in a romance novel or movie with me and Justin. That made me laugh. As if. After the session everyone clapped my back or shook my hand and wished me luck. I nearly cried again.

Friday morning, Justin knocks on the door and helps me carry all my gear to the car. Stopping dead, I blink at the shiny silver Lexus. "You have two cars?"

"No, I hired this one for the trip. It's a long way for the old

Subaru and the forecast is for unseasonally hot weather so we need good aircon." He grins. "You deserve to travel in style."

"You're full of surprises." I murmur, trying not to cry again as I carefully lay the paddle on the back seat. What is wrong with me? I'm so emotional, yet I'm so looking forward to this trip. Am I nervous about it all? Paddling at such a big regatta and Justin meeting Dad?

It is a long day of travel, and I'm glad of the plush leather seats and comfort. Super coach that he is, Justin stops every ninety minutes and makes me get out and walk around for ten minutes. My left arm is growing tight from the lack of movement so I appreciate his concern. As we near Melbourne, the temperature rises to thirty degrees.

"There won't be much shade tomorrow," Justin cautions. "Stay in your team tent as much as possible and keep your fluids up."

"Yes, Coach."

He remains in full coach mode. We check in to the hotel at the Docklands and he insists we go straight to the hotel pool to swim, water-wade and use the spa. I splash him when he swims past until he retaliates and we're both collapsing into the water with laughter. Then he leaves me to do my Tai Chi while he sources takeaway pasta and salads. I text the team captain to confirm I'm here, apologising we didn't make it to the regatta welcome drinks party. She texts back to be at the team tent by eight-fifteen if possible.

We prepare our backpacks for the morning and line up all our gear ready. Justin gives me a physio session. Relaxing into his deft touch, I reflect I must be the luckiest paddler alive to have my own driver, coach and physio. I feel like royalty. When we tumble into bed, Justin holds me close and murmurs, "You got this."

～

By eight, we're walking around the edge of Docklands heading to the row of tents on the other side. The Marvel Stadium looms high on our left, the Bolte Bridge looms in an elegant span across the water on our right. I look at the square of Victoria Harbour water, ending abruptly a mere fifty metres past the race finish buoys at the concrete wall and swallow. How will we stop the boats in time?

We turn the corner and wind our way through paddlers in uniforms of varying shades of pink with yellows and blues. There must be 500 paddlers and the atmosphere is already electric. Upbeat music is playing and a row of bright tents adorns the narrow strip of grass in front of the office buildings. The Canberra team tent is only about four down from the marshalling area. That's good.

"Yay, Hayley!" I'm greeted by cheerful, excited faces.

Justin puts his gear down just inside the tent, gives me a kiss on the cheek and murmurs, "Good luck. I'd better report for marshalling duty."

I grab him in a fierce hug and the team ladies all whoop and cheer. Justin leaves at an almost run, and their cheering turns to laughter.

"He's adorable," says Kellie. "Can you clone him?"

"Yes, by twenty," says Lyndall.

"I want two," says Katherine.

"What do you want two for?" asks Clare.

"You don't want to know." Katherine, who must be seventy, waggles her eyebrows suggestively and everyone cracks up.

My cheeks are flaming as we gather for the team prep talk. I'm thrilled to see there will be six heats, and I'm in row two or three for all of them. We help each other lather up with sunscreen as Susan explains the opening ceremony will start soon, and all teams are to gather on the steps by marshalling. She reminds us to thank the paddlers from Melbourne Pink Phoenix, the first team tent, as our hosts.

We march down to the amphitheatre steps and I'm transfixed as a talented group of youngsters perform the most amazing Lion Dance with a thirty-metre-long pink dragon and stirring drums. I can't imagine how spectacular these dances must be in China. Then there are speeches from the Mayor, the head of Dragon Boat Victoria, and Pearl, the Board Chair of Dragons Abreast Australia.

After a mighty round of applause, we head straight into a lively land warm-up with a designated leader who seems to have a boundless supply of energy and enthusiasm. I wipe sweat from my brow and peer at the group of marshals waiting by the boats. My heart thuds until I spy Justin chatting to a few other men, all dressed in yellow marshal shirts. It will be a hot day in the sun for them as there's no shade at all by the pontoons.

We return to the tent to prepare for our first heat and I watch as four teams stride by, heading to marshalling. My eyes prickle. *All* these women have had breast cancer, yet here they are, so brimming with energy and life. As far as I can see, I'm one of, if not the, youngest woman here. Most of the paddlers range from in their forties to a few that look like they might be nudging eighty. The defining characteristic is their energy and laughter. It's as if they simply took a wrong turn somewhere and corrected course. Humility sweeps through me. I need to be braver; stronger. Live more.

A presence hovers at my shoulder. "You alright?" asks Clare. "The first pink regatta can be overwhelming."

I nod. "So many of … us." I test the word. *Us.* Yes, Hayles, you are one of these vibrant pink paddlers.

"Wait 'til you go to an international regatta with several thousand paddlers. That really brings it home." Elly pats my shoulder. "Grab your paddle, we're up."

I swallow a few mouthfuls of water and fall in with the team. My stomach gurgles with anticipation and I wish I'd trained more with the team. My bench buddy, Kerrie, smiles encouragingly. We file to our assigned boat and my eyes skim the pontoon area for Justin. He finishes helping a paddler into the next boat along then looks our way, spies me and gives a small wave. I return a nervous smile.

Then we're paddling to the start buoys, listening to Lyndall. "We need a smart start, ladies, seven deep and strong, seven brisk and strong, then seven reaching and pulling. Do *not* ease off until I say so and don't worry about the dirty great concrete wall. We won't hit it."

I flex my fingers and get ready. The hooter blares and … whoa! I'm caught out by the speed and power of the start; the strokes are flying. I scramble to get my timing. The pace doesn't lessen for the entire 200 metres with Lyndall calling for lifts and Jenny drumming her arms off and screaming at us. I tune out thoughts of the wall ahead and focus. Driving, driving, driving. My arms are burning. My breath labouring.

"Stop hard!" yells Lyndall and I copy the others as they sit up, lean back and plunge their blades deep. My back is straining against the reverse flow. We stop five metres short of the wall and a tremor runs through my arms and legs.

Kerrie high-fives me. "Good work, buddy. We were second."

Oh my God. We paddle the boat back and I wonder whether I'll make it through six races of this calibre. This might be a 'participatory' regatta, but there are obviously no holds barred.

I've barely recovered when we're grabbing our paddles again. As we head to the start area, I hear my name. I look left and my heart leaps for joy. Dad! I run out of line to give him a brief hug. "You made it! This is our second race."

He holds me at arm's-length. "You look great, Kiddo. Good luck."

"See you after." I race back into line. This race I'm on the right side, and my buddy is Janet, who I haven't spoken with much. "Will we go that fast again?" I ask.

She shrugs. "I expect so. The first race always feels the hardest though."

The second race feels similar to the first and we're a close second again. I hope Dad is impressed. When we get out, I find him hovering near the steps. "Come and meet the team," I say. He follows me to the tent and I introduce him to everyone. He congratulates them on the race. We have a while before the next heat so we go and stand together in a nearby patch of shade under a tree.

"This is astonishing, Hayles." Dad flaps a hand at all the activity. "So different to your running races."

"Mmm. Dragon boating is quite technical, no switch off and just run in your own head space." I smile. "Justin can talk for hours about the sport."

Dad grins. "And where is this handsome young man?"

I squint at the marshals, spying Justin at boat five. "There." I point. "The Chinese guy. We can't interrupt him but you'll meet him tomorrow."

"Look forward to it. I'll watch another race then head off. Let me know how you go, hey?"

The day grows hotter and the team huddles in the tent as much as possible, hydrating and snacking. The sun is ricocheting off the concrete, but it's okay in the boat on the water. I force in water, fruit, crackers and gratefully accept some snakes and jelly babies being passed around, knowing Justin will be grumpy if I don't.

After a brief lunch break about two-thirds of the way through the heats they have the supporters' race. I take Justin's paddle and gloves down to him and burst out laughing when I see the floppy bucket hat he's wearing.

He gives me a sheepish grin. "Susan insisted, said my neck would get burned."

"All it needs is a big tiger emblem on the front and you could be on safari."

He takes his paddle. "Ha ha."

I watch the supporters' race, which is fascinating as about half the paddlers can paddle and the rest look like it's their first time in a boat. The timing is all over the shop but thankfully the sweeps know what they're doing and keep the boats straight. Justin's boat, with Susan at the sweep oar, is third, and I wait while they paddle back. He drips his way over to me and holds out his paddle. My eyebrow arches. "You're soaked!"

"Chap in front of me had never paddled and scooped water over me every stroke." He shrugs. "So refreshing, but I'll need a shower. The harbour water is not exactly pristine like Bar Beach."

I pull my phone out of my pants pocket. "Sorry, Tiger. We need a selfie with you in that hat." He groans and reluctantly stands beside me, pulling a goofy face.

"You'd better not post or send that anywhere," he warns.

"Who me?" I give him a wide-eyed stare and he groans again. I hand him a muesli bar and bottle of iced tea. "See you after the last race."

When I get back to the team tent, I find they're holding a meeting. I scuttle in and try to pick up the discussion.

"So far, we're having an amazing day. Let's hold it together for the final race," Lyndall says and the team murmur agreement and smile. "Susan wants us to prepare a few baskets of petals, and we have twenty minutes now to do this."

I spy wicker baskets full of flowers on the ground behind her.

"Has everyone participated in Flowers on the Water? Does anyone want to?" Her gaze tracks around the group. "Hayley. As this is your first regatta would you like to participate?"

"It's an honour. You should do it," says Denise.

"Okay," I say. "What is it?"

"It's the traditional closing ceremony for any pink regatta." Kathy nods towards the flowers. "We scatter flowers on the water to remember those who have gone."

I swallow. Oh. This is indeed an honour — and could be tough.

~

Flowers sorted, I'm back next to Kerrie for the final race. Lyndall is sweeping. The temperature has apparently reached 33 degrees and as much as I'm loving the regatta, I'm wilting and longing to get out of the sun and into the hotel aircon. Or the pool. Somehow, we hold form for the final heat and although it feels like we paddle strongly we're third.

"Don't worry," says Kerrie. "It's impossible to beat the New Zealand teams. The Boobops from Tauranga are really strong, as are the Taranaki Pinks — and we had both of them in this heat."

We paddle back slowly and as we're waiting to get out, Jeannie reminds me to stay by the boats, ready for the flower ceremony. "It's so hot they're going to move straight into this part."

I hover on the pontoon, seeing Nat and Kathy from my team. They're representing DAC, sweeping and drumming on boat five for the ceremony. I don't recognise anyone else. Soon, the eight boats are being loaded with paddlers from every team in an amazing array of colours and shirt designs. I end up in the eighth boat, and when the paddlers scramble in, I realise I'll be at the front with one of the paddlers from New Zealand.

"Oh my," she murmurs.

Justin looks astonished when he sees me getting in the boat and I shrug. Next, bags and wicker baskets of flowers are loaded into the front of the boats. One by one, we glide away from the pontoon and paddle in a large circle. Stirring music plays from the shore. A buzzing above draws my attention and I glance up to see two drones circling.

"Crap," mutters my bench buddy. "We're being filmed."

One at a time, the boats return to the pontoon, dragon heads facing the shore and the amassed crowd. There must be 800 people with all the paddlers, supporters, locals and media. I gulp, feeling very exposed. Our boat is on the left-hand edge and gradually, the boats shuffle closer and closer, until the paddlers can put their paddles down and link elbows. A knot forms in my throat. Eight linked boats. This must be an impressive sight.

"Take some flowers and pass the bag back," calls our sweep.

We comply, and then the music stops while Pearl, in her role as DAA Board Chair, gives a short speech commemorating the paddlers who have left us, then says there will be two minutes silence while the special song is played. My eyes are already burning and I tug my cap down lower over my face, seeing my buddy do the same as we try not to look at the drones hovering right in front of us.

In all the boats paddlers are crying, some openly weeping. It dawns on me that I'm new, hardly know anyone, but most of these paddlers have special friends and maybe even relatives to mourn. My chest feels horribly tight, and I allow my tears to fall, to grieve with them. Yes, so many of us are here, but many have departed. The song is of course soulful and stirring and I doubt there's a dry eye in any boat or anywhere along the shore.

Once the music stops, we throw our flowers and petals on the water, watching the kaleidoscope of colours bob on top of the brown harbour water. I still can't stop my tears as I watch a dark pink rose petal float away. Will I be a petal on the water one day? Mourned by my teammates? By Justin? My breath hitches and I gulp loudly. My buddy puts her hand on my shoulder and I lean into her, both of us snuffling and blowing our noses. After an eternity, the sweep calls, "Grab your paddles. Paddles back." And we're peeling the boats away to reform the circle, paddle-tap another loop of honour then come in one by one to disembark.

Our boat is last and Justin is hovering anxiously. My face is a blotchy mess and I feel wrung out. Justin grabs my hand, tugs me up from the boat and I collapse into his chest. He holds me tight and strokes my hair. I'm grateful he doesn't say anything; there are no words.

"Can you step back, mate?" a marshal asks. "We need to put the boats away."

With a last sniff, I lift my face and give Justin a wobbly smile. "Thanks."

Justin kisses my forehead. "Come on, you've got a medal to collect." He takes my hand and leads me to the start area, where paddlers are queuing up and being presented with their participatory medal. My heart skips. I adore all my marathon medals, am so proud of them, and this will be my first dragon boat one.

I take the package and smile broadly. The medal is stunning: an intricately carved feminine Chinese dragon on a bright pink ribbon. I *love* it immediately.

"Custom-designed," murmurs Justin. "Apparently Linda, one of the Melbourne Pink Phoenix paddlers, is an artist."

"It's awesome." My spirits lift.

Justin rests his arms on my shoulders and looks into my eyes, his glinting in the shade of the bucket hat. "You paddled magnificently today. Let's get you back to the hotel to rest up. We've still got the dinner and ball to go."

I giggle. "Yes, coach. Although it's much harder to take you seriously in that hat."

Justin whips the hat off and I giggle harder.

CHAPTER THIRTY

PPP Ball

Just as well Justin hustled me along. By the time we'd helped pack up the team tent, walked back to the hotel and had a dip, there's less than an hour to clean up and get ready. I apply my mascara and make-up carefully then peer into the mirror. My nose is a bit pink, but otherwise I don't seem to have got too sunburned. I dab a little more foundation on my nose, then sprinkle my favourite perfume on my wrists. It's been a while since I wore a dress. I've been bold and chosen the close-fitting jade dress with white and cherry-coloured chrysanthemums on. It has an Asian feel to it, which I hope will complement Justin. It has a sexy diamond cut out in the hollow of my breasts.

I walk out of the bathroom and find Justin gazing out the window towards the stadium, which we can see from our high-up room. He turns around and I'm not sure whose mouth drops open widest. Oh my God. He's virtually unrecognisable in a charcoal silk suit shot with threads of midnight blue above an open-neck pale blue shirt. There's a gold chain around his neck. For the first time, I see the son of a powerful businessman.

For a long minute we simply stare at each other. Then we simultaneously step towards each other. "You're unrecognisable," I murmur, fingering his suit sleeve. "This is amazing, so soft and the colour… you look divine."

He gently nudges my hair back over my shoulder. "You too. I love you in jade." His voice is husky. "Almost too good to take to the ball."

Desire ripples through me, and I see how dark and wide his eyes are. "We'd better go immediately then. I paid good money for these tickets!"

Hooking his elbow through mine, he asks, "Got everything? Need a shawl or a jacket?"

I grab my clutch purse and the jade cotton shawl off the sofa back; it might still be thirty degrees outside but the room will be airconditioned. We stroll along the Docklands, and my legs protest at the flights of steps up to the function room. The dolled-up paddlers flutter around like an enormous flock of myriad species of birds with spectacular plumage, and I wonder if I'll even recognise my teammates.

We enter the massive room and there's a podium and lectern set up in front of the windows looking out to the harbour and bridge, a dance floor in front of it, then there must be at least thirty tables spread around the room. A DJ is already playing music. The noise level is rising as more paddlers flow into the room and greet team buddies and friends from other teams with screeches, squawks and hugs. Justin frowns and I feel a surge of love. He probably doesn't like large functions, and this is a stretch for him. "A drink?" I ask. "You look like you might need it."

He focuses on me. "I'll get them."

I follow him to the bar, worrying that if we separate it'll take an age to find each other. My eyebrows lift when he orders two glasses of quality prosecco. He hands a glass to me.

"Not ideal after being in the sun all day, but this is a special occasion." He clinks my glass. "To your first pink regatta."

"Thanks to my super coach." I clink his glass back. The bubbles tingle my nose and the prosecco tastes great. "Thanks for being with me."

"Wouldn't miss it, Hayley."

"Okay you two lovebirds," Susan's voice interjects. "The team table is this way. Come along. Justin, I've put you next to my Danny. You two can talk sport all night."

I stride out to keep up with Susan, difficult in my close-fit dress. Turns out the Canberra team table is on the far side of the room, and yes, I have trouble recognising my buddies in their glam gear and need to eyeball each of them and re-memorise their names. Justin seems happy to sit next to Danny, they recognise each other from being marshals all day, and I sit next to Justin.

Everyone is in high spirits and several toasts are made. The loudest cheer is for Lyn and Kirsten from BCNA. In almost no time, Justin is heading off to collect more prosecco. I tune in and realise Danny and another chap are talking about running. Turns out they both used to run, marathons even, but thirty years earlier. The other chap's wife must be one of our paddlers but I can't recall her name. Her head's down and she's focused on reading through some papers. I listen to the men until Justin returns.

The entrees arrive at the same time as Justin, and my stomach informs me I'm famished. Five minutes later, a red-haired woman goes to the podium. Justin and I swivel our chairs so we can see better. Andrea, from Melbourne Pink Phoenix, thanks everyone for coming to the inaugural Pink Paddle Power regatta. She hopes we had a great day of racing, thanks everyone who helped organise and sponsor the event and says the day was such a success it is likely to become an annual event. Everyone cheers loudly at this news. Andrea says we now have a treat in store with two keynote speakers.

Cassandra is a university academic who has been studying the effects of exercise on chronic disease. She opens with a bold statement about increasing evidence that exercise can slow or even undo the effects of some diseases. This is met with enthusiastic applause — she's talking to a roomful of the converted. She has several slides with an array of impressive data. Justin is listening intently and I watch the flickers of emotion play across his face. I guess he'd like to talk to her later. She finishes to a round of applause and Andrea tells us our main meals will be served in ten minutes.

"You okay?" Justin nudges my elbow. He's taken his jacket off and rolled up his shirt sleeves.

"Yep. This is amazing." I look at the faces around the table, wondering how to get to know them more. Justin's hand steals into my lap and his fingers close around mine. I flutter my eyelashes and lean over to murmur, "I'm looking forward to the dancing."

He grimaces. "You might not be so keen after I've mangled your feet."

"You don't dance?"

"Never needed to." He shrugs.

Our main meals arrive and Andrea taps a spoon against a glass. "I'd like to welcome our second speaker to the podium. Although a relatively new pink paddler, Kaaren has some interesting news to share and I hope you will enjoy her story."

I startle when the paddler across from me gathers up her papers and walks to the lectern. She was checking her speech! "What?" I ask, seeing Justin frown.

He taps his fingertips on the table. "She looks familiar."

The speech is short, but clever in how it weaves several strands of story together.

I feel my mouth open when she mentions being recruited by the club at Moruya. She's from *Moruya*? I look at Justin.

She talks about how she was then recruited by Annie, a DAA

member, to do pink races at her first regatta, which was the Masters Games in 2019. I laugh with everyone at her dry comment about 'why stop at eighteen races for your first ever regatta when you can do 24?' Then she spoke of her abyss, a diagnosis of a recurrence in her spine in early 2021, major surgery and a full year to recover. We all laugh at her animated replay of the expression on her neurosurgeon's face when after being told she'd need a custom-built vertebra and five fused ones she asked if she'd be able to dragon boat paddle.

"I remember her now," murmurs Justin. "She was really keen during the Tuesday night paddles before Covid and then just vanished. I didn't know what happened to her. Wow." He regards me with compassion in his eyes. "Focus on her positives, Hayles."

I focus on her face as she describes her rehab and then getting back in a boat. I swallow hard. She paddles with a part-fused spine. She still goes to regattas. She looks fine. I gaze around the room. How many others here are paddling after recurrences? My heart beats hard. So, even a recurrence is not a death-knell. Look at these paddlers. I tip my chin up. Two weeks until my check-up. I can do this. I will ride the outcome. I will paddle.

I jump when Justin kisses my cheek. "That's the spirit."

I focus on the last few minutes of the talk, and feel my eyebrows rise as she describes using the down time to write a fantasy romance, with dragon boats in it. She's a writer? She finishes her speech by shading her eyes with a hand and saying, "Is that Lake Karapiro I see?"

This optimistic ending is met with rousing approval. I turn to Kerrie. "What's at Lake Karapiro?"

"The international pink regatta in New Zealand next April." She squeezes my arm. "You should go. There's bound to be a spot in a DAA composite team. I'll have a talk to Sharon."

An *international* regatta? I turn to Justin, who's studying my face. "Do it." He grins. "Giulio and Gianni will be thrilled."

I snort and take a mouthful of prosecco, my mind whirring with possibilities. Then I remember the pending scans. The DJ switches to a rousing song and with a massive scraping of chair legs, about fifty paddlers get up and head to the dance floor. The lights dim and a disco strobe comes on, spraying luminescent white rays around the floor. I grab Justin's hand and tug him to the polished wooden square.

"You'll regret this," he murmurs hotly in my ear.

I laugh and shimmy in front of him, laughing harder at the way his eyebrows rise and his eyes follow my hips. He is so gorgeous. I can see the dancers around us sliding glances at him. I'm tempted to tell him my team wants to clone him, but I don't want to freak him out entirely. He's trying hard, but he's not relaxed. I move closer and take his hands so he has to move with me. "Relax into it, Tiger."

He's just getting the hang of it when Nutbush City Limits starts and more paddlers pour onto the dance floor and we're in a large square doing the routine. "Timing!" I say when Justin goes the wrong way and steps into me. He grimaces. Next, we're suddenly forming a massive chain and Justin's hands are on my hips as we bop our way around the entire room, pulling more paddlers up from tables as we go. I feel like I'm a university student again. After another six rousing songs, I'm starting to lather up but the other paddlers look like they could dance all night.

I turn to say something to Justin and find my team buddy Megan grinning at me. Where'd he go? I skim the room and see he's back at our table talking to the Moruya paddler. I weave my way out of the press of dancers and walk over.

Justin immediately twists around. "Hayley, meet Kaaren."

Kaaren smiles. "Sorry, I didn't realise you're a ring-in from Narooma or I would have said something."

I take the seat beside her. "I enjoyed your speech."

We chat for a while and her interest sharpens when I explain my job and how I can work from Narooma for the moment.

"So, you're now basically an editor. I'm a freelance editor as well as an author. We should have lunch and I'll fill you in on the key associations you should join." She rummages in her purse and hands me a business card. "Give me a call, or email me."

"That would be awesome. Thank you." Talk about serendipity. Can anything else more positive possibly happen this night?

A couple of paddlers come to talk to her and I go back to my original seat. Just as I tuck my chair in a waiter places dessert in front of me. Mini fruit tart. Yum.

Justin pours me a glass of water. "Don't forget we've got the social paddle in the morning and it'll be hot again." He leans in. "I bought one of her books for you as she has a box of them here. It's on the floor with your purse."

I choke on my water. Looking pleased that he's surprised me yet again, he pats my back. The room settles into a hum as everyone enjoys their desserts. Glancing at my watch, I'm shocked to see it's well after ten already.

"Would you like to go out on the balcony?" Justin asks, his face oddly intent. "It'll be cooler out there."

"Sure, let's go admire the view." Enjoying his firm grip, I let him lead me around the edge of the room and we slip out the wide glass doors. There are clusters of paddlers outside chatting, and Justin leads me to a far, quiet corner. A breeze stirs against my cheeks and I revel in the cool touch. We lean on the concrete wall and I blink. The Bolte Bridge is a vivid pink. "Er, is the bridge pink?"

Smiling, Justin says, "Yes, pink up-lights. This whole regatta has been a real experience." Pulling me to face him, he tenderly brushes a few strands of hair back and places his lips on mine.

I melt into him, feeling his heart beating strongly through his soft shirt. Behind us, chatting voices approach and then discreetly melt away, respecting our moment. Focusing, I run my hands down his broad shoulders, nestle them in the small of his back and press him closer until his hard cock is hot against my dress, feeding my pooling desire. Justin breaks away and nuzzles my neck, his breath hot and steamy.

"Hayley," he says huskily, "I want to ask you something."

Fighting the urge to say 'not now, let's bolt for our room' I mumble incoherently. What can he possibly want to know right at this moment? Tension ripples through him and I lift my head to peer into his face. His expression is a mix of unreadable and vulnerable and nervous. What's going on with him? I reach up and smooth his pinched frown with my fingertips, then trace his cheekbones and his mouth. With the dark night and pink bridge behind him he looks amazing. More handsome than ever. His dark hair has reflected pink highlights. My heart thuds loudly.

He fishes in his trouser pocket and then presses a small, pink tissue-paper wrapped object into my hands. *Another* present? What have I done to earn this one? Intrigued, I carefully pull the seal off the join and unravel the gift.

"Don't drop it," he mumbles, putting his cupped hands below mine.

I drop the tissue paper into his hands and lift up the fine gold chain to examine the feature piece. My throat closes tight. It is a gold running river dragon clutching a creamy pearl in its foreleg. My vision blurs with tears. Not only is it simply stunning, but I'm sure the necklace is pure gold and that's a real pearl. "Justin," I croak. "You shouldn't have."

His fingers prise it from mine and I'm transfixed as he gently positions the dragon in the centre of my collarbone and fastens the clasp under my hair. Then he rests his hands on my shoulders, the teeny frown back between his eyebrows, his eyes fathomless dark wells. I watch him gathering his nerve. *Oh my God.* My heart gives a massive jolt. Is this what I think? Anxiety wars with soaring hope. I'm not ready!

He kisses my nose. "I know it's only been three months, but I'm certain you are the one for me. Will you marry me Hayley Banks, my FBI agent, my Mu Laohu?"

My heart and stomach are tumble-turning in opposite directions. I want to shriek 'yes, yes, yes' but my mind is hurling obstacles. What about the scans? What about his family? What if I can never have children? My mouth opens but nothing comes out. Tears slide down my cheeks. "I–" I sniff. How inelegant. I stare into his eyes, grappling with my fears. Blinking, I scan his face. Natalie told me to let him decide — and he has — despite everything. So soon. Today. *Now*. It's up to me. *Now*.

My heart wails, *you can't lose him! You know that! Courage, girl. You'll find a way, together.* I nod and cry in earnest at the relief that floods his face. That must've been the longest moment of his life. I didn't mean to put him through that. I nod again and whisper, "Yes, Tiger." His lips find mine and we kiss hard. My heart is rejoicing, while my stomach is busy pushing down the what-ifs. Don't spoil it. I can ask about the what-ifs, the provisos, later. He's crushing me so tightly I can barely breathe.

Soft petals shower over us. Am I dreaming? This is getting silly. The raucous laughter and Justin's low groan cues me I'm not. We've been sprung. Another load of petals flutter down and I turn to find the entire team gathered, beaming from ear to ear. My cheeks are burning. Did they hear the proposal or are they teasing us due to the kiss? God, my face is a mess and I haven't even got a tissue.

"We should recruit more young ones," says Lyndall. "Love the romance aspect."

"Are you saying we're too old?" Katherine demands, hands on hips.

"Only some of us," says Jenny, batting Katherine's shoulder.

Kellie hands me a tissue. "Your mascara's smudged. Smarten up for the team photo."

The night takes another surreal twist as we pose for a zillion photos, reassured that Kerrie is a master at this, and warned we'll be all over Facebook within the hour. By the lack of any comments or congratulations, I realise they didn't hear the proposal. *Phew.* I don't feel ready to make any announcements, I need to absorb what just happened. Justin endures well, summoning up countless grins and even agreeing to a men's shot with Danny and the other partners. Finally, we seem to run out of possible photo combinations.

A town clock somewhere strikes midnight. Justin grabs my hand, and I know he means it's time to go.

CHAPTER THIRTY-ONE
Hayley's Father

I wake first. The sunlight is beaming through the window directly onto Hayley's face, highlighting her delightful rows of freckles, showing up the residual traces of brown mascara on the tips of her curved eyelashes. Her gorgeous hair tumbles around her face and shoulders. Lying still, I study her. How is it possible she just walked along the bike path and into my life and turned it upside down just like that? I did not see her coming.

If I close my eyes, she's standing in front of me – clear as day – holding out the spray of dropped lollipops, an amused glint in her hazel eyes. The moment my world tilted. My heart swells with love and gratitude. Thank you, universe. Thank you, guardian dragons, because I love and adore her. I need her. My heart twists. She said yes … but she hesitated … for an eternity. I was sure she was going to say no. Dare I ask what she was thinking? I swallow. Do I want to know? *Leave it alone, Justin. Be patient.* I can guess: she wants to know her imminent scans are clear and, almost as big an issue, she wants to see what my family will do. I scrunch my fingers. I need to think hard about what *I* will do if they don't accept her.

"Morning, Tiger." Her hazel eyes are studying me. "Yesterday was wonderful. So many surprises."

I kiss her forehead, suppressing a sigh. My proposal is absorbed as one of the surprises? Oh man. I feel like we have a new elephant in the room. Take a breath, we've only just woken up. "What time is the social paddle? We'd better move."

We scramble to get ready and are soon striding along the concrete path around the edge of Docklands, heading to the pontoon area on the far side. The sun is already hot on my legs and, reluctantly, I have the bucket hat on. I need to return it to its owner, anyway. Paddlers are milling by the pontoon and the boats are already loading. I feel an absence and pause, turning to see why Hayley has slowed and find she's stopped about ten paces back and is just standing there with a stricken expression.

I close the gap in four strides. "What's wrong?"

Her throat moves in a massive gulp. "Justin, my answer is yes. I can't imagine being without you." She chokes up. "I love you. But I feel like I can't celebrate properly until after my scans. It's only ten days … can we not tell anyone until then?"

My knees go weak with relief. "Okay." I pat her shoulder. "Then it can be a double celebration."

She gives me a wan smile and resumes walking. Her chin tips up and she strides out as we draw near the boats. I hover to one side as her team buddies high-five her, everyone's spirits high. No evidence they paddled all day yesterday and partied well into the night.

Next thing I know, someone with a camera is nudging me into a team photo. "Love the hat!"

A woman approaches me, introducing herself as Kath. She's sweeping for the New Zealand team, Taranaki Pinks, but they're a sweep short. "You're a sweep, aren't you?" she says. "Boat six needs one."

"I can do that," I confirm, sighing. I'd prefer to paddle with Hayley's team, but never mind. The boats are supposed to travel together down the Yarra River. I tell her what I'm doing and head to boat six.

Soon, nine dragon boats are moving away from the pontoon. As we paddle down the Yarra, we pass below numerous footbridges. People walking or running on the bike paths wave cheerfully, and paddlers wave back. We paddle by several well-known sights and attractions. A welcome faint breeze springs up. I cast occasional glances at Hayley's boat. She looks relaxed, paddling well; this regatta has been good for her.

Everyone swans through the two-hour paddle, we disembark and things get emotional as paddlers hug and farewell each other. Hayley thanks her team for letting her paddle with them, then turns to me with shining eyes.

"Ready?" I ask.

She gives me an impish grin. "You decided to keep the unique hat, then?"

"Crap! I forgot."

"I think you should keep it as your regatta memento. It's growing on me."

I glance around, and failing to see the owner, shrug. "Okay, then."

~

An hour later, we're loading the car. My stomach does a weird flip. Will Hayley's dad like me? How much has she told him? I almost bang my head on the boot door. Does not telling anyone we're engaged include her dad? I guess I keep my mouth shut and follow her lead.

"You right there, Tiger?" Hayley asks. "You're drifting in time and space." Her eyes widen. "Oh. Are you nervous?"

"A bit." I close the boot.

Hayley leans in to kiss me. "You'll be fine." She hesitates, and I can imagine her thinking this will be easy for me compared to her having to meet my family. I can't argue with that.

Another hour later, Hayley is guiding me down a tree-lined street. The houses are a mix of new ones and several refurbished but original-looking heritage ones. Given that she said her father is an archaeologist, I'm not surprised when she directs me into the shaded driveway of a two-storey heritage house. There's a small expanse of lawn surrounded by shaped bushes and colourful roses. The porch is contained by a wrought-iron railing fence and the gate squeaks when she opens it.

The front door flings open and a portly gentleman with a neatly trimmed beard, grey hair and academic glasses folds Hayley into his arms. "Good to see you, Kiddo."

Hayley hugs him back and I notice that she's taller than he is, and much slighter in build. Then my hand is being pumped and I'm looking into alert light-blue eyes behind the glasses. The smile is warm, creating deep creases around his eyes.

"Welcome, Justin. Good to meet you."

"Thank you, sir, likewise." I'm tongue-tied, my brain having misplaced his name.

A grey eyebrow arches and he laughs. "Sir? David will do. Come along in."

I grab our bags and follow them inside. There are middle eastern rugs scattered across dark polished floors, high ceilings, ornate bay windows and elegant cornices. I like the vibes. The walls are adorned with photos of the seven wonders of the world, people working at dig sites, and random close shots of artefacts. Did he find those? Antique sideboards and chests have a mix of ancient-looking pottery on top. Note to self: Don't break anything!

"Come into the kitchen for a cuppa," says David. "Drop the bags by the stairs for now."

I do this and enter a sunny kitchen overlooking a compact, tidy back garden.

"Green tea, Dad," says Hayley, pulling out a chair.

I sit opposite her and watch as David deftly fills a large teapot shaped like an elephant with the trunk for the spout, then piles assorted biscuits onto a plate. He pulls up a chair and pours three mugs.

"So, how was the regatta and ball?" he asks.

Hayley animatedly fills him in, describing the close races, the camaraderie, and how spectacular the ball was with keynote speakers, dancing and the bridge all lit up pink. She stops there, I note, not mentioning my gift and proposal. A small knot forms in my stomach.

David focuses on me. "Hayley tells me you're a really competitive paddler?"

I nod. "It's been my sport since I was ten. My father was a national level paddler in China and he coached me and my brother."

David peers at me through his glasses. "You were born in China?"

"We migrated here when I was fifteen. I lived in Sydney for eleven years, went to university there, worked for a bit and then moved to Narooma."

"And you're a physio?"

I confirm, sure that Hayley has already told him all this and he's just trying to get a sense of me. My turn. "Hayley says you're an archaeologist? What does that involve?"

I sip my tea and munch my way through three biscuits while David describes his routine as a part-time lecturer in archaeology at Melbourne University and the digs he tries to get onto, usually one a year in Australia and one overseas, if possible. He's a lecturer.

An academic as well as a practician. No wonder Hayley is so smart. "Are you a professor?" I ask.

"Professor Banks. Has a nice ring to it." He winks at me. "Still call me David, though." He turns to Hayley. "Roast chicken with the trimmings for dinner. Do you need a rest while I put it on?"

Hayley gives him an indignant look then glances at me. "I'll show you the rest of the house."

"Okay." I stand and help take the mugs and plates to the sink. First, Hayley shows me a sunny lounge area adjacent to the kitchen. The large Persian rug with imagery of nobles on horseback complements the dusky blue sofa. There's an old fireplace built into one wall, and I imagine it is cosy in winter. Grabbing the bags, I follow her up the flight of steep stairs. At the top there's a landing with polished balustrades.

"That's Dad's room," she points to the left-hand closed door, "the bathroom and toilet are in the middle, and we're in here."

The guest room is spacious, with a king bed, ancient Chinese chests on each side, and a small Chinese silk rug. "We're in here together?" I ask.

"You can sleep on the floor if you prefer, but yes." She smiles coyly. "We're not teenagers anymore, in case you hadn't noticed."

I drop the bags and put my arms around her. "I noticed." I kiss her soundly, until she makes a muffled sound. I look up, straight at a professional photo on the wall of a woman in a black coat and top hat riding a large, dappled-grey horse, its neck arched in a perfect frame. I turn Hayley around, seeing there are a series of photos, and nudge her closer. Despite the fancy gear and hair net, the woman's face has Hayley's profile. "Is this your mother?"

Hayley pulls my arms back around her, speaking softly, "Yes. She was a top-class dressage rider. This was her latest and favourite horse, a warmblood mare called Stardust, or technically, Ravenwood Lodge Stardust to identify her breeder." A shudder passes through her. "Mum died a few years ago, unexpectedly. Dad can tell you the full story, I can't."

I grip her to me. "I'm sorry, Hayles. You still miss her?"

"So much," she whispers. "Especially when I got sick. Dad's been awesome, but still."

"What happened to the horse?" I ask, then mentally kick myself. Of all the questions, I ask *that*?

"We gave Stardust back to the breeder. They had two stallions other than her sire, so they could use her to produce more class horses." Her voice drops lower. "I thought about keeping her … but I was in Canberra, working, running marathons and, to be honest, I couldn't face the idea. Too many memories."

Gently, I turn Hayley to face me, my hands on her shoulders. "You rode with your mum?"

"A lot when I was younger." Her eyes dance. "I have my own ribbons from shows and dressage comps. But not really after I moved to Canberra for university and then work."

I hug her close, my mind churning. Maybe she'd like to come to Hong Kong with me, not the first trip, but the second one when we train grooms in the products. Better wait and see how meeting the family goes, but I tuck the idea away.

"We'd better unpack and go downstairs," she murmurs, "before Dad gets unwarranted ideas."

Dinner is delicious, and David opens a bottle of crisp white wine. The evening passes quickly as he asks me many questions about life in China, whether I've been to the Great Wall, seen this temple and that temple. In return, I ask him about fossils and artefacts he's uncovered, what he teaches in his lectures. Hayley chips in occasionally, looking pleased we're getting along. When she gives a massive yawn, David says we'd better decide what to do the next day. We settle for a lunch cruise down the river; nothing too strenuous.

As I'm readying for bed, I see I've missed a couple of calls from

Ethan. I text: *Sorry bro, away in Melbourne. Will call in the morning.* I climb under the sheets wondering whether he has Father's answer re the New Year's Eve celebrations. Man, I hope he has good news. I'm still staring at the ceiling long after Hayley is deeply asleep.

~

Waking early, I slip out of bed and sneak downstairs and into the back garden. When Ethan answers, his voice is all muzzy.

"I suppose I should be glad you remembered." He yawns. "Why are you in Melbourne?"

"We came to an event and now we're staying with Hayley's father. He's really nice." I flex my fingers. "You have news?"

"Yes. Mother worked her magic and Hayley and Li Na are invited to New Year's Eve celebrations. Come just after lunch if you can."

"Just Li Na? Not her family? How long will she stay?"

"Just her. Maybe two weeks … depending on whether I propose to her."

Warmth rushes through me. "I'm happy for you, Ethan. You two look good together." I pause. "I don't care if you get engaged before me … but if the meeting goes well with Hayley, you can definitely propose."

"Well … good luck. See you soon then."

I spin the phone in my hands. I so need this to work. Slipping back inside, I make a tea and before long David and Hayley appear.

The river cruise is wonderful, scenic with good food and interesting commentary.

"I thought you two might like to relax on the river instead of paddling your arms off," says David, lifting his glass of beer to us.

Hayley rolls her eyes at him and gives me such a sweet smile my heart throbs. The day passes quickly and the sun is casting golden lights on the porch railings when we get back to David's house.

A simple dinner after the big lunch then David puts some kind of documentary on the TV. I notice that Hayley is nodding off.

David pats her arm. "Hey, Kiddo, why don't you turn in?"

She yawns again. "Okay, or I might read for a bit."

I go to stand but David makes a sit-down motion. My pulse skitters — he wants a man-to-man talk. I squeeze Hayley's fingers as she wafts past.

David grabs two light beers and motions for me to follow him to the front porch.

"Don't worry, son," he says as he sinks into a wicker chair, "this isn't an interrogation. I like you already. I want to fill you in more about what Hayley's been through as I doubt she's said much."

"Okay," I reply, surprised.

After a pull from his beer, he begins. "She's told you about the breast cancer, which is a big step for her, so she must trust you. She probably also told you she ran marathons, but I'll wager she didn't tell you she *lived* for her running, as did her previous boyfriend of four years."

I sit up straighter.

"Jonathan was an elite runner too. I think Hayley thought they'd marry." He winces. "To be honest, I thought he was far too self-absorbed, but what can you say?" He puts his bottle down. "Then four years ago, several things happened. The first is that Monika and I went on a rugged bush hike in the Dandenongs and we got caught in wild weather. For two days we were cold and soaked, and by the time we made it out Monika was feverish and so ill. I blame myself. I took her to hospital straightaway and three days later she died of complications from pneumonia. She was sixty-one." He wipes at his eyes.

"I'm so sorry," I murmur.

"Hayley and I were devastated. Without her, I'm not sure I would've pulled through. She stayed with me for three months, making me eat, go for a walk." His tone hardens. "In that time, Jonathan found someone else."

"What?" I say in horror, thinking I'm lucky Hayley trusts men, and me, at all. I see by his face there's more.

"Over the next year, her running times dropped, she felt ill, sluggish, and everyone thought it was depression. The life went out of her."

I pinch the bridge of my nose to stop from crying.

"Fortunately, she went to see a new GP, who, despite Hayley's young age, guessed the issue and sent her for scans. So many scans. By then she had a 6-centimetre tumour in her left breast, it had metastasised into her lymph nodes and they worried it was also in her bones."

I swallow hard. No wonder Hayley's terrified these scans won't be clear.

David grips my forearm. "I was devastated — again — thought I'd lose her too. But she rallied, soldiered on through all that risky invasive treatment and staggered out the other side." He wipes his eyes. "But she hasn't been the same since. I want you to know that. Monika was like a bright shooting star that blazed across the sky, and everywhere she went people warmed to her and her rays of positivity." He looks me in the eye. "Hayley is the same; you haven't met her fully yet."

I grin at him. "I've seen glimpses though. As soon as I met her, I could tell something was holding her back."

David grips my arm again. "I am grateful to you, son. Giving her a new sport, a new focus, was the best thing you could do. Not to mention your love and support. I can tell she adores you."

For a moment, I can't speak, can only nod. Taking a breath, I decide to share. "There are a couple of things I'd like to share with you, too." When he sits up alertly, I continue. "I proposed to Hayley on Saturday night."

The look on his face is priceless. "What? Why aren't we celebrating?"

"Because she didn't fully say yes. She wants to know her scans are clear … and she needs to meet my family."

David nods. "The scans I can understand. She won't want to put you through the grief I experienced. Not when there's a known risk." He looks at me with open curiosity. "Your family?"

"My father is traditional Chinese and he wants me to marry a Chinese girl."

"Good Lord!" says David.

I fiddle my fingers together. "I'm happy as a physio down in Narooma … but my father is a multi-millionaire businessman in Sydney."

"Whoa!" says David. "Does Hayley know this?"

I nod. "She Googled him before I got around to telling her."

David laughs, then grows serious. "What happens if your family won't approve?"

I look him in the eye. "I will choose Hayley."

The silence stretches between us until he eventually says, "That's good enough for me."

CHAPTER THIRTY-TWO
Follow-up Scans

I wake shivering and Justin immediately cocoons me in his arms and kisses my forehead.

"It'll be okay, Hayley. Let's get this done."

I snuggle into him, wishing I could believe him. He and Dad insisted on coming with me, Dad shouting us to rooms at The Hyatt again. Justin has worked on the scar tissue every night for the past fortnight and swears it is reducing.

We're in the car at 9 am and collect Dad from the airport at midday. We have a light snack, which I can barely force down, then present at the imaging place. They go for coffee, knowing I'll be forty minutes or so. I drag my feet to the reception counter, then take a seat as instructed. The sonographer collects me, not someone I met before.

"In here, Darl," she says. "Pop into a gown and we'll do the mammogram first."

I'm trying hard not to shiver by the time she retrieves me.

"You alright? You're very pale. Nervous?"

I nod. So much is riding on a good result. The mammogram is as uncomfortable as ever, but she doesn't take any extra images and the doctor is happy with the scans. I feel a bud of hope. The ultrasound person is very thorough, like she's mowing a lawn running the scan device in neat straight lines across both breasts.

"Lot of scarring," she murmurs. She also doesn't need to collect the doctor or take any more images and my hope lifts another notch. But 2 pm tomorrow feels such a long time away to find out.

Justin and Dad are in the waiting room when I emerge.

"Okay, Kiddo?" Dad pats my shoulder.

I shrug. "No extra images, which is a good sign."

Justin looks thrilled.

We spend the afternoon at a movie, then head to The Hyatt to check in and have dinner. I know my quietness is worrying them, but I can't help it; I've gone into a spiral of stress. I rub my temples. The thought of doing this year after year … A tear rolls down my cheek.

Justin grasps my hand. "Talk."

I sniff and another few tears roll down. "Every year. I have to do this every year. It's almost too much."

"It'll get better," says Dad. "Aren't there milestones and when you pass those the appointments spread out?"

True. But you have to pass them first.

Justin and Dad exchange concerned looks. Sensing I can't be cheered up, Justin suggests we turn in. As soon as we're in bed he holds me tight, and I actually bawl into his chest.

Rubbing my back, he murmurs, "Let it out, Hayley. You need to grieve."

He strokes my hair and my face, until I fall asleep.

~

It seems Justin is in charge the next morning, insisting we power walk around the lake, swim in the hotel pool, go for cappuccinos, and then finally head to the hospital. Still subdued, I hear them discussing who will come in to the oncologist with me given two extra is probably too many. Dad wins.

We enter The Cancer Clinic and I smile at the memory of meeting the DAC paddlers in the foyer. Leaving Justin perched anxiously on a lounge, Dad and I take the lift to oncology. It's quite busy and I sigh. However, I feel like a fraud among so many very sick patients.

The doctor calls me at 3 pm. "Hi Hayley. How are you?" she asks, striding towards her consulting room. "You look well."

We sit down and I introduce Dad.

The doctor scrolls through scan images on her computer, and re-reads the report, then turns to me with a smile. "Well. I thought it would be a red herring and it is. No sign of any shadows or malignancy and, if anything, your scar tissue has reduced."

Dad exhales loudly and I stare at her. "So, I'm good?"

"Yes. Keep up whatever you're doing because you look stronger, fitter, and that helps. I don't need to see you until next year, unless anything worries you before then."

"Thank you so much!" I say, standing because she does. "Have a great Christmas."

"You too." She ushers me out the door.

My feet are having trouble feeling the ground as I check out and book in for 12 months' time.

Dad takes my arm in the lift. "Fantastic news, Hayley. Right, slap-up afternoon tea!"

Justin bounces off the sofa when he sees me, and I give him a thumbs-up and a big smile. He looks like he's going to cry. Then he rushes to kiss me soundly, regardless of the number of people in the café area and lounge. When we part, I see a few people smiling, glad someone got good news.

Back at The Hyatt, Dad orders High Tea and watching him choose the petit fours mix for us I realise this is why he likes to stay here. He always did have a sweet tooth. Justin orders Jasmine tea, Dad goes for Earl Grey and I opt for a mix called Turkish Rose. When the food arrives, I'm surprised to see a second waiter bring champagne flutes and a bottle of expensive-looking low-alcohol sparkling Rosé. Justin looks mildly horrified.

I arch an eyebrow at Dad. "We're drinking at 4 pm?"

"A celebration, Kiddo. In style. We can save the rest for dinner."

As soon as we're settled with two cakes each, tea poured, glasses full of Rosé, Dad lifts his glass and Justin and I hurry to follow suit.

"To Hayley! We knew you could do it. Keep being strong, keep believing. Here's to clear scans!"

We clink glasses and take sips. The low-alcohol version is surprisingly pleasant, not too sweet and the bubbles tingle over my tongue. "Thanks, Dad." His expression turns mischievous and my pulse flutters. What's he up to?

Placing his glass down, he leans towards me. "Well, Kiddo, are you going to put your young man out of his misery now?"

I gasp. Then glare at Justin. "You squealed!"

Blushing, Justin says, "Got caught out at the end of a man-to-man talk." He reaches for my hand. "It's okay, Hayles. I can be patient."

Gripping his hand, I travel my gaze over the planes of his face, the almond-shaped eyes, glossy raven hair. God, I love him so much. I realise I forgot to ask the oncologist an important probability question. "One more question: what if I can't have children? It can be an issue after all that treatment."

Justin brings my hand to his lips and kisses my fingers. "It's not a deal-breaker for me, Hayles. It's you I want." He takes a breath.

"Don't stress about my family. It would be wonderful if they like you, but it doesn't change anything if they don't."

I look at Dad. "You approve?"

"Never been happier about anything!" Dad beams at us.

Justin takes the cue and holding both my hands, looks deep into my eyes. "Hayley Banks, will you marry me?"

"Yes, Justin Zhao, it would be my honour."

He pulls me off my chair onto his lap and kisses me so hard I feel heat rising. The tables around us begin to clap, having twigged what's happening. Dad is nodding to everyone and beaming from ear to ear, in his element.

Justin's words buzz in my ear. "I adore you, Hayles. Thank you. You've turned my life around."

I murmur into his ear, "Some women can be bought with lollipops. But only if they're dropped by handsome Oriental warrior-types."

He cracks up.

CHAPTER THIRTY-THREE
The Zhao Family

Christmas in Narooma is wonderful, the best Christmas I've had since Mum died. Dad comes to stay and Justin makes us a delicious Chinese banquet at his place. On Boxing Day morning there's a special paddle and Justin works really hard to persuade Dad to go out in the boat, assuring him he can paddle gently and saying he simply has to experience the inlet close-up. He sits Dad next to Andrew and in front of me, where I can guide him. By half-way through the paddle, I can see he's getting the hang of it and starting to put some pressure on his blade.

Justin is sweeping and he takes us on the most scenic options where we see plenty of wildlife. The inlet is showing off; sunlight glinting on crystal clear turquoise water with great views of the jade seagrass, fish, a manta ray or two and tons of happy birdlife. After eighty minutes Justin brings the boat in and we sit at the tables by the shed to share Boxing Day morning tea, which is a feast comprising Christmas leftovers. I introduce Dad to everyone properly, and Natalie spends a lot of time asking him about his digs. I'd forgotten about her background in science before she moved here.

Giulio and Gianni say the team paddles have arrived, and their parents want to host a club dinner at the restaurant to formally hand them over, with some media coverage. Everyone agrees the first Saturday evening after New Year would work. I study Justin's face, wondering how much he'll freak out if we make it an engagement party too … maybe a quiet word in Natalie's ear. I glance at her and she arches an eyebrow. "Later," I mouth, thinking perhaps I shouldn't give her too much time in case she goes overboard. No pun intended.

At dinner, Dad is enthused. "No wonder you look so much stronger, Kiddo. This paddling is a real workout."

"Glad you enjoyed it. There are clubs in Melbourne, you know."

He pauses with his fork halfway to his mouth. "Something to think about. Could complement digging well, all that arm and core strength."

Justin looks thrilled. "You'd be good at it; you've got the build. Many paddlers keep training and competing into their seventies."

"Ah." Dad waves his fork at us. "Now I feel like I'm being cornered."

We drop Dad at Moruya airport the next morning, and I hug him fiercely. "See you again soon."

He grips me hard. "I presume you'll show me a ring sometime soon?" He stands back, hands on my shoulders. "Unless you'd like Monika's?"

I swallow hard, visualising the elegant gold band with a sapphire set in a wee curved horseshoe of diamonds. "I'd love that. Let me ask Justin."

The flight is called, and he's gone.

~

Time flies over the next few days, and on New Year's Eve I wake with butterflies in my stomach. The final hurdle. *Today.* I open my eyes and find Justin studying me.

"We'd better get moving if we're to arrive after lunch, considering the holiday traffic."

I slide out of his bed, telling myself it will be okay, and head to the bathroom. When I emerge, he's packing a small Esky with drinks and snacks so we won't have to stop and queue anywhere. My small suitcase is already packed. He's hired the Lexus again so we're going in style, and we're on the road by 8 am.

Once we're clear on the highway, to distract my nerves, I ask, "So, tell me more about your family and make sure I can pronounce their names perfectly please."

"Good plan." He patiently goes over each of his family members' names, explaining their significance and meaning. Chaoxiang apparently means 'expecting fortune', Yichen means 'grand sun, moon or stars' and Xin Yan means 'beauty and vitality'. Elegant names for a successful family. Of course, his father's name is the hardest to pronounce, it's so tonal.

Finally, I get it right. "But what should I call them? Their names or Mr and Mrs Zhao?"

He slides a glance at me. "They'll tell you. It's likely to be a formal meet and greet afternoon tea, then my mother will invite you to admire her teahouse. *That* is the important conversation. Father rules the empire, but Mother is in charge of family."

I flex and crunch my fingers, nerves rising. "What do you think I should say?"

Justin reaches over and squeezes my knee, driving one-handed for a minute. "I know this is hard, Hayles, but they need to accept you for you, who you are. I can't coach you, or Mother will detect insincerity. Just be yourself."

I feel like crying. But I can't. This is so important to him. I encouraged him to reach out to his family and I can't be the cause of a new sundering.

"Mother will see your strength and kind heart. I haven't mentioned your breast cancer, so you judge whether to tell her."

We stop for a picnic in a park and I walk a few laps, trying to de-stress. Justin watches me, but doesn't comment. The traffic builds as we near Sydney, and it's after 2 pm by the time Justin swings the Lexus into an opulent, tree-lined street in McMahons Point. My heart thuds louder. Of course they have harbour views. I can see a scenic marina with small yachts and cruise boats bobbing gently and, further out, the Sydney Harbour Bridge. We pull into the curved driveway of a three-storey terrace house, white with ornate windows and shutters and a distinctly Chinese style garden.

Justin parks in a small alcove, then leans over to kiss me. "Remember, just be yourself. Li Na being here will dilute things a bit. You might like her, she's quite bubbly."

I nearly trip over my skirt hem as I get out; the one piece of advice Justin did give me was to dress feminine.

"Don't worry about the bags yet, just come in." Justin takes my hand and leads me to the red front door.

"Red for good fortune?" I murmur.

"And wind chimes to deflect evil spirits, water for tranquillity."

The garden is stunning. "Your mother designed this? It's gorgeous." Inhaling deeply, I aim to absorb the essence of the culture I'm about to enter. *Be calm, Hayles, you adore Oriental history and culture. This will be an experience, a memory. A deeper understanding of Justin.*

Justin looks at me and tips his chin up, then grins. Is he making fun of me? I tip my chin higher and he nods.

The door opens and Ethan steps out to clasp Justin in a hug. "Welcome, Bro." He turns to me and puts his hand out. "Welcome to the Zhao residence, Hayley."

I shake his hand. This is an auspicious start. I follow Justin in, unstrap my sandals and put on the silk slippers, then follow the brothers down an ornate hall. As anticipated, the house is magnificent. A fabulous and elegant blend of Chinese style with a modern touch. The house is large, light and airy, and I love the lattice doors, reminiscent of shoji screens. I'm led into an ornate lounge with magnificent rugs, white leather sofas and chairs, and amazing silk scrolls on the walls depicting waterfalls, mountains and birds.

The family stands as we enter. Justin faces his father first with a deferential bow. "Father, greetings. This is Hayley. Thank you so much for inviting her to join us." He waves a hand, "Hayley, this is my father, Chaoxiang Zhao."

I copy Justin's deferential bow and clasp my hands together. "It is an honour to meet you, sir. Thank you for inviting me into your home."

After an assessing look and grunt, he says, "Welcome, Hayley. Please take a seat."

Justin presents me to his mother, who is indeed beautiful and elegant. "This is my mother, Xin Yan."

His mother reaches out a slender hand for me to grasp. "Welcome, Hayley. I hope you enjoy your stay."

Next, Ethan stands and introduces me to Li Na, his girlfriend, who gives me a shy smile. She is so very pretty and I can see why Ethan fell for her.

His mother pats the sofa beside her and I obediently sit there, Justin squeezing in on my other side. Afternoon tea is served, and the time passes with much small talk and a distinct sense that I'm being weighed and measured. I respond to questions as best I can and try to ask sensible ones. So far, so good.

After about an hour, Mrs Zhao puts her teacup down and turns to me with a serene face. "Would you like to see my teahouse, Hayley?"

My pulse galloping, I smile and say, "I'd love to." Justin surreptitiously pats my arm as I stand to follow his mother. She leads me into an immaculate back garden that's more spacious than I'd expected. I see a cedar tea house in the far corner. Mrs. Zhao still has her figure and the crimson Qipao dress she is wearing highlights her slimness with curves in the right places. She doesn't look like the type to exercise and I wonder how she achieves this. She is every part the wife of a mega-successful man.

When she crosses the ornate red bridge to the teahouse, I spontaneously stop to watch the koi. They are magnificent, and by the size of some of them, quite old.

"You like the fish?" she asks.

"They are gorgeous," I reply. "I'd love to have my own pond one day."

We enter the shaded tea house, which has wind chimes tinkling softly to complement the bubbling water. I spy a row of Bonsai trees on a shelf on the far side and, without thinking, walk past the table and chairs to peer at them. "These are magnificent! Did you cultivate them?"

She glides to stand beside me, her eyes on my face assessing whether I'm being sincere. "I did." She tilts her head and a ray of light catches her jade hairpin. "Which one do you like best?"

I take a step back and slowly run my eyes over the collection. This is a test so I don't rush. Finally, I point and say, "That one. I love the way it is a complete landscape and story within the piece. The water at the base, the sloping moss, the winding path and teeny flowers, the ornate tree and sages reading beneath it. It is … elegant … peaceful … complete."

One of her fine pencilled eyebrows lifts. "A good choice. This is my latest work, to be entered in the Chinese New Year competition in February." Before I can say good luck or any other platitude, she waves a hand at the chairs. "Please, sit."

I perch on the chair and take a deep breath, trying not to roll my shoulders too obviously. Now, we begin.

She angles her legs neatly together, settling in for a long discussion. "Tell me about your family, and you."

"Okay. I'll start with the facts, please ask any questions." I briefly describe my parents, then talk about going to University in Canberra, working in the public service, and being a runner. Speaking quickly, I explain my mother Monika died, noting the flicker of sympathy on her face. I hesitate when I get to the moving to Narooma. Do I mention the breast cancer?

Leaning forward, she probes, "How did you meet Justin?"

Okay, she's opened the door. I take a deep breath and try not to fiddle with my fingers. "Two years ago, I became sick." I tip my chin up and meet her eye. "Although I am very young, I was diagnosed with breast cancer." She sits alarmingly still. "I spent a year in treatment and then went back to work. But I couldn't focus, I'd lost direction … so I decided to take time off to heal fully and live by the sea for a while. Last September, I rented a place in Narooma."

Her eyes narrow. "Are you cured?"

I shake my head. "Too soon to tell, although all my scans were clear two weeks ago. I will be monitored yearly for a while." I stop there, no point sugar-coating anything; she's far too astute.

"Justin knows this?"

"Of course. Not initially, but once we became closer, I told him everything." I tilt my head. "Can I tell you about the day we met?" She clearly has a sense of story from her Bonsai work, so I tell in detail of how on my first morning there a cyclist barged past me and dropped all his lollipops, then when I gave them back to him, he insisted I get in the dragon boat. I have her undivided attention and she even smiles at the end.

"Such an unusual meeting," she murmurs. "Karma, perhaps."

"Mrs Zhao, your son is incredibly talented. He detected my concealed pain from the instant he met me. He also sensed a stronger, underlying person and has been instrumental in bringing me back from the brink. He has made me strong again, has given me a renewed reason for living." I choke up. "I adore him." I wipe at my eye to stop the tear from falling.

She regards me with an unnerving silence. I can't tell what she's thinking. Her next question is a barbed dart. "Will you be able to give him children, us grandchildren?"

I shrug. "I froze some eggs before my treatment so it should be possible, but it might be harder to fall pregnant and there are risks … to me, in raising my hormone levels."

"You would take those risks?"

"If Justin wanted it."

"So, you could leave him a young widower and you may not be able to have children … and you're not Chinese. Do you think you should walk away?" Her dark eyes glitter.

I can barely swallow and my voice comes out as a husky croak. "Believe me, I have agonised about it. Over and over. I even tried to push him away, but a wise friend said that it is not up to me to make the decision for him. It is Justin's choice. If he chooses me *despite* all this, I would love to be with him."

"You make it difficult for me to present your case to Chaoxiang," she says bluntly.

"I am at your mercy. But please consider the effect on Justin. He has just made peace with you all, which I encouraged and helped him with. He will decide his response once you tell him your view, and I will not try to influence him in any way. If we part, I will be heartbroken, but the decision will be his."

She leans forward again. "Are you saying you would walk away if that were the best outcome?"

I chew my lower lip and nod, tearing up. "Justin is a very special man, and I want whatever is best for him." I refrain from saying 'as should you'.

I straighten my spine. "Justin is happy in Narooma, where he is highly regarded and adored by the community there. He is caring, generous, kind and," I smile, "on occasion, very funny. From what I understand, I am the first woman he has been serious about. He may never choose anyone else." I let that hang.

Mrs Zhao smooths her hands down her dress. "Thank you, Hayley. May I suggest you admire the fish for a while?" She stands, nods and walks away up the path.

Finding a tissue, I blow my nose. I'm exhausted. Did I hold my own? Closing my eyes, I match my breathing to the chimes and the water. Afternoon sunlight is trickling in on my face and I lean back in the chair.

I jolt awake when someone touches my arm, relief gushing to see it's Justin. Wordlessly, I stand and let him envelop me. He leans in to kiss me.

"Well, we survived our interrogations, now we wait for the verdict." He peers into my face. "How did it go?"

I shake my head; I don't want to talk about it. Truthfully, I have no idea which way Mrs Zhao will decide. We lean on the railing and watch the koi for a while. "Can we have a pond?" I ask. "The fish are so tranquil."

"Sure," says Justin.

"Oi!" Ethan shouts from the back door. "Are you two coming in? How about a game of Mahjong?"

"Have you played?" Justin asks.

"Only twice, but I'm happy to learn."

The next hour passes quickly as four of us play. I'm no match for their speed and am glad we're not playing for money. At 6 pm Li Na excuses herself to help Mrs Zhao in the kitchen. Ethan explains there will be at least twelve courses. He seems friendly, no sign of the animosity when we first met. I excuse myself to go upstairs to freshen up and change into a smarter dress. Justin has brought the bags in and I see we're in separate but adjacent rooms.

My nerves are bubbling by the time we're called to the dining table at 7 pm. My eyes widen at the extensive spread. Surely, we can't eat all that? There's enough to feed a whole dragon boat team! Once we're all seated, with Ethan having poured everyone rice wine, Chaoxiang clears his throat and lifts his glass. All eyes fix on him at the head of the table.

He stands, so we all do too. "Thank you for sharing this feast with us. May the next year bring continued prosperity, good fortune and good health." He waves his glass at Justin and Ethan. "I am pleased to be joined by both my sons this year." He drains his glass, then waits while we do. Ethan hurries around to refill the glasses.

My stomach is churning. How much longer do we have to wait? At this rate I'll be drunk before the verdict lands.

"Next," says Chaoxiang, with an air of pomposity, "I welcome Li Na and Hayley to our house — and to the Zhao family. Congratulations to both my sons on their engagements."

The strength leaves my legs and I plop inelegantly onto my chair. Did I hear that right? Grinning, Justin hauls me upright. Li Na is smiling broadly and bowing to everyone and Ethan looks like he's fit to burst, or start doing cartwheels.

Gripping my elbow, Justin levers me to my feet so I can drink a toast. I manage this, then smile and bow at everyone and congratulate Ethan and Li Na.

The banquet is convivial, each dish divine. Mrs Zhao is an amazing cook. The evening passes quickly, although sometimes they speak in Chinese and I can't follow. At one point, Mr Zhao turns to me, his breath laden with wine, and says, "Justin tells me you can ride horses."

I explain about my mother being an elite dressage rider and how I borrowed ponies from the agistment centre and rode for many years, going to shows and events with her.

"This is good." He nods sagely. "You could help Justin with the horse products."

My mouth drops open. "I'd like that."

He assesses me. "Maybe you'd like to go with him on the second Hong Kong trip and help manage the horses."

My heart almost stops. Mr. Zhao is clearly an all-or-nothing guy. "It would be my honour," I gasp.

At eleven-thirty we all go up to the third floor, and into an ornate study at the front of the house, with a small balcony. The Sydney Harbour Bridge is lit up and I can hear lively music and announcements. Our own private view of the fireworks at midnight. Justin keeps sliding me pleased glances but is restrained in front of his parents. He holds my hand when the fireworks start. The display is spectacular; this has turned into a magical evening. I have a lot to learn about the Chinese culture, but I will try.

"Well," says Mr Zhao, "that is Australia's New Year done. The celebrations will be bigger for Chinese New Year."

We go back downstairs and Li Na and I help Mrs Zhao to tidy up. Finally, I slide into the bed, wishing Justin were not in the adjacent room. But the next year looks bright.

CHAPTER THIRTY-FOUR
Celebrations

The next morning, we go for a walk around the marina with Ethan and Li Na. I can see Hayley is tired, but she chats happily with Li Na.

Ethan sidles next to me and says lowly, "She's nice, Bro. You have chosen well."

I pat his shoulder, "Thanks, that means a lot."

We have family morning coffee together, then Hayley and I leave, with much bowing and smiling. Mother has packed a picnic lunch for us. As I take the box, I lean in and say, "Mother, thank you so much. For everything."

She kisses my cheek. "I want to see you happy, Jun Jie. This will keep the family together."

I hug her and she squirms and smooths her dress.

On the drive back, Hayley and I share the details of our interrogations. I can't believe how bold she was with Mother, but it worked. I glance at her. "Are you happy?"

She twists to stare at me. "How could I not be happy, you crazy Tiger?" She fiddles her fingers. "I have something to ask. Dad has offered me Mum's engagement ring. It's stunning, a sapphire in a horseshoe of diamonds. Did you want to choose a ring or would it be okay if we use my mum's?"

I squeeze her knee. "That sounds special, Hayles. We can choose the wedding rings together."

She leans over to kiss my cheek.

~

A week later, and we're dressing ready for the dinner at Delizioso to celebrate the sponsorship. At Hayley's request, I wear my charcoal-blue suit, and she has chosen a flowery dress with a low neckline to show off the dragon necklace. At 6.30 we enter the restaurant and find most of the team is already there, most with their partners. The Clear Water Dragons banner is prominent across the back wall, the tables are all laid with crisp white tablecloths, candles, single roses and several bottles of wine.

Hayley rushes over to hug Akiko and my eyebrow raises. Why are Kraig and Akiko here? Then I see Simone, my receptionist, with her husband. My stomach niggles: something is afoot. My suspicion increases when I see the smug looks on Natalie and Sandi's faces.

Sandi rings a bell and tells everyone to take a seat. Giulio, Gianni and Francesca are seated at a table under the banner with their parents. I head over to meet them and thank them profusely.

Giulio leaps up. "These are my parents, Tony and Phillipa, this is Justin our head sweep and coach."

They shake my hand and I babble profuse thanks. The pile of gear piled up behind their table is impressive. I assume they will present gear to each paddler.

Tony says, "I thought we'd have entrees then do the presentations."

Most of the younger paddlers have drifted to the Italian table, and Hayley insists we sit between Kraig and Akiko and Natalie and

David. The food is aromatic and delicious. Akiko leans in to whisper something to Hayley, who squeals in response, and Kraig blushes.

"That's awesome. Good luck!" She turns to me and whispers, "They're going to try for another child."

I look at Kraig and nod.

Sandi stands and rings the bell and we hush up. "Tony and Phillipa are now going to present the sponsorship gear. When I call your name, please come over to this table."

Amid much frivolity and bows of thanks, the team collects their sponsorship package of a paddle, paddle bag, team towel and team jacket — Amalia, Andrew, Greg, Mara, Elena, Giulio, Gianni, Francesca, Chloe, Rose, Pippa, Natalie, Nigel, Simon, Nick, Hayley.

"Finally," says Sandi, "Justin and me as the sweeps."

I go to stand with Sandi as we jointly receive our packages from Tony and Phillipa, who kiss us on both cheeks. All the paddlers are admiring their paddles, which are gorgeous, with a blade of turquoise water, a small trim of jade seagrass at the bottom and a crystal white dragon. I couldn't have designed anything better.

"I now propose a toast to Phillipa and Tony. Can everyone please be upstanding," announces Sandi.

We toast and give them three rousing cheers and a massive round of applause. We sit down and our mains are brought out. I can hear Giulio and Gianni discussing how we're going to train to go international. Sandi rolls her eyes at me. I tuck into my lasagne, trying to ignore the way Natalie and Hayley are murmuring to each other. I pause my next mouthful: she wouldn't, would she? I look at the glint in her eye. Oh no. She would.

～

I watch Justin's face as he pauses eating and looks at me. I suspect he's worked it out. How much will he freak out? Yet this was definitely too good an opportunity to pass up. Once the plates are cleared, Natalie reaches behind her chair to collect another banner and beckons to Giulio and Gianni to hold it up behind her. Nat stands and bangs a spoon on her glass.

"This has been a fabulous evening so far, but apparently we have one more thing to celebrate."

The paddlers twist in their chairs, intrigued.

"It's been a long time coming, and we thought we were going to have to create a Tinder account for Justin." That raises a laugh. "Then last September, this random pretty paddler turned up. Justin threw lollipops at her feet to make sure she noticed him … which she did, big time. It's been absolutely fascinating watching them dance around each other, will we, won't we." Natalie wipes at her eye and flaps a hand at the brothers, who unfurl a magnificent sparkling banner with *Congratulations Hayley & Justin* in cursive writing, with embroidered balloons and champagne glasses.

A loud gasp and then a massive cheer goes up and people bang their glasses. Justin is blushing a deep crimson so I lean in to hug him. "Come on, Tiger, got to do this in style."

"Couldn't we do style in private?" he moans.

"Nope, come on. Stand with me in front of the banner." I tug him to his feet to stand next to Nat. I see Tony is taking photos. Excellent.

"Then, after all that circling, the dark horses snuck off and got engaged! Three cheers for Hayley and Justin!"

The team stamp their feet and yell congratulations, and waiters emerge from the kitchen with champagne and fresh flutes, and a towering Tiramisu cake with sparklers and figurines on top.

Once everyone's glasses are filled, I hug Justin to me and tip my face up, revelling as his mouth meets mine. Ignoring the catcalls and whistles we kiss long and hard.

"I like this part," murmurs Justin.

"There can be more of this part," I grin against his lips.

The celebrations continue until midnight, with each paddler coming to individually congratulate us.

Sandi pokes Justin's shoulder. "I told you these muscles were too good to waste. Looks like Narooma's most eligible bachelor is off the market."

Justin laughs, seemingly recovered from the limelight.

Next, everyone is picking up their gear, stowing it in Justin's car and hugging everyone good night. We wander outside the restaurant, drive to his house and stow the gear.

He takes my hand. "Remember our first kiss?" His eyes are deep and dark.

"Walking on a moon beam, how could I forget?"

We amble over the road to the golf course, and head to the cliff edge. The night is balmy, a thousand stars twinkling. A three-quarter moon casts enough of a silver swathe to imagine a path across the water surface. We stop close to the edge, where we can hear the water rushing over the rocks below.

I snuggle into his arms.

Kissing my hair, he says, "I can't ever thank you enough for walking into my life. I am a better and happier person because of you."

"Tiger, you saved me. You turned my life around too."

"We had some challenges, didn't we?" He brushes his lips down my neck and I shiver.

"True. But when the going gets tough, I now know the answer is to paddle harder."

He licks my neck, "A great motto, Hayles."

My body heating, I mumble, "Enough philosophy. More of the good part …"

I plant my lips on his, slipping my tongue into his mouth. He groans and responds, and we stand there forever with moonlight washing over us.

About the Author

Kaaren loved stories.

As a child, she was often sprung reading by torchlight long after 'lights out'. At the age of twelve, she decided she'd write and illustrate the eighth Chronicle of Narnia. She won the Year 12 section of the inaugural Canberra Times Short Story Competition.

Always a storyteller, Kaaren went on to publish three children's books, a fantasy duology and two fantasy trilogies – the most recent being the acclaimed *The Mage and the Bird Caller* series, which showcased her love of dragon boating. Although fantasy was her first calling, and her Mage series did include romantic elements of increasing 'chilli' intensity, in her heart Kaaren wanted to write a contemporary romance – and she never shied away from a challenge.

A mad keen sportswoman, Kaaren lived for horse riding and long-distance running. A breast cancer diagnosis in 2005 did not stop her, but its return during 2021 in her spine meant she had to give up these two pursuits. She turned her attention instead to dragon boating, which features in the *Mage* series as well as in her final book, *Paddle. Live. Love.* – a four-chilli contemporary romance that embodies everything and everyone Kaaren valued.

Kaaren passed away in August 2024.

Dragons Abreast Australia

Many tears are shed over a breast cancer diagnosis. The disease robs us of many things – our energy, our appearance, our confidence. Once a survivor has had surgery and other treatments, we need hope and connection with those who understand and others who have this lived experience. We need to be physically active; to tread a new life by learning something new; to attain peace through mindfulness. And we can give advice and support to help other survivors. Then the tears will be of happiness, while we power down many rivers and waterways of the world.

Founded in 1998 on the principles of participation, awareness and inclusiveness, Dragons Abreast Australia is a national charity with groups spread across the country. We are a network of paddling groups comprising breast cancer survivors of various ages from a great variety of backgrounds, athletic abilities and interests. High on our list of priorities is having fun and travelling across the rivers, lakes and harbours of the world to help restore ourselves.

Being able to paddle and socialise in the company of others who have travelled the same path help to restore our confidence, spark and sense of adventure we need to permit a full and active life after treatment.

We invite you to join us in the boat at www.dragonsabreast.com.au

Many regattas hold designated 'pink' races, where paddlers combine to form 'pink' teams and meet new people. There are numerous Dragons Abreast clubs around Australia. To find a club near you, go to https://dragonsabreast.com.au/location/

For readers who are not breast cancer survivors but who wish to experience the exhilaration of paddling, visit <u>www.ausdbf.com.au</u> and follow the links to find your state's Dragon Boat Federation.

Kaaren Sutcliffe participated in 'pink' races at the Masters Games in Adelaide in 2019 and had an absolute ball! After major surgery for metastasised cancer in her spine in 2021, Kaaren was thrilled to be back in a dragon boat and once again able to participate in 'pink' regattas. An absolute highlight of 2023 was paddling for Dragons Abreast Australia Team 'Hope' at the International Breast Cancer Paddlers Commission regatta held at Lake Karapiro in New Zealand.

Kaaren always donated some of the proceeds of her book sales to support Dragons Abreast Australia, and requested that the same be done for this, her final book.

Editor's Note

I knew Kaaren for a short but action-packed two years, meeting her via our shared passion for dragon boating and quickly discovering we were both writers and editors.

In July 2024, Kaaren sent me the manuscript for *Paddle. Live. Love.* with a request for general feedback and then a proofread. With that also elicited a promise from me that, should the worst-case scenario eventuate, I would ensure this book got published and launched. I think, deep down, she knew she wouldn't be here to hold the book in her hands and launch it herself, but still, we made great plans and then went on to plan our future Australia-wide book tours and author talks – such was Kaaren's refusal to ever say 'never'.

Sadly, 'never' eventuated but I was determined to honour my promise – something I could not have done without the support of Kerrie Griffin OAM, Susan Pitt and Susan's partner, Danny, all of whom read and reread the manuscript, offering suggestions and gentle 'did you realise …' comments.

The fact that Kaaren managed to finish writing *Paddle. Live. Love.* while she was so sick is testament to her strength, willpower and downright stubborn nature. I can only hope that we've done her justice and produced a beautiful, feisty legacy story her husband, Andrew, and daughters Elena and Mara can be proud of.
We miss you terribly, Kaaren. Paddles Up!

Kellie Nissen
Just Right Words

Family's Note

Kaaren has left us with a final gift in *Paddle. Live. Love.* We remember her for her beautiful dedication to her crafts and perseverance in all aspects of her life, from on the water paddling in a dragon boat or kayak to writing in her study surrounded by mementos, books and art.

She enjoyed bringing people together with her book launches. She faced every challenge with a bravery we admire and she is remembered as having the heart of a dragon.

Kaaren spoke of the joys of writing, of setting off with a plan, yet not knowing exactly how things will unfold. She spoke of how her characters would come to her as the story developed and nudge her in a certain direction. It was a privilege to see her return to writing and finish the contemporary romance she wanted to write, in the scenery she loved and spent so much time in.

A big thank you to Kellie as editor for all her work in getting this book published. Thank you to everyone who supported Kaaren along the way. A portion of each book sale goes to the McGrath Foundation and Dragons Abreast Australia.

Kaaren would have loved knowing this book found its way to you. All our best,

The Sutcliffe Family

Other Books by Kaaren Sutcliffe

The Mage and the Bird Caller trilogy

- *Undercover Mage (Book 1)*
- *Fugitive Mage (Book 2)*
- *Eminent Mage (Book 3)*

The Prophecy of the Sharid trilogy

- *Kered's Cry*
- *Kered's Call*
- *Kered's Crown*

The Ambitious Mage series

- *The Pegasus Touch*
- *The Scales*

Children's books

- *Samarkand's Road*
- *Four Fabulous Fantasies*
- *Catch Me a Friend*

Kaaren's books are available via her website:

https://kaarensutcliffe.com.au/books/